The Broken Hearts Society of Suite 17C

LEIGH ANN KOPANS

*For Tara —
Sometimes broken
hearts bring us
the best
of friends
xoxo*

Copyright 2015 by Leigh Ann Kopans

All rights reserved.

This book is a work of fiction. References to real people, events, establishments, organizations, or locations are intended only to provide a sense of authenticity, and are used fictitiously. All other characters, and all incidents and dialogue, are drawn from the author's imagination and are not to be construed as real.

"The world will break your heart ten ways to Sunday, that's guaranteed. And I can't begin to explain that, or the craziness inside myself and everybody else. But guess what? Sunday is my favorite day again."

~ The Silver Linings Playbook

For Jamie and Trisha – my very own Writers' Broken Hearts' Society. I can't imagine making it through one day, let alone all these years, without you.

And for Lisa, Real Life Arielle's mom, and all the parents out there just like her, who will never break their children's hearts because of who their children love. You are making the world a better place, one soul at a time.

Chapter 1

Rion

Rion Burke's ex-boyfriend Tate Sullivan was an asshole. A totally gorgeous asshole who could charm the pants off the most raging of lesbians, and who was the best fuck she'd ever had. Rion added "no more hot guys" to her mental notes-to-self list. Apparently, they clouded her judgment way too much.

It wasn't the fact that he smoked pot, or even that he sold the stinky shit out of the back of his car, that bothered her. It was the time he'd left five fucking pounds of it in the trunk and then told her the car was okay for her to drive to the store to pick up munchies. On top of that, he'd been too fucking stoned to remember—or care—that there was a police checkpoint on the back road they almost always took on their quest for munchies.

Rion had only smoked one joint in her life, about five minutes before the stink of it made her want to vomit and she swore her lips would never touch that shit again. Not that this fact mattered when the police officer pulled the Wal-Mart bag full of zippered sandwich bags full of the greenish-brownish curling dried leaves, took in her tattoos, nose piercing, and bleached hair with a sweeping gaze, and decided Rion needed to be in handcuffs, right then and there. Most likely, her trademark glare and the low growly voice that only came out in moments of extreme stress didn't help her argument that she was a totally sober kid just heading out to pick up Cool Ranch Doritos and microwave pizzas for her friends.

It wasn't the look that Mom gave her from across the Indiana minimum security women's correctional facility metal table that bothered her. Mom's third DUI in as many months had erased any room she might have had to criticize Rion.

No, what bothered her was the judge telling her that she was lucky she was only getting a ten thousand dollar fine and losing her federal college funding, plus spending hundreds of hours in community service. That killed her. Hearing the bullshit from her court-appointed lawyer about how lucky she was for an eighteen-year-old offender with such a sizeable stash found on her person didn't help a bit.

Ten thousand dollars and a lingering promise that she'd graduate college was all that was left between her

The Broken Hearts Society of Suite 17C

and Dad after he died in that wreck two years ago, and Tate Sullivan had ripped that away from her before she even saw it coming.

Rion should have known shit would just go downhill from there, especially with Mom's history of alcohol issues. With one parent dead and the other in the slammer, Rion's last year and a half of high school were pretty well fucked over before they even started.

Luckily, the staff of the group home where she'd been living turned out to be good for something. At the last minute, Rion's exit counselor had dug up an unclaimed private scholarship for foster kids going to college to major in fine arts. So Rion had made it to Indiana Northern University, where she hoped to make her love of music into a career and ride out the State's support for foster kids just a little bit longer.

She stood outside Harrison, Suite 17C, after a long and snarling battle with the admissions office to convince them that, even though her name sounded like "Ryan," she was not, in fact, a guy, and did not have to sign up for the selective service to complete her admission. Though the prospect of Army service was fearsome, it had nothing on the group home she'd just escaped from. She'd seen enough of how disgusting guys' personal hygiene could be after living there for the last six months.

A used duffle bag and a cheap backpack held all the important stuff she had to her name. Every item in her parents' house, which Rion was seriously considering selling off, held too many painful memories for her to lug to the dorm room. The one and only upside to having just a suitcase, a purse, and a laptop bag to unpack was that she could skip move-in day and all the dumbass roommate introduction bullshit. Just as she'd hoped, Rion arrived to an empty three-person suite. Evidently her roommates were out participating in what looked like a combo meet-market and extracurriculars clusterfuck on the quad.

Rion wasn't afraid to snoop around a little to figure out what kind of roommates she'd be dealing with. She crossed over to the space between the doors to the other two bedrooms and nudged each open with a toe and peered inside. One of the rooms was already unpacked with the same methodical, obsessive order as Rion's social worker's desk. According to the embroidered name on the fluffy white bathrobe draped across the bed, it belonged to someone annoyingly named Amy. The other room was also taken. It looked like a damn hurricane had blown through it. The only visible signs of humanity were a cork board with endless pictures of the same girl tacked to it, and a brand-new planner splayed open with a color-coded class schedule filled in on the first page.

So many other things had been chosen for her lately. Why should her bedroom at college be any different?

A dozen t-shirts, three pairs of jeans, a pair of shower shoes, and a secondhand laptop all sat in their new places within minutes. It didn't matter that Rion didn't have a lot

The Broken Hearts Society of Suite 17C

of stuff, because she really only needed one thing. This laptop, and her headphones.

These babies shut out the world Rion hated and took her to her favorite place at the same time. A world where she could shuffle together, speed up, and remix half a dozen digital sound files, each of them pretty good on their own, into something truly transcendent.

If there was one beautiful thing left in Rion Burke's fucked up world, it was mixing, combining, twisting, and making new music out of songs that already existed, ones people thought were finished. And she'd be damned if she didn't make it into a career, one that would take her out of White Trash Woods, Indiana, and give her back a normal, peaceful, trouble-free life.

Rion settled into the hard plastic desk chair, leaned back, plugged in the headphones, and got so lost in the sounds that she almost didn't notice her phone ringing three feet away. The thin, bright white letters announcing the caller caught her attention at the last minute, and she lunged for the phone. She'd ignored two of Mom's last three calls, and missed the other. Between brooding over her lost scholarship and getting her shit together, Rion had given herself a pass. Still, she knew damn well Mom only got one call a week. The guilt had been eating at her, and even though she hated to admit it, it would be pretty bitchy to ignore another one of Mom's calls.

"An inmate from the Indiana Department of Correction is trying to reach you, do you accept this call?"

The bored recording of a woman's voice was the one familiar thing in this strange, empty dorm room, and Rion's heart jumped. "Yes, I accept." The familiar click and then emptiness of dead air set her on edge for the three seconds it took for the approval to go through.

"Rion?" Mom's voice came clear enough over the staticky line.

"Mom," she sighed, trying to hide the sense of relief that washed over her at the sound of something, anything, familiar in this stuffy, empty dorm room.

"Hi," she said.

"Hey. Sorry I missed your last few calls. I was…" Rion's voice trailed off.

"Pissed off?"

Mom's language had gotten progressively rougher with each month of prison. Even minimum security was a pretty tough place to live, apparently. "Um…for a while, yeah." Rion had needed her, and she hadn't been there. She didn't have to say it.

Just like everyone else, Mom thought Rion was a tough, hardened bitch who didn't give a shit about anything, who lacked so much care for her own future that she would do some dumbass thing like sell pot out of the back of her boyfriend's car. Yeah, Rion had been a pain in the ass for a couple years—since that night the police came to the door with news of his accident. There were only two ways to deal with that much pain—inflict it on others to make yours hurt less, or make yourself tough enough to hold it all in. Rion had tried both. Neither had worked too well.

Unfortunately, that didn't change the sentence, or the fact that Mom clearly believed she'd committed the crime. It was only when Rion had screamed her ear off about how she'd never been high, let alone sold pot—which was only a little bit of a lie—that she'd felt the slightest bit bad about it.

"I know. I expected you to be. I…I'm sorry, Ri. I don't know what else to say." Mom's voice broke the slightest bit before she recovered. Then she cleared her throat, and said softly, "It's no excuse. But I'm still learning how to be a mom in prison."

Too bad she *couldn't* be a mom in fucking prison. Rion had lost her mother two months after she'd lost her father. For that, Rion could never really forgive her.

She was on her own now. Time to fucking put on her big girl panties and deal with it.

Rion sighed. "What's up, Mom?" Always better to ignore her pathetic fishing for compliments. Rion knew Mom wanted her to say, "You'll always be my mom." She also knew Rion well enough to know that it was never going to happen.

"Uh…well, I'm calling because I managed to get a hold of Olivia. Wrote her snail mail, I actually didn't think she'd get it."

"Who?"

"Oh, you remember Olivia. She used to visit all the time, back when…"

"When, Mom? When I was a baby?" She'd always been bad about this—letting her love of nostalgia interrupt her goddamn common sense. She knew how easy it was to want to rewind to a time when Rion was a little kid, dad was alive, and she was sober, but Mom was the one who'd fucked things up. Not her. She wasn't going to pull this passive aggressive Indiana guilt bullshit. Not on her first day at school.

"Well, uh…maybe. Maybe it was. Now that I think about it, I remember her bouncing you on her knee. Doesn't seem that long ago to me."

"So?"

"So." Mom cleared her throat again. "She owns a place near campus. 'The Studio on High?' And since we're old friends, and I told her about our, uh…situation, and that you could use a job that's kinda flexible around your classes…"

"Wait, wait." Rion's stomach flipped. "You got me a job?" This was a part of the whole mess she'd been avoiding just because she didn't have any idea in hell how she was going to resolve it—how to pay for college now that her federal funding was gone. Her scholarship covered her classes, and an allotment from a state fund from former foster children paid for her board. But there was still the cost of the dorm, books, and everything else she might need. No sane person would hire her with her

The Broken Hearts Society of Suite 17C

record. Not with a campus fucking overrun with upperclassmen and upright citizens shoving their applications at every retail manager in a ten mile radius.

Mom chuckled, and a smile spread across Rion's face. It had been so long since she'd smiled that it actually felt unnatural. "I suppose I did. Livi has always been an entrepreneur, and I haven't seen her in ten years, or more maybe. But I knew she had been buying up some businesses near campus, so I thought I'd check in with her. When she mentioned she ran a studio, I jumped on it. She says she's got a lower level receptionist position for you but she'll up your pay grade to what she pays her second level artists."

Rion's head spun as she glanced at her headphones and shitty, slow computer. Could it be possible that Mom had done something right for once—gotten her a job in the field she hoped to work in, for life? "An artist at a Studio." An uncharacteristic gushiness fought to get out of her, but she tamped it down. She couldn't turn soft with Mom now, not yet.

"Well, um. Thanks, Mom."

"Do you want her number?"

"Oh. Um. Yeah." Embarrassment flared in Rion's cheeks. Sixteen months in a group home should have taught her to fucking focus and keep her head on straight.

Thank God, the prison's one minute warning message came on a second later, not leaving too long for Mom to go through her list of awkward goodbyes. The kicker was the way she ended. "I'll call you next week, okay honey?" Her voice shook.

Rion sighed. Mom wanted to hear that Rion would pick up when she did. But with all the shit that had gone down in the last month, Rion was having a hard time promising anything to anyone anymore.

"Take care, Mom," she mumbled before she hung up.

Rion called Olivia right away, but hadn't expected her to tell her to come in for an interview "any time." Rion was used to having her life run for her at the group home, with specific times for waking up, going to work, and lights out. The freedom stretching in front of her felt huge, and she hadn't yet decided whether that was in a good or terrifying way. Someone trusted her to manage her own life. Rion wasn't even sure if she trusted herself.

She glanced at the clock. Already 4:00 PM. Too early for dinner, and nobody was here. The floor had just been buffed and the cheap area rugs still had vacuum lines in them. The suite had slightly more charm and less of a moldy smell than the waiting room outside juvenile court, but the emptiness of it made something deep inside Rion twist. She hadn't been really, truly alone for a very long time. She thought that was all she wanted, but now that she was, the emptiness of her surroundings made her feel restless.

The Broken Hearts Society of Suite 17C

She sighed. Now was as good a time as any to wander around looking for a random music studio somewhere along campus's main drag.

New students filled the sidewalks on either side of Francis Street, a meandering road that curved down over a hill and was lined with shop after shop hawking college spirit wear, antiques and knick-knacks, cheap beers, and everything in between. All these kids were new here—had to be. At least one thing about each of them was more than necessary—more polished, more flirty, more desperate, more excited. She'd gritted her teeth and determined to avoid being a stupid freshman, or at least looking like one.

She rolled her eyes as she watched a girl far too dressed up and painted for textbook shopping giggle at a guy like she'd literally never heard anything funnier. A cluster of three assholes in khaki shorts and boat shoes pushed past her, leaving a noxious cloud of cologne in their wake.

Finally, near the bottom of the hill, she found it, on the corner of a small street full of older, less flashy shops, and a bar or two. The Studio on High, 420 Francis.

A black plastic sign, with chunky neon lettering, creaked gently on two hooks above the door. Obviously a nod to the famous Doors album. She nodded appreciatively. Maybe this wouldn't be so bad after all. A long, red desk with a cutout Pinpoint records logo greeted her, and she breathed out as she stood at the desk. "I'm here to see Olivia?"

Some guy in a white t-shirt with a mess of dark hair sat behind the desk, sketching with a thin Sharpie on plain white paper. He didn't look up, but kept sketching manically, the tendons on the back of his hand dancing in time with the flick of his wrist. Rion rolled her eyes, fighting the urge to bark, 'Hey, are you deaf?' She cleared her throat and leaned over the desk, casting her shadow over his paper.

Only then did he stop drawing, look up, and show her the most gorgeous fucking ice-blue eyes she'd ever seen.

"Oh, Jesus fucking Christ," he stammered, standing up and toppling his chair to the floor at the same time. "I'm so sorry. How long have you been standing there?" At his full height, he stood easily two heads taller than she was. His plain, dark sleeveless shirt and tattoos and stretched earring holes made him look like a rocker, but he didn't have the skinny-guy body of a typical front man. No. He filled that shirt and, despite her better judgment as far as thinking about any guy's body, Rion guessed that his ass probably filled the back of his jeans equally well.

Do. Not. Drool. You desperate horny bitch. She'd become used to berating herself for her stupidity, but now there were new stakes. This job might be her last chance to stay at Indiana Northern. She couldn't fuck it up.

"I'm here to see Olivia," she repeated, tearing her eyes away from his biceps. "There's a job opening?"

The Broken Hearts Society of Suite 17C

Something clicked in the guy's head, and his face relaxed into a friendly smile, showing off a shining lip ring. If Rion believed in God, she would have cursed him for sending a guy that embodied literally everything she found attractive, but who she couldn't have because he worked in a fucking head shop.

"Holy shit," he said. "Please tell me you're going to be our new receptionist. Me and the rest of the artists are beyond sick of this answering-phones shit."

Rion's eyes flattened into a confused glare.

"Not that it's a shitty job or anything. It's not. It's a good job for a freshman. Totally."

"What makes you think I'm a freshman?"

"Christ," he said, jerking his hand back through his hair. "Just that…I mean…I've never seen you here and…Christ," he said again. "You look young, okay? You caught me."

Rion grunted a short laugh. "Well, you look old." He did, but not in a bad way.

"I'm twenty-one. Not much older than you."

She'd been right. Their eyes locked and Rion lost her breath again. Damn him. "So you're a senior."

"I might be," he said, dipping his head, "if I was in school."

A buzz punctuated the air, sharp, mechanical, and loud. It must have been some weird kind of speaker feedback. "Can I just talk to Olivia?" she managed, pretending to look for something in her bag. It was empty except for a bare keychain and a tattered wallet, but she carried it for moments like this, when she had to look like she was important. When she had to get the idea across that she had something else to look forward to, something important to hold onto. "I don't have all day," she said, even though she actually did have all day.

"Yeah, totally. Totally. I'm sorry." The guy ambled around to the front of the desk and Rion walked to meet him. He reached out to shake her hand again, and Rion half smiled as she breathed in his scent—some citrus, something woodsy. Like the best things about guys' cologne without the annoying heavy chemicals. "I'm Crash," he said. His eyes searched hers for a moment and he swallowed.

Rion didn't answer. She couldn't. It was like her vocal cords, her movements, every thought she had, were paralyzed by what she saw hanging on the wall now that she'd moved closer into the store. Not only were there no guitars, amps, or mixing boards in plain sight, there was an entire wall in front of her stacked with bongs. Every color, size, shape and material you could imagine, right there waiting to be filled with some disgusting-ass dried leaves and then to ruin people's lives.

Desperately, she tried to smooth out the tremor in her voice. "What kind of studio is this?"

"We do piercings, mostly. A few tattoos. That's why I'm here."

The Broken Hearts Society of Suite 17C

"And that?" She couldn't tear her eyes away from it. Mom wouldn't have sent her to place that sold marijuana paraphernalia, and probably had a hook up to the real thing out of its basement or something, willingly. Would she? "This is a head shop, isn't it?"

Was this how her life would always be? Intertwined with the technically, but not really quite, legal, because she wasn't any better than that? Was she really just a piece of white trash shit who'd never amount to anything, like hundreds of other kids who left the foster care system?

Nope. Not if she had any say in it. Mom had fucked her over once, and she'd survived. Still, a woman who drowned her sorrows in a bottle of cherry vodka and nearly killed herself and half a dozen other people because she felt like going for a drive afterward didn't deserve Rion's trust. She wasn't going to survive by letting Mom fuck her over again.

"Oh, that? I'm not sure about that side of the…hey! Where are you going? How are you going to interview?"

She shook her head as the heavy glass door shut behind her. As she stalked back down Francis, she closed her eyes and tried hard not to think about Crash, his easy manner, and his incredible, inquisitive blue eyes.

She wouldn't be seeing any of them again.

Chapter 2

Arielle

The quad of Indiana Northern buzzed with energy, but Arielle knew she was more excited than every other new student at this school combined. Soon, the nervous trembling in her limbs would stop, and the rest of her life would begin. Soon, she'd see Rachel for the first time in almost two months, and then every single day after that.

Rachel and Arielle had been stealing kisses and whispering in ears and letting hands wander every time Rachel could make the two hour trip home to Indianapolis, which, lately, had been far less often than Arielle would like. That made the blow of getting waitlisted for Northern, where Rachel was starting her second year, that much worse, and the high of getting the letter that she'd been pulled off that waitlist that much more exciting.

The Broken Hearts Society of Suite 17C

She'd found out three weeks before school started that she'd actually be attending, but tried to keep a sad face while Rachel stroked her hair before she left, told her it would be okay, that they'd see each other for the holidays. Rosh HaShanah wasn't the most romantic of holidays for most people, but given that the two girls had first hooked up in the synagogue coat check room on that day a year ago, Rachel's words were extra swoony.

For the entire month of August, Arielle had kept the news to herself. She'd be going to Northern after all. They could finally, really, seriously be together—a normal couple. See each other every day, meet up for coffee, go on dates. And today would be the day it all started.

"You ready to jump in there?" Amy asked in her soft, patient voice.

Arielle had agreed to walk with her new roommate, just because it would have been weird if she'd refused to. The girl had an odd air about her, like she was made of lambs' wool and bemused contentment, like life was a fairy tale unfolding around her and she was happy to be part of the ride. But she wiped down the sink every time she washed her hands and she'd been really sweet about letting Arielle choose which room in Harrison Suite 17C she wanted. (The one with the view of the quad, obviously.)

"Yeah. I think the Greek life stuff is that way."

"Okay. I'm headed just over there. Church stuff," Amy explained with a nervous smile.

Arielle nodded, then craned her neck to find the group of tables representing different sorority houses on campus. Rachel had been pulled into one during informal Spring recruitment last year—something that started with "Delta." Delta Pi…something? Arielle had grimaced when Rachel breathlessly told her about the whole process when she came home for Passover, but soon it became clear that Rachel loved sorority life. There was some invisible connection that lived in the Greek letters that Rachel seemed to have emblazoned on everything, something that Arielle just couldn't grasp. But Arielle loved Rachel, so she would hang out at the sorority parties. No problem.

A flash of long, shining chestnut hair caught Arielle's eye, and her heart stuttered. It started up again when she heard the laugh. She'd know that laugh anywhere—the one that made her feel safe when she was uncertain and put her on top of the world when she was sad. The one that had helped her figure out her place in her messed up little corner of Indiana. Even though Rachel's gorgeous smile was aimed at some guy as she handed him a flier, Arielle knew it as the same one that made her fall head over heels for this beautiful, ambitious, about-to-be-ecstatically-surprised girl. Arielle's legs couldn't carry her to the Delta Pi table fast enough.

With every step Arielle took, the noise and hustle of the crowd melted into slow-motioned, muffled, meaningless activity. As the guy turned away from Rachel and kept walking along the quad path, Rachel's eyes roamed over the crowd.

Come on, look this way. I'm here. All you have to do is turn a little more...

And then it happened. Their eyes locked, and Arielle's heartbeat counted the fractions of seconds it took for Rachel's eyes to go wide with happy surprise, for her smile to crook the corner of her mouth up and deepen the adorable one-sided dimple next to it.

Their gazes connected with so much electricity that it nearly knocked Arielle off her feet. Rachel's eyes flew open wide and Arielle's steps quickened. She was almost there. Instead of the smile Arielle had waited for, Rachel's total shock had made her jaw drop, and her feet cement to the ground. So Arielle closed the distance, standing on her tiptoes so she could fling her arms around Rachel's neck.

God, it felt so good to have her right here—real and warm and right here to touch. Rachel's hands rested loosely on Arielle's shoulder blades instead of gripping her in a hug—she must have been so surprised she'd lost her strength.

It was only when Arielle buried her face in Rachel's neck, breathing in the deep, flowery scent of her perfume and sighing at the slip of Rachel's perfectly straightened hair against her cheek, and Rachel stiffened, that she realized something was wrong.

Rachel didn't laugh, or squeal, or cry, or kiss her. There wasn't even a happy hug. Instead, Rachel dropped her arms and stepped back. And when she asked Arielle, "What are you doing here?" her tone was confused instead of happy.

Arielle's hands trembled as Rachel took another step away, still holding them loosely between her fingertips. Her intuition told her that this wasn't shaping up to be the happy reunion she'd fantasized about.

"Waitlist," she said breathlessly, commanding herself to calm down. She had to give her a second. Rachel always did need a second to get used to new things. "I applied and I was waitlisted, and I never told you, because it was already hard enough, knowing we'd have to be apart. But I got the letter three weeks ago, and..." She couldn't stand it any longer. Arielle stepped in, craving more contact.

Rachel stepped back, then scanned her sorority's table. "Hannah? Okay if I duck out for a few minutes?" The girl stopped her conversation with a hulking guy carrying a football under his arm to nod and wave at Rachel. "Follow me," she said to Arielle, dropping one of her hands and holding the other low by the pinkie and tugging her gently through the crowd.

Less than a hundred feet away, a university building loomed over the quad, framed by pillars and arches that reminded Ari of something she'd see at Hogwarts. It wasn't the reason she'd wanted to come to Northern, but it definitely didn't hurt. Rachel dropped Arielle's hand when they reached the gray stone stairs, and glanced back at her as she tugged the heavy wooded door open.

The Broken Hearts Society of Suite 17C

The shining floor sent echoes to the roof with each of their footsteps in the empty entranceway. Rachel pivoted to turn into an equally empty hallway, then leaned against a wall to face Arielle.

The tension in Arielle's chest dissipated somewhat. She just wanted to go someplace private to make out. Arielle slid her hands over Rachel's hips, pulling her up toward her. She just wanted to feel her again, just wanted Rachel to cup her jaw and stroke her lip with a thumb, the one thing that always totally undid her.

But Rachel's body stayed glued to the wall. Her fingers whispered against Arielle's and she asked again with sad eyes, "What are you doing here?"

Just like that, the tension returned. "I thought I would surprise you," Arielle said softly, this time without a smile.

A deep sigh blew through Rachel's lips as she stood and again held Arielle's fingertips loosely between her own. "At the Student Activities Fair? With all my friends there? While I was working the table?"

"I knew for sure I would find you there." Stinging tears began to prick at her eyes.

"Listen," Rachel said, trying and failing to look into Arielle's eyes. God, this was getting worse by the millisecond. Arielle willed her body to stop shaking. "Things are different here at Northern. So different from back home."

"Yeah," Arielle said, forcing a weak smile. "I know. You're really busy, and you have a ton of extracurriculars, and I totally respect that. I swear. I'll be the best college girlfriend. I'll bring dinner to the house when you have to study late. I'll bake cookies for all your sorority sisters, and they'll all love me. And we can figure out which classes we can walk to together, and then on holidays we can drive home together. It'll be…"

"Impossible." Anger flashed across Rachel's face as she let the word out in a huff.

It was just one word, but it had a hundred possible meanings. That didn't change the fact that none of them made a bit of sense to Arielle. "What do you mean?"

"Ari," Rachel said softly. "We can't be together. Back home? That was fun, that was messing around. Home is a holding pattern. This is real life."

"But I'm real. The way I feel about you is real." Panic overloaded Arielle's senses, letting her focus only on each individual word as it came out.

"I've never told my sorority sisters about you," Rachel said, staring at the floor. "They don't know, and…" she blew out a breath and raised her eyes to Arielle's. "And I don't want them to. They've never let a gay girl in before, and…you know."

"But you are gay. And…"

"No," Rachel interrupted, her eyes hard. "You are gay. I am Rachel. I liked hooking up with you, yeah. I liked spending time with you. But that can't be for the rest of my life. That's not…that's not who I want to be."

The Broken Hearts Society of Suite 17C

Rachel was lying to herself, and she didn't even realize it. Arielle knew the look on Rachel's face when she came, she knew the stroke of Rachel's hand over her stomach. She knew the tone of the quiet conversations they had, fingers running through hair and lips pressed to throats. She knew the way her heart felt so full it might burst. That was love.

"I love you," Arielle said, calling every ounce of conviction to her words. "And you love me. You can't possibly tell me you don't. I didn't imagine everything between us."

"You don't love me, Ari." Rachel kept staring at her feet and slowly lifted Arielle's hands from her waist. "You love my pussy. And we did have fun together. But now…now we have to grow up."

Hadn't they talked about building a life together? Hadn't they mentioned "someday" in their delirious after-talks? "I don't understand how your sorority sisters don't know. You're gorgeous. How did you get through a whole year going to parties with them and not dating any of these stupid frat guys without them asking you what the deal was?"

Rachel's eyes flicked to Arielle's, then she covered them with both hands and slumped back against the wall. Ari staggered backward, the realization hitting her like a Hulk-punch to the stomach. "You did date someone, didn't you?"

She fixed her eyes on her shoes. "There were so many parties during rush, and I got invited to one. And then I really started to like him. A lot."

"Him?!?!" The pain of imagining Rachel with a guy threatened to completely undo Ari.

"I'm sorry, Ari. I am. I thought…"

"You thought what? Did you have any idea how much I loved you?"

Rachel's milk chocolate eyes went stormy "God, Ari, I don't know. You just…you can't blame me for making the decisions I did. Everything is different here. Our real lives are starting now. You'll see. Everything will change for you, too."

A thousand thoughts whipped around Arielle's head, none of them formed into anything coherent, none of them making any sense. After all, they came from senselessness. This was wrong, this was all wrong. Nothing would change for her, ever. She and Rachel belonged together. They were the same, from their obsession with perfect grades to their overbearing Jewish mothers. College was where they were supposed to grow into adults together. Indiana Northern was where their relationship was supposed to really start, not end.

But the hard truth was that Rachel had already started to back away, toward the door. "I should get back," she said, pointing a weak thumb at the quad. "The girls need me." Arielle's legs were the ones glued to the ground now.

The Broken Hearts Society of Suite 17C

And then, just before she rounded the corner out of the hallway, "I'm sorry, Ari. I am. I…I'll see you around, okay?"

Arielle's knees hit the floor and pain sliced through them. A sob ripped through her chest, and she swallowed it, forcing the tears to run silently, their only accompaniment the quick breaths that took hold of her lungs.

Arielle's life was over. She would never love anyone as much as she loved Rachel. It was impossible.

Chapter 3

Amy

Amy's small town, church-girl life had been seamlessly perfect until exactly two weeks ago. Which was why it was such a relief she was finally settled at Indiana Northern—it gave her the chance to forget about the single misstep she'd made back home and focus on the next four years of doing well in classes, cheering Adam on at every single football game, and planning for their life together once he'd either gone pro or earned his business degree. Or both.

She was a lucky girl, and she knew it. Hardly anyone had the luck to be spending four years with the love of their life, to have a plan in place so that the sailing would be smooth the whole way. Yes, thinking about what had happened was still a bit fresh and painful, but Adam's words right after they'd found out—"We can get through anything, babe. I know we can,"—rang through her memory like a prayer. He was the only other person who

The Broken Hearts Society of Suite 17C

knew about it, what it meant they had lost and gained at the same time. She believed him, because he was her future. He was all she'd ever really wanted, and he would make anything her heart desired happen for her. He'd promised.

She hitched her purse over her shoulder and glanced at the framed picture on her desk one more time before heading out—she and Adam at prom, just three months ago. Everything about that day had been perfect—from the corsage to the DJ playing their song for the last dance, to the hotel room Adam had surprised her with afterward. Even though that was the night everything began to change, and so much was different now, at least their relationship would never show it. Amy's phone buzzed against her palm, and she turned the screen out to see a message from Adam.

Hey baby. Meet outside admissions at 5? I want us to have dinner.

He was always thinking of her. Amy could barely keep the smile off her face as she turned toward the door, nearly walking head first into Arielle, one of her new roommates. The girls laughed, but Arielle's excitement to get out the door was obvious.

"You going to the Student Activities Fair?" Amy asked, scanning Arielle's outfit. She dressed in trendy jeans and left a trail of just-showered scent with every move she made, even though Amy knew neither of them had ventured down to the showers yet. Compared to

Amy's small-town style, Arielle's outfit looked like it had come straight off a runway. It made Amy regret not giving more thought to the way she dressed. She tugged at the hem of her cheer squad t-shirt and chanced a tentative smile at Arielle.

Arielle nodded. "Yep. I'm going to surprise someone, actually. Doesn't know I'm going here. Yet." This girl's smile was so full of joy that it lifted Amy's heart.

"Want to walk down together? I need to meet someone at admissions and I have no clue where that is."

Arielle laughed. "I have no clue either."

Amy nodded and smiled to herself as she left the Suite first, holding the door for Arielle. Yes. Everything was going to be just fine, after all.

When Amy had envisioned life at Indiana Northern, she saw a large-scale version of high school. But this was different in so many ways. For one, crosses were everywhere.

Amy had gone looking for the "religious life" section of the Activities Fair, sure. Dad would definitely be wondering whether she'd settled on a church for weekly services, and sending a flier with a worship schedule home should be enough to appease Mom and Dad, as well as Adam's parents.

But she hadn't expected there to be this many Christian groups. She scanned the crowd. Adam had told her he'd meet her outside Admissions, which was straight ahead, but he was nowhere in sight. Arielle had already run off toward some girl she knew from home, and it made Amy nervous to be alone.

She craned her neck over the crowd. The quad was an interconnected web of paths, all meeting in the middle where the information booth had been. Arielle had been looking for the section with the sororities, and the guide had sweetly explained the color-coded system. Amy had heard "religious life" and zoned out after that, only half-noticing which direction Arielle had gone. She'd thought for a second about asking for Arielle's number, so they could meet up later, but once she touched base with Adam she probably wouldn't be back at her own room for awhile, anyway.

She pulled out her phone and texted Adam: **Where are you?**

She stood, jittery, until the little dots indicating he was typing popped up on her screen, then furrowed her brow when they disappeared. A minute later, nothing.

Apprehension twisted in her gut, but she quashed it down. Everything was going to be fine. Perfectly fine.

If he wasn't standing in front of admissions yet, Adam had to be in the religious life section. He was a pastor's kid—*the* pastor's kid. He went to church every Sunday and Wednesday, not to mention every youth group and outreach event. She walked tentatively down the sidewalk lined with cheap, six-foot folding tables, trying not to be too obvious about looking for him. One girl handed her a glossy handbill promising a "Coffee and Christ" Bible study, a man in a short-sleeved shirt and priest's collar handed her a small potted plant and a schedule of masses on campus. When she smiled politely at the table for Hillel, which she assumed was Jewish because of the stars, the kid working that table handed her a pen. She grasped for the right words to tell them she was a Christian, but didn't want to offend anyone, so she wrote her name on the signup sheet the kid pointed out to her and kept walking.

She scanned the crowd again. Where in the world could he be? She'd made it to the end of the walk with an armful of fliers, the plant, and a few candies and pens, but no boyfriend.

Finally, a reply came through on her phone. **At the activities fair. I'll find you.**

She blew out a breath. Maybe he'd been recruited to help the football players with their table, or maybe he'd gone to grab some fast food for lunch.

Way to be a crazy psycho girlfriend, Amy. You know he loves you. What are you worried about?

She slung her backpack to the ground to drop her armful of stuff in, wondering how much longer she was going to be out here. There were so many people, and she suddenly felt she was making an impression on all of them at once. She should have worn one of the cute new outfits Mom had taken her shopping for—skinny jeans, flats, and a little cardigan. She'd never forget how Mom had held her out at arm's length, brushed a copper wave back over Amy's shoulder, and pronounced her 'perfect.' She'd needed to hear that this summer, since everything that had happened since prom suggested otherwise.

Amy sighed again and shook her head. She was in a different world now, and she was determined to put all that nonsense behind her. Except for Adam.

Then it occurred to her—maybe he'd gone to the cheerleading table looking for her. Of course. She really should get to him.

Amy pushed from squatting over her bag to standing so quickly that she rammed her head into some poor guy's crotch.

"Holy crud!" he grunted, doubling over and backing up at the same time. Amy blushed in mortification, rushing to pick up all his dropped papers.

"Oh my gosh, I'm so sorry. Here, let me…"

The guy puffed as he stood up to full height—just one or two inches taller than she was, his head topped with hair almost as orange as hers was. His mouth twisted into a grimace as he adjusted his dark-framed glasses, and he moved toward Amy with a slight, but obvious, hobble.

Amy's heartbeat slowed. Thank goodness, he seemed like he'd recover.

When he finally spoke, it was with the beginnings of a smile. "They told me this year's Activities Fair would be challenging, but man. They didn't tell me it'd be a gauntlet. A surprise one, at that."

"I'm so, so sorry. I didn't…I mean, do you think you'll be okay?"

He laughed again. "I can't say for sure. I've never taken a direct hit to that…uh…area, but I know a lot of guys who play sports have, and they end up just fine."

Of course he would be. Adam had been knocked between the legs more times than she could count, and he was certainly no worse for wear. She almost reassured the poor guy she'd just headed in the crotch by saying just that, but something held her back. Maybe because something else entirely occurred to her.

"You didn't swear," she blurted.

"Huh?" the guy asked, finally looking sort of normal instead of wincing in pain.

"When I…you know. Ran into you. You didn't curse, even though it obviously, um…hurt."

"Oh, right. Weird, right? I've always been weird. But, you know…" he gestured around to all the crosses and shirts mentioning Jesus in some capacity or another. "I was raised in a super Christian house. My parents would have killed me if they'd heard I'd cursed, and our neighborhood was pretty small. So I kind of trained myself not to." He chuckled. His eyes were rich brown with flecks of moss-green, like if she could go inside them

The Broken Hearts Society of Suite 17C

she'd be standing in a lush forest. A feeling of inexplicable, complete safety bled through her. "I think I adequately expressed my pain regardless, though."

"Are you sure you're okay?" she asked again, her voice helpless and small.

He opened his mouth to respond, but at that moment, a girl approached and thrust a flier at them. There, in glossy magazine-print glory, was a picture of an eight-week-old fetus with the words "It's not a choice, it's a child" in bold black lettering beneath it. "Come to our meeting for support of pre-born rights?" the girl asked in a voice too high and cheerful for the picture she held hundreds of copies of in her hands.

Amy's mouth dropped open and she stammered. She tried to make words come out—simple words like "no thanks" or "I'm busy that night"—but came up empty. The brown-eyed guy's eyes swept over her face and saw something that made him step forward and take the paper, then examine it.

"Are you a Christian group, or a political group?" His eyes narrowed at the girl.

"Our table is in the political activism section, but..."

"You shouldn't be here. This is for churches, prayer groups, and Bible study groups. Not gross shock and awe campaigns."

"Listen, pre-born rights are..."

"Not for this section," the guy repeated. "If I see you here again, I'll report you."

The girl snatched back her paper, glared at him, turned on her heel and marched away.

"You okay?" the guy asked softly.

She wasn't okay. "Yeah. Yeah. I'm just…" What was she? Suffering from PTSD? Was she pro-choice now, after everything that had happened to her?

"Pro Choice" was among the dirtiest of phrases back home. But she wasn't home anymore. "Those pictures just gross me out," she said quietly, trying to maintain eye contact with him but staring at his ear instead.

"Yeah. I had a class last year about the psychology of political campaigns. We spent a while on those. There are more gross things about that than just the picture."

She nodded gratefully. "You know, it's my first day here. And I was only here looking for—"

Then the sound of an anguished sob ripped through the air. Nobody else seemed to notice, but her head turned in a flash. Mom had always said that Amy felt everyone else's suffering ten times more than her own—it was what made her the star of every mission trip her church sent them on. Sure enough, there on the stone steps of one of the old buildings sat a girl with her head bowed and bobbing as she cried. Amy's heart twisted when she realized she recognized that head, covered in dark brown curls highlighted with streaks of burgundy. Arielle, her new roommate.

The guy with brown eyes stood closer to her now than he had a few seconds ago, watching her. "That's my

The Broken Hearts Society of Suite 17C

roommate," she explained, hitching her bag over her shoulder. "I should...Maybe I'll see you later?" How did you end a conversation with a random, ridiculously nice, non-swearing guy you just head-butted in the private parts?

"Definitely," he said. "You'd better go," he said when Arielle lifted her head to reveal tears running down her cheeks in rivers.

Amy plowed through the crowd toward her.

She only looked back once, and when she did, the guy was still watching her with those patient, calm brown eyes.

Amy didn't have to ask what was going on. She knew from the second she saw Arielle sitting on those stone steps, lonely and despairing in the middle of the busiest day on campus, that the surprise she'd been so excited about less than an hour ago hadn't gone as well as she'd hoped.

Had gone disastrously, by the looks of it.

Amy fumbled in her purse for the little packet of tissues her mother had taught her to carry everywhere—she wouldn't want to be seen with smudged makeup or a runny nose. She found three wrinkled ones left in the packet, and handed one to Arielle, who noisily blew her nose, then sat there, no longer crying, but taking deep, shuddering breaths as her red eyes stared blankly out onto the quad.

She said it almost without hesitation, like it was totally natural. "Let's get you home." Something deep and satisfying warmed in her when Arielle nodded and grabbed onto her for support when she stood. "There's a path behind this building that'll let us go around the quad instead of through the crowd. Okay?"

Arielle just nodded and took another shuddering breath.

The girls walked quickly together, Arielle looking at her feet and Amy sneaking a glance at her every now and then. Arielle moved purposefully in the direction of their dorm, but Amy doubted she would have ever moved if she hadn't told her to. The look on her face expressed nothing but emptiness.

Up the elevator and inside their common room, Amy dropped her bag of fliers to the floor, and coaxed Arielle's messenger bag down from her shoulder. When it was gone, Arielle crossed the room like the weight of it had been the only thing keeping her from moving. She collapsed on the couch and resumed the same pose she'd had on the quad—staring into nothing.

Her tears had stopped. Amy couldn't decide whether that meant she was better or worse. Back in June, when Amy had lain on her bed weeping for days, the tears stopping meant that she was so exhausted with grief and confusion that she felt nothing anymore, and had nothing left to put forth, not even her pathetic, snotty tears.

When Amy was in that situation, the one thing she'd needed was for someone to sit beside her, keeping her company and understanding that she was in the midst of a

The Broken Hearts Society of Suite 17C

horrible, endless expanse of sorrow. So that's what she did.

Cautiously, she raised her hand and put it on Arielle's back, moving it back and forth just a bit. With that, Arielle's whole body convulsed, and the tears started again.

"Shhhh. Shhhh. It's okay. I mean, maybe it's not, but I'm sure it will be. Eventually."

"It was the whole reason I came," Arielle sniffled in a voice just above a whisper, which was somehow even sadder than the twisted sound Amy expected. "So we could be together."

"Oh, honey," Amy crooned, surprised at her own easy affection for this girl she had only just met two hours ago and knew next to nothing about. "It can't have been that bad. Maybe he was just so surprised that he...didn't know what to say? What were his exact words?"

Arielle raised her eyes to Amy's, and stared at her while she took another shuddering breath. "Yeah. *She* was surprised. And it really is that bad. She said we can't be together—that nobody can know."

Amy's stomach sank. After all those sermons Adam's dad had given about the homosexual agenda, how it was going to destroy families, the very fabric of the country, she had a lesbian roommate.

Suddenly, when that agenda was sitting beside her and heartbroken, it seemed a whole lot less scary. A whole lot less other and a whole lot more human.

Amy gave Arielle a pitying look, and reached further around her back to hug her at the shoulder. Arielle's head fell onto her shoulder, and she sniffled. After a few seconds, the sniffles got wetter, and Arielle asked timidly, "Do you think you could get me another Kleenex?"

"Yeah. Of course." Gingerly, she stood up, and Arielle slumped back onto the couch, drawing her knees up to her chest and staring at the front door.

Mom had packed 20 tiny packets of tissues in with her stuff, of course. The instant she emerged from her room with one in each hand, their common room door swung open, revealing a girl in a leather jacket, despite the heat, short shorts, and combat boots, with the most rage-filled scowl on her face that Amy could imagine. The girl looked from Amy, standing stunned in the doorway, and Arielle, still looking at nothing on the couch, dropped her bag on top of the pile Amy had started, and sighed heavily. Her eyes burned into Amy's. "What the fuck is wrong with her?"

Amy flinched, seeing a flash of Mom's judgmental brow-wrinkling in her memory.

"Um. It's just…she saw someone from back home, and it wasn't…"

"Breakup. A breakup happened," Arielle's voice ground out, low and hopeless.

"Fuck." The girl actually looked sorry now. "Um. Whoa. Okay. Well, I'm Rion, and I'm in the other room. So."

The Broken Hearts Society of Suite 17C

Amy put on a smile that was hopefully friendly while being respectful of her new destroyed friend on the couch. "Amy," she introduced herself.

Rion's eyes swept over her body, then over to Arielle, then across the room. Amy was being evaluated, and Rion's cold stare didn't give a single hint of what her verdict was.

"Okay. Well I'm gonna…I mean, I should…my stuff is still everywhere…" Rion jerked her head toward the only room with a closed door, and quickly disappeared into it.

Just then, Amy's phone buzzed. She flipped it over.

Adam: **Waiting in the lobby of your dorm.**

Butterflies filled Amy's stomach. It was amazing how Adam could still do that to her. Maybe they'd be one of those couples who still felt their hearts skipping a beat when they looked at each other, even after 50 years of marriage. Everyone deserved to love someone like that.

"Arielle?" she asked softly, trying to meet the girl's gaze. "I promised someone I'd meet them for dinner," she said softly, leaving her words purposely vague. No need to rub it in Arielle's face that she was in a happy relationship, not now or ever. "Can I bring something back for you? Or…do you want to come with us?"

"I'm good," Arielle said in that same strangled whisper of a voice.

She was definitely not good, but Amy didn't think she was going to slit her wrists either. Not right now, anyway.

"Okay. I'll come back soon, okay? Make sure you're alright?" And she wasn't lying. Amy knew the kind of pain that made you stare into nothing, and at the very least, it deserved to be checked up on. Arielle's nod was barely perceptible. "Alright," Amy said on her behalf. She quietly picked up her purple backpack embroidered with her initials and slunk out the door.

Amy slumped against the elevator wall, watching the glowing red numbers slowly tick down from 17. She flipped her key card over and over in her hand, letting the plastic rasping against her skin bring her back to the moment at hand. She was about to see Adam again, and she really couldn't wait.

She had understood when Adam hadn't been able to hang out during move-in day. Saturday had been a whirlwind of hauling things in from cars, unpacking, decorating, orientation tours and hall meetings. She thought she'd seen him once in the crowd at one orientation event—he was so big and bulky, it was hard to miss him—but he'd been talking to someone else and she'd only glimpsed his profile before he'd turned and walked the other way. She'd texted him, but sometimes he'd been so busy he hadn't even been able to reply for hours.

The elevator dipped down, then stopped, and Amy held her breath as the doors slid open. There he was, waiting at the desk for her. As an offensive lineman, Adam was of course a big guy—six foot four and two

The Broken Hearts Society of Suite 17C

hundred ten pounds—but he was a gorgeous, muscled kind of big. Huge in the best way, that made her five-seven frame feel petite and feminine. There was nothing like being engulfed in his hug, as though she could completely disappear in it—be completely hidden from the world. And in just four years, it could be just the two of them. That future began now.

Adam turned at the ding of the elevator door closing, and Amy practically skipped toward him, beaming. "Hey, you!" Her voice lilted, automatically becoming higher pitched in his presence. She waited for the big grin to spread across his face, like the one she was used to seeing. Those beautiful straight teeth, the dimple that only showed on one side. He was perfect.

But that smile never came. Instead, it was one with lips pressed together, like the one he gave to the guys on the losing team when they lined up to shake hands, murmuring "good game." It was the smile that meant, "Sorry you lost. I'm being a good sport by shaking your hand."

Amy tried to ignore the sinking feeling in her stomach and turn it into concern for whatever was upsetting him. "What's wrong, babe?"

"It's good to see you, Ames," he answered, pulling her into a soft hug without even trying to kiss her.

What in the world was going on? They were away from home now, out from under the watchful eye of her dad. Adam was almost always a gentleman with his kisses, saving the really passionate ones for rare private occasions, but this was college. Amy pulled back a little and stood on her tiptoes, stretching her lips to his. But he just gave her that same weird smile again and stepped back from her, too. "Can we talk?"

Now the pit in Amy's stomach was really heavy. The last time she'd said those words, she was sitting Adam down for a talk, and the news wasn't good. But she'd been so scared then, and right now he looked…calm. Resigned. Sure of himself in a way she'd never been.

He tugged her toward the common area tucked inside Harrison tower's entryway, filled with decade-old furniture pre-arranged to encourage freshmen to socialize. She sat on one of the loveseats, the swirled, office-grade fabric rasping against her thighs when her sundress hiked up. She tugged it back down toward her knees, but the fabric stubbornly rode up.

Adam sat in the chair opposite her, and reached both his hands out. Instinctively, she wove her fingers with his.

"Amy," he started, "I'm glad we're finally getting a chance to talk."

"I've been trying to get a hold of you, but I thought—"

"It's been busy," he cut her off. "We've both been busy, but in the past couple days, I've done a lot of thinking, too."

Amy's eyebrows furrowed. "Thinking about what?" All the thinking, all the planning, had been done before they got here. All during senior year, as they completed

The Broken Hearts Society of Suite 17C

their applications at the same cafeteria table and went out to dinner together to open their acceptance letters. As Adam held her hand two weeks after graduation and promised her everything would be okay, that this was just a bump in the road that they would get over without a hitch.

"I've been thinking, and praying, Ames. And talking to my dad. The thing is, everything here at Northern is so new. It can be overwhelming, and a little confusing, too. And I really want to do the right thing."

Okay, this was seriously confusing. "I know you do, babe," Amy said, "You always do the right thing. Always."

He blew out a breath. "It's so good to hear you say that." His eyes darted around the common area, and seeing nobody else there—it was nearly time for dinner—he looked at her again, squeezing her hands gently. "I think it would be best if we took a little break."

"Break from...what?" Amy gave him a gentle smile even as her stomach went wild. She could guess what he meant, knew it, probably, deep down. But taking a break from their relationship was not a concept she could begin to wrap her head around, so she asked the question anyway.

"I've been meeting a lot of guys here, and they all broke up with their girlfriends—and boyfriends—before they moved here. College is meant for experiencing new things, and I really want to give that my best shot."

"But we talked about this, we—"

"I wasn't lying when I told you I'd prayed about this," he said, lowering his voice and giving her a pitying look. As if that helped the giant fist slowly squeezing her ribs together so that she couldn't breathe. "God wants something bigger for us, Amy, and I'm pretty sure it's for us to be together. But don't you want to be sure yourself? Don't you want to know what it's like, to be apart, before we decide to be together?"

"What do you mean, to be apart? What would be the difference, Adam? We'd have the same classes, the same roommates, the same everything, except we wouldn't have each other. We wouldn't have anyone."

Adam's eyebrows furrowed down further, and he pulled one hand away from Amy's to slide it over the back of his neck, shaking his head slightly.

"I'm saying I think we should…you know. See other people for a little while. See who else is out there."

"You're saying…I'm sorry. You're saying you want to go out with…other girls?" The words felt too strange rolling off her tongue, because she had never even entertained that concept. There were no other girls, not for Adam. He'd told the story a hundred times, how they'd shared a football field since he was on the Kindergarten PeeWee team and she bounced around with the Tiny Tigers cheer squad. Her mom joked that it might be love at first sight, but they'd never know, because the first time they'd seen each other they were infants, gurgling at each other across the church pews. Their

The Broken Hearts Society of Suite 17C

relationship was a given, like the rotation of the Earth or ham on Easter. Adam loved her and she loved him and they were going to be together forever.

Most of all, they were going to complete the family they'd accidentally started. They were going to make the whole thing right.

Now he dropped her hands entirely, and sat up straight. "I talked to my dad, too. I told him what I was feeling." His deep blue eyes with flecks of gray, the ones she'd marveled at so many times between kisses, flashed into hers, then looked down again. "He agreed that you're a great girl, and that you're perfect for me, and that I owe it to you to be completely certain. In my heart."

Amy wanted to be sick. No, she was definitely going to vomit. The thought of Adam being with other girls in the same way he'd touched her...kissing them, slow dancing with them, running his hands through their hair...it was unnatural. "You can't," she whispered. "After everything that happened to us...you just can't."

"No, Amy." Adam's voice took on that tone that meant a decision was being made, whether Amy liked it or not. "After everything that happened to us, I need to."

Hot tears clouded her vision without warning. She looked toward him, but couldn't see him. It was like he was fading away before her very eyes, with the rest of her future. With the one they'd started back home, and were supposed to be picking up right now.

"You need to go now," she whispered. She wasn't even sure what made her say it. She didn't want Adam to leave, but this wasn't the Adam she knew—the one who was, above all else, devoted to her. Loyal, honorable. Steadfast. This wasn't the same Adam. Whether it was his roommates, his father, or his own confusion, something had changed him, and she couldn't look at him anymore.

"Baby, are you okay? Can I walk you back up to your room?"

Amy's stomach lurched. "You need to go now," she said, her voice a little stronger. A couple other thoughts ran through her head—like how she wasn't a baby, and obviously not his anymore, and how she could walk herself back up to her room—but she couldn't bring herself to say them in a way that didn't draw attention to herself.

With a shaking arm, she pushed herself up from the chair, and forced her legs to turn from Adam and toward the elevator, the only place that offered any certainty or comfort now.

"Amy, please. I want you to know how much I love you."

But he didn't. She'd thought he loved her, but here was the evidence, plain as day. He didn't. You couldn't do something like this to someone you loved.

She let out a shuddering breath, and forced herself to walk to the elevator. Punch the number. 17. Her suite. The only thing that felt anything close to safe right now. She could barely see Adam's outline in the lobby when she turned and rested against the back wall of the elevator. He'd gotten so much smaller, so far away. He wasn't moving, but she was. Up, up, and away.

To get over one breakup, I went out to a drag club for mardi gras. It wasn't about male attention, it was about remembering how to have fun without it.

~L.S. Mooney

Chapter 4

Rion

Rion sat down hard on her bed, wincing as its springs squeaked beneath her. The girl on the couch in their common room—Arielle, she thought—was obviously a fucking mess. Maybe a head case, too. Whatever was going on with her, Rion did not want to disturb the silence that Amy, the chipper pretty one, had left in her wake as she bounced out of the room to dinner with God-knew-who. At least it had gotten her smiley ass out of the room.

A sigh escaped Rion's lips as she stared at her own blank walls. Fucking pathetic. What had she gotten herself into, anyway? She should have known better than to think she could share a living space with two entitled college brats without wanting to kill them.

The Broken Hearts Society of Suite 17C

Her stomach grumbled, loudly, almost echoing off the gray concrete blocks that surrounded her. For a split second, panic shot through her as she wondered what time dinner was, whether she had missed it—then she remembered that she was at college now, that her scholarship covered her food, and that on a campus this big, there was some kind of dining hall open at pretty much any time. She could do whatever she damn well pleased. At least, when it came to meals.

She hoisted herself up and gingerly opened the door to her room, again. Arielle still sat on the couch, staring at nothing. Jesus, she could have at least put the fucking TV on. Anything to fill the horrible silence punctuated by her pathetic sniffling.

Rion didn't know this girl at all, so she had no way to know whether she would or should like her. But so help her God, she would murder whatever asshole prepubescent son-of-a-bitch pussy college boy had turned her into a red-faced, sniveling, awkwardness-oozing roommate on her first day at school.

Should Rion tell her where she was going? In the group home, she rarely spoke to her roommates—for one, she didn't dare, because she was legitimately worried the bitches would knife her. But for another she didn't have to. They had a curfew, and set times for meals. More importantly, they didn't give a shit about each other. In a group home, you could only afford to give a shit about yourself.

"I'm going to get something to eat. I'm starving." She left out the part about what a goddamn long, awful day it had been finding out she had to work at a head shop just to stay in school. This girl's day had obviously been worse, even though Rion didn't know what it would really take to get her to cry that much anymore. Cry at all, really. The last time she'd let herself had been Dad's funeral, and even then she didn't know exactly what the tears were made up of.

"Could you bring back something? Anything. I skipped lunch but I don't think I can leave the room."

Dramatic, much?

"You have swipes, right?"

Rion's mouth dropped open. "I..." the presumptuousness of a kid asking her to buy dinner meant that this kid never had to worry about money. Ever. But then it occurred to her—not only did her 21-meal-a-week meal plan give her enough to eat, but there would almost certainly be leftover meals she could share. And Rion had had bad days, days where she would have given her right arm for someone willing to bring her dinner.

Not to mention all the crying had made the poor girl look like a fucking leper, her skin was so blotchy and swollen. She really shouldn't be leaving the room. "Yeah. I do. I'll be right back."

Rion took the stairs. Only sixteen flights, and they were all down— it gave her a good excuse to stretch, and

The Broken Hearts Society of Suite 17C

to kill time. Who knew how long bouncy Amy would be gone?

The dining hall in the basement of Harrison Tower was one of those a la carte places, where everything was made to order or pre-packaged and could be taken away in boxes. A moody introvert's dream, Rion thought, smiling wryly. It was one of the things that made her happiest about being assigned this dorm in the first place.

A bored-looking girl in a University polo and black visor took her order for three personal cheese pizzas. The gaping pit inside her stomach growled in approval. Had she seriously forgotten to eat lunch?

She absentmindedly grabbed a bag of carrot sticks and a little container of ranch dressing to make them more palatable. A couple packages of Oreo cookies and a couple bottles of pop should do it. She loaded it all onto the tray and handed her card to the bug-eyed cashier. "What?" Rion snarled when the girl tipped her head down at her tray. The girl quickly swiped the card.

"Wait," Rion said, her eyes going to a cooler just behind the checkout. "Is that ice cream?"

"Yeah, it's Jeni's. We get it sent in from Ohio."

"Is it any good?"

"Oh, it's the best."

"Okay, give me one of each flavor."

"You sure?"

"Positive. I have the biggest meal plan."

"Scholarship?"

Rion glared at her.

"All the scholarship kids get the biggest one, and always buy pints. RAs, too," the girl rushed to explain, her voice full of apology. Rion realized for the first time that this girl was scared of her. Jesus.

So, she forced a smile. "Makes sense." She snagged a white plastic grocery bag from the end of the line and tossed everything in. Thank God her room was only an elevator ride away.

Back inside Suite 17C, Rion dropped the bag on the wobbly particle board coffee table in their common room, and got to work spreading it out. Arielle had finally left the couch, but came back a few seconds after Rion slammed the door. She had on a huge t-shirt and a pair of yoga pants, which made Rion want to get into her own giant comfy pants. She'd brought a pair of Dad's that she couldn't actually remember him wearing, but they made her feel closer to him anyway. Arielle clutched a thin blanket around her shoulders and resettled on the same spot on the couch, picking up the little pack of tissues Amy had brought out for her.

"Oh my God," she moaned. "Pizza. You are the best. Seriously."

A smile twitched at the corners of Rion's mouth. "See? Things aren't all bad."

Now even Arielle cracked a smile. "It's been pretty much the worst day of my life, but pizza always makes things better. Seriously, thank you."

"Yeah, me too."

Arielle's eyes went wide. "You got dumped too?"

"No, I just had to take a shit job I really didn't want to take." Rion had stormed out of the Studio determined to find some other place, any other place, to work. But all of them had online job applications that asked whether she'd ever been convicted of a crime. The little voice at the back of her head that said the Studio was the best opportunity she had was right. Dammit.

Rion needed to change the subject before she got all melancholy. That wouldn't help anyone. "So which of these douchebag college guys do I have to murder?" The words were out before she thought about what she meant by them. Why did she give a shit about which Indiana Northern asshole had broken Arielle's heart? It seemed like the crying was over, and hopefully so was the food-ordering. They could go about their lives going to different classes and moving past each other from the door of their suite to the doors of their rooms, and before they knew it, freshman year would be over.

But she still had some strange pull toward wanting to know. Wanting to care.

"None of the guys. But a two-faced sorority girl would be good."

Ah, lesbian romance drama. Fucking fabulous. In the group home, Rion had seen more than a few gay girls making out one day and throwing punches the next, and that shit was never pretty.

Still, she caught herself guarding her words. Caring what Arielle would think of her. "Well, give me her stats and I won't let her into the Suite. You have my word."

Arielle cracked another smile as she reached for a pizza box. "Tall, willowy, straightened reddish-brown hair, wearing her sorority letters. Fucking gorgeous. And full of herself. You know, the usual."

"Done and done. If you have a picture we can hang it on the wall and throw darts at it."

But now the girl choked back a sob. "I have so many pictures."

"Okay, okay. Too soon. Sorry." Rion fumbled through the bags. "Look. I have ice cream too. It'll be okay."

And then the door to Suite 17C flung open, and the previously bubbly, bouncing, smiley Amy came in, her face dripping with tears and a total fucking mess.

Chapter 5

Arielle

Arielle had been just about to shove a bite of hot, cheesy comfort food into her mouth when the door swung open. Shoulders shuddering, Amy let the door slam behind her, and slumped against the wall. She slid down to the floor in time with the tears sliding down her cheeks, her purse softly thudding against the office-grade carpet a moment before her butt did.

The pizza dropped on the plate, leaving a hot smear of pizza sauce on Arielle's hand, which she absentmindedly wiped on her clean yoga pants. She'd have to find the laundry room sooner rather than later, she guessed.

"Jesus fuck," Rion murmured, slowly taking steps back toward her room.

Amy gasped and whipped her head, with eyes wide with shock, over to Rion.

"She's really…Christian," Arielle mumbled at Rion while she moved across the room to slide her arm around Amy's back and pulled her to standing. "Come sit on the couch," she said to the still-weeping girl. The haze of the headache that her own tears had left behind minutes before still pounded behind her eyes. If Arielle thought she'd looked bad, Amy multiplied that tenfold. "Are you okay? What's going on?"

Maybe she was called down to the lobby because there was bad news from home. Maybe one of her parents had been in a car accident or something. Arielle would lose her shit if anything happened to her mom, no matter how much the woman could annoy her sometimes.

"He…he…he said he loved me, but…" Amy managed, gasping, before she collapsed into tears again.

"Motherfucker." Rion swore again, but when Arielle shot her another scolding look, she shrugged and slumped into a chair, watching Amy, who was beginning to calm down enough to hiccup instead of gasp.

"Oh, honey," Arielle said, channeling her mom's calming tone as much as possible. Her hand hovered in the air above Amy's back, uncertain as to whether she should rub it like Amy had rubbed hers. A couple girls back in high school had flinched any time Arielle's hand came close to touching their bra—she'd learned to be careful with touching girls.

But when Amy let her head fall onto Arielle's shoulder, the choice was thankfully made for her. Arielle

The Broken Hearts Society of Suite 17C

put her arm around Amy's back, and squeezed her shoulder. "What did he say?" She asked, softly. Carefully. She couldn't repeat Rachel's stupid excuses right now if she tried.

"He just said...everyone he had met had broken up with their girlfriends when they got here...and he wanted to see other girls? I guess? Because he prayed about it, and he's pretty sure I'm the girl he's supposed to be with, but he just wants to be totally sure?" Her voice twisted higher on the last few words, and she started to sob again.

"What is wrong with these nut-clutching, mansplaining dickheaded assholes?" Arielle and Amy went quiet at Rion's outburst. "Well, seriously!" she said, throwing her hands in the air. "You," she said, motioning to Amy, "were obviously like about to get married, and you," she pointed at Arielle, "fucking transferred to this school to be with that dumb bitch."

"She's not a..." Arielle started, her stomach twisting instinctively at anyone referring to Rachel that way.

"Oh but she is," Rion said. "Nobody can know you're together? Suddenly lesbians are this horrible thing? Is she living in fucking 1994 or something?"

Amy's stomach pulled in as she gave a short, slight laugh, and her mouth twitched up at the corners. Arielle had to admit she was right—Rion was outspoken, but at least she was making this a little more bearable.

"And your guy. Who does he think he is? You're obviously pretty, and sweet, and the two of you had something really serious. And now he wants to fuck other girls, just because he saw all the fresh Indiana Northern meat?"

Amy's mouth dropped open, and she stared at Rion. "You think he's going to—I mean—do you think he's wanting to make love to other girls?"

Arielle shot a dagger-eyed glance at Rion, and quickly but firmly shook her head.

"No…no," Rion stammered, giving Arielle a panicked look. "I'm sure he just wants to…you know. Kiss them and stuff?" she checked her response with Arielle, who rolled her eyes at her when Amy wailed.

"Okay, look. Let's just calm down, okay?" Arielle said in the soothing voice again. She had definitely learned more than she'd thought. Mom hadrubbed Arielle's back through a few crying sessions when she was fourteen and just starting to come out at school. Ninth grade girls could be brutal in their teasing, and Arielle had learned not to give a shit mostly by Mom teaching her how to deal.

Teasing was one thing, and Rachel was another.

After a few quiet moments, while the girls waited for Amy to start taking deep breaths again, Arielle put slices of pizza on napkins for each of them. She handed one to Rion first, with a slight smile, then nudged one down the coffee table in front of Amy's face. "Eat," Arielle said, smoothing her hand over Amy's long hair before she pulled it away and picked up her own slice.

The Broken Hearts Society of Suite 17C

The girls ate in silence for several moments, and then Rion let her napkin drop to the floor, half the piece of pizza still on it. "Listen," she said, leaning forward with her elbows on her knees. "Guys are assholes. Girls too, I guess. I swear to God."

Amy whimpered.

"It's like they don't know how to be decent human beings. Do you know what happened to me, literally three weeks before I left to move here?"

Arielle and Amy waited for her to continue.

"I was with this guy, and he was cute, and fun, and really really good in bed, and he just happened to sell pot on the side. And then I fucking got stuck driving his car, with a trunkload of the shit. Nothing like trying to explain to the cops that it's not your pot and knowing they don't believe you."

Arielle whispered "whoa," and Amy's eyes were the size of saucers. "So," Amy's timid voice broke the silence. "I mean…weren't you smoking that stuff too? If he was? Or didn't you at least know it was in there?"

"Of course you'd think that. Everyone else did. It makes sense." Rion scoffed. "But no. I wouldn't touch the shit. My only real crime was being stupid enough to drive the car without searching it first. Anyway, I had to go to court. Got a ten thousand dollar fine. Lost all my federal loans. Asshole completely fucked me over."

"So you broke up with him?" Amy asked quietly.

Rion scoffed, weaving her fingers together and staring down at them. "Didn't have to. When he saw me after I got out of court, he figured I wanted to kill him. He was right But it's hard to kill someone that you're used to kissing, you know?" Now Rion's voice had gone from hard to broken and quiet.

Arielle shook her head. "You loved him, didn't you?"

"Well," Rion grumbled, "I wouldn't say...I don't know. Maybe. Yeah. I lived in a state run group home for the last year and a half. He was kind of the only person I had." Rion stared down at her hands some more, and Arielle thought she heard her sniffle, too. Clearly she was done with that conversation, for now at least. They were all quiet for a very long few seconds.

"Okay," Arielle finally said, tossing her pizza down onto the coffee table with a dull thump. "This is pathetic. We are pathetic."

Yeah, she still felt completely devastated, like Rachel had permanently poisoned the part of her that could feel happiness. But there was another feeling too, the one that insisted that this was utter bullshit.

Just like Rion, she knew she was worth more than this. And from what little she knew of Amy, and from what she could see of Rion, she knew the same thing about them.

"Jesus, give her a minute," Rion said, crossing over to the chair next to Amy and sitting down. She looked the girl up and down, as though she was wondering what to do with her. Then she reached into the bag, pulled out a pint of ice cream, cracked the top off, and handed it to Amy, who took it, looking lost. Then Rion mumbled, "Sorry," and pulled a spoon out of the bag, too. She barely had time to hold it out to Amy before the poor, sniffling girl snatched it and started to dig in.

"Seriously," Arielle said, watching her two roommates strike up a camaraderie before her eyes. "People screw with us, and we cry and eat ice cream? What the hell are we doing?"

Amy sniffled. "You guys are swearing a lot."

Rion snorted and pulled another pint out of the bag.

"I'll be right back," Arielle said, pushing herself out of her chair, "Be ready to hand one of those over to me."

In her room, Arielle dug through one of the three huge duffels she'd crammed in her dad's trunk before the drive up to Northern. She was a sucker for two things: color coding and office supplies, and even though she'd be using her laptop for almost everything in classes, she'd stocked up on a few cute notebooks and fancy pens. She found a notebook that was absolutely perfect—a composition style, so that pages couldn't be torn out—and had three birds in some artsy-collagey configuration on the front. She grabbed a pack of new gel pens and stalked back into the common room.

"We are not going to let this happen again," Arielle said.

"And we're going to do that with a notebook and cutesy pens?"

Arielle glared at Rion, but Amy cracked a smile.

"We all know this is bullshit, right? Sorry, Amy—" Arielle said as she wiggled her yoga-pantsed butt back over the cheap dorm furniture upholstery.

"We all know our exes"—she swallowed—"totally screwed us over. We know we didn't deserve that, right?"

"And we're never going to put up with anything close to it ever again," Rion said.

"Exactly," Arielle said, willing certainty into her shaky voice. Unfortunately, at this point, she couldn't promise she wouldn't jump back into Rachel's arms and pick right back where they left off on their happily ever after, given the chance.

But deep down, she also knew that that happily ever after had been totally destroyed by whatever it was that made Rachel embarrassed to be her girlfriend.

"Adam said…he said he thinks we belong together," Amy's voice cracked as she fought to get some volume into it. "He just wants to be sure. So probably, we'll…"

"No," Arielle interrupted, slamming her hand on the cover of the notebook, then fiercely opening the cover and tearing the cap off the pen with her teeth. "You will not be getting back together. I'm sorry, because I don't really know you at all, but I know that any guy who promises a girl forever and then comes to college with her and then dumps her ass is not forever. He is not The One."

How much was she talking about Amy, and how much was she talking about herself?

The Broken Hearts' Society of Suite 17C

Arielle shook her head. It didn't matter. "Listen to me," she said, trying to infuse every word with conviction, "The three of us were put in this Suite together for a reason. I know we were."

Actually, Arielle had been put in the Suite because she was a late transfer.

"My best friend backed out of our double last month," Amy said. "Decided to start at the community college close to home instead."

Rion swallowed another bite of ice cream. "And I'm here because—"

"Shut UP!" Arielle said, beginning to scribble furiously. "I'm serious. We're all here for a reason, and I'm going to tell you what it is right now." The ink from the green gel pen was especially shimmery, and it pulled a spark of happiness through the darkness threatening to take over Arielle's whole experience at Northern. The words formed under her pen almost by themselves, and when she finished writing, she held up the notebook for the girls to see.

Amy blinked hard, clearing her eyes of the last of the tears, and Rion let out an exasperated sigh as she leaned forward to read.

"The Broken Hearts' Society of Suite 17C?" Rion read.

"Yep. We've all ended up on the wrong end of some really bad breakups, and we're having a hard time dealing. It's true. And you know what that means?"

"We're pathetic?" Amy offered.

"Yes, okay." Arielle rolled her eyes. "We're pathetic, today. That's why we're never going to let anything like that happen ever, ever again. We're going to have such an amazing, jerk-free year, that we're going to make our exes look like pathetic losers at the end of it. And we're all going to hold each other accountable." Arielle swallowed down the doubt rising in her chest. She doubted that gorgeous, confident, social butterfly Rachel could ever look like a pathetic loser, but now that she'd given the whole speech, she owed it to her roommates to at least consider it a possibility.

"So how are we supposed to do that?" Something like hope sparked inside Arielle as she heard a hint of willingness in Rion's question.

"We're going to hold a meeting. Every other Sunday. Just like this, with ice cream and pizza, but without the crying."

"My mom only packed like a month's worth of tissues anyway," Amy joked, finally letting a real smile creep onto her face.

"It's only going to work if everyone's in. We all have to help each other." Arielle looked straight at Amy, who swallowed hard, then nodded. She moved her eyes to Rion. She stabbed her plastic fork into the ice cream, taking a long time to twist out a scoop, then shove it in her mouth, then swallow. She looked up at the girls, letting her gaze shift from one to the other. "I'd probably

The Broken Hearts Society of Suite 17C

have to listen to you girls talking about exes and crushes and dating and love no matter what, right?"

"Right," Arielle nodded, keeping her face solemn.

"Fine," Rion said, passing a pint of ice cream to Arielle as promised. "How's this going to work?"

"Concentrate on your ice cream," Arielle mumbled, trying to catch hold of the stream of words jumping up in her head like magic. She flipped open to the second page of the book and wrote so furiously her hand ached when she was done. The notebook made a hefty thud when she dropped it, open-faced, on the floor right next to the pizza.

Rion leaned in to read aloud:

> We, the residents of Harrison Tower Suite 17C, hereby promise not to enter into a relationship with any individual possessing the qualities of our exes, who tore our hearts out and smeared them across the Indiana Northern quad, specific to each of our members as follows:
>
> Rion Burke: Hereby swears never again to date any motherfucking asshole who has had any involvement, association with, or history of using illegal drugs, or behaving recklessly under the influence of alcohol, or

participating in any legal infraction or crime that would result in disciplinary action. She is not that kind of girl, and refuses to be brought into that shit by association ever again.

Arielle Duval: Hereby resolves never again to date any girl who is not confident of, secure in, and proud of being a lesbian. The ideal girlfriend will have had enough experience dating women to know with 100% certainty that she is sexually attracted to, and sees herself having a future with, another woman. Furthermore, she will be fully out and secure with anyone in the universe knowing about her sexual orientation.

Amy Bauer: Hereby promises never again to fall so deeply in love with a guy, and become so wholly attached to him, that she loses any idea of who she is without him. She will not discuss commitment or a solid future with any guy before she has her own plan for a future, independent of any relationship.

The Broken Hearts Society of Suite 17C

To this end, we resolve to meet on a semi-weekly basis to report our dating behaviors (or lack thereof) and hold one another accountable for our backslides, pitfalls, and slip-ups, and to cheer on our successes.

Because one soul-destroying breakup is more than enough for one lifetime.

Chapter 6

Arielle

Arielle squinted at the large metal sign planted in the ground in front of a cement behemoth of a building. She double-checked her schedule. It didn't look like the sort of building that would hold a women's studies class, but more surprising things had happened since she'd arrived here. She nodded when the name matched up with the one on her schedule, relieved she wouldn't have to backtrack halfway across campus like she'd had to after this morning's statistics class.

Of course, it probably didn't help that, with every step across the quad, she was desperately hoping that she wouldn't look up to see Rachel approaching her. Or hoping that she did see Rachel. She really didn't know. The memory of her still felt so real, down to the smell of her peach perfume, and the swoop of her warm blonde hair. The girl invaded her dreams almost every night. Arielle always woke up expecting Rachel to be warming the narrow space left in her twin extra-long mattress, but when she opened her eyes, it was always cold.

At least, after the first week post-breakup, she had stopped crying over the empty bed. Well, most of the time. And at least when she had cried, letting out sobs so loud she sounded like a dying hyena, she had her own room so that Rion and Amy wouldn't hear it. Thank God for Harrison Tower.

The motley collection of girls in the classroom confirmed she was in the right place—Womens' Studies 272. In fact, there were *only* girls in this class, most of them looking more like Rion, with weird hair, clothing, piercings, or some combination of the three. One wore a t-shirt emblazoned with the words "FEMINIST KILLJOY" in all caps, and another was discussing a protest at the Statehouse this past weekend, and her subsequent arrest. Two girls in the back corner were having an animated conversation about something...intense, and Arielle flinched when one of them practically screamed, "Since I have a vagina." It became painfully obvious to Arielle that what she'd thought would be a large entry-level class was almost entirely populated with upperclassmen, passionate about the subject at hand.

Not to mention that the women's studies major she imagined she'd be so perfect for might not have been such a great idea after all.

Of course, she'd come one minute before class started, leaving her with a choice of three seats in the second row, or any seat she pleased in the first row, directly in front of the instructor. Awesome. She focused on the floor, tucking a loose curly strand of hair behind her ear and counting the number of pairs of combat boots and Birkenstocks and watching her ballet flats walk past them. And then, all of the sudden, a pair of gold sequined canvas shoes caught her eye. And they were next to an empty seat, too. Arielle practically grinned at the feeling of relief. She wasn't the only normal girl in this class. Or abnormal. Whatever.

She slung her bag to the ground and settled into the empty seat. "It's left-handed," a soft alto voice warned her. Arielle smiled and followed the gold shoes up a long, toned, smooth-as-silk pair of legs, and solid yet curvy-in-all-the-right-places torso to one of the most captivating faces she'd ever seen.

The girl had perfectly clear, amber skin, free of any freckles or blemishes except for a beauty mark an inch below and to the right of her left eye. And her eyes—deep brown, almost black, but with so much depth, like they held a million points of light. The top lid was so delicate, curving and smoothing into the top of her cheekbone, that Arielle had to fight the urge to reach out and touch it.

Thanks to a less-than-diverse Indiana upbringing, Arielle hadn't met very many Asian people in her lifetime, and she had never before wondered what kind of Asian

The Broken Hearts Society of Suite 17C

someone was. Korean, Japanese, Vietnamese, Chinese—she'd never cared, until now. She had no explanation for it, but she wanted to know every single thing about this girl. Being around Rachel had felt like transforming herself into a dam against a flood of hormones that would eventually break her down. It was out of control, it threatened to consume her. With just a few words, this girl had infused her with calm.

Arielle took a deep breath, trying to stop the telltale lazy flip of her stomach. She smiled politely at the girl, then talked herself into looking up at the board, getting out her computer, tucking her hair behind her ears, all in an effort to avoid staring. When she looked again, the girl was looking back at her. Goddamn, she was gorgeous.

"I don't mind," Arielle managed as she slid into the desk.

"Good. It's nice to have company up here. Do you think sitting in the front of the class is the same as sitting in the front of the bus? Accepting that you just aren't one of the cool kids?" The girl's subdued smile could have been friendly or just polite, but somehow it felt like something more. Arielle's brain went a mile a minute. Introducing herself had never been one of her strong suits, as ridiculous as it sounded, and when she was this mesmerized by someone's face, it was a recipe for disaster. But there was no way she'd ever meet anyone here if she couldn't manage to say her name out loud.

So, as Arielle slid her bag to the ground, she turned to the girl and reached out a hand. "My name's—"

A sharp, confident voice sounded from the back of the room. "Welcome to Women's Studies, Feminism in Film. This is a 200 level writing class, which is not entry level but a required gen-ed." The professor strode into class on sharp heels, which clicked against the floor with such precision they sounded like a metronome, interrupting every conversation in the room. Including Arielle's almost-introduction to the stunningly gorgeous girl beside her.

The entire lecture was just as forceful as her entrance, with the professor glossing over the film and writing content, and ranting about some definition of feminism the New York Times had just used in a front page article that was apparently going to take women a peg even further down the corporate ladder. Or something.

Even though this was only a two hundred level class, and it fulfilled a gen-ed, most of the girls in the class appeared to have registered for it because they were fans of the professor. She knew most of them by name, and participated in the followup discussion much more like a friend than like a teacher. By the end of class, Arielle had aching fingers from trying to type notes on everything they said, and a spinning head from trying to make sense of the vast majority of it.

When the professor, Dr. Bennett, finally said, "Okay, see you on Thursday. And don't skimp on the reading,"

Arielle leaned forward, raking her fingers back through her hair while trying to massage away the dull headache that had started between her eyes halfway through class. Only after a few seconds of deep, calming breaths did she realize the other girl was still sitting beside her. At some point in the class, she had slumped back in her seat, staring blankly at her computer.

Like she was thinking exactly the same thing as Arielle.

Arielle sat up and slowly closed her laptop, sliding it into her bag. *Please say something. Please introduce yourself.*

"Did you get any of that?"

OhthankGod

"Uh...most of it?" Arielle managed. "Or some of it? Depends on how much comprehension counts for 'getting it.'"

The girl laughed, her maybe-polite smile from earlier widening into something friendlier, more genuine. "I always get nervous before a new class, but usually it turns out to be okay. Guess this is not usually."

"Thank God I wasn't the only one," Arielle laughed.

"What are you going to do?" the girl asked, picking up her own bag—a paisley-patterned quilted backpack—as she stood to leave. "About the class, I mean? Tough it out?"

Arielle was on her feet in a second, lifting her canvas messenger bag over her shoulder. She shrugged. "I don't know what else to do. I don't think I can switch now. It was hard enough trying to get my schedule to work in the first place."

"Good point. Mine is the worst. Like, now, I have exactly an hour and forty-eight minutes before the next class. Too long to eat a quick lunch, not long enough to go back to my room for a nap or even to get any homework done when I'm starving and I have to eat lunch first."

Arielle checked her phone—she was starving, too, and no wonder. It was one-thirty. She hadn't had the luxury of scheduling classes around all-important meal times, since she'd gotten in to Northern at the last minute. She forced her thoughts away from the bitterness that rose in them when she thought of everything that had brought her here. In her first six days on campus, she'd realized that she liked Indiana Northern far more than she'd ever liked Wesleyan.

It had surprised her, especially because she thought she'd hate the huge campus, huge classes, huge everything. Suddenly, Northern was looking even better.

"Are you? Hungry?" Gorgeous Girl asked.

"Oh, um…yeah, actually, I am. I was just going to…" Where was she going? She'd mapped out her classes and tried to memorize the paths she'd take, but hadn't bothered to think about stopping for food. Brilliant.

"I'm going to Peabody if you want to come," the girl continued.

The Broken Hearts Society of Suite 17C

Arielle's phone buzzed in her hand and she mumbled something to the girl while checking it. Her mom wanted to know how her first two classes were.

Fine, Arielle answered, **but now I'm starving and I don't know where to eat. LOL**

Want me to look up the best dining halls? On the Google?

Mom. Seriously?

I'm just saying…

Arielle shook her head and smiled. "My mom," she said to the girl, who she'd kept pace with as they left the building without a second thought.

The girl smiled, holding up her phone. "Mine too, though I mostly ignore her."

"Aw, no!" Arielle laughed. "She can't be that bad."

"She's ridiculous. She means well, but…yeah."

"What do you mean?" Arielle asked as they pushed into the dining hall, one of the old-fashioned ones where you went through a line to get hot food.

"I don't know. She's always trying to, like, connect with me, but…it never really works. You know? We just don't have a lot of things in common, no matter how badly she wants us to. That's why I'm here, I guess. It just made me feel too guilty all the time."

Arielle's grumbling stomach told her to get an extra piece of garlic bread to go with the lasagna the lunch worker served up, which looked surprisingly delicious.

"What do you mean, why you're here? You're not from Indiana?"

They slid into seats across from each other and the girl laughed. God, she had a beautiful laugh. Light and full at the same time.

"No, I'm from California. Silicon Valley."

"Hold on. You're from California, where it's all green and blue on Google maps, to the wasteland of cows and corn and flat highways and gray winters? To stay here for four years?"

The girl smiled and stabbed at a cherry tomato with her fork. "Yep. I just wanted some distance, I guess."

Arielle nodded as though she understood, even though she really didn't. Which was why she shoved a bite of lasagna into her mouth, blushing when some of the cheese stringed over her chin and she had to fumble for something to wipe it away.

"Can't believe I haven't introduced myself yet. Lauren," the girl said, holding out her hand just as Arielle crumpled the sauce-smeared napkin. Arielle's hand jumped at the opportunity for contact, and slid into Lauren's. "Arielle," she managed to squeak out.

If her phone hadn't buzzed against her thigh, she never would have let go. She flipped it over. Mom. Again.

Did you find some food? #Jewishmother

Arielle scoffed, and put the phone back down.

"Mom again?" Lauren asked.

"Yep. Hold on." Arielle's fingers flew over the phone's keyboard, letting mom know that she found a place.

Mom: **That's good. It's the worst when you can't find food. Once I went on a day trip to some outlet mall that Aunt Sharon said was the absolute best.**

Arielle: **And?**

Mom: **And there were no good bargains, but worse, the only place to eat anywhere close to the stores was Chick-fil-A.**

Arielle: **So?**

Mom: **So I can't eat there.**

Arielle: **What are you talking about? You don't keep kosher.**

Mom: **No, but they lobby against gay rights. And I love you.**

Arielle stifled a laugh with her fingertips and shook her head at the phone.

"What?" Lauren asked, a small bemused smile on her face as she picked at her own lasagna.

"She just…she really loves me, and she tries so hard to be supportive. She just misses the mark a little bit." Arielle giggled again.

"Okay, but doesn't that annoy the hell out of you?"

"Not really. Most of the time it's just funny."

"Let me see," Lauren said, reaching across the little table and snatching the phone from Arielle.

Immediately, Arielle froze up. Did her messages with Mom scream "big fat lesbo?" She didn't think so. Mom loved the word 'ally,' but Arielle didn't think she'd used it just now. Had she?

Lauren's eyebrows made a funny wave across her forehead as one went up and the other went down. Jesus, that was adorable. "I don't get it."

"Oh, it's just…she has a political thing against Chick-fil-A."

This is stupid, Arielle. Just tell her. You're out, you're proud, for Christ's sake. What do you care if she knows?

But Arielle knew that what she wanted most in this moment was to spend more time with Lauren. She also knew that she was terrified this enchanting girl wouldn't ever hang out with her again if she knew. Irrational, stupid, against everything she stood for, yes. That didn't change the absolute truth of it.

"Oh, the gay thing?" Lauren asked, and Arielle's heart dropped into her stomach. All that stress for nothing—the girl wasn't stupid. "Assholes. That reminds me of one of my best friends back home, though. Neither of her dads would buy Barilla pasta, and the week after that Honey Maid commercial with two dads and a baby, they bought every box in the store. Sylvie—my friend—hates graham crackers."

"Oh my God, that's like exactly the same thing," Arielle laughed, still keeping a careful eye on Lauren. What did she think about gay people? Did she understand them at all? If she understood, was she freaked out that Arielle was gay? Had she made all the connections yet?

The Broken Hearts Society of Suite 17C

Lauren chewed and swallowed before speaking again. "Anyway, obviously your mom loves you. There's not a lot of activism to do these days, I don't think. People don't really mind gay kids. Half the gay kids at my high school were out by the end of freshman year with no problem. But I think for parents…they want to protect their kids, and fifteen years ago, gay kids needed that. You know?"

"Okay, so you think my mom is legit, but your mom annoys you?"

"It's…different. I mean, not to diminish your mom's LGBT fixation, but my mom wanted a daughter so badly, and never could get pregnant, so she adopted me from China. And then like once a year, at the Chinese New Year, there would be a dragon cake, and sometimes she'd take me for a photo shoot in traditional Chinese clothing."

"So what? I bet you were adorable," Arielle said, realizing how that might have sounded only after the words left her mouth. She was still adorable, but not in an *awwww* way. More like Arielle could watch her smile and eat and talk for hours, and not get tired of her.

"Oh, I was," Lauren said. "But that was it. No Chinese school, no meetups with other adopted girls, no trips to China. So she was kind of making me into this Chinese poser. When I was little, she put me in karate classes, and I only realized karate was a Japanese thing after I'd earned two belts."

"Belts, huh?" Arielle asked, chewing another bite. "Sounds like something a karate master would have."

"No, that's the thing!" Lauren said. "I wasn't even good at being *fake* Chinese. I sucked at karate—couldn't stand how controlled it was, how subdued. It was like it was challenging and boring at the same time, I guess? Anyway, my sensei saw how crazy the stances and poses were making me, and put me in striking class instead. Thank God."

"That sounds terrifying. Is that where you break boards and shit?"

"Nope. It's just the formal name for kickboxing."

"You're a kickboxer? Like you wear gloves and everything?"

Lauren laughed. "Yep. Usually people are surprised because I'm kind of…quiet, maybe? And a little shy?"

"You don't seem shy to me."

Lauren's grin had melted into a soft smile as she looked right in Arielle's eyes. "Maybe that's because I like you. With most people, it takes me a while to get comfortable with them, but for some reason, you're different."

Well hell. That sounded like a come-on if ever Arielle had heard one. *Get your head on straight, you crazy person. Most of the world isn't gay. Chances are, this girl isn't either. Most people don't think twice about saying something like that. She probably just wants to be friends.*

Thank God she had a mouthful of food. She could chew and swallow before responding. Maybe she could wipe her mouth with her napkin, and breaking eye contact would break this weird hold Lauren seemed to have on her.

She did just that, and looked up at Lauren again. Had her clear, steady eyes turned down the slightest bit? Was she sad?'

"Yeah. I…umm…me too. I don't make friends easily."

"Well, sounds like it's a lucky day for both of us. Should we do this again Thursday?"

Was she asking her out? "Um…okay. What time?"

"After class?" Lauren asked, her eyes seeming to sparkle with some kind of amusement now. "Because I'll see you then?"

Of course. In class. When Lauren would see her whether she wanted to or not. Not a come-on, just a convenience. Arielle's heart sank, even though there was still one big thing she had to figure out before she could let herself get truly interested in this girl—was she gay?

Her stomach was back to twisting, and she pulled on the fake-cheery smile she'd gotten so good at in the two weeks—God, had it already been two weeks?—since Rachel had broken her heart.

And then she realized—Rachel's gorgeous eyes and sweet smile hadn't crossed her mind in hours. Ever since she'd first seen Lauren.

That was a good thing, romantic prospect or no.

Thinking about the next time she'd see Lauren brought Arielle's thoughts back to that insane class they'd just attended. "I so wish I could drop that class."

"No! Why?" Lauren looked at her like she had just told her she was going to stay in bed under a blanket for the next five years. Like she was already planning on seeing Arielle twice a week for the next fourteen weeks, and would be crushed if she didn't.

Arielle's lips twitched. "I don't know. I thought I was interested in women's studies, like maybe for a career? I thought I was really passionate about the issues, but after listening to Professor Bennett, I think I'm pretty ambivalent."

Lauren scoffed. "I think Virginia Woolf would look ambivalent compared to her. What kind of a career would you even get with a women's studies major?"

Arielle screwed up her mouth in thought. "Um…teach? Lobby? I really have no idea," she finally admitted. "I just figured I would really like the class. Enough to make it my major." When she said it out loud, it sounded like the dumbest thing possible. "Academics weren't my first priority in coming here, exactly," she rushed to explain. And that just made her sound even dumber. Awesome.

"You didn't come to Indiana Northern, one of the best schools in the Midwest, for academics? Then why are you here?"

Arielle pressed her lips together and shook her head.

"Ugh," Lauren said. "Didn't get in where you wanted? That's tough. I know how that feels. I didn't get into

The Broken Hearts Society of Suite 17C

Harvard, and my dad didn't want to pay for Columbia, even though it has an amazing premed program."

Arielle tried hard to keep from choking on her pop. Those were schools she hadn't even considered. Even if she did find out that Lauren was the proudest of lesbians, and therefore dateable, she'd be out of Arielle's league. On every level.

"No, I did, I just…decided not to go there." God, this was going downhill fast. She stuffed a bite of pie into her mouth.

"Well, if you want, I can help. I mean, with the whole major situation."

Arielle's eyebrows went up. "No, you know exactly what you're doing with your life, and I'm not going to do that. At all." Arielle could barely remember the chemistry class she'd barely earned a B in last year. Pre-med was definitely out of the question.

Lauren laughed. "We could tackle it together. I mean, if you want. We can, you know, research a lot of different jobs, maybe. Go see what they're like."

Arielle stared at Lauren, her heart skipping a beat. She had only just met this girl and she was willing to put up with Arielle's chronic indecision, and possibly a gross lack of ambition? The fact that Arielle had at least a year to figure out what she wanted to do was irrelevant. Her stomach flipped again.

"I mean…I'm sure you have friends and everything, so. I don't know." Lauren stared at her fingernails. Were her cheeks flushing? "I just thought it might be fun to…you know…"

Arielle had never tried to date out in the wild. She wasn't one hundred percent sure of the line between flirting and friendship, especially with other girls. Lauren probably wasn't gay, and if she was, why would she flirt with Arielle when she was so perfect?

But something whispered in the back of Arielle's mind that Lauren was more than a California girl at an Indiana school, and she was doing more than trying to make a new friend.

Arielle's phone buzzed, and she growled, "Mom," secretly grateful to the little glowing screen for the interruption. It was Amy.

Meet you outside Watkins in five?

Shit. They had bio lecture together, along with about five hundred people. The first day of classes, they'd hunted for the lecture hall on the edge of the vast campus together, and on the second day, they'd run into each other on the way. Arielle smiled at the offer, and texted back **Sure.** On a campus this humungous, it was nice to have someone you knew walking beside you.

"You know what? That sounds great," Arielle said, standing up and gathering her things. "The jobs thing."

Lauren perked up, her smile a mix of happiness and relief. "So, Thursday?"

"See you then. I've uh…I've gotta go. To my next class. I'm meeting someone. She's just a friend, but…I mean…it's across campus, and…" God, she was an idiot.

"See you then," Lauren said, pulling out a tablet and a laptop, the motion of her body waving her scent toward Arielle. She breathed it in and smiled. It was beautiful, happy and light. And it was definitely not peach.

I was dating this guy this past summer, and I was debating ending things. He was supposed to help me move into my new apartment and didn't. When he called that night, he said he wanted to end things. I said "oh okay sounds good" and he said "that's it?" and I responded with "oh, wait, do you want me to cry or something? I can cry if that makes you feel better about yourself." It was Halloween and I just went out drinking on a drunk trolley with my friends dressed as the ever-so-fabulous Audrey Hepburn.

~Taylor Mandel, Ohio State '13

Chapter 7

Amy

It had been thirteen days since he'd broken up with her. Thirteen days since he'd turned her upside down and inside out; since every one of her emotions, spoiled hopes, and dashed dreams hung around her neck like a gaudy necklace, weighing down the real her and visible to everyone.

Hopes and dreams didn't even cover it. Adam had been her everything. In those first few moments when she had tried to process what he was actually saying, she was devastated. She loved him, and he tore a gaping hole in her heart that threatened to bleed out every time she thought his name.

But as Arielle had pulled out the notebook, and started preaching about the Broken Hearts' Society, those tears and anguish had quickly turned to something black,

The Broken Hearts' Society of Suite 17C

intangible, and scary—her life without Adam. He had been the defining factor in her past, present, and future, and when she imagined her life without him, it was nothing. No plans, no ambitions, no dreams that didn't hinge on being with him.

What had really surprised her was how she felt when she realized that. There was no sadness now. The more she thought about it, she wasn't angry that he had destroyed her future, but that he had ever been her entire future in the first place.

That she had allowed him to be her future.

So when she'd promised the Society that she wouldn't ever again be with someone who encompassed her life, her plans, her identity so completely, she'd meant it. This pain, this blackness, this embarrassment and shame, that she was eighteen years old and had absolutely no life-plans independent of him—this was not okay. This could not happen again. She'd felt strong in that moment, being angry about the blackness, the pain that half of her had ripped itself away and left the other half bleeding. But anger took a lot of energy, and the blackness by itself was stubborn. Amy sighed, letting the blackness know she saw it, and she felt it, and she didn't really know what to do right now.

Her eyes wandered to the stack of brightly-colored pamphlets she'd picked up at the Student Activities Fair, featuring crosses, *ichthus* fishes, and catchy phrases using puns on "The Word" and "His ways." The idea of sitting in church hurt. Amy and Adam had sat together week after week, singing praise songs beside each other, praying together. They'd even recommended sermon podcasts, blogs, and books to each other.

Amy knew two things: The blackness of losing Adam covered church just as much as it covered eating, sleeping, and walking through campus, and that, just like those things, she couldn't give church up. Church had been part of their relationship, yes, but her connection with God was all her own.

At the same time, she couldn't go to the same type of church she always had, with the passionate sermons warning against sin and the testimonies from people who wouldn't even imagine doing the horrible things she'd done. Even when she did have a chance to make the three-hour drive south to Tripp Creek, she didn't think she'd ever be able to go back to the pews where she'd held pinkies with Adam under a hymnal, or the building where they'd snuck their first kiss during a lock in.

That didn't change the fact that she'd need to do a lot of praying to get through this statistics class. She leaned over the textbook, digging into the tiny-print pages with her elbows. Maybe she thought that if she leaned on it, the formulas would somehow migrate to her fingertips and make her at least work the problems correctly, even if she couldn't understand them.

High school had been so easy. Maybe it was the post-breakup blackness or maybe it was just because her school

The Broken Hearts' Society of Suite 17C

had been easier than other Indiana high schools, but here at Northern, she was actually going to have to work for her grades. Which would be okay with her, if she even knew how to study. She already felt hopelessly behind with all the labs, assignments, and readings she had between her five classes, and it was only the second week of school.

At least she could count on the Broken Hearts' Society to keep her love life in check. As if she'd ever date again—as if any guy had ever been interested in her besides Adam. Maybe her roommates swore too much, and maybe her parents would have a heart attack if they found out one was a lesbian and the other had tattoos and a mother in prison. But they were kind, and they'd rubbed her back when she'd cried her heart out. She even felt like, eventually, she might tell them about the rest of the story with Adam, the one that started at prom and ended in the cold, white walls of a clinic an hour and a half from home.

Her parents were back home, and she was here. In the real world.

Amy was learning more and more that "back home" and "the real world" were more different than she'd ever imagined.

Like pretty much every evening, Amy's brooding while staring out the Library's top floor window carried her hours after dinner. But tonight, just as real dark was settling over campus, the alarm on Amy's phone started chirping. Amy jumped and flipped her phone over. Rion's shift at The Studio was ending in—oh, geez—ten minutes, and Amy had promised she'd meet her there and walk her back to Harrison. "If they see someone waiting for me, they won't ask me to hang out. I uh…I really have to study," Rion had said.

Amy knew it was about more than that, but she didn't push. In their founding Society meeting, Rion had been the most reserved, probably because she was the only one who wasn't a red, snotty mess of tears at that moment, and Amy had no interest in alienating the girl she had to share a couch with for the next eight months. Besides, Rion seemed to be freakishly talented, academically— Amy had seen her scrolling through quiz and assignment grades on her phone, and they were all 90 and above. Whenever Amy saw her in the Suite, she was bobbing her head and moving her lips slightly to something piping through her giant headphones.

The alarm chirped again with a five-minute warning. "Darn it," Amy muttered as she threw her phone and wallet into her bag and her hair into a ponytail. She'd sat around all day wearing sneakers, worn jeans, and a t-shirt from that past spring's youth retreat. She'd absolutely loved the thing when she'd helped design it—the front said in all caps, BODY PIERCING SAVED MY LIFE, and the church's slogan was printed on the back, very small, so that it was hidden by most girls' hair. She remembered loving the small feeling of power when she helped present it to Adam's dad, and he'd protested at first, but listened

The Broken Hearts Society of Suite 17C

to her arguments about how kids were looking for subtle Christianity with enough humor to make them look cool. He'd approved it, and thanked Amy at the end of the meeting.

That night, she'd had fleeting ideas of getting involved in church leadership in bigger ways than she'd ever imagined. When she mentioned something about it to Dad the next morning, he'd seemed to agree. She'd been so excited that Dad believed in her ability to lead, until he suggested Amy look into shadowing the Director of the church's preschool program. Since obviously she'd want to work with little kids.

Seven weeks and two days after that retreat, her whole world had turned upside down and inside out.

When she'd promised Rion to meet her after work, she'd imagined changing into something that didn't make her look like a bum first. But whatever. It wasn't like she had anyone to impress.

Of course she'd kept tabs on him—Facebook still existed, and he still posted updates and photos like nothing significant had changed in his life. There was nothing interesting about the photos, and Amy wavered between being really happy about that and really annoyed. Happy, because no matter how angry she was at Adam, those few sentences that said maybe, just maybe, they could still have a future together wouldn't leave the back of her mind. Annoyed, because she so badly wanted tangible reasons to be angry with him. Maybe she'd judged him too harshly, imagining him kissing other girls, whispering the same promises to them as he had to her in the still dark of summer camp or tented under her covers that one game-changing night. Maybe she owed it to him to let him be for a little while.

From the updates she saw on Facebook, and what little she could get out of friends back home who still talked to him, Adam was playing football and sitting at study tables outside of class, and that was pretty much it.

Amy hurried out of the library lobby and into the early evening air. Here in Northern Indiana, summer seemed to cling on to its last days harder and harder as the end of September approached, holding the humidity in the air even after the heat had receded. Amy breathed the dampness into her lungs anyway, wanting to feel something different, something more real, than the doubt that had surrounded her for the last two weeks.

Amy whipped out her phone and typed in "The Studio on High." She and Arielle had the name memorized by now, since Rion had been ranting about it for days—how her last boyfriend had made it impossible for her to get a decent job, and how she had been hoping The Studio on High had been a music studio—something that would help her bounce back from her conviction and move on, live a normal life. Instead, she'd be surrounded by marijuana pipes all the time, surrounded by the exact same kind of people who'd practically ruined her life.

But nothing came up on her phone's map. Amy took a

The Broken Hearts Society of Suite 17C

deep breath, and started walking in the direction of Francis Street: a long sloping street packed with neon signs, sportswear shops, bad Chinese and hamburger places, and the campus book store. Even if she couldn't find the address, Indiana Northern made up most of this sleepy Midwestern town. If there was a tattoo and piercing shop, it really couldn't be anywhere else.

Amy's strategy of following the road from her dorm to Francis failed when she ran into a dead end, up against a huge lecture hall. She hitched her purse over her shoulder and set out to go around it, but was then blocked by a courtyard edged by trees that didn't allow much view of anything beyond. But Francis had to be just through there, didn't it? As long as she kept walking in a straight line…

Speedwalking toward the trees took a couple minutes—as much as she wanted to be there for Rion, there was no way she was going to run— but when she reached them and peered through, she saw only the back of a row of off-campus student housing. Two guys walked down the alley coming toward her. One carried an enormous pack of beer cans, and one of them whistled at her. "Hey baby, you free tonight?"

Amy froze. The only person who had ever called her that had been Adam, and it was much less forceful than the question these guys were asking. "You sure, honey?" the other one asked. "We'll take care of you." Then he put his fingers up to his mouth in a "V" formation and stuck his tongue through them, wiggling it back and forth. Amy had no idea what that meant, but the way his eyes flashed as he did it made her skin crawl. She took a step backward, stammering syllables that made no sense. She wondered if she could run backward, and her heart started pounding when the guys took slow, purposeful steps toward her. They were laughing, telling her they'd get her someplace nice and warm, then laughing some more. For the first time in her entire life, a guy was making her feel exposed, and scared.

"Come on, sweetie. You don't have plans tonight. Not better than this." His hand flashed down to below his belt, then up again, and Amy shuddered.

"No, actually…I'm…uh…"

"She's with me."

Amy's breath caught in her throat at the words, which flashed out hot and angry towards the guys and carried a tone she didn't recognize. She whipped her head around and was met with warm brown eyes piercing into hers, and lips that whispered, "Play along," so quickly she could have been dreaming them. Given what the two guys in the alley had just said to her, she should have been scared, but calm flooded her as the guy slid his arm around her. As his forearm curved around her waist, she could feel every muscle in his arm, strong and tense.

The guys in the alley stopped in their tracks and started shaking their heads. "Whoa, sorry bro. We thought she was alone. We didn't mean anything against you."

"No," the voice who had just rescued her, the one that was holding her up on now-shaking legs, replied. "But you did mean something against *her*. Here's an update on how to be a good guy. You see a girl alone, you ask if she's okay and if you can help her."

The beer guy's mouth dropped open. "But that's what…"

"And you fucking mean it," the guy said, growling. Amy's cheeks went hot at the curse word—she'd always hated it when people swore. It could have been the curse word, or it could have been that they were just giving up, but the guys started to mutter to the ground and get back on their way.

The guy's hand remained tight on her waist as they shuffled away, finally starting to joke loudly again when they were almost out of sight. And that's when he moved his hands to each of her shoulders and turned her slightly, looking her face over carefully, tilting his head and checking her eyes. His brows knit together. "You okay?"

That was when she realized–she'd seen these eyes, up close, before. Sienna brown mottled with olive green and specks of yellow. Now it was Amy's turn to gasp. "Oh my…wow. Hi. Again." The guy smiled in return, dropping his hands, suddenly seeming to struggle with finding a comfortable way hold his body while he looked at her.

"Hi," he replied, his face finally relaxing.

"Did you…I mean…how did you know it was me?"

"I didn't."

Amy flushed. Of course he didn't.

"I mean, I'm glad to see you again. But, ah…I heard them hassling you, and I saw that you looked like you had no idea where you were going, and there's nobody else out here, so…yeah."

"Well" Amy said, acutely aware that her legs still felt like Jello and that her hands would probably tremble if she raised them, "Thank you. I would say I would have been fine, but I probably wouldn't have been."

"A freshman girl versus two huge drunk fraternity guys? I'm sorry, but no matter how strong you are, you'd have had nothing on them. And what makes it even worse is that this school totally sucks at dealing with sexual harassment and violence." His gaze darted up to hers. "If the administration admits it happens, they have to deal with it, and taking steps to prevent it would be admitting it happens…I'm so sorry."

"What for? In case you missed it, you pretty much just rescued me." Because she was a damsel in distress—a thought that disappointed her more than she would have expected

"For…you know. Crude language."

"Oh. Oh. I…hardly thought about it." It was a lie—words like 'suck' and 'blow' and 'hell' always made her a little squirmy, but she'd grown used to hearing them, hanging out with the football team so much during high

The Broken Hearts Society of Suite 17C

school. Those guys tried to be polite around their girlfriends, but everyone knew that they saved the crudeness for the locker room, and sometimes it slipped out after a game, especially if it had been a good one. More serious profanity, however, made her feel on-edge, like someone's feelings had been so nasty that they'd had no choice but to spill over into their words. That kind of harshness had never been part of her world, and she never wanted it to be.

"So…where were you headed?"

"Just to meet my roommate after work?"

"Because it's not safe for her to walk alone?"

Amy laughed. "If that was the case, would I have been going to meet her on my own?"

Now it was his turn to flush. "Guess not."

"Just…I think…my legs are kind of shaky."

"Oh, geez. Of course they are. Come on," he said, raising his hand as though he was about to touch her back again, then letting it fall at the last minute. Instead, he lightly put a hand on her shoulder and steered her toward a group of benches in the little courtyard framed by trees. Each of them was big enough for about two and a half people, and Amy settled herself to the far side of one of them while he chattered on about how this courtyard was beautiful for studying, or doing anything where you needed to get a little quiet in the middle of a crazy school day, but in the middle of the night it became a great place for guys looking to mess with a girl.

"It's just far enough away from the buildings that security cameras aren't practical. Stupid," he said, shaking his head. He settled himself on the opposite side on the bench, leaving a little less than six inches between them. "Are you going to be okay?" he asked, furrowing his eyebrows at her.

Amy stared out at the line of trees, trying to calm herself using the horizon trick Daddy had taught her that one summer on the boat. Her world started to calm, her legs to feel more solid. Amy swallowed, nodding slowly. "I am. Thank you, really. So much. You can go."

The guy sat up a little straighter. "Do you want me to go?"

"No, but…I don't know. You were obviously on your way somewhere too."

He laughed, shaking his head a little bit. "No. I mean, yeah. But it's really not a big deal."

"Well, in that case, maybe stay with me a little bit longer?" The words slipped out before Amy even could think about how they sounded. She'd known this guy for a total of 20 minutes, but being with him felt like cuddling under an electric blanket in the dead of winter—like moving into a safe haven. She knew she sounded like a pathetic little girl, scared of her own shadow. Frustration flashed through her. "I mean…"

"Of course," he replied, like she'd asked him if he brushed his teeth at night. He, leaned back into the seat and tipped his head to the sky. "I'm Matt, by the way. I know we've known each other for a week, and now that I've defended your virtue, it feels kind of silly that you don't know my name."

Amy forced her lips up into a smile, despite the adrenaline still licking at her insides.

Matt must have noticed, because he kept talking after a single beat. "Look, we even have something to do. It's clear out tonight. The stars are out."

"That's unexpected, with the humidity," Amy blabbered, hoping the mundanity of the conversation would help to calm her insides and steady her limbs enough to get going. Rion's shift was certainly over by now, and it would only take her a minute or so to get all her stuff together. If Amy was lucky, she'd be good to go in just a few more minutes, and Rion wouldn't have to wait that long.

Amy had to admit she was slightly scared of what Rion's mood would be like if she was super late. She didn't know the girl well enough yet to know how she'd react.

"I don't know. I'm from Chicago, so I hardly ever see them."

"Why?"

"Too much pollution. But this is one of the things I loved about Northern when I came to visit. There's space, all around it. Room to breathe. I love watching the Indiana Northern stars at night almost as much as I love watching the clouds during the day."

"So, do you take all the girls star watching?" The

question made Amy's head spin with confusion as soon as it left her mouth. Even if she was thinking about looking for a relationship right now, which she so definitely wasn't, he was not her type. Only a couple inches taller than her, wiry frame, light brown hair tinged ginger. He was so…unexceptional. She'd always been attracted to tall guys with lots of muscles, guys who could make her feel like Thumbelina when they gave her a bear hug. Guys who were so larger than life that she practically disappeared when she stood next to them.

Except there never had been guys. There had been one guy—the guy, or so everyone had thought.

"Yeah," Matt said, and Amy found herself surprised at his reaction. "I've brought one or two out here. That's why I like you. You're the one who brought *me* here."

"I didn't—"

"And I have to say, I'm very glad you did. I'm just now noticing that constellation, right there. It spells your name. "S-A-R-A-H."

Oh, so he was a joker. Amy smiled even as she wondered how much of what he'd just said was part of the joke. "Excuse me. That is not my name."

"No, of course not. My mistake. There's your name. J-U-L-I-E."

Amy's smile stretched muscles that hadn't been used for weeks. "What makes you think there are five letters in my name? Do I seem that complicated to you? I'm a three-letter girl. Simple. Unremarkable."

Matt shook his head slowly, catching her eyes again. "Not unremarkable in the least." Amy looked, suddenly, down at her fingers, which were woven together, and bit her bottom lip. "Okay," Matt continued. "Duh. There it is right there. S-A-M."

A laugh bubbled out of Amy's throat, and Matt let one loose to match. "Well?" he asked, turning to her. He was only a few inches away from her now, and Amy wondered when he had gotten closer to her. "Three letters. An M, a Y, and an A."

"Oh, that's a beautiful name. Delicious, in fact."

Amy's eyes flared wide. "Excuse me?"

"Y-A-M. My favorite at Thanksgiving."

Now she was grinning, and let the laugh move down to her belly. He looked at her with a mischievous sparkle in his eye, and she smacked him on the shoulder in response.

"Obviously, Amy, your strength and resolve have returned. Where are we going next?"

"Oh, no. I can make it to the Studio by myself."

"Of course you can. But the only thing left on my to-do list today is sleep, and I won't be able to unless I see you safe back in your dorm at the end of all this. Okay?"

Amy took a deep breath, pushing the night air, which suddenly felt clean and new, down into her belly. She relaxed back onto the bench, mimicking Matt's pose. "Well, only if it'll help you sleep better."

Chapter 8

Rion

"God fucking dammit," Rion whispered as she slumped against the rough brick of the Studio. She'd managed to keep her head down for her entire shift, answering the phone and completely re-organizing file drawers on her first day. If she had to work there, she was determined to avoid contact with any of the tattoo artists and piercers, half of whom reeked of pot. She thought it would be no problem.

Ignoring people was harder work than she'd anticipated. These people loved to talk, and especially on weeknights, the Studio could be pretty empty. That gave them even more time to loiter around Rion's desk and talk her ear off. One of the piercers, Stephanie, spent 20 minutes bent over her shoulder clicking through a Facebook album that only showed furniture her husband

The Broken Hearts Society of Suite 17C

had designed for some famous supplier in New York City. Rion knew she was supposed to 'ooh' and 'aah' and probably say how adorable the two little kids photobombing half the pictures were. Rion knew damn well what that would do, though. It would make Stephanie think they could be friends—and they definitely could not. She only had enough energy to give a shit about herself.

Ultimately, that was why she'd taken the job at the Studio, even after the idea of working in the same square footage as the wall o'bongs had sent her storming out of there on her interview day. After a quick job search, she'd realized that every single application included that tiny box you could click if you'd ever been convicted of a crime. Everyone knew what checking that box did to your application—got it tossed directly into the circular file. The Studio really was her only chance, so she'd have to make it work. If she stayed behind her desk, and didn't get involved with any of the loser employees, it would almost be like she wasn't even associated with them, like she wasn't even really in that building at all. Almost.

She had let out a huge sigh of relief when her shift ended at nine and Crash hadn't showed once. He might as well have been sitting beside her the whole time, though, for as often as he crossed her mind. She scolded herself for her ridiculousness as she packed up her stuff. He'd told her he only worked at the Studio occasionally, which turned out to be correct—if "occasionally" meant "every fucking time Rion was working." His presence, and his unending glances her way, seemed to scream "I'm a copy of Tate Donovan with extra hotness and extreme fuckability, and if you get involved with me, I'll ruin your life even more than he did."

Rion knew exactly why she'd thought that, too. Crash was try-to-get-a-selfie-with-him-so-you-can-look-at-his-gorgeous-face-any-time, could-probably-work-as-a-romance-novel-cover-model, make-your-pussy-wet-just-by-looking-at-him attractive. It wasn't just that he was everything that she had always found hot in a guy—beautiful art on his arms, subtle inked designs just under his collarbones—but that the tattoos she could see hinted at the ones covered up by his clothing. And what she couldn't see was clearly delicious.

Because Crash worked out. If he was really an artist, and all he did was paint or take pictures or whatever, there was no way his job could give him a body like that, with muscles obvious in every inch of his arms, and a flat stomach that showed ridges through his thin t-shirt. He definitely pumped iron on the side.

Gym rats were really not typically Rion's thing, but the more she let her mind wander on the glorious piece of art that was Crash, the more she thought of what he might look like lifting weights, and the more her animal-girl instincts took over. And they told her that she wanted to see Crash again, and that if she did, she'd probably be forced to jump him.

The Broken Hearts Society of Suite 17C

Which was not, of course, ideal. Because guys who had tattoos and jewelry like that, worked in places like this, and gave themselves names like Crash, clearly had at least one thing wrong with them. At best, it was a humungous self-constructed ego of badassery, and at worst, it was rampant delusions of grandeur bolstered by getting stoned off his ass every chance he got.

Rion shook her head at her own stupid thoughts as she hitched her bag back up on her shoulder, impatiently scanning the sidewalk for Roommate Goody Two Shoes. It didn't matter, because there would be no getting stoned, or even drinking. No falling for guys who are clearly punks. No getting wrapped up in shit that could land her in the same lame ladies' prison as her mother. No negotiation. The deadly combination of pot, stupidity, and being broke had almost ruined her entire education as it was. She wasn't going to open herself up to it again.

She picked up her phone and checked for a text message, email, hell, Facebook post, anything from Amy to tell her why the fuck she wasn't here on time. Amy was the kind of girl who was endlessly careful, who worried that maybe even seatbelts didn't make a car safe to ride in, and maybe she should drive around wearing a helmet, too. Rion hadn't realized nine o' clock would be so fucking dark in the last week of September, but the blue sky was quickly turning navy. It cast an ominous haze over the roads and deepened the shadows in the Francis Street alleyways.

Rion's body tensed. If there was one thing spending those sixteen hellish months in the group home had done for her it was teaching her how to throw a punch. College town skeezebuckets couldn't be more dangerous than group home douchebags. She would have bet her scholarship that Amy had no clue how to fight, though, and Rion suddenly felt a twinge of guilt for asking her to meet her after work. She'd been desperate for some plan to buffer her from any interactions with Crash.

It didn't help that Amy really didn't seem like the kind of girl who was okay with saying no. And Rion really felt like a giant piece of shit for asking her to meet her now, in the dark, alone, just to avoid some pothead, aimless, loser-ass, completely gorgeous guy. A guy who smelled just as delicious as he looked, and—now that she thought about it—not at all like pot.

Fucking shit, Rion. Focus on avoiding him. Who's controlling you, your brain or your pussy? You're worse than a guy.

She pulled a pack of cigarettes out of her bag, closed her eyes at the familiar feel of the smooth paper cylinder passing between her fingers, and lit up.

Ever since the arrest, she'd been trying to cut back on these cancer-causing sons-of-bitches, and she'd been doing pretty well, too. Three a day the week after she left the group home, then down to two. She'd passed up one and only had one the day after the first Society meeting, and another couple days after that when she couldn't figure out some dumbassed reading comprehension question to save her life. And now. Now when her head was swimming with a hot guy with full tattoo sleeves. Now when she was surrounded by bongs when she never wanted to see another one in her life. And freaking out over keeping a scholarship that she needed, absolutely needed, to survive.

Because surviving meant graduating from college, and that meant being able to go it on her own.

She took a drag off the cigarette and let the sweet, sharp smoke fill her lungs, closing her eyes to take in the feeling and letting herself lean against the building again. She was smoking a cigarette after three days of nail-chewing and willpower. She hadn't seen Crash today. Amy would be here soon. Things could be much, much worse.

"You know, those things will kill you," a smooth baritone voice rumbled out right beside her. She startled and opened her eyes, and the sight of him made her jump. His dark brown hair covered his left eye and made her want to run her hands through it. His lip ring caught the light, calling into focus the sharp angle of his jaw, the beautiful lift of his cheekbones. Worst of all, that art— crisp and decisive, yet intricate art, covering every inch of firm, strong arm— it was like Crash's entire purpose on Earth was to get Rion to touch him. Her fingers twitched.

Don't do it, you bitch. Don't even think about it. He's only trouble.

"We're all gonna die," she drawled, fighting to keep her words smooth as butter. "I just might go a few years sooner than I would have otherwise."

Crash scoffed. "Okay, sure. Coughing up blood and in incredible pain."

Rion's eyebrows pinched together. "Okay, Principal Buzzkill. Is there anything else I missed in health class?"

"Yeah. You need to eat three meals a day, especially breakfast."

"What makes you think I don't?" She didn't. Communal dining situations always made her anxious, almost certainly a holdover from the group home, where mealtimes were a prime setting for fist fights. She hadn't really considered that when she'd scheduled classes that kept her away from her dorm for a whole day, but with breaks only short enough to let her eat in a dining hall, not take anything back to her room.

"You're thin." He shrugged, letting his eyes sweep down over her.

"Not where it matters," she mumbled. She had a great rack and a great ass even if they had shrunk in size too. Crash raised an eyebrow while looking down at her chest.

"Eyes up here, asshole," Rion said, and it surprised even her when it came out through a smile, a large part of which was a knee-jerk satisfaction that he was definitely not gay.

"You mention your boobs, I have to look."

"I didn't say boobs."

The Broken Hearts Society of Suite 17C

"But you must have meant them, because you're right. You're not thin where it matters." a slight smile twitched at his lips. "Regardless, I have a weird sort of sixth sense about food. I know when people are hungry. I feel it."

Was he standing a little closer now? Her skin prickled at the thought. Control your breaths, Rion. But with him standing so close, she couldn't help but breathe in his scent. It was sharp and boy-scented, not musky, clean. And absolutely no pot. Huh.

"What magic is that? Is it the same magic that gave you the name Crash even though that's not even a real name?"

"Now that," he said, standing up, "Is a great philosophical point. What *is* a real name? Something to think about, isn't it? What did we read in high school with that theme? Great Expectations? Gatsby? The Count of Monte Cristo? No, I don't think it's any of those…"

Rion glared, forcing her smile back, but sure it was still right there where he could see it. "I have no idea what you're talking about."

"Well if you aren't familiar with those bastions of classic literature, then I certainly wouldn't expect you to pick up the reference to the classic 1996 video game featuring a wily yet undeniably charming anthropomorphic bandicoot named Crash."

"I…um…"

"I thought not." Crash shook his head as though it was the biggest disappointment of his day. "But to answer your question, yes. It does come from the same place. My Catholic mother, who passed on her food-pushiness AND named me something so boring, bland, and proper that I could never use it to do the kind of art I want to do.

"Okay," Rion said, letting her head loll to the side, hoping the rough texture of the bricks against her scalp would ground her. She stared off down the street, not looking in his eyes, pretending not to be interested. "I'll play. What's your real name?"

"I don't think I should tell you that," he said, stepping toward her. Where the air had felt damp moments before, it was now charged with electricity—a pull toward him that she fought against. Rion commanded her feet to stay planted on the concrete and forced the corner of her mouth to quirk up in a smile. He was probably right. If she knew his real name, she'd know that much more about him, be that much closer to him. Which she really, really wanted to do, even though she didn't.

She licked her lips and swallowed. *Dammit, Burke, now he's going to think you want him.*

But the only reaction from Crash was a quick flick up of his eyebrow, like she was interesting, but not compelling enough for him to say more. "I'd better not," he said, shrugging. "I don't want to ruin the mystery."

"What mystery?"

"Well, it's always good to have a little mystery on a first date."

Rion's heart dropped into her stomach and started flopping around like crazy. She fought the urge to wrap her arms around her waist. She normally had guts of steel. What was this guy doing to her?

He was being gorgeous and flirting with her, when nobody had ever done that. Ever. In the last two years, the most romantic thing that had happened to her was Tate offering to share some of his "good shit" with her during a late-night basement pot party. She'd rolled her eyes and made out with him anyway.

And look where that had gotten her.

"Look," Rion said, pulling every ounce of resolve to the fore, forcing herself not to look at those tattoos covering every inch of his arms, not to let her eyes follow his impeccable cheekbones to his—what color were they? Holy shit. Bright blue eyes. "I don't date."

Every word was painful.

"Well that's a shame," Crash said, closing the space between them in one long step. "Because I don't kiss girls that don't let me take them out at least once first."

He reached his hand up, slowly, toward her face. Jesus fucking Christ, if he touched her jaw, she would melt. She would seriously die right on the spot. She would beg to kiss him.

Instead, he brushed a bleach-blond strand away from her forehead. She fought against letting her eyes flutter closed, but he smiled like he knew exactly what he was doing to her. "You gonna be okay walking home?"

"Yeah, man, we've got her."

The spell was broken. Every tense muscle in Rion's body relaxed, which was kind of crazy considering a guy's voice she didn't recognize was speaking for her through the dark. But when she turned around, relief swept over her. Amy.

"Fucking finally," Rion said, smiling. Amy's eyes flared like Rion had just called her a ho-bag or something. She came to stand beside Rion anyway.

"Sorry," Rion said under her breath. "It's just that you're a little late."

"I got a little lost," Amy said, her eyes darting to the alley behind Rion.

"And a little sexually harassed," Mystery Guy piped up. Rion looked him over. He was a ginger, but an unusually decent-looking one, even if he wasn't very tall. Normal jeans, generic brown oxford shoes, and a t-shirt with a bust of Jesus on it. Underneath it said "BRB."

Rion grinned. "Your shirt. Fucking hilarious, man," she said.

"Thanks," he smiled back. "And I believe it, too." He met her eyes, still smiling, but she felt the warning. Don't fuck with this guy's religion. She smiled in response.

"Cool," Crash said.

God, she'd almost forgotten he was there.

"Well, since you've recovered, I'll start my shift. You'd be amazed how many college students get drunk and then

The Broken Hearts' Society of Suite 17C

come in to talk to me about tattoos. Too bad I can't actually do the art on drunk girls, or I'd be a rich man."

Rion, Amy, and Random Guy stared at Crash. Rion tried to glare, but she couldn't.

"See you later, man," Random Guy said, sticking out his hand to shake Crash's. Holy hell, he'd just activated Crash's forearm muscles, which flexed his tattoo in a way that made Rion's mouth water. Rion bit her lip and looked down. She watched Crash's feet as they walked his deliciously chiseled ass into the Studio, and exhaled.

"Are you okay?" Amy's voice was gentle as she nudged Rion's elbow with her fingers. Rion forced her own legs to move. Holy shit, why did one stupid guy have this much of an effect on her? She gritted her teeth. She'd worked her ass off for the past two years to make sure nobody, and nothing, would be able to mess with her emotions ever again.

Dealing with one parent's death and another's betrayal in a three-month span was enough of that to last her a lifetime.

"Yeah, I'm…yeah." She stumbled over every syllable. "Crash is just…" *Just what? Gorgeous? Captivating? Infuriatingly charming?* "Annoying."

Amy smiled. "Okay."

Rion felt the teasing in Amy's tone, and her mouth twisted into a frown. "Seriously. He's the guy I wanted you to meet me here so I could avoid him."

"I sense I probably shouldn't be in on this conversation," the ginger guy said.

Oh, that was right. Amy had her own guy to be interrogated about. The satisfaction of the realization almost made Rion smile. "Who's this?" Rion asked, tipping her head toward him.

"This is Matt," Amy said offhandedly. "He says it's maybe not the safest for girls to be out walking at night."

Matt nodded. "Which is ridiculous, but yes, definitely the case at Northern. We're working on increased police presence, stronger penalties for sexual assault, but it's all…I don't know. Missing the point? Doomed to be ineffective? Really discouraging."

"Who's 'we?'" Rion asked.

"Student Government. It's kind of a joke, actually. You'd think things would have changed since sixth grade, but it's still just a popularity contest where the biggest change we could hope to affect is slightly tastier lunch selections. Sometimes they ask us about big stuff, like building a new parking garage."

Both girls looked at him. Rion had no idea what to say without going on a rant about how all government was corrupt, and he shouldn't be surprised, and he was being a fucking misogynist if he thought all women needed male protection to walk through campus, but she didn't for two reasons. One, Amy seemed to be cool with him, and even if she'd been late, she had kept her promise to meet Rion after work. And two, Rion's insides still felt all rumbly, and her hands slightly shaky, from talking to Crash.

Exactly why she'd been so desperate to avoid him.

I had a boyfriend all freshman year who lived in Florida. He came up a few times to Ohio and decided the next year he would move up (he was a year younger). So we found an apartment with two other girls, so we had three bedrooms but each of us would pay a quarter of the rent. Well, mid-summer he just said he wasn't coming and I never heard from him again (until almost 5 years later.) So the kicker was I got the biggest room but had to pay double the rent the next year.

He still tells me to this day that I'm the one who got away. He was just young and scared. Crazy how life changes.

Because of that living situation the next year I decided to live in the sorority house. That didn't end well. And then I left OSU. I think that one breakup completely changed my life. Not for better or for worse, just…changed.

~Jessica Wadler

ated data}
Chapter 9

Arielle

Arielle loved her mother. She really did. She loved that Mom supported her no matter what, loved that she held her hand through every step of the college selection roller coaster—first the application to Indiana Northern, the acceptance to every school except Northern, and the ensuing heartbreak, then the whiplash of getting into Northern after all.

Mom had known why Arielle had her heart set on Indiana Northern, and had held her tongue against warning her to pick a school just because the girl she loved went there. Instead, Mom had made a list of everything she thought Arielle would love about it.

Mom had been a self-proclaimed LGBT ally from the moment Arielle came out at age 15, when she realized that, when she was with the boy she'd been dating, she didn't get worked up at all. No nervousness, no sweaty palms, no jittery anticipation of whether and when he would put his arm around her, touch her, try to kiss her. She Googled ridiculous shit like "How do I know if I'm gay?" and she came across one man's explanation of how he knew: When he imagined himself in a room full of both boys and girls, he realized the only ones he would want to see in their underwear were the boys.

That day, while trying to dodge flying kickballs and otherwise completely disengage from gym class, she tried it out. The boys were all gangly limbs, acne, and bravado, trying to keep their still-sometimes-breaking voices in check. They also stank, which Ari knew from experience with her little brother was usually due to deodorant management issues—she often had to yell at Ethan to put deodorant on before bed, too.

Then, she'd surveyed the girls. She'd gone to school with most of them since kindergarten, so trying to figure out if she would be sexually aroused by any of them in their underwear was just…no. But then…the curve of that one girl's hip was so beautiful, and the way the other girl's neck gracefully curved up into hairline and down into collarbone looked almost…kissable. Like if these girls were new girls, ones she didn't know from sleepovers and tee ball and ballet and synagogue youth group, she would want to get to know them. She would want to touch them, and, yes, see them in their underwear. Probably less than their underwear.

She'd never forget the feeling when she realized what that thought meant. After all, she'd always known it deep down inside, but now it was a truth, one she'd uncovered from deep inside her that she just knew couldn't be hidden. She motioned to the gym teacher that she had to use the restroom, and tried her best to jog, instead of sprint, off the gymnasium floor.

Her butt landed on the first hard-wood slatted bench she saw, and she put her elbows on her knees and head in her hands. Her heart raced, her chest burned, and her stomach was tight. It was scary, this shift, but Arielle could feel a sense of relief starting to take over, the very same place inside of her that she'd just uncovered telling her that she was going to be alright. And, letting her hands smooth over the back of her neck, she'd smiled.

She'd come out to Mom that night, when she was lying in her low twin bed and mom was sitting on the floor beside her. Since Arielle was a little girl, mom had had a series of questions she asked her at bedtime because "How was your day?" had annoyed Ari as long as she could remember. "What was your best thing today?" "Who did you hang out with?" and "Are your classes what you expected them to be?" all preceded the final question—"Is there anything else you want me to know about?"

Arielle had answered Mom's questions that night, but she could sense that Mom knew something was different. Before the last question, Mom had reached up and stroked her hair, something she hadn't done in years. "Anything else, my Ari?"

"I think...I think I figured something out today."

Nothing from Mom. The silence, instead of being scary, gave her room. Let her breathe. Made her feel like she could speak anything, and it would fit perfectly into the space between them.

"I think I like girls. In that way. Like most girls like boys? That's how I like girls."

She'd expected Mom to come back with a barrage of questions about how, when, why, who. She'd heard coming out stories, and they were all far more dramatic and tense than this one, with parents in tears, asking stupid questions, stubborn in their denial.

But Mom had just done what she'd done every other night. She'd raised up on her knees, bent over, and kissed Ari on the forehead. Most nights, Arielle had hated that, but tonight, it felt like a promise. Not a seal of approval, but something deeper. Something that told her that Mom saw her, and heard her, and loved her.

"You okay?" Mom had murmured.

And Arielle had smiled into her pillow. "Yeah. I think I am."

That memory was one of those Arielle carried with her everywhere, always, one of the most precious of her life. After that, Mom's show of support had started small. Mom searched online for articles about how to be a good parent to your gay kid, what signs to look for that she needed to talk. But quickly, she realized that nothing really had to change. Arielle had never liked talking about boys or romantic stuff anyway.

So, aside from changing her Facebook profile picture to a square-shaped rainbow with ALLY written in big letters across from it, and attending the Rainbow Seder at their synagogue, which board members were all encouraged to do anyway, nothing much changed.

Until Rachel.

Rachel's family had moved from Chicago to Indianapolis when she was in eleventh grade, and Arielle would never forget seeing her on the first day of school. Ari's first reaction wasn't how beautiful she was, or how tall, or how new—their small suburb hardly ever saw new students—it was how scared she looked. Her hands trembled at a locker three spaces down from Ari's, and Arielle had just wanted to make it better. She'd slammed her shoulder into the locker and pulled up quickly, smiling up into Rachel's warm brown eyes and explaining, "This row sticks."

And then Rachel's smile had completely taken her breath away. And then they'd talked, and she'd helped Rachel find all her classes, and Arielle had thanked God and everything holy that she wasn't a freshman, because that meant she knew enough to show Rachel around. When she'd found out that Rachel was Jewish, she'd just about lost it right there in the hallway. She was perfect. They were perfect.

All those Disney Princess movies where the girl is floating around on a cloud after meeting her Price Charming? That was Arielle the day she met Rachel. And Mom had known something was different—something big and important.

Which made telling her about the breakup that much harder. Mom had loved Rachel—probably more for what she had done for Arielle than Rachel herself. Arielle knew Mom well enough to hear the conversation in her head— she didn't want to upset Arielle more, and she didn't want to seem like she didn't care. But Mom was upset, too.

Arielle's phone buzzed in her pocket, and she knew from counting the buzzes and repeats enough times that she had six text messages, all sent back to back. Mom's most annoying habit, by far, was writing a novel of a text message and sending it all at once, so it got split up and jumbled and hard to assemble. But it didn't matter. Ari knew what she was texting to lecture about.

It was that time of year.

Mom: **Do you want me to rent a car for you to drive home for Rosh HaShanah?**

Okay, I just checked. You can't drive a rental car.

Arielle rolled her eyes. Obviously, everyone knew that.

Mom: **I'll come pick you up.**

Arielle: **Mom, don't be ridiculous.**

Mom: **It's ridiculous to want my daughter home for the holidays?**

A tear rolled down Arielle's cheek. She hardly ever went to Friday night services, didn't keep kosher—not eating shrimp because the texture grossed her out didn't count. Jewish stuff happened a handful of times a year—at Passover seder, at summer camp, and at High Holiday services at the synagogue she'd been named in, had her bat mitzvah in…and met Rachel in.

She hadn't been back to that building since last year, when Rachel had come back home after her first three weeks at Northern. Those three weeks, Arielle thought she would die if she didn't see her soon. Then she'd managed to sit through *Unetaneh Tokef* before texting Rachel, underneath cover of prayer books, to meet in the coat closet. They made out for what turned out to be a little under an hour.

Thankfully, Mom hadn't noticed. Or, more likely, hadn't cared. Arielle and Rachel had agreed to keep their relationship under wraps, since it had started in adverse conditions—Rachel was leaving for college in four months—and would only get more challenging over the course of the year. If they could do long distance for that long, then Rachel promised they could tell everyone. Their mothers were friends. Everyone knew them. Hell, probably everyone had known about them, but Arielle was too ensconced in her own stupid bubble of love to realize it.

The Broken Hearts' Society of Suite 17C

Their entire relationship was based on a future that would never exist. The worst part was that home was such a big part of that future, and its loss still stung like hell.

Mom: **It's only six days away, Ari. We need to make plans for getting you home.**

Arielle bit her lip and swallowed the lump in her throat.

Arielle: **I already made plans. I can't miss class that day or the day after. I'm going to Hillel. Already paid for dinner.**

Amy had dropped a flier on Arielle's desk a week or so ago. Arielle had looked at her with questioning eyes. "You're not Jewish." Amy had shrugged, but when Arielle had seen the name scrawled on the front, right above 'Harrison 17C'—Amy Bauer—it had made sense. Of course the most Christian girl Arielle had ever met would have a Jewish last name, while she was firmly stuck in a sea of WASPs with Dad's French surname, Duval.

That flier was the only reason she knew that Hillel on campus—which she hadn't thought about since Rachel had told her how lame it was last year—was hosting dinner for the low price of $20 for Rosh HaShanah evening.

Which, given that she would rather listen to nails running down a chalkboard than sit in a huge dinner surrounded by Jews she didn't know, there was no way in hell she'd be attending. Just like there was no way in hell she was going to go home. Which just made her pathetic, and scared, and homeless for the New Year for the first time in her entire life.

Arielle's phone trilled one last time.

Mom: **Oh! Shelley's son is on the student board there. Do you want me to have him meet you there? She says he loves it.**

Ari: **I'm sure I'll find him. Thanks Mom.**

Arielle had no idea who Shelley's son was, or whether she would even want to shake his hand, let alone spend hours sitting through services next to him. That just got her thinking about services, about how she'd have no idea what they would be like until she sat down, and then it would be too late. Would the chairs even be comfortable? Would the prayerbook have translations? Would she know the tunes? Would the rabbi be weird?

She stewed over it for the next five days, feeling her heart sink each time she came to the inevitable conclusion. Rachel would definitely be going home, which meant Arielle couldn't go home. She couldn't think about Rachel without feeling her heart twist and sink—if she saw her, she knew she'd lose it. Sorority row and the two blocks around it were off limits for that very reason, which is why Amy had agreed to meet Rion after work the other night. The chance of running into Rachel on her way in or out of her sorority house was too risky if she wanted to make it through the semester in one piece.

The day before the holiday, she kept her nose in her book and her focus on her professors' lectures, swatting

The Broken Hearts Society of Suite 17C

away thoughts of home and brisket and the Temple Beth Am coat closet like the annoying blood-sucking mosquitoes they were. That period of her life was over, and even if Rachel had wanted to get back together, Arielle had enough self-respect to know that she would never, ever allow that. Some wounds could never be stitched back together.

Her phone buzzed one more time.

Mom: :(**We'll miss you. Will you call me after?**

Arielle knew what Mom's easy acquiescence to the whole 'I can't come home' solution meant. She was delighted that Ari had decided to go to Hillel all on her own. In Mom's ridiculously optimistic brain, which thought much more highly of Arielle than she ever would think of herself, it would be easy for Ari to make friends. Everyone at the Jewish student center would love her, and soon she'd feel more at home on campus than at Temple Beth Am.

But Arielle knew the truth, deep down in her soul, and it stung like a bitch. If she ever had been the kind of cheery, sweet girl who made friends instantly, that had certainly been wiped away in the last three weeks. Indiana Northern had gone from being her biggest dream to her worst nightmare, all in the five devastating seconds it took Rachel to break her heart.

Still, maybe Mom was right. Maybe after four weeks of pure pain broken up by college classes and lunches with one very cute girl who may or may not have been interested in her, it was time for Arielle to, at the very least, try. The image of Lauren sitting across from her in the dining hall, flashing a smile and coaxing one out of Arielle, too, lingered sweetly, bringing Arielle to the edge of a daydream.

Maybe one walk over to Hillel couldn't hurt. Just to take a look.

Arielle's boring-as-hell bio lecture was actually only a block away from Hillel, which was tucked into an alleyway just off Francis. Around the corner was a coffee shop, which Arielle told herself she could easily duck into if she chickened out at the last minute.

Get a hold of yourself, Arielle. It's a bunch of Jews in a nice building. They won't bite.

The smell of burnt wood laced through the air, which had turned from muggy to sunshiny and crisp at twilight in just a couple of weeks. This was Arielle's favorite time of year. She commanded her feet to stop outside the building and forced her lungs to open up, fill with the smell of chilly air and leaves turned brown and new beginnings. Something that just might bring her peace.

Okay. She could do this.

She knew where the Jewish Student Center was, since mom had insisted on a tour of it when they'd visited, over a year ago now. She let her legs carry her there, commanding her shoulders, full of tension and nervous energy, to chill the fuck out.

The Broken Hearts Society of Suite 17C

Hillel took up half a block on one of the streets bordering campus. It was made of white concrete and glass, and stood three floors high, dwarfing the church that sat to one side of it and the tattoo studio nestled beside it around the corner. Arielle sighed. Temple Beth Am back home was all brick and stained glass, carpet, dark corners, and musty prayer books. This didn't look like a place she could pray, let alone feel at home.

Behind the humungous window on the third floor, students stood in rows, holding prayerbooks. Apparently, services had already started. There was a whole community of Jewish kids here at Northern, doing their thing, praying, celebrating, eating, and forming a community on the Jewish New Year without her. Just like they were doing at home.

The ache that had moved into her heart, making it leaden, in the week after Rachel had dumped her, came back and sat heavier than ever. She slumped down on one of the concrete stairs that led up into the monstrous building, and swallowed back what she knew was an inevitable onslaught of tears.

You need to get your shit together, Duval. You have a whole life to live on your own. Be a grownup.

A tear rolled down her cheek, and watching it plop onto her jeans only emphasized how pathetic she was. Arielle refused to let it get out of hand. She focused on a row of buildings just at the end of her line of sight—ironically enough, sorority row—and tried to blink clarity back into her eyes. The messy jumble of anger and sorrow surged through her chest, pushing a roar into her ears, but she wouldn't let it show. If she had a nervous breakdown on the steps of Hillel…well, she couldn't think of anything more pathetic than that.

She wouldn't have ever noticed someone sitting down beside her, if she hadn't sucked her snot back in and smelled that perfume. Something flowery with a hint of fruit that was distinctly, irresistibly feminine.

And there she was. Lauren, who she hadn't breathed a word about Rosh HaShanah to when they'd smiled over sushi yesterday at lunch. But here she was, sitting beside Arielle at the saddest moment she'd had in weeks, watching her with kind eyes.

"You're Jewish," Lauren said. Not a question, but an invitation to start a conversation.

"Yeah. But they didn't find me."

"Who?" Lauren asked, her eyes narrowing.

"Hillel. The Jewish Student Center?" Arielle motioned over her shoulder at the imposing building, and Lauren nodded her understanding. "I just think it's amazing they didn't find me, with my first name and all."

"What do you mean?"

"Nobody from Hillel found me," Arielle repeated. "Like, I didn't get the auto-Jew email that I would have gotten if my last name was Cohen or Shapiro or Rosenbaum."

The Broken Hearts Society of Suite 17C

Lauren's face twisted up, reflecting vaguely interested confusion.

Arielle sighed, feeling that little point of emptiness inside her expanding. "The last names. They can tell who the Jews are because there are last names that are almost always Jewish."

"And you're Jewish. But you don't have one?"

"My dad isn't Jewish. He's French."

Lauren's eyebrows stayed suspended slightly higher than normal above her eyes as she watched Ari. "So…?"

"So…it's the New Year—Rosh HaShanah—but nobody invited me."

"Someone has to invite you? Doesn't the holiday just sort of happen?"

Arielle sighed, trying to mask her mild frustration. This is why her youth group friends said dating non-Jews could be frustrating. "Yeah, which is why I decided to walk by, I guess. But Jews are usually pretty decent at outreach—finding Jews and letting them know what other Jews are doing. Trying to guilt them into coming, I guess."

"Well, obviously you accomplished that for yourself. You're here, aren't you?" Lauren nudged Arielle's shoulder with hers, and Ari looked up into her warm smile, teasing, but patient.

"Yeah, I'm here," Arielle grumbled, scuffing the toe of her shoe against the concrete stair.

"But you're not actually sitting in services."

Arielle shook her head. "This is going to sound stupid."

"You could never sound stupid."

Arielle's cheeks flushed at Lauren's words, at the velvet softness of her voice when she said them. "I hate the prayers. I don't understand the words—most Jews don't, actually. But when we pray in English, it feels lame. It's a no-win. I can't stand to be in there." It wasn't a lie, but it wasn't the whole truth. She'd hated services at home, too, but the fact hadn't ever prevented her from attending. Everything else about being home made that one annoyance bearable.

"But you would have gone to prayers, or whatever, at home?"

Holy shit. Was this girl reading her mind?

"Yeah," she smiled at her shoes. "Home is apple cake, getting my hair fussed over by my mom, and playing rock paper scissors with my little brother behind the prayer book during the fourth hour of services. Home is…home. This isn't home, so it's not Rosh HaShanah." Arielle searched Lauren's eyes, begging her to accept the weird logic of her brain's war with Jewish guilt. Lauren nodded.

"And you can't go home." Not a question, but a statement. A challenge.

"I…have a midterm."

"No you don't," Lauren said calmly, as though she was observing the shape of a passing cloud. "Professors aren't allowed to give midterms until next week."

The Broken Hearts Society of Suite 17C

Embarrassment bloomed in Ari's chest for having been caught in the lie, though it made absolutely no sense that she should even care what Lauren thought. "What the hell? Did you memorize the academic calendar?"

"Yes I did."

She was serious. "Are you insane?"

A hearty laugh boomed out of Lauren. "Possibly? But if I'm going to be a pre-med major, I have to get used to a very regimented study schedule. I mapped it all out before I got here."

Now it was Arielle's turn to look at Lauren like she'd just spoken Martian.

"Well, I wasn't going to sign up for the classes if I didn't know I could handle them!" Lauren laughed. "I don't do anything without a plan," she said, her smile falling, her tone going softer. It sounded more like admission than pride in her voice, and looked that way too, from the way she stared down at her hands now. Her long fingers ending in smooth, neatly curved and painted nails danced around each other, cracked the knuckles on the opposite hand.

Arielle could understand that—needing to be prepared. Needing to have a plan for every possibility. So why hadn't she thought about what would happen if Rachel dumped her? Especially when Rosh HaShanah came?

Arielle stared off into the distance, fighting back tears when the reason came to her. Because Rachel dumping her was never a possibility. They couldn't have been more perfect for each other.

"I'm trying to change that, though," Lauren said. Arielle looked up and their eyes met, Lauren's dancing with light like they had the day they'd first met.

Arielle pressed her lips tight and managed a smile. "Maybe I should, too."

"So are you going to go in, or not?" Lauren's words pulled Arielle out of the pit of self-pity quicksand. It was a genuine question, and for a second Arielle got lost in her deep brown eyes that somehow caught the light in the way she'd never really seen. They held a challenge, but a gentle one.

It totally sucked that she couldn't even manage to walk into a stupid building.

"I...no. I don't think so. No."

"You don't want to, or you can't? Or you won't?"

Now anger flared through Arielle, just for a second. She didn't need one more person guilting her, especially a person who wasn't even Jewish. But she heard the real question behind Lauren's soft words and patient eyes. She was asking whether Arielle was willing to be in charge of herself.

"I want to," Arielle said slowly. "I think. I want to do something. It's, like, the most important holiday of the year. For my family, anyway. For me. It's a new beginning, you know? A fresh start. I've always loved that."

"But?"

The Broken Hearts Society of Suite 17C

"But I can't go in there."

"No fresh starts for you this year?" Lauren asked, her eyes searching Arielle's. Ari hadn't told her anything about Rachel, but the way Lauren looked at her right now...it was like she could tell Arielle had lost something.

Arielle smiled sadly, and shrugged. "I don't know. I hope there will be, I guess. Maybe."

"Well then," Lauren said, standing up and dusting off her butt. Two seconds of ogling later, Arielle pried her eyes away from its perfect muscular roundness. Her cheeks flushed red, but a sinking feeling in her stomach edged out the terror of saying something. Now that Lauren had found her here and challenged her, she didn't want Lauren to leave, and the feeling was so fierce that it forced her to stand, too.

"I'm sorry," Arielle blurted. Obviously she'd said something wrong, to make Lauren want to get away from her so quickly. She had to say something to get Lauren to stay here, to keep doing whatever she was doing that made Arielle feel grounded and just a little calmer than before.

"For what?" Lauren said, dipping down to pick up her backpack, and turning to face Arielle. Her stomach started to flip at the soft, delicate, slightly sweaty feel of Lauren's hand slipping into hers. Absolute heaven. "I was just going to say that I don't know anything about the Jewish New Year, but I know every stupid thing there is to know about the Chinese New Year. At least the way white people in California with Chinese daughters do it. So, maybe I can help."

Arielle cocked her head at Lauren, narrowing her eyes, trying to figure out if she was serious or making fun of her. A girl who sat down with her outside a random ridiculous building, who asked her questions and listened patiently, wouldn't be making fun of her. Would she?

"I mean," Lauren stammered, drawing her hand back and holding it awkwardly at her waist. "I know it's not the same thing, I just thought…you look so lonely, and I know a good Chinese restaurant nearby…obviously that's not a Jewish thing, but, you know…"

She looked mortified, and Arielle pushed to her feet, wanting to be at eye level. "I would love to."

"Yeah?" A grin spread across Lauren's face, even though she still kept her hand close.

"Definitely," Arielle said, her hand twitching with wanting to reach for Lauren's. She wanted to feel those fingers brushing against hers again so badly. But there was one thing she wouldn't be able to bear—messing up this tiny seed of whatever this was, too soon. Instead, she leaned in and nudged Lauren's shoulder, then took the first step away from Hillel, and toward her first ever grown up, all-her-own Rosh HaShanah.

Chapter 10

Rion

Rion had made it almost two weeks without seeing Crash.

In her first two weeks working front desk at The Studio on High, he had shown up at some point during every single one of her shifts. Sometimes he tried talking to her, sometimes he just looked at her from across the room with an unreadable expression. He never tried to upset her, but his mere presence seemed to infuse something in Rion's very being that made her jittery and off-center. Two things that she absolutely could not stand to be.

So she'd sweet-talked Olivia into letting her see The Studio's shift schedule. Then she'd snapped a grainy cell phone picture of it for reference. Olivia's eyebrow had gone up, and Rion had felt herself starting to get flustered. "It's just easier for me to see it next to my class schedule."

Olivia raised an eyebrow. "Don't I already know your class schedule?"

"Well, yeah, but…I might be changing it."

Olivia had lifted a doubtful eyebrow and handed the schedule over anyway. "Just let me know what changes."

Relief swept Rion at the opportunity, and she pored over the schedule. Crash tended to work late, so scheduling her shifts to end well before his started was tricky, especially with how much money she had to make to write that tuition check to Northern every month. Luckily, Olivia was patient enough to let her pull a two-hour shift and race to her 12:30 class, then come back afterward.

Rion knew she was being a pussy and she hated herself for it. She certainly needed to learn to handle herself around guys like Crash, since they were abundant in the music industry. Which, by the way, the Studio just might contribute to. After a lunch break that just happened to coincide with Olivia's, Rion had been given the job of picking and playing the music for the shop. Nobody would notice if she switched out the typical boring playlists for a couple hour-long mixes she'd spent every second of her free time working on.

It was only six, but Crash was getting in at 7 tonight. Rion huffed in frustration as she pulled on her jacket and signed out of front desk computer. Having the schedule

The Broken Hearts Society of Suite 17C

on hand had been useful, but also annoying, since it meant that she always knew when Crash was coming in and going out too. She called goodbye to Olivia and pushed out the heavy glass door, shivering with the blast of cold air. It was early October, and the air was already getting frigid with the sunset. She quickened her steps and reached down the back of her jacket, groping for the hood of her sweatshirt. "Dammit," she muttered when it became clear she'd have to take off her jacket to make it happen, looking back over her shoulder.

And smacked dead into a tall, lean hunk of muscle in a leather jacket, dark jeans, and heavy black boots. Her heart dropped into her stomach. She knew it was him, mostly because of the smell of leather and aftershave that made her all fluttery inside. Only now the smell was slightly better—it was laced with the faint whiff of a cigarette.

She raised her eyes, and there he was. There was no explanation for how badly she wanted to touch his thick hair. When he smiled, her gaze trailed down to his mouth, and dear God in heaven, that lip ring took her breath away every damn time.

"I'm sorry," he said, but the gravelly-soft tone of his voice and that sexy smile told her something different. He flicked the lip ring with his tongue, and she couldn't not stare. Couldn't stop imagining what it would be like to flick her own tongue against it.

"What are you doing here?" she asked, willing her own voice to convey annoyance. Judging by his smirk, she didn't think it worked.

His eyes sparkled as the corners of his mouth pulled up even more. "You mean, why am I early? Because our schedules aren't supposed to overlap?"

Rion's eyes flared and her heart hammered against her chest. "I…uh…I mean, how…"

He shrugged, never breaking eye contact. "Olivia told me. We've been friends a few years, and she's not afraid to ask me weird questions. Told me you asked to see the schedule, that you were obviously avoiding me. Wanted to know if I'd groped you or something." He rolled his eyes and smiled at her again, and a small part of Rion's brain wished that he would, in fact, grope her. Damn him. That look of his, dragging over her curves and connecting with her eyes like flint against steel, was going to melt her on the spot. "I'm coming in to reshuffle some of my shifts anyway. Stephanie's husband was in a work accident, something involving a forklift. He can't work, and she needs better shifts where she'll get more tips."

"What about you? You need cash, too."

Crash shrugged. "I'm okay. I don't have two little kids to take care of."

"Oh." Not only was he not stalking her, he was here to do something nice for somebody else. All she'd tried to do was avoid Crash, and the part of her that wanted him to say he'd been looking for her screamed. She wanted to strangle it.

"Plus, I was hoping to run into you. You're not the only one who memorized the schedule."

Goddammit. Bright blue eyes, staring right into hers, waiting for a response. Shining lip ring forcing her to stare at his lips, and think about kissing him. Gravelly, low voice saying such beautiful words.

"When did you quit wearing your nose ring?" He asked, just as casually as he might have wondered about the forecast for tomorrow.

Her hand flew up to the spot on her nose where the hole had healed over, the one she'd convinced herself would be completely unnoticeable to anyone else.

She'd had her nose pierced when she'd moved into the group home. She'd always wanted one, and reasoned that this would make her look like more of a badass anyway. One day, a swift punch to the septum from a girl down the hall when they fought over the shower had torn it so badly that she finally gave up on it. She missed it, though.

No guy had ever spoken to her so straightforwardly. Sexy looks always progressed to a hookup instead of conversation, and in the past two years said hookup was either initiated while drunk or high. She always had tried to lose herself in the making out, to tell herself that the groping felt good, but could never shake her annoyance that the guy wouldn't remember any of it in the morning.

"So you did have one. Thought so. I bet it looked incredible."

"It did." She let her hand move to touch the spot again. Jewelry wasn't something that lasted long in the group home, and it was the one thing that had added a little sparkle to her face that couldn't be ripped from her neck or traded for cigarettes.

Crash nodded. "You should get it redone." Then he blew out a cloud of smoke. Damn, that smelled incredible. Half of Rion ached for a long draw on the cigarette. The other half was proud of herself for kicking such a nasty habit to the curb.

"So, are you waiting for Amy again?"

"Who?" Damn, this guy was one annoying-ass question after another.

He chuckled. "Your roommate? The one walked you home with Freckles the other night?"

"Oh, right. No, I don't think so. I didn't ask." She should have made Amy meet her. Begged her. Whatever it took to avoid standing alone in the dark with Crash and thinking thoughts she couldn't afford to be thinking.

"So who's walking you home? It's getting dark."

"Thank you, genius. I might never have realized that if you hadn't said something. It's a damn good thing I'm not helpless."

"Rion. No way." Her heart stuttered when he said her name. "Seriously, I understand that you're Miss Tough Girl, and I admire that. I do. But you are also barely over five feet tall and probably a hundred and ten pounds soaking wet. Whatever you dealt with back home, it's no match for drunk-ass frat guys letting their dicks lead them down Francis."

Rion rolled her eyes and gave him a look that said *Please, asshole.* He didn't relent.

"You heard what Freckles said about campus, and I've been here awhile. I know he's not wrong."

Dammit, why hadn't Mom ever made her take karate? Why hadn't she focused more on fighting in the last two years, and less on hiding and dodging trouble? She met Crash's eyes, desperately wanting to say something smart, strong, independent—but totally failing to come up with anything. Instead her face fell and she shook her head, frustrated.

She expected Crash to strut and gloat, or at least talk to her like a child. Instead he just took one more drag, then dropped his hand, letting the cigarette smolder for several long seconds. He pushed off the wall and motioned for her to follow him with a tip of his head. "Come on. It's a free country, right? I can walk next to you on the sidewalk if I want."

Rion bit her lip, turned, and started walking, setting her sights on the straightest path back to the safety of Harrison Suite 17C. She'd never thought someone so annoying could be so damn cute.

True to his word, Crash fell in step with Rion, clouds of breath puffing out in the cold night air. They walked for several silent minutes, their breathing growing slightly more labored, falling into pace with one another. With each flash of her feet over the sidewalk, Rion grew more resigned that they'd have to come up with something to talk about, so this wouldn't be the most awkward walk ever.

Maybe she could give in, invite him in for a quick fuck in her XL twin dorm bed. Scratch the itch she had for whatever it was about him that went so deep under her skin.

Hell, maybe he was even a nice guy—nothing about him said he would be bad dating material. Well, besides the tattoos, and the punk clothes, and really long hours working at a tattoo shop that seemed to get half its business from bong sales. And the completely opting out of school. One or two of those things didn't mean much, necessarily. But all in one guy? He had to be some kind of a loser.

Still, she couldn't stop replaying their last conversation in her head. The way he'd noticed her, even her missing nose ring. The way he'd wanted to take care of her. She couldn't shake the feeling that Crash would never be content just to be a quick fuck.

"Can I ask you something?"

"Anything." His answer was so quick, his expression so open, that any impression of cockiness she'd gotten when she first bumped into him kind of melted away.

The Broken Hearts Society of Suite 17C

"Why did you say something to me about my nose ring?"

"Did it bother you?"

"I'm the one asking you the question." He laughed, then shook his head and stared down the street. "But seriously. You say you're shy around strangers, and here you are giving this girl you've met once random fashion advice."

"You and I both know it wasn't fashion advice. It was life advice."

Rion's eyebrow raised.

"A nose stud…it's not normal. Not for girls at Indiana Northern University, anyway. If you like it, wear it. Normal is overrated."

Rion let that sit with her for a few seconds, letting the motion of his thumb against the butt of his cigarette mesmerize her. She knew how gross smoking was, but the smell and the glowing orange embers and the casual motions of smoking added up to a memory of the last ten months of her life. A good memory. One of something that relaxed her, made her feel like she was happy in her own body for a fleeting moment.

"I hate smoking," Rion lied.

"Really? I find that hard to believe since you're walking closer to me now than you were two minutes ago."

"I am not…"

"You are. When we first stood out here I noticed how cool the street lights looked reflecting off that gorgeous bleach job. Now it's all in the shadows and so close I could touch it."

A lump rose in Rion's throat. "Gorgeous" was a word that nobody had ever applied to her hair. A pressure started to squeeze at her chest and she knew exactly the words she had to say to relieve it. "You're flirting with me." Except the lump didn't go away, and the tension didn't dissipate, because Crash slowed his pace, then stopped. She stopped too, and faced him.

He considered her with a slight smile and tilt of the head, and then moved close enough to touch her.

Everything was amplified, from the near-silent hiss of the misty drizzle that had begun to fall to the reflection of the main drag's lights in the wet asphalt to the sounds of the cars as they glided over the shallow skin of dampness on the road.

And the cool metal glide of his rings against her eyebrow as Crash reached up and brushed the long blonde bang, the one she'd considered turning pink or purple but never had the cash to make it happen, away from her eyes. Instead of dropping his hand, he moved his fingers along the line of her jaw and lightly trailed them over her throat before pulling away. His touch blocked everything else— her emotions, her speech, her breathing. She tried to make her stuttering sigh as quiet as possible, because he was still considering her, looking at her like a tattoo he had almost, but not quite, finished.

"Yes. I am flirting with you." The corner of his mouth crooked up and he raised his eyebrows at her as if he was waiting for some answer.

God fucking dammit, how could he stand to be so patient? Did he know she felt like she would burst just from those gorgeous eyes studying her face? Maybe he did. Maybe he was just messing with her. Maybe he got his rocks off making passes at girls he never intended to actually do anything with.

"Look. Uh…Crash." There was no way that was his real name, but now wasn't the time to push. "I don't date guys like you."

His short laugh broke the still air between them. "I wasn't aware there were other guys like me."

Jesus. He may have been cute, but he sure as hell was cocky. "You know what I mean."

His eyebrows raised again. "Tell me."

"Guys who sell bongs. Guys who drink, who party," she said, gesturing to the cigarette. "Guys who smoke."

"First, I don't sell bongs. I do tattoos in a shop that sells bongs. I don't drink. The most exciting party in my recent history was a 48-hour Netflix binge. And by 'smoking,' do you mean my once a week cigarette?"

"You're not serious." Nobody smoked just once a week.

Crash smiled flicked the cigarette again. "Serious as death. I look forward to one or two after a hard week. They relax me without making my head fuzzy, like alcohol or drugs would. If I ever did them."

The guy had to be lying. Working where he worked, inked to high heaven, sporting a lip ring…you only looked like that if you were heavily into the drugs and alcohol scene. She took a step forward and blinked at him. Maybe she could catch him in his lie. Rion got closer and lightly ran an index finger along the curving lines of one of his tattoos, starting halfway up his neck and trailing over his collarbone, then dipping below the collar. Quieter than a whisper, his breath hitched, and Rion knew she had him right where she wanted him.

"You don't do drugs? Don't drink? Nothing illicit besides this one little cigarette?"

His Adam's apple bobbed as he turned his eyes to hers. "Neither. Not ever. And I'll do you one better—I don't date girls who do, either."

Rion's heart sped up. She reached down and pulled the cigarette from his fingers, lifted it to her lips, and took a long drag. Then she dropped it on the concrete and snuffed it out, still looking at him. His lips were so close to hers that if she leaned forward just a few inches…damn him. What if he was telling the truth?

She let her hand drop, and stepped back, putting some air between them once again so that she could maybe take a deep breath. Air filled her lungs, but her heart kept hammering away, pushing heat over her chest and up to her cheeks. Damn it all, how could she keep him in her sights while making sure that he was actually dateable, as he claimed?

"Then why…?"

"Why do I have so much ink? And dress like a punk?" He shrugged. "I like how it looks." He lowered his voice. "And I think you do too."

Shit. She had to break this spell and get an answer about him, one way or another. "Pee in a cup," she said, letting the words rush out before she thought better of it.

"Excuse me?" Instead of the indignation Rion would have expected, his eyebrow and lip twitched in annoyingly attractive unison again. He stepped back, and Rion ached to be closer to him again.

"Prove it to me. Do a drug test at the student health center."

Both of Crash's eyebrows flew up, betraying very real shock. "What the…?" His quick recovery only took away some of Rion's satisfaction. He crooked his lips into a smirk and hooked one thumb into the waistband of his jeans. "Do you need to watch, or…?"

Rion rolled her eyes. "I just need the results."

"Alright, but you'll be missing out. Probably not the most romantic setting for your first time seeing…me, though."

She couldn't help but crack a grin at that. "Okay, if you're planning on there being a first time for me seeing your dick, you're making a lot of assumptions."

Crash nodded. "I am. In fact, I'm assuming you'll say yes to going out with me the minute I pass that test. If I'm not mistaken, the center opens Monday at 10:00, so…brunch?"

A slow smile spread her lips. Considering how hard she'd worked to put a defensive wall up against the types of guys she found most attractive—guys with tattoos and lip piercings and combat boots who- fuck her against the wall-obviously worked out, that wasn't too likely. "We'll see," she said, turning away from him before her grin made her look like a fucking cheerleader at a pep rally. "Monday?" she called over her shoulder as she walked into her dorm.

Rion didn't even try to calm her grin as she walked into Suite 17C.

Chapter 11

Amy

Amy would be lying if she said she hadn't been looking for Matt for the past two weeks.

He wasn't hard to find, either. His brownish-red hair turned out to be more unusual than Amy would have expected, and he always seemed to be crossing the quad when she was getting out of class, or studying at his usual table in the just-off-campus coffee shop when she was ducking in for a latte on her way back to the dorm.

He also almost always had a Jesus shirt on.

Whenever she saw him, she smiled, and he smiled back, and before she knew it she was heading over to ask how he was doing, and to answer his questions about her search for a decent worship service to go to.

Which, honestly, wasn't going too well.

Back home in Tripp Creek, Shiloh Tabernacle Southern Baptist Church was small and familiar, where everyone knew everyone and Sunday services were just as much a chance to gossip and to gather gossip material than to be religious. She'd never thought much of it until this past summer, when the pastor—Adam's father—had spoken in his rumbly voice about heaven and hell and sin and she had felt as though he had seen into her thoughts. The things she had done with Adam, the secrets they had kept, must have been written all over her face. She always felt like Pastor Mason was speaking directly to her. She'd never been able to understand how Adam could look so calm during those same sermons, and when she'd asked him how he made it through services, he'd just shrugged and changed the subject. Or pushed her into a dark corner of the church and started making out with her.

When she arrived at Northern, she'd given finding church services to attend the same level of thought as finding a place to get her hair cut. It would be good to have one on hand, but if all else failed, she could definitely get what she needed the next time she went home. But when Adam dumped her, church had turned from something she should do into something she knew she needed, but felt hopelessly separated from. She'd gone looking, of course, attending three Sunday services so far. One of them the ultra-hip-with-electric-guitars variety, one at a church mostly populated by seventy-year-olds,

The Broken Hearts Society of Suite 17C

and one with the same roaring sermons that had terrified her back home.

None of them made her feel close to herself, let alone to God.

She wasn't going to do that anymore, she'd decided. If she was going to find that connection with Jesus that everyone always talked about, but she had never quite felt in the way she thought she was supposed to, it wasn't going to happen via someone screaming into a head mike, or swooning to the sound of his own voice with long guitar solos. Not for her, anyway.

"You know," Matt said one early-October day as she sat explaining this while sipping her half-caff macchiato, "you could always come with me."

"Come where?"

His eyes crinkled with his soft smile. Even if either of her roommates had asked her to describe his eyes, she wouldn't have been able to. Amy just knew that the greenish-brownish-gold made her heart, and then her shoulders, relax every time she saw them.

Rion had teased her at each Broken Hearts' Society meeting about Matt, who she insisted on calling Carrot Top, or Goldfish, or Big Red. Even Arielle had commented that Amy hung out with him an awful lot for just being friends. But she assured the girls what she'd been thinking about Matt since the first moment she met him—he wasn't her type. He just wasn't. The fact that she didn't drool when she saw him, didn't feel the urge to plant her lips on his, was just part of it. Each time she ran into him in that coffee shop, new evidence mounted. He was unambitious, floating through a philosophy degree, still unsure about his career goals at the beginning of his sophomore year.

Besides all that, he may have been a Christian, but he didn't really take religion seriously. In fact, Amy felt a little squirmy over every new t-shirt she saw on him. The bust of Jesus and "BRB" was just the beginning of it. Last week, he'd been wearing one with the Virgin Mary on it. The text said, "Abstinence—only 99.99% effective." Another featured Jesus in hockey gear and said "Jesus Saves." Amy got the jokes, but something about them felt more like mockery and less like professing faith.

"Go with you where?"

"To church."

"You go to church? I thought these shirts were a joke."

Matt started laughing, covering his mouth with the back of his hand and leaning over his open textbook.

"What?" Amy asked, suddenly feeling embarrassed. "What's so funny?"

"Go to church? I work for church."

"What?" Panic rose up in Amy, fluttering around her chest. Was he a pastor? A deacon? There was no way. "But you're a student!"

"I'm also a pastor's kid who's passionate about community service. Well, priest's kid. I grew up Episcopalian. My parents know one of the pastors out

The Broken Hearts Society of Suite 17C

here, and he got me a job working with the youth group kids. Fourth to sixth graders are a pain in the ass, but they can be sweet, too. Especially when they're doing volunteer work."

Amy's jaw dropped as she took all this in. "Okay, okay. Back up. You're a pastor's kid? Where is this church?"

"Francis Street United Church of Christ? Used to be Methodist. It's the oldest church within forty miles."

"Ohhhh, the huge stone one with stained glass?" Amy had seen it. She'd also been thinking that it was probably old and boring, filled with locals and no students. Old people. So, she asked him.

"That's right. Almost no students, but that's kind of what I like about it. If that makes sense. I don't have to worry about anyone else but myself, and what I'm thinking. What I'm saying. What my purpose is supposed to be that week. Besides, the congregants are old but the prayers aren't. The pastor there is cool."

Purpose. Such a calm word, and he looked so calm talking about it, too. There was a peace about him when he mentioned church, and volunteering.

Which, Amy now realized, was exactly what she had been wanting. She imagined sitting beside Matt during services. They would probably sit side by side, their legs almost touching, which they hadn't done since that night watching the stars. The thought made her anxious. What if she accidentally touched him? She had always insisted on sitting far from Adam during services for that reason. And, geez. There he was again. Always in the back of her mind.

"So, do you want to? Come with me?"

"I...it sounds great. Maybe I will. I guess."

"What's your hesitation? Didn't think a guy like me could work at a holy institution? Or don't think a holy institution that would hire me could be that holy? I'm perfectly normal." He held his arms out and leaned back in his chair. He really was normal. Normal jeans, normal brown guy shoes. All except for the t-shirt that screamed, "Jesus is my Love Machine." A t-shirt whose sleeves pulled back when he spread his arms out, and showed what she hadn't noticed before—Matt may not have been as tall or as large as Adam was, but his muscles were seriously defined.

"Do you work out?" she blurted, and her eyes went round when she realized what she'd said. Out loud. "I mean...um...it's just...I hung out with the football team at school. The guys who were the heaviest lifters? They had arms like that." She held a breath in her belly, waiting for his response. She tried to ignore how much she suddenly itched to touch those biceps.

"Funny you ask. I had to lift for soccer at school, but since I got to Northern I've hardly worked out at all. But now one of my old friends from when we were little goes here, and she teaches some kind of self-defense class at the

The Broken Hearts Society of Suite 17C

rec center. So I promised my mom, who promised her mom, I would go."

"Self-defense? Like, street fighting?" Amy raised an eyebrow. "You don't seem like the kind of guy to punch and kick and yell."

"What, because I'm a pacifist? Does that mean I can't work out? I need a t-shirt. 'Satan can't handle these guns,' or something. I should write that down." His eyes sparkled with mischief as he fake-leaned toward his bag.

Amy swatted his shoulder with her hand. "Stop it. If you wear that t-shirt I am not going to be seen with you again."

He sat up straight. "You were planning on being seen with me? Again? I thought these were all just chance encounters."

They were, weren't they? "Um...they are."

He leaned forward. "So you're telling me you come to this coffee shop every other day after my last class because you love the lattes?"

"Yes," she said carefully. "That's what I'm saying." She might have been saying that, but her heart was going a mile a minute. *He is not your type. You're just happy a guy is paying attention to you. You are pathetic, Amy. Get a grip.*

"Okay. Well, how about this. If I promise not to get the 'Satan can't handle these guns' shirt, will you go out with me?"

Amy startled. "I can't," she blurted.

He looked at her, taking in her expression, examining her face as it twisted in reaction to emotions not even she understood. He nodded slowly, and slumped back in his chair. "Okay."

She knew what he was thinking. She had told him about Adam. "Don't...I mean...it's not you."

It was true. She fumbled for something, anything to say that made sense. But he jumped in.

He started shaking his head and sat up again. He moved his hand like he was going to touch hers, which he sometimes did, but now he pulled it back. "Listen to me. You don't owe me a single explanation. I've taken women's studies."

She raised an eyebrow at him.

"I don't believe in the friend zone. You don't have to go out with me just because we happen to spend a lot of time together. Or, um..." he cast his eyes down at his paper coffee cup. "Maybe it just seems like a lot of time to me. Anyway, I like spending time with you because you're you, not because I'm hoping to eventually make out with you."

Amy's stomach dropped as the image of Matt leaning in to kiss her flashed through her mind. And she really liked it. She bit her lip and pressed the back of her hand to her cheek as it flushed. What in the world was wrong with her? He was so patient and charming and funny and, seriously? A committed Christian? Maybe she should go out with him once. Give him a chance.

The Broken Hearts Society of Suite 17C

"Seriously. Let's be friends. Come to this martial arts self-defense class with me, though, so I can stop feeling so pathetic hanging out at this coffee shop waiting to run into you."

Did he just wink at her? Amy was about to turn into a puddle, and she didn't even like Matt. Did she?

"You want me to come to self-defense class," Amy said in a measured voice, pretending to be interested in few dregs at the bottom of her long-empty latte cup. "Basically, you want me to learn to fight."

"Yes. I want you to learn how to punch someone in case you ever run into assholes like those guys I yelled at a couple weeks ago. And I don't want to be that asshole friend who thinks you need him to protect you just because he's a guy and you're a girl."

Amy stared into her coffee. "Yeah, I know those guys." Her voice was more bitter than Matt's dark roast must have tasted. Amy had grown up with nothing but the idea that girls needed to be protected by men. Protected, kept, and led by them. People hardly said as much, but it was everywhere. Mom always listened to whatever Dad told her to do. Women never preached at church. She had always been encouraged to start a career where she would be able to follow Adam.

"Oh. An ex-boyfriend?" Matt's eyes trained on her, like if he didn't watch her carefully he'd miss some vital information.

"Yeah. And every guy in my home town."

"No wonder you're not thrilled with the idea of dating. And that sucks. But, Ames—" Matt leaned forward like he was about to tell her a huge secret. "If it inspires you to be my self-defense class buddy, I can't say I'm that upset about it."

Amy bit her lip, reached down to loop her bag around her hand. Thank God there was a Society meeting tonight. "Okay. I'll come," she said.

Matt's face lit up with a grin. "Yeah?"

"Yeah," she said, standing. "Probably." The feeling stirring in her belly was familiar, even if it was distant—excitement. Anticipation. Uncertainty.

He held out his phone. "Give me your number? Just so I can text you details? I don't know them yet," he explained hastily.

Amy thought it was pretty unlikely that he didn't know the details of a workout class he'd already committed to. But the idea of him texting her suddenly seemed pretty good. One way to move slowly closer, maybe. Her belly flipped as she reached out and her fingers typed in her number on auto pilot. "Thanks," he said as she handed it back to him.

She bit the inside of her lip harder, unsure of whether she wanted to suppress the smile for him, or for herself.

The Broken Hearts Society of Suite 17C

October 5th – Society Meeting

"Rion's here!" Arielle clapped when the doorknob to Suite 17C turned. Amy arranged the paisley plates she'd bought especially for the meeting and tried to find a comfortable way to sit on the thinly-carpeted floor.

"I brought four pints this time," Rion proclaimed, dropping the white plastic shopping bags emblazoned with "THANK YOU" in red letters on the floor. "The dining hall chick was really excited because of the flavors she called 'seasonal,' or some shit."

Amy barely flinched at the curse word, and smiled to herself as she reached into the bag and pulled out a pint and a spoon. She had never tasted sweet potato ice cream, but the way Jeni's Ice Creams made it almost convinced her to stuff her freezer with every pint on campus. She whimpered as the sweet, cold spiciness filled her mouth. It was almost enough to forget that she'd just turned Matt down for a date.

Arielle pulled out the Society Notebook, stared at the blank page for a moment, then looked sheepishly at her roommates. "I don't even have an agenda."

"That's okay. Amy has something she wants to tell us," Rion said, unboxing the personal pizzas.

"I...what?" Amy stuffed another spoonful of ice cream in her mouth, realizing almost instantly that she'd been found out. She swallowed and mumbled, "How did you know?"

"Okay, I guess we can just…um…open up the floor," Arielle said, scribbling the date and "Meeting #2" at the top of the page.

"Hold on. You didn't say you wouldn't date any guy. You said you weren't going to get *serious* with a guy," Rion pointed out, blotting the grease off her personal pizza with a stack of napkins. "And he's not even your *type*. You said that after you met him."

"Which is why I shouldn't go out with him!"

"No. That's why you should. Because you can spend time with him without worrying about falling madly in love with him," Arielle said, nodding like she'd just said the most logical thing in the world.

"I saw him," Rion said, nodding. "He was very nice, but Red Rocks is not your type. Nothing to worry about."

"Red Rocks?" Arielle crinkled her nose. "What, is he a redhead too?"

Amy's gaze flicked between them. "I…I guess. Is that bad? Or good? Or…" The smiles on both girls' faces crept wider. "Listen. He's SO not my type," Amy repeated.

"Are you sure?" Arielle asked in the same way her mom would when she knew she was lying.

"Do you think his dick has freckles on it?" Rion piped in, the edges of her mouth twitching and her eyes crinkling.

"Huh. I guess I never thought about a dick having freckles before," Arielle mused.

"Yeah, cause you only ever think about pussy." Rion grinned at Arielle, who snorted, choking on the big swig of pop she'd just taken.

"Okay, STOP IT!" Amy yelled, letting her slice of pizza slap down onto her plate. "He is not my type, I do not like him, and I don't care if he has freckles…down there." Heat flooded her cheeks as she tried, and failed, to keep from picturing what was below Matt's belt. Were his abs as defined as his biceps? Did his chest move down into a cut stomach? She swallowed. "So neither should you. Anyway, he just wants to be friends. He said that."

"Hold on. He actually said that? He said, 'I just want to be friends,'" Arielle raised her eyebrows and stared into her with the question.

Not exactly.

"Yes," Amy said. She returned to her prim feet-tucked-under-bottom, knees-together, and back straight position. She picked at a corner of her pizza crust. She was suddenly not hungry.

"So there's no problem," Rion concluded. "You don't like him, he doesn't like you, there's no way this is going to turn into a relationship, much less a horrible, all-consuming, attached-at-the-hip one, so you go to the self defense class, throw a punch, break a board, shake hands goodnight, and meet him for Jesus time the next day. Hell, it's not even a *date* date."

"Seriously, Ames. What are you worried about?" Arielle glanced at Amy's pizza with a napkin crumpled on top, and pried the top off another pint of Jeni's, handing it to her. Amy hadn't felt very hungry, but suddenly dark chocolate ice cream felt like exactly what she needed. She licked the rest of the sweet potato ice cream off her spoon and dug in.

"Nothing. I'm worried about nothing." That was the simple answer, but really she was worried about a lot of little somethings—the way her stomach flipped when Matt said something sweet to her, how she was actually thinking about buying one of those Jesus shirts of his, the nagging need to know more about his job at the church and what he wanted to do with the rest of his life. The way his smile made her feel warm and the way heading to Francis Beans coffee shop after class was almost automatic now.

"Nothing," Amy repeated. "I just don't need to take a self-defense class, so I'm going to stay home."

"Says the girl who almost got mugged coming to meet me after work" Rion pointed out, polishing off her second piece of pizza and reaching for a pint of salty caramel. Amy had no idea where she put all that food, as tiny as she was.

Arielle gasped and swallowed a mouthful of Diet Coke hard, then coughed. "You what? Jesus, Amy."

Amy's eyes flared. Swearing, she might get used to, but that? Maybe never.

"Aw, holy shit. I'm sorry."

Rion stifled a laugh.

The Broken Hearts Society of Suite 17C

"I'm just going to shut up now. I suck," Arielle growled. Amy didn't have the heart to tell her that even that last word would have made her squirm a couple months ago.

"You do not...um...you know," Amy said, "In fact, I was going to ask you. Will you come with me, to the class? Just in case...you know."

"Just in case you finally freaking realize Freckles is your type and you decide you want to jump him on the way into the locker room?"

"I wouldn't...I mean, I don't...argh!" Amy said as she clapped the lid back on the ice cream and let her shoulders fall in defeat.

"I know," Arielle said, putting a gentle hand on Amy's shoulder. "We know. Besides, you're still dealing with the whole Adam thing, I'm sure."

"I saw him the other day," Amy said, remembering the way her breath caught and her legs froze in place when she saw Adam walking toward her on the quad, with his hand not only around the waist of some girl, but with his fingers hooked in her front belt loop. Something he'd never ever done with her, saying he wasn't into PDA. The girl was petite, more willowy than Amy would ever be, and her smile flashed white and perfect up at Adam, like he was a god.

Adam had seen Amy, had noticed her staring. She knew it because his mouth dropped open like he was going to say something, and for the briefest second, he stopped in his tracks. But the girl tugged him along, asking him a silent question. He leaned down and whispered something in her ear, and Amy would have sworn she saw him kiss just below it. Amy's heart twisted, remembering when he'd kissed her there.

That was always a sign with him that things were about to go farther than she really wanted them to go.

Amy remembered when she'd looked at him that way, like he was worthy of her worship, and believed it. She'd still be doing it, believing that, if he hadn't broken up with her.

Now, she wasn't sure whether she was grateful to him for leaving her, or just trying to dull the still-gaping wounds. But she knew one thing—the depression that had taken over in the week right after he'd broken up with her had faded, little by little, every day. Now, four weeks into the semester, she couldn't remember the last time she'd dreamed about him.

In fact, when she'd finally told Mom about the breakup, she could have sworn that Mom had been more upset than she'd been. With Dad as Adam's football coach, and Adam's dad her pastor since childhood, the families had always been so linked that the two of them being together felt like the last puzzle piece of their families' story clicking into place.

That was what accounted for the strange, empty feeling when Adam left her. Maybe when that one piece was gone, the rest of the puzzle would stop making sense. Maybe that was why she couldn't find a church she liked.

Maybe that was why coffee with a guy with freckles was the thing that made her look forward to going to class every day.

"Amy? Earth to Amy? I'll go to the class with you, if you really want me to. Then at least I won't feel guilty for skipping another work out. Which I would definitely do either way." Arielle reached back and tied her shoulder-length waves back at the base of her neck.

"Maybe it'll be fun." Amy forced a smile. "Maybe Matt's right when he worries about how dangerous this campus can be at night."

Rion grabbed another pint of ice cream. "Matt's right. Mmmhm. Okay."

Amy pushed her lips into a hard line. "Time to talk about you, Rion? What's the update on Crash?"

"Yes, Rion. Give us the update on Crash." Arielle grinned, letting his name roll off her tongue in a teasing lilt.

Rion's expression hardened. She looked like she was debating whether to call in nuclear launch codes before she uttered a word. "He…is definitely interested."

"In what? You?" Amy pushed her. If she had to open up, she was definitely going to push Rion to do the same.

"Fucking me, definitely."

Amy winced.

"Sorry, Ames."

Amy shook her head, trying to brush off the coarse language. Admittedly, it got easier to hear every time. Rion's bluntness was something she could appreciate, at least.

"Is he interested in me? Like, being with me? I'm not sure, but my bet is on no."

Arielle frowned, and so Rion gave her a little more. "Nobody's ever been interested in me for more than my tits." Rion shrugged and stared at her hands.

She didn't say it, but Amy could tell by the look on her face that this wasn't a statement she was super happy about." So what are you going to do?"

Rion shrugged like her particular genius in this situation was no big deal. "I'm testing him."

"Ooooh. How?" Amy asked, while Arielle quirked an eyebrow. "Standing him up for a date? Asking him about the future?"

"Making him actually take you out on a date after running away from him for a month?" Arielle snarked as she started to stack the used paper plates.

Now it was Rion's turn to roll her eyes. "No. Like, literally testing him. I told you guys—after what Tate did, any guy who touches drugs is not allowed to touch me. At all. I told him he had to piss in a cup before I'd go anywhere with him."

"Whoa," Arielle said, with an exaggerated slow clap. "Impressive. What about alcohol?"

The way Rion's eyes flared in response said she obviously hadn't thought of that.

"The only way you could know that for sure is if he was still drunk," Amy said.

Rion quirked an eyebrow at her.

"I had…friends who got in trouble. With a breathalyzer." The football team was far from squeaky-clean on the alcohol front, despite Adam the Pastor's Kid being the captain.

"So, anyway," Rion said. "I told him to be at the Student Health Center tomorrow morning. I have class two buildings down before it, so I'll be walking by anyway. If he's there, I'll know he's interested. If he's not, I go to lunch and forget I ever let him bother me."

"This is a really weird sort of romantic," Arielle cooed, pulling up her shoulders and giving Rion puppy dog eyes, like she'd never heard of anything sweeter than a guy who was willing to pee in a cup for a chance to date someone. "Can I come? Amy will come too. It's right after the ridiculous self-defense class she's dragging me to so she'll owe me one."

Rion's eyes narrowed at Arielle, and for the first time Amy found her biting look amusing.

"What's with you? Last time you broke out that notebook I thought you were going to use the pages to wipe snot and tears until our next meeting."

"It's been a month," Arielle said, concentrating on her ice cream.

"Sorry, but you're doing a really bad job of deflecting," Amy giggled. "Might as well tell us why you're not miserable."

"Oh, I don't know. It's nothing. Probably," Arielle said through a mouthful of Brambleberry Crisp.

"It's a girl. You had *sex*," Rion said, leaning in and peering at Arielle with a look that was half jealousy and half amusement.

Arielle laughed shortly and shook her head. "No. Nope. No, I definitely did not. Not even close."

"But you met someone," Rion persisted.

Amy had spent much more time with Arielle than Rion had, and her heart froze at Rion's easy conclusion. She looked at Arielle, her eyebrows furrowed.

"I…sort of. I mean…maybe. I don't know. It's nothing. Probably." Now Arielle twisted her fingers together and stared at them, speaking just above a murmur. Definitely uncharacteristic.

Amy hadn't even thought about the possibility of Arielle kissing another girl, let alone having sex with one. How did lesbians even do that? The thought made Amy swallow hard, because she couldn't even begin to grasp it– she'd spent her whole life being taught to never, ever even think about same-sex couples as anything besides an abomination, let alone considering them kissing.

Arielle looked up at Amy cautiously, as if she'd been reading her mind. Amy's heart twisted, because she realized that when she looked at Arielle, she didn't see a sinner or someone disgusting. She saw a friend, who'd had her heart shattered just like Amy had. Most of all, she saw someone who clearly had someone she was interested in, and needed a way to talk about it.

It was Amy's turn to tease. She cleared her throat and smiled. "This person you've been meeting for lunch before we walk to Biology. You're always so happy when I meet you after that. It's her, isn't it?"

"We're just friends..." Arielle started, when Rion cracked up.

"Bullshit. You are crushing so hard. Is she hot?"

Arielle's eyes flashed to Amy's, then focused on Rion. "Yes. I mean...definitely." Then a grin broke out on her face. "We really are just friends. Nothing's happened. And she's nothing like Rachel. But...I don't know. Amy's right. She makes me happy."

Amy's cheeks stretched with a smile, like Arielle's happiness was pushing right through her, too. She let it sweep over her, and reached a hand out to squeeze Arielle's. "You'll keep us posted, right?"

Arielle caught Amy's eyes and nodded, still smiling. She blew out a long breath that sounded like relief and contentment mixed together. Then she looked at Rion. "So. This test you're giving poor Tattoo Guy. I want to be there. You know, for moral support."

"For me?" Rion said. "Because, what? You think I care what the results are?"

"Not for you, for him. Poor guy." Arielle's eyes danced with laughter, and Amy giggled. She did feel bad for the guy, even though she totally understood why Rion wanted the test.

"Sure. Might as well bring the whole fucking Broken Hearts' Society Welcome Wagon," Rion grumbled. She hoisted herself up to standing and looked down at the other two girls. "Are we done? I have to go…" She clamped her mouth shut and shook her head. "Whatever."

Then she stalked into her room and slammed the door.

Arielle smiled at Amy like they had a secret. Amy shook her head, smiling too. "I thought the Society was supposed to keep us from getting our hearts broken," Amy said. "Not finding us new boyfriends–er…sorry. People to date," she finished when Arielle's eyes flashed to hers at the word "boyfriend." Even though Amy wasn't entirely comfortable with the idea of two girls being romantic with each other– even talking about that kind of thing could cause trouble in her hometown–Amy liked Arielle. She liked her good-natured teasing, admired the way Arielle seemed to be willing to drop everything for her roommates. The idea of making her into a real friend was more attractive than the whole lesbian thing was disturbing, by far.

"I don't know," Arielle said, offering a small smile to Amy. "I think letting the right person get away could be just as heartbreaking as getting dumped."

The Broken Hearts Society of Suite 17C

Matt's words bounced around in Amy's memory. How he liked her because she was her. She had never even asked Adam why he loved her, and he'd never offered to tell her. And here was Matt, giving her this gift without expecting anything in return.

Amy sighed.

"What?" Arielle asked.

"Nothing," Amy said, determined not to put words to thoughts that she couldn't even grasp. She pushed herself to standing and started collecting the tops to the pints of ice cream. "It would be heartbreaking for the rest of this ice cream to melt, don't you think?"

"Devastatingly," Arielle agreed as she bent down to help.

My roommate sat me down one day & gently told me that it was OK to cry... but could I please cry in private because the vet suspected the amount of my tears in the living room was the cause of her cat going bald from stress.

~Jen Ellision

Chapter 12

Arielle

"I don't even have workout clothes," Arielle protested, trying to keep her voice in a complaint tone instead of a whine. Theoretically, she didn't really care what anyone thought of how she looked. At least, that's how she had been back home, when she was with Rachel. So proud, so sure of herself. So certain about who she was, and what she wanted.

She didn't even know why she had agreed to go to this damn class. Yes, she wanted to be friends with Amy, and obviously her infectious smile given over several pints of ice cream had convinced Arielle that self-defense class would be a great building block. Now she and Amy were standing outside the humungous Indiana Northern athletic complex. Arielle was wearing stretched out, baggy yoga pants, which she was pretty certain had at least one

The Broken Hearts Society of Suite 17C

tiny hole in the butt. And the t-shirt mom had bought her when she'd gotten into Northern off the wait list. The soft, deep burgundy v-neck with distressed lettering was cute, at least.

She sighed as Amy tugged her by the upper arm. "Just remember, you're doing this because we're in the Society. I need you." Her face didn't match her words—she grinned, as if mocking Arielle's misery.

"I don't work out," Arielle repeated for the fifteenth time since they left their dorm.

"Just…try to do the moves. And maybe smile a little bit. You know, so people don't think you're completely miserable. Plus you have such a pretty face when you're not scowling." Amy beamed at Arielle, like that was supposed to be a compliment or something.

"Just because I'm a girl doesn't mean I have to smile," Arielle grumbled.

Amy rolled her eyes and pulled Arielle into a side hug. "Oh, Ari. I know."

"Well look who actually showed. I seriously was not expecting to see you."

Matt had a tenor voice that sounded almost musical when he talked. Arielle's eyebrows tented up when she turned to see him. Rion's nickname for him, 'Freckles,' was overkill—he definitely had them, but just a modest spattering across his cheeks. In fact, he had really great skin—it was fair, for sure, but he didn't have a trace of acne, and that ruddy brown hair offset his brownish-green eyes perfectly. Even for a girl who wasn't attracted to guys at all, Matt was attractive.

That didn't change the fact that Amy's claim that she wasn't attracted to Matt at all was so obviously bullshit. The closer he got, the bigger Amy's smile grew, and her 'hi,' had a breathy quality. Her shoulders edged up, her head tilted to the side, and she giggled at least three times in one minute. He looked at her from under his eyelashes, pulled a nonexistent loose hair from her hoodie, and listened to her words like they were gospel.

Their obvious infatuation with each other would have been disgusting if it wasn't so damn adorable.

Amy and Matt melted pretty quickly into small talk about a statistics professor they apparently shared—some paper, some bad joke the professor constantly made. All of a sudden, Arielle was a third wheel.

Great.

She followed them to the third floor of the rec center, then wandered over to the class schedule to figure out where the hell they were supposed to be going. This was some kind of martial arts, Amy had said—self-defense. Theoretically, feminist Arielle was all about it. Defending herself. Taking back the power.

But real life Arielle had fallen down at the ballet barre, tripped over her own two feet at second grade soccer practice, and never gotten past the easiest moves in some yoga class her mom had begged her to take. Her stomach started to twist as she went down the list.

The Broken Hearts Society of Suite 17C

Yoga...spinning...power core...Zumba? What the hell was that? There was no self-defense, no tae kwon do, no muy thai listed. No Krav maga, even. Oh, this last class had to be it.

Cardio kickboxing? She shot a glance over at Matt, who noticed and started heading over to her. "Cardio kickboxing? Amy. Seriously. Sleep is my cardio. And I am serious about that. So serious I have a t-shirt that says it." Arielle had imagined self-defense class teaching her a few swift punches and kicks, no sweating involved.

Amy glared at her. "Arielle. *Seriously*. I already signed you up. And paid for you. The instructor is expecting you."

Matt chimed in. "And I promised my mom that I was bringing two girls. I trust Amy and Amy trusts you and my mom trusts me, so you have to kickbox. See?"

"What is the relationship here, exactly?" Arielle asked as they walked down the hall. The room Matt led them to was covered in thick gray mats and studded with huge punching bags. A pile of humungous rubber bands sat in one corner and a rack in the corner held a dozen wooden poles. This looked more like a torture chamber than an exercise studio.

"My mom used to teach karate at a dojo before we moved to Chicago," he explained, stepping out of his shoes and leaving them on a tray. The girls followed suit. Amy was watching him like every word he said came out of the goddamn Bible. Arielle's mouth twisted. "So?"

"So this girl, the one leading the class today, was in one of Mom's classes, but she was a total failure at it. She stuck with it for awhile anyway, switched to MMA, and won some championship or something."

"I thought your mom was a pastor. She's a karate teacher, too?" Amy asked.

"No, my *other* mom is a karate instructor."

"You're...adopted?"

Arielle tried not to smirk. Poor Amy was so confused.

Matt shook his head and smiled gently, like he was totally used to answering this question...one Arielle already knew the answer to.

"Two moms. One is a pastor, the other is...well, let's just call her an athletic entrepreneur. She owns a dojo, a yoga studio, and a women's fitness center."

"Two moms," Amy repeated, clearly trying hard to assemble all the puzzle pieces of Matt's very interesting family life.

"Yep. My moms are gay. Most of mom's congregants think it's pretty funny that her wife is a black belt. She's even taught classes at the church."

Amy looked like someone had just told her that the earth was flat and losing a couple inches off the edge every day. "But I thought...I mean...for a pastor to..."

"It's okay, Ames," Arielle said, chuckling as she pulled her sweatshirt off. "You're living with one of them too."

"No, no, I just…seriously? A woman pastor? With a wife?" She didn't look horrified, scared, or grossed out…more like her brain just needed some recalibrating.

Matt laughed. "Sorry I didn't mention it before."

"No, it doesn't matter. I just…pictured your mom and dad. I've never met a female pastor, so I just assumed…"

"You pictured meeting my folks?"

"I didn't stay that," Amy said, concentrating way too hard on getting her own lace-up shoes off her feet.

Arielle bent down to take her shoes off, and a shriek came from the other side of the room. "Matty!" A tall, muscular blur of a girl with shining black hair pulled back into a ponytail barreled across the mat and jumped into Matt's arms. After a tight squeeze, she stepped back and grinned.

And Arielle's heart stopped. The squealing, hugging girl was Lauren.

Not only was Lauren here, but she seemed to be Matt's childhood friend. Which meant she was the one teaching this class.

Which meant the girl that Arielle was slowly falling in love with was almost certainly going to be watching her fall on her ass in about five minutes.

"Hey there! Geez, it's good to have you here at Northern. How long has it been since I've seen you? You got so tall," Matt said, standing on his tiptoes to try to gain some height on Lauren. Amy laughed.

"Just a couple years, crazy."

"Nah, it's been at least seven or eight. Look at you! I knew you were a champ, but geez. You're buff."

"Well, you know how it is. If you want to be a fine physical specimen like myself, you have to eat your veggies. And kick ass at Nationals."

Jesus, Lauren's smile was beautiful. Arielle's stomach flipped and flopped and twisted into knots.

"I'm going to show Amy all the equipment," Matt said, motioning for Amy to follow him.

"Be my guest," Lauren said, finally turning and giving her full attention to Arielle.

Arielle's ears rang with a soft tinny strangeness when their eyes met, like the whole rest of the room, or the whole rest of the world for that matter, could just disappear and she wouldn't care a bit.

Lauren's grin stretched wide as she stepped close to Arielle and said, "Hey. You found my class."

She looked so freaking happy about it that Arielle hated to tell her that she'd never been looking for her class, hated to explain the chain of connection between her and Amy, Amy and Matt, Matt and Lauren. And suddenly, with their eyes connected and Lauren's gorgeous muscled shoulders just…out for her to look at…she couldn't think of the words she would need anyway.

After a couple seconds of baffled silence, though, Arielle had to say something. "I guess I did. I mean, it's not like I was looking for it, but…"

Lauren's smile turned down just a bit, at the corners, and watching her go from happy to sad made Arielle's heart twist again. "I mean, I wasn't looking for *you*."

Now Lauren frowned.

"No no no! That's not what I meant. I mean, it is, but...oh, God..." Then, a gentle, cool hand rested on Arielle's shoulder. She looked up and Lauren's soft, understanding smile was back.

"I'm glad you're here," Lauren said softly, looking into Arielle's eyes for a split second longer than she really had to. "I was starting to think I would only see you after class. I mean, I was happy you didn't drop it after all, but, you know..."

No. She didn't know. She wanted so badly to know what Lauren was thinking, but she also really, really wanted to be able to just...be around her.

Arielle would be lying to herself if she thought she'd stayed in the class for any reason other than Lauren. There was something about being close to her, the combination of the easy way she laughed, the strong, graceful way she held her body, her habit of calm, quiet listening with all her attention, like Arielle was the only other person in the world when they were together.

Arielle refused to think of it as a crush. It wasn't—not the head over heels, all-consuming feeling she'd had for Rachel. That was love. This was...something else. Something easier, but something less certain than Rachel, too. Like at any moment, Arielle would be happy to have

Lauren around, but at the same time, she had no idea how Lauren felt about her.

It was lovely and heart-pounding and happy and maddening all at once.

After all, Arielle was too busy waiting for Lauren to grab her, passionately kiss her, and start pulling her shirt off to even start thinking about trying to be anything more than just friends.

Jesus. She had to stop running all these thoughts in a loop. If she was going to manage that, she probably had to stop hanging out with Lauren, too. She really couldn't imagine doing that. Not at all.

When Lauren was around, Arielle didn't feel like a tiny guppy in the huge ocean of Indiana Northern. Lauren didn't make things better, exactly, or even easier, it was just that when Arielle was with her, she felt like she had finally found a place where she really fit.

Could one single person be the same as a place? The same as a life? The same as home?

She shook her head to bring her back to the moment. Lauren squeezed her shoulder, and Arielle tried to keep a straight face despite how heavenly it felt.

"Matt!" Lauren called .

"What's up?" he said, hustling over to her from across the room where he'd been going over the equipment with Amy. As he walked, Amy's eyes raked up and down his body like she was a hungry wolf and he was a piece of steak. Arielle tried to hide her amusement, even though

The Broken Hearts Society of Suite 17C

Amy's questioning look at her told her she wasn't very successful.

"Here's the thing, Matty," Lauren said. She jerked her head back toward the door. "Hattie did not do her research. Or my mom wasn't listening to me when I told her about the class I got assigned to teach. This one is women's only."

Arielle looked at the half-dozen other girls who had trickled into the room. They all eyed Matt like he was a humungous centipede—almost certainly not dangerous, but gross and unwanted anyway.

"Seriously? It didn't say that on the sign."

Lauren rolled her eyes. "Of course it didn't. A couple of these girls are here because they have a history of violent relationships. Teaching them kickboxing empowers them. They don't want their exes or whatever to be able to find them. So, I'm sorry, but you're going to have to partake of my brilliant instruction another time."

Matt's mouth twisted in disappointment as Amy reached them. "What's up?"

"I can't stay," he said. "Girls only."

"Oh, no big deal," Amy said. "We'll just take a different class."

"I don't teach any other ones," Lauren said, frowning. "Maybe just tell Hattie you came and that I was amazing, as expected. The first one's not a lie and the second, everyone already assumes." Lauren beamed, and Arielle giggled at her cockiness.

"True," Matt said, ruffling the hair at the back of his neck. "Okay, so obviously I've gotta go. Ames, coffee after?"

"No, no. I'll go with you. I have work to do, anyway. And maybe you can give me some pointers on that bio professor."

Amy didn't need pointers on biology class. Arielle didn't know if she had a photographic memory or what, but she retained more information about single-celled organisms and the cellular structure of plants than Arielle could ever imagine learning.

It was all she could do not to roll her eyes at Amy. They would be having a talk about this, though. Either she was lying to the Society about her crush on Matt, which completely defeated the purpose of meeting, or she was totally deluding herself. Either way, this wouldn't end well. But, goddammit, Amy was already headed toward the door with Matt.

She glanced back at Arielle when she was almost to the door. Arielle spread her hands, palms up. "What am I? Chopped liver?"

"What's the problem? This is the same Lauren you told us about from class, right?" Damn her, that little small town church girl was perceptive. And just sent Arielle a wicked wink over her shoulder.

With Lauren standing right there, listening for her answer, maybe even caring whether she wanted to stay or gof…there was no way she could say no.

The Broken Hearts Society of Suite 17C

Did she want to take a kickboxing class, and have Lauren watch her sweat and stumble all over herself? Absolutely freaking not. Did she want to make Lauren think she wasn't interested in spending time with her? Nope on that front, too. Did she want to have the conversation with Lauren about how conflicted she was, and why? Hell no. There was really nothing to be done. She had to stay.

She sighed.

"Everything okay?" Lauren asked, genuine concern on her face.

"Yeah...I mean, no...I mean...geez, it's like I can't even talk whenever you're here." Had she seriously just said that? It was like she was admitting to Lauren's face that she couldn't think straight around her. Arielle took a deep breath. *Get it together, Ari.* "I just...I've always been pretty unsuccessful at exercise."

"Okay..."

"I mean... I've tried ballet, swimming, spinning, running, pilates, yoga. I usually end up falling or hurting myself somehow, and ending up worse off than I started. I'm a disaster. I mean, you should see my legs. They're full of bruises. I can't even walk without injuring myself."

"Well," Lauren said, her eyes sparkling with quiet amusement, "luckily, we mostly stay in place in this class. Hardly any foot movements required."

"You're not serious."

"Dead serious. Stay, okay? I really want you to stay."

Oh God, Lauren's hand was on her back now. Brushing down the strap of her sad excuse for a sports bra.

"If you're horrible, you don't have to come back. And I'll personally make sure you don't hurt yourself."

Arielle was absolutely mesmerized by the way Lauren's lips moved when she said those last words. "Okay. Just this one class."

"Okay," Lauren smiled, then crossed the mat, where a whole row of girls was busy stretching. They bent over and flattened their palms to the ground, then stood and pulled their heels to their butts, then crouched into deep squats, making all of it look effortless, even relaxing. Any one of those movements would make Arielle tip over like a drunk elephant.

Lauren motioned for Arielle to join them, then said in her ear. "Just follow their lead. You'll be great."

Then, as she moved away, Lauren's voice morphed from her soft, patient one into that of a drill sergeant after three cups of coffee. "Okay ladies, warm up is on the wall! Let's get it done!" The mat wasn't large, but when the girls started jogging laps around it, Arielle suppressed a groan. She fell into line and copied their movements. By the time they'd jogged around the mat twice, side shuffled up one side and down the other, done the same with lunges, and finished 20 jumping jacks, Arielle had broken a sweat and badly needed a drink of water. All the other girls looked ready to start punching something.

The Broken Hearts Society of Suite 17C

Lauren was literally the only reason she was still standing there. And as she thought that, Arielle was surprised to find that the idea didn't bother her that much.

"Now find your bag!" Lauren tossed a pair of boxing gloves to Arielle, and she fumbled to get them on her hands like everyone else in the class. Each of the girls took their place in front of a big punching bag, bouncing on their toes and holding their gloves up to their faces. Lauren clapped and let out a loud whoop.

"Okay girls, we're gonna kill it today, am I right?" Lauren's voice was solid, strong, and commanding. Energy vibrated off of her, seemingly transferring to every other girl in the room. They kept bouncing, and one or two glared at their bags.

"Imagine your person or thing, okay? We're gonna kick the shit out of it today and make it wish it never messed with you. Hands up, ladies! Our first combination is jab, jab cross. Nice and easy to start out. And...go!"

'Person or thing?' What in the...? But all Arielle had to do was glance around the room to figure out what Lauren meant. Each of the girls was furiously whaling on their punching bag with looks ranging from rage to determined hatred. This was the same as tossing darts at a photo of your ex, but with far more practical application. This was actually teaching them to fight, if they ever felt like they had to. Making them stronger.

Arielle stepped up to the bag and held her gloves up in front of her face, trying to mimic what she'd seen Lauren do. The obvious face to imagine plastered on that bag was Rachel's. Rachel, who had so seriously screwed her over, who had ruined her life, who had gotten her stuck here at a school where she couldn't possibly find a place to fit in, where she didn't really belong. Who had blinded her to any self-interest other than the one that involved a future with Rachel, together. Forever.

In the second it took for her to think all that, she knew she was angry—no, royally pissed off—at *herself*. For being so stupid, for being so…*in love*. She'd thought it a million times, but hadn't really felt the implication. She was rapidly falling in love with someone with no proof that she was actually out of the closet. She'd banked her entire future on someone who wasn't comfortable enough with herself to envision her own future.

Rachel had loved her—she was sure of it. But she hadn't loved Arielle enough to risk her own future to be with her—or what she saw as risk, anyway. And Arielle hadn't respected herself enough to find that out about Rachel before she'd gone all in.

Yep. There was only one person Arielle was royally pissed off at, disappointed in, maybe even hated—herself.

The anger bubbled up as pure hot energy, shooting through her body and exploding out through her gloved hands. The horrible stew of pain, grief, regret, self-

The Broken Hearts Society of Suite 17C

realization, and blame had simmered for too long, and started to boil over—and the bag was the perfect target.

Her fist shot out and slammed against the bag. She winced, expecting pain, but all she got was the solid thud of her glove against the firm column, which gave a little when she pushed. Oh, damn. That felt good. She couldn't imagine Rachel's face there, and she certainly couldn't imagine her own—even she didn't hate herself that much—but instead, the bag held a list of every stupid decision she'd made, every immature presumption she'd held about who she was and who she wanted to be. Then, every indecision—she was such a dumbass for not knowing what she actually wanted to do with her life when she came here, for counting on one single person to shape her entire future. Sure, she'd made excuses and reasoned—her mom and dad met in high school and married pretty much right after college. Why shouldn't she and Rachel have been the same?

"Aaaand, stop!" Lauren's voice broke her train of thought, and as all the girls stepped back from their bags, Arielle did too. She was surprised to find herself out of breath, with burning arms and belly muscles, her chest already breaking out in a thin sheen of sweat.

"Your next combination is jab, cross, hook, hook."

When Lauren called for everyone to go, the girls started to bob and dance around their bags, their fists flashing around and to the side, their feet pivoting so fast Arielle couldn't catch the movement.

"Looking awesome!" Lauren called as she walked down the mat, right up to Arielle. Lauren hovered behind her, and that light flowered scent of hers made it almost impossible for Arielle to focus on hitting the bag.

Once again, Lauren's fingertips brushed lightly on her shoulders, almost making her forget where she was. "Pause for a minute. You want to use your torso to twist and propel your shoulders around. Then your arm can punch forward instead of twisting in that weird way. Otherwise you could end up pulling something. Let me see you try again," Lauren said, stepping back and watching.

"I told you I'm hopeless. I have no idea what you were talking about with the jabs or whatever."

"I kind of figured that from watching you on the first round, but you looked so into it I really didn't want to kill your mojo. Looked like you had some steam to blow off." There it was again, that sparkle in her eyes that was so gorgeous, yet maddening, because it told Arielle there was more behind her words. Maybe the kind of "more" she was hoping for.

Do not do this to yourself again, Arielle. Don't move too soon, too fast. Don't make one girl your everything, without even making sure this is what she wants.

But that was damn hard to keep thinking when those cool, delicate hands rested so lightly on her shoulders again, sending the kind of electricity down her shoulders that would make someone swoon and beg for more.

"Let me help you out," Lauren said. Arielle could swear her voice was lower, softer. More careful. "Think strong arms, okay? You want that bicep to be focused, strong. Not flopping around like a fish out of water."

Arielle grimaced. A fish out of water was exactly what she was, and this class was a spectacular example. It was hard to stay pissed off at Amy for dragging here here, though, when her little puppy-love-induced oversight had resulted in Lauren running her hands over Arielle's bare shoulders. *Stop it, you bitch hormones.*

"Try again," Lauren said, a bit firmer. "Twist from here." Lauren's hands moved down to her waist, and Arielle had two choices—focus on the bag, or say to hell with it and turn around to kiss Lauren. Arielle darted an arm out, keeping tension in her muscles, and was rewarded with a much more satisfying smack.

"Good. Now do the same with the back foot."

"The what?"

"When you do this," Lauren said, moving a quarter turn further behind her and moving her hands so quickly and smoothly that Arielle barely saw it coming. But, oh dear Lord, Lauren's hands were now firmly gripping her hips. Just like they'd be if she was about to…no. There was no way she could think of that. Not here.

With firm hands, Lauren twisted her hips to the side, making Arielle's knees twist awkwardly. A sharp pain stabbed through the top of her shin.

"Okay," Lauren laughed. "You are definitely going to have to loosen up." Lauren's hands slid down the outside of Arielle's thighs, past her knees, over her calves. Arielle wondered if Lauren could feel them turning to wobbly jelly right beneath her fingers. Lauren's fingers wrapped around her ankles, cool and sure. Why hadn't anyone ever told her the ankles were erogenous zones? How had she never realized that someone gripping her ankles could send her into a tailspin of a sex-crazed stupor?

Before she knew it, Lauren had twisted her feet to line up with her hips, and Lauren was saying something about strong arms and hooking around the bag like a bear hug. Arielle nodded like she was taking it all in, but Lauren's touch had managed to bewitch her so intensely, that she didn't even really care that she had to exercise to get it.

Arielle wanted more.

Well, at least there were—Arielle glanced at the huge clock on the wall and groaned inwardly—thirty minutes of this class left. With her arms burning and her legs starting to feel like rubber, Arielle wondered what more these girls could possibly handle. But they did.

Every time Lauren called, "Break!" the girls stepped back from their bags, but no more than thirty seconds later, she barked "Lunges!" or "Sit ups!" and the girls fell into whatever activity she called at such a frantic, automatic pace that Arielle would have sworn they were cyborgs. Especially because she moved at about a third the pace as they did, and with so much difficulty that she

The Broken Hearts Society of Suite 17C

seriously couldn't understand how they did a squat more than once. In their lives.

But at least, between the excruciating rounds of crunches, lunges, leg lifts, pushups, wall sits, and some horribly torturous thing Lauren called burpees, there were more kickboxing rounds. And the way Lauren laughed and smiled every time she had to grab Arielle's hips and wrench them back into position, or circle her wrist with one hand and grab the elbow with the other, those amazing shivers went through her whole body.

Better yet, even though the combinations that Arielle was attempting to do well only involved three or four moves at a time—jab, side kick, knee, or elbow, roundhouse, front kick—the movements were so far from natural for her that it was all she could do to keep up the pattern consistently. Repeating the names of the moves over and over took so much mental energy that everything else was blocked out—that is, until Lauren touched her.

So, even though every second of physical activity was excruciating, the rhythm of the absence of all the anxious thoughts that had consumed her for the past four weeks, then the all-consuming sensation of Lauren's hands on her body, was almost intoxicating. It was like she'd stepped into a dream world where the only things that mattered were physically discharging her frustrations, and being aware of just one other person.

Finally, Lauren called, "Aaaand, you're done! Strong work, ladies! I'll see you in two days!"

Arielle looked down at her shirt, which she'd had to repeatedly tug down throughout the session as it crept up her hips. She made a face at the wet half-oval of sweat that had formed at the collar and arched down to her boobs. She wondered if there were stripes of sweat on her back or—oh, God—on her inner thighs. These were cotton yoga pants, looser and floppier than the tight capris the other girls wore. And her toenail polish...chipped to oblivion. She was such a mess.

And yet, as the other girls called their thanks and goodbyes to Lauren, Lauren was quietly watching Arielle.

Suddenly, Arielle felt shaky, but not because of the workout.

She fumbled for her messenger bag, reflexively checking for her phone, her keys, her ID holder. Trying to give herself something to focus on while she waited to see what would happen. She wanted to talk to Lauren. Wanted to spend more time with her outside of class. Kickboxing class would be one way to do it—she should be grateful to Matt for the connection.

But instead, she was acutely aware of how gross and smelly she was. How, if she was going to dream up a way to get closer to Lauren, this would have been at the bottom of her list of ideas.

Arielle brought herself back to full height, and realized that the room was empty except for her and Lauren. Who

The Broken Hearts Society of Suite 17C

was standing two steps away from her. Because she'd walked over, by herself. Because she'd wanted to.

Arielle's head spun even as she commanded herself to keep it on straight. *Don't say anything stupid. Maybe don't say anything at all.*

Her mouth betrayed her, though. "Well that was—"

But at the same time, Lauren blurted, "I'm really glad you—"

"I'm sorry," both girls said again, in unison. They laughed, even though Lauren's gaze seemed dead serious.

Arielle finally had a brilliant thought—drink water. Probably it was scientifically impossible to blurt out stupid shit in front of your crush when your mouth was full of water. Hopefully.

"You're gonna want to make sure you drink a lot of water today. It'll take your body awhile to make up for all the hard work you did."

Arielle sighed. "Yeah. Eight cups a day, right?"

"Even more for you, since you're not used to this kind of thing."

"Hey, how do you know? Didn't I look like a killer out there?" Arielle gave her a teasing smile.

Lauren threw her head back and laughed, then reached up to pull out her ponytail, refastening it in a slightly more put-together looking bun. The length of her hair—halfway down her back—and the practiced movement of her fingers as they flicked around the elastic seriously took Arielle's breath away. How could one girl be so smart, so funny, so sweet, so athletic, and so graceful? "You look good," Lauren said. "Don't get me wrong. Clearly you're in shape."

Lauren's eyes skirted down the curve of Arielle's hip and she could have sworn they lingered on her butt. She was *not* in shape, but coming from Lauren, there was no way in hell she was going to argue.

Yeah, she had it bad.

"Clearly I'm a disaster. Sorry you had to spend so much time, uh…you know. With your hands on me."

There were a million ways Arielle could have said that—'helping me,' 'positioning me,' 'fixing my horrible form'—and instead she said it in the damn sexiest way she possibly could have.

But her words seemed to bring out the sparkle in Lauren's eye again. The one she had when she was amused, patient. Waiting for more. Could she…?

"I didn't mind." Lauren's slight smile stayed steady, her eyes focused on Arielle's. Arielle waited for the followup—"It happens to lots of people," or "Most people start out needing help," or even "This stuff can be tough." But there was nothing. Just Lauren's waiting. Watching.

"Well, you won't have to worry about it again," Arielle chuckled, pointing her eyes to the floor. "Clearly this was not my kind of class." She started off toward the door, and Lauren quickened her steps to catch up.

"Wait. What do you mean?"

The Broken Hearts Society of Suite 17C

Arielle's stomach flipped and she slowed to let Lauren fall in beside her.

"You have to come back. The second time is easier for everyone."

Arielle raised an eyebrow. "If you can tell me that again and promise you're being completely honest, I will."

Lauren's eye contact dropped. She looked to the side and let out a breath with a telltale fall of her shoulders.

Arielle grinned triumphantly. "I knew it! I knew I was a disaster!"

"Well, I had to keep moving you around the whole time just so you wouldn't hurt yourself," Lauren admitted. "If you don't stand the right way, pivot your hips enough, you can seriously get injured."

That just brought Arielle's mind back to the memory of Lauren's hands firm on her hips, and she swallowed. *Keep talking.*

"Exactly. I'm a disaster, and I'm not going to do that to you again." She started back toward the door. So close now. So few seconds for the direction of this whole thing, whatever it was, to remain static or change everything.

"Please," Lauren's voice was soft, patient again, but the way she grabbed Arielle's wrist was anything but. Arielle hoped the wide eyes she looked back with told her just how hopeful she was—against all reason. Lauren stepped closer, and Arielle didn't back away. "Your punches were okay. If you remember to keep strong arms, they'll be pretty decent, actually." Her voice was getting softer as she inched closer. She didn't drop Arielle's hand, even though the grip of her fingers had loosened. Arielle fought against letting her eyes drift shut as she felt the light graze of Lauren's nails against her palm.

"So," Arielle said in an equally soft voice, "You wouldn't mind holding my legs the entire time? Just so I can get pissed off at a punching bag?"

"That, and other reasons," Lauren answered, searching Arielle's eyes for something. She was only a step away, and yet her shoulder turned, then her foot followed. Half a step away now, and from what Arielle could tell, holding her breath back just like she was. Testing. Waiting.

Arielle was too cynical, too doubtful, to imagine it—Lauren slowly, slowly leaned forward, her eyelids moving down the smallest touch. It couldn't be anything else but the look of someone who was going to kiss her.

And so Arielle let her breath out, and let her heart hope, and leaned in, centimeter by centimeter to match Lauren. She was so close she could feel her breath against her cheek. Arielle took in a stuttered breath and…

The door to the room opened with a whoosh. Arielle jumped back, her heart thundering against her chest. Lauren clapped her hands down to her sides. "Hey, Lauren." A middle-aged guy in a polo and khakis stuck his head in. "If it's okay, I'm gonna put Zumba in here. They're starting in fifteen. Don't worry about cleanup, I'll send Chris in here to handle it."

The Broken Hearts Society of Suite 17C

Arielle was already out the door, down the hall, and in the elevator when she heard the guy leave.

Running away again, Ari. Awesome.

Arielle took every turn through the rec center that she could, just in case Lauren was following behind—hoping she was following behind, but not wanting to talk to her again. Not just yet. Rooms full of happy exercising students, apparently experiencing no misery and certainly not any ridiculous relationship drama, or non-relationship drama, flashed before her eyes. She passed the elevator and shouldered her way through a heavy metal door, sighing with relief when she exited into the stairwell. Something about the solid gray concrete, smelling blank and looking empty, under the steady, cool fluorescent lights, helped her take a deep breath. She had to focus on one thing at a time. Had to make sure she was okay before she involved anyone else.

She wanted to slump against the cool concrete wall, maybe stay in this stairwell until the rec center closed, just to guarantee that she wouldn't see Lauren on her way out. But she'd taken enough twists and turns through the center, and there were at least two doors exiting from these stairs to different halves of campus, North and South. Arielle lived on South, but more students lived North. She'd have to take the gamble that Lauren did, too.

Arielle shook her head. She hated that she was even thinking this much about which door she should exit. She knew one thing—whatever Rachel had done to her, she couldn't live her life afraid of who or what might be on the other side of every door she opened.

Drawing a long breath into her lungs, feeling her muscles, already sore from the class, Arielle pushed out the rec center door and was greeted by a cold gust of wind. She pulled her hands into her sleeves, put her head down, and started walking.

The light was waning fast. Instead of the intense wind she'd expected from that first step out of the building, the air was mostly still, with an edge of chill—and then she felt the first stinging drop against her cheek. Dammit.

Arielle knew that Indiana weather could change on a dime—after all, she'd grown up here—but freezing rain? In the middle of October?

She put her head down and quickened her pace, counting steps. Every ten was closer to Harrison. Almost halfway there now, and...

"Arielle? Arielle!"

One of the only times she had heard Lauren's voice raised was in the kickboxing class she'd just taught. Still, like everything else about her, apparently, Arielle had internalized it, memorized it. So she knew instantly that the girl calling after her was the one girl she really wanted to see, and didn't want to see, at the same time.

She stopped in her tracks, but a prickliness in her chest kept her from turning back. The mix of emotions she had for Lauren was too much to handle.

The Broken Hearts Society of Suite 17C

And yet she was here. And Arielle wouldn't run away from her. And she was calling Arielle's name. Right now. In the stinging, freezing, rain.

It wasn't until Arielle turned to face Lauren that she realized that there were warm tracks of wetness running down her cheeks through the chill. Dammit.

She took a shuddering breath inward.

"Hey," Lauren said, for one of the first times ever with her face twisted in worry, instead of calm and smiling. "You didn't have to…I mean, I wanted to…talk to you."

Arielle gave a short laugh, trying to keep the edge off her words. "I…listen. I need to be honest with you. I can't do this."

"What do you mean?" Lauren wrapped her long arms, covered only in a thin hoodie, around her torso and shivered.

"I don't know what I mean. That's the problem."

Lauren just tilted her head, kept looking at Arielle. Waiting for more, in that horrible, perfect patient way she always did.

"I just…I like hanging out with you. Maybe too much. I don't know. Some things have happened with…someone from home. Recently. And I don't want it to…affect us. I mean, this. I mean…me." Arielle's head fell as she realized she'd just totally betrayed her feelings.

"This thing that happened…was it with a friend?" Lauren breathed this more than asked it, and her chest rose slightly more noticeably.

Arielle's own indecision enraged her. "Not really a friend," she said. "More than a friend."

"It must have been a big deal if it's still making you cry."

Arielle's hand flew up to her cheek. Dammit, the girl had noticed. This ever-perceptive, always patient, mysteriously caring and attentive girl had noticed she was crying, and cared enough to stand in the freezing rain to talk about it.

"Yeah. It is—it *was*—a big deal."

"Okay, well drama from home or not, and whether you want to be friends with me or not, you are wet and freezing and my dorm is close. You're coming back with me."

"It's close? Really?" Arielle said, fighting back more fat tears from rolling down and stalling with a stupid question at the same time. Harrison was two minutes' walk away. She'd have her stuff, and her roommates. She'd have the sanctuary of the Society to unload everything.

But more than all that, she knew deep down, she wanted more time with Lauren.

"I'm in Crawford," Lauren said, touching Arielle's elbow with her fingertips, gentle and at the same time insistent.

Arielle nodded and swallowed hard. "Okay. Thanks."

She didn't tell her that she lived in Harrison, which was two buildings from Crawford. Instead, she quickened her pace to keep up with Lauren's long legs, and followed her home.

Inside, Arielle realized that she was really more damp than wet, hardly in need of a towel. She waited for Lauren to notice the same thing, but instead Lauren looked her up and down and said, "Come on. You're soaked and freezing. Let's get you dried off and warm."

Arielle wasn't soaked or freezing, but she nodded anyway. There was every reason not to let herself be alone with Lauren but she wanted it now, more badly than she'd thought possible. Even though she knew damn well that things could get too out of control, too fast, especially since they hadn't even had the "Are you gay?" talk.

But Lauren had followed her out of the rec center. Called after her. Touched her wrist in that way that sent warm waves up and down her arm. Brought her home, offered to clean her up. Lauren *had* to like her, didn't she? Had to be interested in something more than just lunch buddies, even more than friends.

Still, she couldn't forget what had happened the last time she'd made assumptions about a girl's feelings for her. That had backfired in the biggest way possible the day after she'd arrived at Northern.

Lauren was like a magnet, tugging Arielle along behind her and all but erasing her hesitation. Lauren waved hello to the person working the desk, then grabbed Arielle's hand and pulled her into step beside her. "Technically I'm supposed to sign you in, since it's past seven," Lauren said under her breath. "Stupid Northern rules. I mean, I would if I had to, but it's just a pain in the ass."

"Breaking the rules, Lauren…oh shit. I just realized I don't even know your last name."

Lauren laughed as she punched the 'up' button on the elevator, dropping Arielle's hand in the process. Again, her heart did that sinking thing, like the break in contact was pounding her heart down. "You're going to be disappointed."

Arielle laughed back. "I don't see how I could be disappointed by a last name."

"Nelson."

Arielle gave her a confused look.

"It's just so normal," Lauren explained.

"So?"

"Well, yours is so exotic. Arielle Duval. It sounds like royalty, or a movie star."

"Or a mermaid?" Arielle asked, smiling a little.

"Oh! I mean…okay. Maybe that's where I got both of those."

"Because those are the two things Arielle is," Arielle sighed with a resigned smile, slumping against the wall of the elevator as Lauren punched the button. Floor seven. "I got it a lot growing up. A mermaid princess. It was especially hilarious when I completely sucked at swim team."

Lauren rewarded the small story from Arielle's childhood with a hearty laugh, meeting her eyes when she did. Whether Arielle liked it or not, whether Lauren intended it or not, the connection between them was intense. Almost overwhelmingly so. The doors closed, and they were alone.

Normal girl procedure was to take the opposite wall of the elevator, but Lauren leaned against the wall and against Arielle. Arielle's eyes roamed around the perimeter of the elevator—it had room for at least ten more people. Yet Lauren was right here next to her. Touching her.

And she'd just admitted that she'd been thinking extensively about Arielle's name.

Crawford was an older building, its walls made of cinder block painted over with thick off-white, its doors a pale green-coated metal. And the doors were so close together. Lauren pulled her keychain from her bag and shoved a key in the lock of room 712.

"Keys? Seriously?"

"Yeah," Lauren said, grunting as she shoved the door open with her shoulder. "It's a little stuck. And, obviously, it's old, but check this out."

Lauren's room was the neatest, tidiest, most put-together, perfectly matchy-matchy college room, or any room for that matter, that Arielle had ever seen. It looked exactly like the college dorm rooms on the advertisements in department stores. It was completely put together, not a single thing out of place. And the fleeting thought ran through Arielle's head that, because of that, it looked a little empty. She took a couple steps over the flawless, seafoam area rug, the one that went perfectly with the bedspread, the green swirled together with a white and purple paisley.

Then, suddenly, Arielle understood what Lauren was telling her to check out. She gasped. "You got a single. How in the…"

Well, Lauren said, letting the heavy door close behind her and practically causing Arielle's heart to stop completely, "Obviously, like I said, it's old. Like, the floor tiles are cracking, the ceiling has water stains, we have radiator heat, and the bathrooms are…interesting."

"Wait, wait. You have your own bathroom?"

Lauren beamed. "Yep. I told you I accepted early decision, and into the combined undergrad/M.D. program?"

Arielle nodded, remembering how awed at Lauren's intelligence she'd been.

"Well, part of the deal was that if I was in those two programs, and if I chose a learning-focused living community, I'd get a single. The argument is that I need to be able to keep my own hours for studying, without risking roommate conflicts. I guess since the University is making a big investment in me." She shrugged like everything she'd just said was totally no big deal. Not

The Broken Hearts Society of Suite 17C

impressive at all. Really, she was a genius, a valuable brain to the university, a gem among the student population.

"Well, I came here off the waitlist," Arielle chuckled, "So I guess I'm lucky I only have to share with two roommates."

"Do you at least have your own bedroom?"

Arielle nodded. "There's like a common room and bathroom, and yeah, we have our own teeny tiny bedrooms. You can barely fit two people in there, but…I mean, not that I've tried to fit two people in there. But if you imagine it. Not that I've been imagining it, but…" Oh, God. Now she felt like she was going to throw up. What was it about this girl that turned her into a bumbling, idiotic fool?

Arielle looked around the room, praying that Lauren would fill the dead air. After a couple weird seconds, she did. "Um, okay. So my dresser's right there," she said, waving a hand toward a wooden chest of drawers. "You're totally welcome to whatever. I'm just gonna…" she leaned her head toward the bathroom.

"Yeah, yeah. Of course." Arielle had to let the poor girl pee.

But one second after Lauren shut the bathroom door behind her, Arielle heard the unmistakable hiss of a shower turning on, full force. Wonderful. The girl she was infatuated with was getting naked, right on the other side of a metal door. And they were totally alone. No roommates as buffers, as insurance against what Arielle suddenly felt was a train barreling toward her on the tracks.

She was almost totally sure that Lauren had been about to kiss her in that workout room. Eighty percent. Maybe fifty. That combined with everything else from tonight added up to a pretty good chance that there was something between them. Now she had about five minutes to figure out what that was.

But first she should probably stop being a total doofus, and change her clothes. The thing she'd come up here for.

She pulled open the top drawer slowly, for some reason trying not to make so much noise, and was met with the sight of pair upon pair of lacy panties with bras to match. She caught her breath. Dammit, being alone in the room with Lauren was one thing, feeling the touch of Lauren's soft hand against hers, listening to her strip on the other side of the door…but actually seeing the panties that covered the pretty damn perfect ass Arielle had appreciated so many times? Heat shot through Arielle and she had to take several deep breaths to get her hormones and the thoughts they dredged up back under control.

She blew out a long breath as she pulled open the next drawer, and was greeted by the unmistakable smell of Lauren's perfume wafting up from the clothes inside. Lauren smelled good even when she was working out…

Arielle's eyes fluttered closed, remembering the feel of Lauren's hands on her hips. How in the world was she going to deal with eleven more weeks of class with this

The Broken Hearts Society of Suite 17C

girl? She snapped them open again, and examined the shirts she had to pick from. Lauren's taste was simple—solid cotton shirts, soft to the touch and, Arielle knew, clinging in all the right places. She may not have ever noticed the exact details, but she damn sure had the image of that curve under Lauren's breast, or the strong, graceful line of her collarbone, burned into her brain.

Arielle breathed in through her nose, slowly. She fumbled through the drawer until she found a deep purple tee, a great color for her, with three-quarter length sleeves. She let her hoodie fall down her arms and tugged her tank off, leaning down to stuff it in her bag, then sniffed her armpit to make sure she didn't stink too badly. The sweat was definitely there, she decided, wrinkling her nose, but the deodorant would mask it well enough with a shirt on.

And there would definitely be a shirt on.

She tugged on the t-shirt, then stepped out of her flip flops and yoga pants. She didn't even register that the shower had turned off until Lauren swung the bathroom door open a few seconds later. Then Lauren was suddenly, adorably there, in a blue terrycloth bathrobe and a huge white towel turbaned on top of her head.

And staring at Arielle in one of her own t-shirts and black cotton bikini panties.

Arielle scrambled to pick up her yoga pants from their damp pile on the floor and hold them in front of her.

"I was just…I couldn't…I didn't know you were going to take a shower," she finished lamely. As if that explained anything.

Lauren didn't laugh or rush to fill the awkward space this time. She just watched Arielle carefully, letting her eyes trail down to the clothes half-hanging out of Arielle's bag, her bare toes, and finally, up her legs, torso, and back to her face. She didn't move, but just said, "There are some sweats in the bottom drawer, if you want to warm up."

The look on Lauren's face was dead serious, like a challenge instead of a joke.

Arielle couldn't move. Something had taken hold of her, frozen her every nerve, from her feet to the hairs on her head. The air between them crackled with something, and right now Arielle was convinced that there was a very fine line between awkwardness and tentativeness.

But then, Lauren stepped toward her. Steadily, purposefully, stopped just a foot in front of her, then bent down. Arielle's mind went to another place entirely, thinking about the position of Lauren's head combined with the memory of how it felt to have the gorgeous girl's hands running down her calves just half an hour ago. Of course, instead of touching Arielle, Lauren pulled open the drawer and dug out a pair of worn-in black sweatpants, the old-fashioned kind with elastic at the ankles. Lauren stood up to full height and held them out to Arielle. There was no way Arielle could take them from her without their fingers touching, and when they did, more fizzy warmth spilled through Arielle's body.

"These are my favorites," Lauren said in an even quieter voice than was typical for her. "I got them before my last growth spurt, so they should be perfect for you."

Arielle should have made a joke about her height. Instead, her heart just sped up at the realization that Lauren had noticed it at all. Just another thing to add to the list that made Arielle think that maybe, just maybe, Lauren had been checking her out just as much as she'd been memorizing every curve and angle of Lauren's body.

Arielle laughed lightly, breathlessly, but couldn't smile. She had to step back to put on the pants, and she hated moving away from Lauren, but standing there staring at her while pantsless wasn't really an option. The cotton was soft, worn, speaking of a million quiet, relaxed moments in Lauren's life that Arielle was now connected to. Arielle pulled herself back to full height and spoke again.

"I'll give them back," she managed.

"I know," Lauren said, still looking at her steadily, with the slightest tilt of her head, and the touch of a smile. Like looking at Arielle was the only thing she really wanted to be doing at that moment.

And damn her, Arielle felt exactly the same way.

Then Lauren reached up to the towel wrapped around her head, and Arielle's eyes skimmed down from Lauren's eyes, to her lips, then back again. Her skin was flawless, begging to be touched by Arielle's trembling fingers. But she was still frozen, waiting for something she doubted would happen, yet was desperately hoping for. Lauren's hair tumbled in heavy wet strands over her shoulders, smelling like pear and adding one more layer to her scent.

"Your hair is still wet," Lauren said, in an even quieter voice this time. She took another half step toward Arielle, then lifted the towel and reached down, pulling it around her back and wrapping it around her hair. She knew Lauren was wrong. It wasn't wet, not even close to dripping. Maybe the top layer looked damp. But the feeling of Lauren's thumbs grazing against her neck, her pinkies brushing her temples, was too consuming for Arielle to spend an ounce of energy on anything else, even protesting Lauren's unnecessary closeness. Not that she would want to.

After a few seconds, Arielle felt the towel graze heavy against her shoulder blades, then heard it slump to the floor. She didn't break eye contact with Lauren—couldn't pull herself away from the dancing light of her eyes. Lauren amazingly, terrifyingly, didn't pull her hands away from Arielle's face. She just let them skim down, fingertips light against her jaw, then her neck. Then, for a split second, her collarbone.

Arielle's breath was broken, quiet gasps. Something shattered out in the hallway, followed by a voice yelling, "Shit" and that was the one thing that tore her eyes away from Lauren. And when she did, over Lauren's shoulder,

The Broken Hearts Society of Suite 17C

she saw a corkboard studded with photographs. One near the middle was of Lauren standing with some guy. The fact that he was kissing her on the cheek wouldn't have been the biggest problem, if his hand hadn't been obviously wrapped around her waist, skimming under her cropped shirt, fingertips pushed beneath the waistband.

Air rushed into Arielle's lungs faster than she thought possible, and the spell was broken. Every muscle tensed, every nerve was on edge, as she went into autopilot mode—focus on your backpack, get to the door, get the hell out of there. It briefly occurred to her that she was running away from this girl for the second time in one night, and that the drama factor of this relationship was seriously high, but she didn't even care.

What kind of a horrible person clearly tried to kiss you when she knew you were gay and she was, or had been, in a relationship with a guy? Judging by that picture, Lauren was straight as a fucking ruler.

Arielle tried to talk herself down, but it was no use. Her emotions made her feet move, even though logical thoughts fought against them: *She could be bi. There's nothing wrong with a bi girl. Except I said that I'd only date an out-and-proud lesbian. And I stand by that. I think.*

Mercifully, the elevator opened within seconds, and Arielle slammed her palm against the "door close" button, resting her head on her forearm against the wall and letting a miserable, tinny buzz fill her ears, slowly but surely blocking out everything else.

October meant that it got darker outside every minute, and she'd been up in Lauren's room for at least fifteen. The sky was a velvety navy, not a single cloud, the stars beginning to poke dim pinholes in the expanse above. Arielle glanced up for reference—Crawford was only two buildings from her own, the new freshman dorms built to hide the once-shining facade of the twenty-year-old ones. The result of zoning codes was a secluded courtyard between them, which was empty of students now because of the rain, lit only by a yellowish street lamp.

Arielle briefly thought of what Matt had said about campus at night, and vowed never to come this way again. Based on how epically she'd failed at that kickboxing class, it wasn't a safe bet that she could take anyone down, no matter how threatened her life was.

Hell, she couldn't even keep herself away from a girl who was so obviously straight, it should have slapped her in the face. Instead, she'd pushed it away, seeing only the signals that might mean that Lauren liked her, no matter how obvious it should have been.

The rain was coming a little harder now, the drops growing bigger as the sky darkened. Arielle squinted at the back of Harrison tower, hoping she wouldn't have to leave the courtyard, go all the way around the new wing, and enter through the official entrance, made of shining

The Broken Hearts Society of Suite 17C

plate-glass. Every time she walked into Harrison she felt like she was on display from all angles—the courtyard in front, the person working the desk, anyone who was watching the huge TV or cooking in the little kitchen.

And in her five weeks on campus, she'd never looked or felt worse than she did at this moment. The thought startled her—she'd always thought she'd never feel worse than when Rachel smashed her heart into teeny tiny pieces in front of half the student body.

Was it possible for a girl she'd never really kissed, and certainly never loved, to make her hurt this much?

She was so close to the building now, and lifted her eyes to see a heavy metal door, like those in the back of shops for unloading merchandise, with a long bar to push in and open it. Arielle hustled to reach it in a few more steps, pushed her forearm flush against the bar, and pushed her whole body into it.

And was met with only hard resistance. The goddamn door was locked.

It was only then that she realized that she was crying. Again. Jesus, what was wrong with her? Lauren was just a girl. Just one, stupid straight girl who was really friendly and really sweet and really, really goddamn beautiful. She was no different than any of the other girls at her high school who didn't mind being touchy with each other, said "I love you," all the time, and yeah, once in awhile wanted to experiment with kissing another girl.

But Arielle had never put up with that, and here, in the chilly rain with big fat tears running down her cheeks, stuck in a courtyard and unable to move her aching quads a step further, she knew one thing more than ever—she was going to stick with her Society pact if it killed her. No more making out with, or falling head over heels for, girls who didn't even really know if they were gay or straight.

She held back a whimper when she thought about dodging Lauren after class every day for the rest of the semester. It would be really damn tough. Arielle angrily swiped at one more tear, looked up, and realized that, no, it would be impossible. Because Lauren was jogging toward her, keys dangling from one arm, another pushed up under her boobs. Long black hair laying in limp ropes down the front of Arielle's hoodie, the one she'd left in a stinky clump on Lauren's floor.

"Arielle! Oh my God. You have got to stop running away from me like that."

"Well, actually, that was kind of the plan." Arielle laughed ruefully when Lauren got within earshot. She didn't give a shit now. She had to find some way, any way, to make this less painful.

"I'm sorry about what happened back there," Lauren said breathlessly, swiping some wetness off her forehead, maddeningly adding nothing else to the thought.

Arielle stood and took her in, feeling the heaving of her own chest. She tried to come up with something that would cut ties and explain to Lauren that they couldn't

The Broken Hearts Society of Suite 17C

hang out. But all that was shot to hell when Arielle saw the tears welling at the bottom of Lauren's eyes. She stepped forward, wanting so badly to stretch her arms out, stand on her tiptoes, and squeeze Lauren tight to her.

"No, listen. It's my fault. Here's the thing," Arielle said, blinking against the rain, which was somehow less important than getting these words out, right here, right now. "You know I had a bad breakup when I got here. With my ex-girlfriend."

Lauren swallowed and nodded, listening.

"Well, it was because she didn't want her sorority sisters to know about me. Didn't want them to know that she was gay," Arielle continued, watching Lauren's expression turn down even more. Somehow, Lauren felt Arielle's pain as it spilled out of her mouth. A part of her melted as she went on. "Anyway, my roommates and I…I promised them…promised myself…that I would never date anyone…never *fall* for anyone," she said, turning her eyes to her shoes when she said the last bit, "who wasn't one hundred percent sure. Anyone who wasn't proud that they were gay, anyone that wasn't out. You know? Because then…I couldn't get hurt that way again. I guess."

Lauren took in a sharp breath, like something had whacked her in the chest. Then she nodded, slowly. "Also because you deserve better than that. That was shit," she finished with a whisper.

"Yeah, it was." Arielle's tears were starting to come back, too. Somehow, it hurt even worse that Lauren knew exactly why she'd run away. Because what she was really saying was, "Yes, Ari, you matter. You deserve so much." Which sucked, because all Arielle wanted was Lauren.

"Anyway, I saw that picture of you with that guy."

Lauren's brows pulled up, her head tilted toward her shoulder. "What…?"

"On your bulletin board," Arielle's voice lowered. "He has his arm around you, he's kissing you?"

"Oh, him? Oh my God. Arielle. He's…he *was* my boyfriend."

Arielle's heart sank. She knew it.

"We went through a lot together—a whole lot. We're still really good friends. And for some stupid reason that's the only picture I have of him that's actually printed off. But I swear, we are not together. Haven't been for a long time."

A million thoughts warred in Arielle's head. What Lauren had just said didn't change anything. She still wasn't saying, 'Yes, I'm gay, here's my lesbian membership card.' She had dated a guy. Maybe even loved him. Maybe slept with him. How could she be gay? How could this ever end well? Arielle opened her mouth, hoping that something would come to her to say, but nothing did.

But then, Lauren started to talk again. "Look. I'm only eighteen. I've been with a couple guys, and yeah, we kissed. Yeah, I even told one of them I loved him."

The Broken Hearts Society of Suite 17C

Arielle pressed her lips together, shook her head, looked away. There was no way she could handle this conversation for a second longer. "Yeah, I get it, okay? It's fine. You're straight. I'm not. The end." Arielle knew she should add, "We can still be friends," or "We can still study together," but that wasn't true. Best case scenario, she'd be able to avoid obsessing over Lauren for the rest of the classes of the semester. Maybe get a new hobby, inside, in the dark. Where her ridiculous hormones couldn't' be unleashed on anyone else.

"But listen. Arielle."

Goddammit, there was something about hearing Lauren say her name with so much force behind it that made her want to melt into a puddle there in the dimming courtyard. Arielle locked eyes with her, summoning every ounce of bravery so that, this time, she wouldn't run away. She would listen first, then leave.

Lauren swallowed, her face twisted into a desperate look. "I don't know why I would run after you without shoes or a bra on, but it has to be because I like you. I may not be able to scream from the rooftops that I'm a lesbian, but I do know I really, really want to kiss you. More than I've ever wanted to kiss anyone. *Ever.*"

Lauren's words were like a match to Arielle's soaked-in-kerosene heart. Her chest burned, and she pulled her head up, suddenly brave, maybe even careless. As she stepped up to Lauren and pushed her fingers through the hair at the back of her head, tangled and wet and smelling absolutely delicious, she only knew one thing. She felt exactly the same way. But she forced herself to ask one more thing. "So is this the first time? You've ever wanted to kiss a girl?"

"It's the first time. But I seriously doubt it'll be the last." Lauren's breath caught as she leaned down, and Arielle's did the same as she pulled herself closer to Lauren, begging herself not to lose this fire. Because this would be the most awkward run-away of all. Then it became impossible, because Lauren's hands cradled her head once again, her fingers playing at Arielle's stringy curls like they were something treasured. It was all so surreal, being this close to Lauren, fulfilling the fantasy she'd had for weeks, nearly having the chance to taste her. Between her twisting belly, her pounding heart, and her absolute desperation to press her lips to Lauren's, there was absolutely no way she could walk away now.

So she didn't. She closed the gap, brushing her lips against Lauren's, nearly wild with the flawless soft skin, igniting a hundred points of electricity in her own, coated by a cool dampness that only made her want to push in for more, harder, faster, deeper. Anything to stop the absolute insanity of the feeling rushing through her. She'd known she was attracted, she'd known she'd had a crush—she didn't know that nothing she'd ever felt before would compare to kissing Lauren.

Nothing. Not even kissing Rachel.

The Broken Hearts Society of Suite 17C

The realization slammed into her chest like a ton of bricks, stunning her with surprise, then filling her with gratitude. Whatever this girl was—gay, straight, bi, the devil in disguise—she was filling an empty place inside Arielle that had been empty for a long time. Even with Rachel.

And then—oh, God—Lauren's fingers ran back through her hair, and then her lips were hard on Arielle's, buzzing with the slightest of whimpers from deep in Lauren's throat, setting every nerve in Arielle's body on edge. So she moved one hand to Lauren's jaw and another down to her waist, groaning when she gripped the toned curve that molded so perfectly to her palm. Lauren pressed her stomach against Arielle's, solid warmth against soft curves, the touch Arielle had been craving since that first lunch they'd had together. Everything else, even the freezing rain, went away. Arielle parted her lips and traced her tongue, for the barest of seconds, over Lauren's bottom lip, which brought another, slightly strangled noise from Lauren as she flicked her tongue out to taste Arielle's.

Arielle's thoughts were lost in the complete wonder of holding Lauren, kissing her like she meant it, finally being able to do what she'd wanted to for so many weeks. Lost thoughts meant lost fear, only the complete and total wonder of being wrapped up in Lauren's smell, her taste, her touch.

Finally, after Arielle thought her heart would beat out of her chest, she set her heels back on the ground, breaking contact, slowly dropping her hands. She watched Lauren, examined the way her eyes slowly fluttered back open, memorized the sound of her slightly ragged breathing. Her eyes met Arielle's and a smile tugged at her lips. Lauren blinked, and let out a breathy, "Wow."

Arielle gave a little laugh, suddenly overtaken by the intensity of the moment, and dragged her toe against the ground. "Yeah," she chuckled.

Lauren's hands had fallen to her sides, too, but now one of them reached out, brushed the inside of Arielle's pinky so gently it could have been a dream. Arielle's fingers twitched to grab on, hold onto this moment. But she knew what had to happen next so completely, so deeply, that she wouldn't do anything to stand in the way of it. She froze. Waited. Maybe even prayed.

"Will you…I mean, can we…I mean, I really…" Lauren stuttered and blew out a breath. "Dammit."

"It's okay," Arielle said, pulling the tips of Lauren's fingers ever so slightly with hers. "That was…"

"I want to know you better. I want to spend time with you. I can't really explain it, but I just want to be with you more. I don't want to break your rules or whatever, but I…I don't want to let whatever that was go."

Arielle's heart screamed a million things it could have been: Lust, love, hunger, need, desperation, pure hormones. But only one word kept running over and over through her brain. It was *right*.

So she laced her fingers with Lauren's, pushed up on her toes, and brushed a kiss, light as a whisper, at the corner of her mouth. "I don't either," she said, forcing herself to let go of Lauren's hand. She'd started to shiver, and knew they couldn't stand out in the rain forever. She also knew that if she actually went home with Lauren, or took Lauren home with her, things might go too far, too fast for either of them. "I should get back inside," she said.

"I guess I should too," Lauren said, her face uncertain, flicking around the dark courtyard.

"The door's just around the corner. I'm in Harrison."

The sounds of chatter from a group of girls drifted into the courtyard. "There's the gaggle from floor 5," Lauren laughed. "I'll follow them back," she said, starting to step away. "Since it's getting dark. See you next week, I guess?"

Shit, their next class wasn't till next week? "I…" *Don't make yourself look crazy, Arielle.* "Yeah. That's perfect," she smiled. Then Lauren was gone, hustling off toward the street-lamp-lit sidewalk. Arielle wrapped her arms tight around herself, put her head down, and walked around to the front of her building, feeling her grin grow wider with each step.

Even though Arielle knew that this might be breaking the promise she'd made to the Society and to herself, she tried to hold the doubt at a distance. No, Lauren wasn't an out-and-proud lesbian, but she also wasn't straight. And they weren't a couple, exactly, they were just two girls who'd kissed once. And who'd implicitly planned to do it again.

Arielle finally made it to Harrison, wrenched open the heavy glass door, and ducked into the elevator to take her to floor 17. She let her forehead fall against its wall with the heavy jerk of the floor upward. She was definitely in trouble, because she'd definitely broken that promise.

And right at this moment, she definitely didn't care.

Chapter 13

Rion

It was too goddamn fucking early to be awake. Rion cursed herself and her pounding head for agreeing to be at the Student Health Center at 10:30 in the morning just to be there when Crash pissed in a cup.

Now that the possibility that Crash really was clean was in her head, she couldn't think of anything else. Because if he was clean, she'd have to date him—she'd promised. And if she went out with him, she seriously doubted she could keep from kissing him. And if she did that…well, she was in a shit ton of trouble.

Not to mention that Amy and Arielle were supposed to be here with her. And even though her voice had been grumpy when she told them they'd better not flake, the twisting in her stomach confirmed that she'd been dead serious.

The irony of a girl who'd survived a group home, a drug bust, a night in prison, and a hearing before a judge needing her roommates to be with her when she met Crash again wasn't lost on her. She was tough, but only when it came to closing herself off from other people. Anything remotely related to opening up to them? That was the real problem.

Well, that and Crash had seemed pretty damn confident that he'd pass the drug test, and then she'd have to hold up her end of the bargain.

She checked her phone and cursed herself again. How the hell was she five minutes early to an appointment she'd never wanted to keep anyway? Her stomach twisted further, then exploded into butterflies when she saw him walking up the hill.

Brown corduroy pants, fitting exactly the same as his jeans—hugging his butt, sitting low enough to imagine his abs, but not low enough to see them underneath his soft cotton t-shirt. And, dear God, that leather jacket. Her hands twitched with the thought that she'd love to feel it. The tattoo peeking out from the collar of his shirt, the gently rising, sculpted cheekbone. His full lips and the glint of the ring that curved around the bottom one.

As he got closer, he looked up, giving her a lazy smile that shot through her middle. The glint of that lip ring took away her purposeful thoughts of annoyance, and made her smile back at him. She'd been standing beside a bench, and took his arrival as an excuse to sit down, expecting him to stand and talk to her. But he made himself at home, scrunching in next to her. He was tall, and solid, but not too big to fit beside her. She liked that.

She pulled back to look at him, against her better judgment. Jesus Christ, it was like a master marionette was handling her when she was around this guy, making her act like she was more attracted than she actually was. Or should be. Her eyes desperately searched for something out of place—bloodshot eyes, the smell of alcohol on his breath or pot on his jacket, the twitching fingers that were telltale signs of so many illicit activities. But there was nothing. Just Crash, serene as fuck, waiting to piss in a cup for the chance to date her.

"Hey, sweet Rion," he said, looking at her like it was only a matter of time before he'd be seeing her naked.

Ah. There was the one thing that infuriated her about him, something for her to latch onto. His cockiness. "What did you call me?" she asked, injecting a growl into her words. "Am I like a fucking cupcake or something?"

"Wow, you haven't had your coffee yet, have you?" Arielle asked in a singsongy voice.

Dammit. Rion had momentarily forgotten her roommates were meeting them here. She sighed. Introducing Crash to them felt like rolling out a welcome mat for him straight into her life.

"Crash, this is the girls. Girls, Crash."

Arielle strolled up to the bench, with Amy at her elbow, holding out a steaming cup of dark roast coffee.

She stood in front of Rion and bounced on her heels, smiling as she nodded to Rion to take it. Arielle rarely smiled, not in the six weeks that Rion had known her anyway. "What's with you?" Rion asked, taking the coffee and holding it to her lips. It was too hot to drink just yet, but the cup felt good in her chilled fingers.

"Something's with her," Amy said, her mouth twisting into a slightly put-out expression. "But she won't tell me yet."

"I don't know what it is yet!" Arielle protested as she elbowed Amy in the side and giggled. Christ on a fucking cracker, Arielle never giggled. "But it's pretty good. Was. Good. I think. I mean…oh my God, Rion. This is about you." Arielle slid her eyes to Crash and smiled again. "Hello."

Amy looked around awkwardly at the one or two students clutching coffee cups, heads down and backpacks heavy on their way to the first class of the day. "It's not about me," Rion growled. "It's about Crash."

"Right," Amy said slowly. "Hey, Crash."

"Nice to see you again," Crash sat up from his reclined position, which Rion couldn't help but notice pushed the barest outline of his dick into view against the crotch of his pants. He shook hands with Amy, then Arielle, turning his charming easy smile on them, too. "Nice to meet someone else named after a cartoon character."

"Vintage video games meets vintage Disney," Arielle said, letting out a hearty laugh. This somehow pushed a

The Broken Hearts Society of Suite 17C

flash of rage up through Rion's chest, flushing her cheeks with heat.

So what if he flashed a flirty smile at her roommates, made them laugh? Why did she even fucking care?

Crash clapped his palms together, and rubbed them back and forth twice. "Okay, I have an appointment. C'mon, Ri." He stood up, stretching his long legs even though he'd barely been down one or two minutes, and strode to the door, holding it open for Amy, and Arielle, who still had that fucking annoying silly grin on her face. Maybe Arielle was high. Maybe that bitch who'd broken up with her had finally really broken her.

Rion didn't have the time or energy to think about that now. She had a class to get to, and her favorite one, too—basic audio engineering. Getting this over with would free up more brain waves and let her focus in there.

She rolled her eyes at Crash to make sure he knew how much his insistence on dating her was inconveniencing her life. He flashed her a teeth-baring smile, like her every annoyed expression would be so worth it when she finally had to break down and go out with him.

Leave it to Rion to antagonize even the guy who wanted to go out with her.

She sighed, and took a seat in the waiting room as Crash sauntered up to the desk and checked in. "Just a drug test, ma'am," he said, loud enough for the whole waiting room to hear. Rion slid lower in her seat. At least it wasn't as embarrassing as an STD test.

"Is it for an employer?" the receptionist asked.

Crash shot Rion a wink over his shoulder, fast and sly. "Not exactly," he said with a smooth nonchalance.

"So you're paying for it."

Crash nodded and handed over a credit card.

"Okay then. Fill this out and we'll call you back when we're ready for you."

Crash took a seat at the end of the row, right next to Arielle. Crash bent over the clipboard, scribbling his information into the blanks, and a thought flashed through Rion's head. She leaned over to Amy and whispered, "Tell her to look at his name." She looked confused for a second, but then pursed her lips into a little 'o' and nodded.

She leaned toward Arielle and whispered in her ear the same way, but Arielle's head was clearly somewhere else. She shook it and said, "Look at his what?"

At that second, Crash clicked his pen shut, stood up, and returned the clipboard, grinning as he made his way back to his seat. "What do you want to know, Rion? I'm an open book. Ask me anything."

"Nothing," Rion grumbled. "Whatever. Shut up."

He nodded seriously. "Great response. Nuanced. Definitive."

Rion glared and was about to tell him to shut up again when a young nurse in blue scrubs walked out.

"Williams?" And Crash nodded again, stood up again, and Rion watched his ass move against his corduroys again. She sighed. The beauty of that butt might make his cockiness bearable.

"I'll be right back," he called over his shoulder.

The minute he left the room, Arielle bolted upright and craned her neck around to look at Rion, who had slumped down in the chair and let her neck loll around on its back. "He is *cute*," she hissed, looking at Rion like she'd lied to her about there being free ice cream or something.

The mask she'd been trying to put on around Crash since the last time she'd seen him, since he'd touched her face so tenderly and nearly knocked her off her feet, fell away. Rion closed her eyes. "I know. Goddammit, I know. It's awful. And I have to work with him." She gripped the top of her coffee cup with one palm. She didn't feel like drinking any of it, but knowing it was there was good.

"I mean, I'm gayer than Christmas, and even I think he's attractive," Arielle said, nodding. "Like, there aren't many guys on the planet I would make out with, but he's one of them. If I was drunk."

"Girls," Amy said, lowering her voice. "We're at the health center."

The look on the receptionist's face confirmed that lesbians drunk-kissing hot tattooed guys was not acceptable material for conversation in this particular waiting room.

"And," Arielle continued, "He seems kind of nice. He's funny."

"He's cocky. It's like oozing out of him."

"That's what she said," Arielle said under her breath, and Rion couldn't help but give her a chuckle at that one.

"What?" Amy asked, looking to either side. "What's the joke?"

Rion took one look at Amy's perplexed face and started full-on laughing. Soon, both she and Arielle were in the throes of belly-shaking laughter, with Amy sitting between them looking a little pissed off.

Then, the door swung open, and Crash came out just ahead of a preppy-looking lab tech in form-fitting scrubs. "Thank you," he murmured back towards her, and the tech giggled in response. Jesus fucking Christ. Was this guy releasing pheromones into the air around him that obliterated college girls' willpower?

Crash walked over to Rion with the tech at her side. She had a clipboard with a form and some scribbling on it. "Well?" Rion said, standing up to meet his eyes. He had to have smoked something in the last couple weeks. Something that would at least register on the positive end of the instant test, and require further testing.

The tech looked up at Crash. "According to HIPAA, I can't say anything unless…"

"It's fine," Crash waved his hand. "I want her to hear."

"Okay…Um, well, everything came up clean. No drugs in your system, nothing to worry about."

The Broken Hearts Society of Suite 17C

Rion waited for the sinking feeling of defeat to take over, but instead, the butterflies returned. She'd promised to go out with Crash if he was clean, and she'd known the whole time that deep down she really wanted him to be. She just didn't actually think it would happen.

"Thank you so much, Merilee," Crash said, shaking the girl's hand and leaving her with a starry look in her eyes.

"Well, that settles that," Arielle said, shouldering her messenger bag and tugging at Amy's arm. "We're going to be late for bio if we don't get moving, Ames." Arielle grabbed Amy's arm and spun away, giving Rion the most obvious wink of the century.

Rion was caught, and she knew it. "Thanks, guys. See you tonight."

"Yes! Tonight! There's a Doctor Who marathon on. I'll buy the munchies if you watch with me, Rion," Arielle chattered, never losing the loopy grin on her face. Rion gave Amy one last *"What the hell is going on with her?"* look, and shook her head when Amy shrugged.

"Nice girls," Crash said as he waved to the receptionist on the way out.

"Surprisingly, yes," Rion said. She did appreciate her roommates, the way they put up with her swearing and her dark moods, which, she was well aware, greatly outnumbered the lighter ones.

"What do you mean by that? What's surprising about your roommates at Indiana Northern, the nicest school in the Midwest, being...nice?"

"Oh, I don't know," Rion shrugged.

"You do know," Crash said, nudging his shoulder into hers, which made her stomach go fluttery again. "You try to deflect, you try to end conversations by acting like you don't know or you don't care. But you know exactly what you were talking about."

Rion cursed herself for having left her coffee cup on the table on the waiting room's side table in the midst of all the activity. She could really use it to warm her hands now, or throw it in Crash's full-of-himself, fucking beautiful face. She looked up into his eyes and, yep. Confirmed. He was an incredibly gorgeous specimen of a man.

Dammit.

She sighed. "I've never met a rich girl, or a girl from a small town high school, that I liked. I've never met someone who had a totally easy life that I actually got along with."

"Until now," Crash said, watching her.

"Yeah," Rion said, staring at the ground. "That's all I meant."

"So, what now?" Crash asked.

"What do you mean, what now? I'll go out with you, just like I promised I would."

The Broken Hearts Society of Suite 17C

Crash laughed. He turned and gave her a weird little bow as they walked. "Yes, I understand that. And I appreciate it. So what would you like to do?" He stuck his hands in his pockets and looked around casually, like she was supposed to hand him a fucking itinerary or something.

"I don't know...I figured we'd...go out? Sometime?" Rion raked her eyes down over him. She hoped it was somewhere public, or she might not be able to resist touching him for another minute.

"So let me get this straight. You made me take a drug test, and now you want me to plan a date, too?"

"I mean...I guess you don't have to plan it. I don't really...know much about dates."

"How in the world is that possible?" Crash asked, turning to walk away from the health center, down the path that led straight through the quad. Thank God. In a second, they'd be engulfed in a sea of people.

"I just...don't go on dates?"

"Nope. I won't believe that for a second. That is, pardon my language, fucking impossible."

"You don't know what you're talking about," Rion said with a slight edge to her voice. The guys at her high school had been crass degenerate assholes, and the ones at the group home had been the same, with the addition of being high, drunk, or violent half the time. Tate Sullivan had been the most worthy guy there, and even he turned out to be a force of ruin in her life. The most romantic thing the guys Rion had known did was remember the condom. "Kids don't exactly date where I come from."

"Which is...where?"

"Northwest Indiana. Close enough to Chicago that the City gangs spill across state lines, spreading through the Section 8 housing. And in group homes."

"You were in a group home? Can I hear more about that?"

Rion's heart stopped and sunk to her stomach. "Maybe. Sometime." Crash had just proven he was clean—a Good Kid. It was Rion's turn to wonder whether she was good enough for him. Maybe she'd been wondering that all along. "It was a foster home, not a juvie home," she hurried to explain. A ball of anxiety twisted itself into being. Was leaving out the fact that she'd been arrested and sentenced lying?

"Well, whatever you've been through, and whatever kinds of guys you've met, I can't believe you've never been taken on a date. A beautiful, interesting, mysterious girl like you, and nobody ever gave you the kind of attention you deserved."

Rion bristled. "How do you know I *want* that kind of attention?" One of the reasons she'd never fit in with the group home kids was that she wanted to be by herself, lost in her music. She couldn't help it that Tate had been so charming and hot, and she'd just wanted someone to hold her, and the way he'd touched her had made her feel important, valuable. It wasn't her fault that one thing had

The Broken Hearts Society of Suite 17C

led to another, and then suddenly they were a couple. She couldn't help it that she'd just needed to feel wanted by somebody.

And look where that had left her.

"Okay. So you've never been taken on a date, but you've never really wanted to be on a traditional one either. I guess a nice dinner and a movie are probably too cliché for you?"

Rion smiled. "Not the number one way I'd want to be spending my time, no."

"Well, since you're obviously waiting for me to figure out a solution to this little conundrum, I have a suggestion. You're hungry, right?"

At that second, Rion's stomach grumbled. "How did you…?"

He shrugged. "I figured you didn't roll out of bed until right before I was supposed to meet you. Right?"

"No. I rolled out of bed right before my class. This is just a stop on the way," she said.

He clapped his hands together and blew into them. " When does your class start?.."

Rion pulled out her phone, glanced at the time, and raised her eyebrows. "I still have 45 minutes to get there." Dammit. She needed to learn to think before speaking, especially in front of hot guys that threatened to confuse her thoughts as it was.

"Perfect. You're going to call me a god after this."

Rion laughed shortly. "Don't count on it, buddy."

"Buddy? Did you seriously just call me Buddy?"

"Did you seriously just tell me I was going to end up worshiping you after whatever you have planned?"

"Well," Crash said, turning his ice blue eyes on her and flicking an eyebrow up. "Maybe not after breakfast."

A shiver ran down through her body as a half-second image of what might make her worship him flashed through her mind. Rion may have been stand-offish, she might have been a loner with a mile-high wall around her heart, but she was a still a red-blooded eighteen year old girl. And it had been way too long since she'd properly gotten off.

"Jesus, I'm sorry. It's cold," Crash said. Before Rion could protest, he shrugged out of his jacket and swung it around her shoulders. The scent of him, the sharp guy smell, practically made her swoon. She almost protested that she wasn't cold, but she couldn't exactly tell him, "I shivered because I imagined what it would be like to scream your name with you inside me."

So she just said, "Thanks," and let him pick up her hand and blow on her fingers, trying not to let how amazing his breath felt on her skin show. And then she looked into his eyes, only giving half a damn about whether it looked like she was coming on to him, and said, "Lead the way."

The Broken Hearts Society of Suite 17C

"Holy shit," Rion said as she leaned against the rigid back of the cheap plastic booth in the Hole in the Wall diner that Crash had taken her to. Yes, it was actually called that. Yes, she was actually charmed by that, as much as she hated to admit it.

"Banana chocolate chip waffles," he responded, leaning back to mirror her. "Fucking blow my mind every time."

"You're not kidding. I have to say, I might go out with you again if it involves this place." She would never have said it so easily if the past hour hadn't been filled with the best conversation she'd had in—well, years. All it had taken was Crash knowing, and loving, the vast majority of her favorite bands to get her to start talking. Before she knew it she was tearing up when she told him about the stark, simple beauty of Jim Morrison's lyrics, and Crash responded by quoting The Ghost Song: *"We have assembled inside this ancient and insane theater to propagate our lust for our life and flee the swarming wisdom of the streets."*

It was a line she'd always loved, and had never thought could sound more beautiful than it did in the original song. But coming from Crash's lips, with his head softly bobbing to the unaccompanied rhythm of the words, it made her head spin and the world feel unsteady, in flux, all around her.

Rion simply couldn't manage any words. She let out a soft sigh and felt a smile creep on to her lips.

"You smiled. Rion Burke, you smiled at me for what I think is the first time ever."

"How do you know it was you? What if it was the pancakes?" she said, nodding toward her plate, which was empty except for wide smears of syrup and a streak or two of chocolate.

"If the pancakes make you smile, I will bring you here every day," he said, his expression dead serious, his body still relaxed. He rolled his shoulders back, pushing his pecs out so they stretched his shirt, and Rion had to blink hard to get the image of licking a line all the way up his torso out of her head.

He held the door open for her on the way out, leaving a narrow space for her to pass through. Goddammit, if she accidentally touched him one more time she really would tackle him.

"Okay, well…I had a good time. Thanks." Rion tried not to make eye contact with him, just to make sure there was no way he could see how badly she wanted to kiss him. She could see Harrison from here. If she was lucky, she could be back home and under a blanket, wallowing in her own patheticness, within 15 minutes.

Because no matter how clean Crash was, falling for him felt more dangerous than any drug.

"Oh…okay." Crash said as he let the door swing softly shut behind him. "Do you have class now? I thought you were on the schedule for a couple hours from now."

"I…" Dammit, she couldn't lie to him. *What the fuck is wrong with you, Rion? Spending another hour with him won't push you head over heels.*

"There was just something I wanted to show you. Do you have a minute?"

"Where?" Rion surveyed the street. There were people here and there, ducking out of Starbucks or into Northern's bookstore.

"Just down the street, actually. You're not too cold, are you?"

Rion wiggled her arms inside his jacket, which she hadn't taken off the whole time they were in the diner. "No, I'm good," she smiled.

"Looks cute on you," he said.

"I…"

"Come on. It's just a few blocks this way," he said before she could think of anything remotely coherent to say. So lightly, but with a firm hand, he brushed his fingertips down two inches of her spine, turning her to the right.

The freezing rain had turned to a freezing downpour the night before, and dingy puddles filled the trenches between Francis Street and its curbs. The air whipped into a mild breeze, lifting Rion's hair into wild tendrils and making her shake the heavy arm of the jacket down so her fingers were free to fix it.

"Okay," Crash finally said after three blocks of Rion's short legs rushing to keep up with Crash's long ones. "It's right down this alley."

Rion raised her eyebrow at him. "You want me to walk down an alley with you."

"Yep. In midday, with tons of people around. And look," he said, pointing up and to the right, "even a security camera, which tracks everyone who goes in and out. Hand to God, I'm not dangerous. As if you couldn't be sure of that by the fact that Olivia hired me in the first place."

Crash tugged Rion by the fingertips around the corner into the alleyway. She gasped when she looked up.

The two-story expanse of bricks was an explosion of color, texture, and impossible light. Flowing shapes pierced by sharp angles and filled in with everything from fish scales, ombre effects, and miniature scenes within scenes all combined into something that covered at least half of the wall, and completely took her breath away.

"Holy fucking shit," she breathed, gaping at the beauty of it. She knew her mouth was hanging open, and when Crash saw it, he laughed.

"That's a good thing, I guess?"

"Yeah. This is incredible. This is like…every cool art technique possible combined to make one perfect piece of art."

"Okay, are you reading my mind or something?" He shook his head at her, a bemused smile on his lips.

"Well it's true, right? When did you discover this? I've been here for weeks and it's not like everyone knows this is here. Not like all those lame sculptures the campus is so damn proud of."

Crash chuckled and scuffed the dusty ground with his toe. "I do love a girl who has her opinion about art."

"I don't know much, but holy shit. This is incredible," she repeated, well aware at how dumb she sounded re-using words. She didn't care. "So," she asked again. "How did you find this?"

"Promise you won't tell?" he asked.

She raised her eyebrows and dipped her head down. "I guess."

"I painted it." He beamed now, and for the first time she noticed how perfectly even his teeth were behind those kissable lips.

"Shut up. You did not." She pushed him on the shoulder, the firm muscle under her touch not lost on her, but she couldn't resist getting closer to the art. She moved up close to the wall, as close as Crash had been to her when he almost, she could swear, kissed her the other night. This mural felt more like him than the pompous guy who made her want to hiss and swear. This was simple and complicated all at once. She ran her fingertips over a couple bricks covered in a pattern of circles within circles, small and large, looking kind of like the slides of cells she and Amy and Arielle had been analyzing for biology class.

"Yeah, I did. This is what I really want to do—large scale public art. The tattoos make sure my rent and my bills get paid, but this is what I bust my ass for. And spend half my money paying for paint for."

"I seriously thought you were bullshitting me when you told me you were an artist." She looked at him, then looked up at the wall. Pride lit up his face, and seeing it, knowing that her words had brought it out, made Rion's heart jump. She wanted to do it again. "This is real art. Just fucking gorgeous. I mean, not that tattoos aren't art, but…"

"No, I'm not only a tattoo artist. Though my tattoos are awesome."

There was the cockiness. But for the first time, it made Rion smile instead of bristle. She stepped back and moved a few paces farther down the wall. There, in one of the trapezoids that slotted perfectly into a curving oval shape, was a painting of the same alley she was standing in. Two people holding hands. One of them a tall guy, and one a petite girl with long, bleach-blond hair topped with dark roots. Holding hands.

"You painted us," she said breathlessly. There was no way he could have known what the weather would be like today, gray and misting, injecting a chill into your bones even though it was well above freezing. "You painted us, here, today. You knew we'd be here."

The Broken Hearts Society of Suite 17C

"I didn't *know*," he corrected. "I *hoped* you'd come with me. Sometimes I like to think...I don't know, it's stupid."

"No, it's not," Rion said softly, turning and looking intently into his eyes. She knew he had her mesmerized, and she didn't even care. "Say it. Whatever you're going to say isn't stupid." She was never this sentimental, but being here with him, staring at the one thing this near-stranger had poured his heart and soul into, made her own heart feel like it was stretching and twisting and growing back a part that let her feel things she'd lost a long time ago.

For the first time, he didn't meet her advance. Instead, he gazed at the wall, his eyes moving smoothly from one panel to another. "Sometimes I think that if I paint something, it'll happen. Some things are more abstract, like that blue and white panel? That's from a memory—a family vacation on a lake. It's for calm. I needed to be calm when I painted this."

"And you painted us looking at this wall because..."

"I've been hoping it would happen since the first time I saw you."

It was like all the air had been sucked out of that alley. Rion heard the words, but couldn't translate them into meaning, into an appropriate response. They washed over her, like something strange and warm and entirely right, but alien all at the same time.

Crash stepped toward her. "I don't know a lot about you, but I know that whenever I'm with you, I feel a little better. A little steadier. I know you're funny, and I can tell you're smart. I feel at home at the studio, and as far as I can tell, you do too. I just want to get to know you a little better. It might not make sense to show you my art, this thing that I've only shown one or two other people. But I wanted you to know…I'm not all talk. I like you. When I found out that you won't get high or drink, that we have that in common…well, that's not a small thing. That means a lot to me."

"Really?" Rion's curiosity suddenly went into overdrive. She didn't think staying away from substances would mean a lot to anyone at Indiana Northern except for her.

"Yeah. I have my reasons. I didn't say anything at first, and then you told me, so I didn't really have to," he said, motioning to her to follow him back out of the alley. Now she hung on his every word, needing to know how he came to the exact same brand of unlikely misfitdom as she had.

"But," he continued, moving his arm around to her back in the same so-close-yet-too-far-away way he'd done earlier, "Yes. I won't date girls who use either."

"You're shitting me," she said.

"I shit you not," he replied, smiling gently at her. He pressed his hand in just the slightest bit, so now his palm pressed against the small of her back instead of just his fingers.

The Broken Hearts Society of Suite 17C

Rion fought to keep her breathing even. They came to the end of a block and waited at the crosswalk. She tried to focus on the light.

Watch for the "walk" sign to come up and you'll feel calmer. You'll be able to talk to him again.

What would she even say, once she regained some sense? *My opinion of you has totally changed? Have you been tested for STDs because I'm pretty sure I'm about to force you to fuck me silly? Please tell me you have your own place?*

Okay, that was too far. She was horny, not stupid. As shitty as things had been lately, she wanted to stay alive, and going home alone with a guy you barely knew was grade-A stupid. The opposite light turned yellow, and Rion realized she had no clue what they were doing next. Was the date over? Did she want it to go on longer, or should she take a moment to cool off?

"Crash, I—" and then, with her mouth wide open, a humungous blue pickup truck barreled past, slicing through the water puddled against the curb, splashing right into Rion's wide-open mouth. She was frozen solid for a second, then whimpered, then wailed. Freezing cold water dripped from her hair, now flattened against her skull and plastered against the outline of her neck.

"Holy shit!" Crash screamed at the pickup, throwing his hands up in the air in a "What the hell?" gesture.

Rion stared down at herself, taking in the completely soaked front of her jacket and jeans. The front layers of her hair hung stringy and mud-streaked against her threadbare Chemical Brothers concert shirt. She shivered in the breeze, which kicked up right as the cold was hitting her and made her shake to the bone.

"Oh my God, fucking bastard!" Crash yelled after the truck, which was long disappeared from view.

Rion managed a laugh. "I appreciate the outrage. I'm just sorry this cut things short." Leave it to Rion to find her courage to speak when she was soaking wet and looking like a drowned rat. And feeling even worse.

"No. No way we're ending things like this. You need to change." Instead of crossing the street back toward campus, now he turned and led her back toward Francis. Back toward work.

"Are you taking me back to the studio? I don't have any spare clothes there or anything."

"Yeah, sort of. I live right above it, and I have spare clothes."

Rion fumbled for her phone. "Just need t-to tell my roommates," she said, the shivers rippling through her words. She texted Amy:

Headed to Crash's place. Got caught in the rain. Back soon.

She winced with how stupid that sounded, but she trusted him. Dammit, even that thought sounded stupid. So she added **Above the Studio.**

Amy's return message came screeching through almost immediately.

ABSOLUTELY NOT. BACK TO HARRISON.
Then, after a second, **You barely know him.**

Rion sighed. Arielle was right, damn her.

She'd read somewhere that you should always tell your girlfriend where you were going, and how long you were planning to be there. She'd scoffed when she read the advice to beginning college students in the waiting room magazine. She didn't have any girlfriends at all—it was best to watch your own back in the group home, never to rely on anyone else. She knew she'd have roommates at Northern, but seriously doubted she'd ever be friends with them.

She didn't know if she could possibly be friends with anyone. Well damn, she'd even managed to surprise herself.

She was about to shoot back a reply about how Crash was fine, really. But then he looked over her shoulder and saw the screen. "Dammit," he said, turning around and nudging Rion along with him in a split second. "She's right."

"No, she's not," protested horny Rion. Suddenly all she could think about was getting in Crash's pants. It had been so long, and she had felt so alone, and she could really use a really good orgasm…

"Yeah. I don't piss in a cup for a girl and then show her my best work in the city if I'm going to fuck her and leave her." He snuck a quick look down at her. "Not that that's, like, a thing I do. I'm not an asshole."

Warmth bled down through Rion's body as a smile pulled up the corners of her lips. "Okay. Well, um, Harrison's not that far away."

Not that being soaked to the bone didn't make it feel farther away. By the time they arrived in the lobby, Rion was shivering even more, despite Crash's coat. Maybe because of his coat, since it was damp too. When she realized that, she groaned. "Shit, I'm sorry. Your coat. Do you…want it back?" She looked up at him, waiting for his response to dictate what would come next. She didn't want to say anything, even though he'd made it clear that he liked her.

After a few very intense-feeling seconds, Crash chuckled. They must have made a strange sight, her soaking wet and him a tall, tattooed, clearly older-than-freshman guy. Looking at each other awkwardly, in the middle of the lobby, where nobody hung out. "I don't know what to do," he said. "Your shirt's white, so you really should keep it on till you change clothes."

"Yeah. I should." Somehow, she ignored how disgusting she must have looked and felt, how damn unsure she felt about this whole thing, and looked back into his eyes, daring him to make the next move.

"Do you…want me to walk you up?" He said slowly, carefully. Giving her space to say "No, maybe next time," and not have it be awkward.

But she wanted to be closer to him now. Wanted to put an end, once and for all, to her questions about this

The Broken Hearts Society of Suite 17C

beautiful guy and whether he wanted the same thing from her as she wanted from him.

"I could show you my secret...thing. I mean, hobby. I mean, passion. I mean...oh, Jesus Christ." How did she explain how she felt about her music and what it would mean to share it with anyone, let alone Crash, without making it sound like an innuendo? "I mean, my thing. Like the street art is your thing."

"Whoa," he said, smiling. "Yeah. That would be good."

Rion knew Amy and Arielle would both be in class until 3:18, which meant she'd be alone with Crash for three hours. Maybe he'd leave after ten minutes. Maybe he'd stay the whole time, and they'd walk to the Studio for work together. Maybe she'd finally get to see the tattoo-and-muscle gorgeousness that was underneath that shirt.

Damn. She needed to get a fucking grip.

Now that she was leading the way, Crash's fingers no longer lingered against the small of her back. When he'd first rested them there, it had annoyed her, felt like an extra appendage she hadn't asked for and hadn't wanted. But now that he was standing all the way across the elevator from her, not really staring at her but definitely watching her, it didn't feel close enough. Now the *not* touching was the thing that made her feel uncomfortable. Unsettled.

So when the door slid open on floor seventeen, Rion forced the slight trembling from her hands and darted one out to catch his. She gave him a smile as she pulled him forward, just to let him know it was friendly, inviting. Trusting. The door clicked shut behind her, heavy, filling the air with the tension of Crash's waiting.

They were on her turf now. She gestured around. "This is the common room," she said. Crash took in the decorations Amy and, a little bit, Arielle, had filled the walls with. A random movie poster on one wall, a white board with a giant cork board on either side, filled with whatever flyers and takeout menus the girls had deemed relevant. Conspicuously, no snapshots of any of the girls with anybody else. It seemed like most of them had wanted to start with a clean slate when they were here.

"Looks like you guys are pretty close," Crash said, pointing to the one snapshot Arielle had made them take after the first Society meeting. A selfie. They looked so together, and, actually, happy.

"Um...I guess we're friends. Like I said, it's kind of unlikely that we're getting along. And lucky." She dropped her bag and sized him up. Rion had never seen Crash look uncomfortable, even when he was about to piss in a cup. Now he stood in the middle of their common room, fidgeting like he didn't know what to do with his limbs. "Just...have a seat. Read a magazine or something. I'm gonna shower."

"And you want me to wait?"

"For your coat," she said with a smile. "Yeah."

The Broken Hearts Society of Suite 17C

She ducked into the bathroom and let his coat drop to the ground with a thud. She picked it up and examined it, sighing. It was soaked with dingy water. Hopefully she hadn't ruined it.

Soon, she was wincing as the hot water hit her chilled skin, and after a few minutes, standing in the blissfully warm steam of the shower, staring at her feet, trying to get her scrambled thoughts together on what to do next. She towel-dried her hair, thanked whatever deities were out there that Arielle had a supply of hair elastics in her disordered pile of crap that had pissed Rion off just that morning, and swiped on some mascara and lip gloss. She nodded at the mirror. Yeah, this was okay.

If only she'd remembered to bring some clothes in with her. She sighed, thankful that at least she had a small frame that would be mostly covered by the towel. If Crash was going to see her naked, the first time wasn't going to be when a heavy strip of terrycloth happened to fall or slip.

That thought alone sent a surge of heat through Rion. It wasn't embarrassment or fear. It was pure lust.

She knew he'd be all over her, and that she'd feel his lip ring graze places of her body that would send her over the edge.

An edge that threatened weakness, one she hadn't even allowed herself to get close to for a very long time.

Rion gripped the top of her damp towel with both hands and pulled it apart, blowing out a pent-up breath slowly and looking down. Moving from the shower to the chilled air had hardened her nipples, and she admired how cute they looked over the heavy roundness of her breasts. Her stomach was smooth, and the navel piercing there was pretty damn cute. And she'd just trimmed her pubes. She wouldn't look too bad naked, not too bad at all.

And she had at least three hours in this suite with Crash to herself.

What a strange feeling to be happy to be here alone, instead of trying to be alone in some other place, some crowd of people she'd never seen before and would never see again. Her heart twisted in two when she realized—being alone with Crash was what she wanted. Being alone with Crash was enough.

Stop it, you sentimental bitch. He's probably getting impatient waiting. Maybe he wants to go home.

But she knew he didn't.

Her hand didn't tremble as she reached for the door handle. In fact, there wasn't an ounce of hesitation in her body. It was like her instinct had taken over, and for once, she was mindlessly, steadily, doing exactly what she was supposed to be doing.

Slowly she stepped out of the bathroom and back into her room, forcing another door handle down, more steps into a perfectly certain uncertainty.

She walked into her room to see Crash, his heavy boots all the way up to his hair flopped over his brow, fast asleep on her extra long twin mattress.

The Broken Hearts Society of Suite 17C

She let out a sigh, full of steam and keyed-up sexual tension, escaping from her body in that one breath. Once again, Crash had foiled her. He'd taken every image she'd had in her head of tearing his clothes off, licking his abs, and moaning as he thrust into her, and met it with a completely different sight—one that told her to take care of him.

His head turned to the side and he made a low moan from deep in his throat, his eyebrows knitting together in his sleep. Across the cheek that had been on the blanket was the clear indent of a spiral notebook binding, and Rion rushed over to pull it gently out from under his head. When her fingers brushed his temple, his mouth twitched up in a smile and a soft sigh rose from his lips.

Goddammit, if she wasn't careful, sleeping Crash would melt her cold, dead heart to a puddle before she even got a chance to fuck him. In her short dating life, sex was first and feelings were closely guarded, most likely not explored or given at all.

Rion shivered. The air in her room was even colder than that in the bathroom, probably because it sat on the outside wall of the suite. She reached her arm out to brush Crash's fingers, and his hands were like ice. On tiptoes, she pulled a heavy blanket from the top shelf of her closet. It was rough and an ugly gray, but it had come with the room. Rion knew it was clean, because Amy had offered to wash everyone's linens the first week they were at school. Crossing the little space quickly, Rion draped it over Crash, marveling at the way it left the toe of his boot peeking out, while she had been able to curl all the way up inside it like a turtle hiding in a shell.

No emotions before fucking, she reminded herself, smiling a little at her admission that fucking Crash was inevitable, even if it wasn't going to happen right now. But when she pulled it up over his chest, and felt the hard muscle beneath it, her body started moving independently of her brain again. She let her fingers trail down his shoulder, across his strong forearm, down the back of his hand. And when her fingertips grazed his, he closed them into his palm, gripping them firmly.

Rion's eyes darted to the humungous sleeping guy's face. Eyes still closed, lashes still fluttering in the deepest of sleep. And then a low hum from his lips, the beginning of words.

"Mmmm, baby. Come here. So cold." She could tell there was little effort in the way he tugged her down toward him by the hand, and yet it would have been impossible to break away even if she'd wanted to. If she let him pull her down on top of him, he'd wake up, and whatever wonderful thing he was seeing in his dreams would be ripped away from him.

"Everyone deserves sweet dreams," Rion murmured, and let her body, still wrapped only in a towel, fall perfectly into the narrow space between his body and the edge of the bed. Lying there stiffly, she waited for Crash to say more from the dream world. But the only change was a relaxed expression, instead of the drawn eyebrows he'd had a second ago, and the slightest of smiles.

Rion toed up the edge of the blanket and wiggled her body underneath it, making the towel fall away from her thigh as she did. Then she tried to control her brain at the one monumental thought that kept skittering through it— *You are in bed with Crash. You are in bed with him, and his arm is around you, and you're sharing a blanket, and you, my dear, are naked as the day you were born.*

More naked, in fact, than she'd ever been with Tate. Probably closer, too—he always liked to fuck in a position that let him see her body, then disengage as soon as he could. This full-body touching was weird. Very weird, but very nice.

The room was bright, but pressed against the hard curve of Crash's body, she felt warm, and held, and secure. When his arm wrapped around her waist and tugged her even closer, she only tried to resist for a second before realizing that, as much as she'd programmed herself to resist being squeezed, penned in, weakened—his arms felt like they belonged around her.

And then, exhausted, she fell slowly, peacefully asleep.

Chapter 14

Amy

Talking to Mom had been almost impossible lately.

Dad was no problem. Ever since she'd turned nine or ten, she'd stopped being Daddy's little girl in his eyes and turned into a little woman. Amy would never forget the first time she'd asked him a question—probably about some boy or another—and he'd awkwardly chuckled, then called to her mother. "Leslie? Your daughter has a question for you." He'd patted her on the head and turned back to his football game.

Amy knew that, on some level, she'd been a disappointment to her father. The second child who had not only been another girl, but had such a traumatic birth that her mother wouldn't be able to have any more children. Amy had taken away Dad's chances of ever having a son.

The Broken Hearts Society of Suite 17C

Which was why, she was sure, he'd loved Adam so much. The day they started dating in eighth grade, she'd seen it in his eyes. It was like she'd gotten married a decade early, and she was going to spend the time still living at home, but belonging to Adam. Which meant that Adam would belong to her family, too. Since that day, Dad's interaction with her had basically involved giving her a side hug, kissing her head, asking how her day was, and then talking to Adam about football over dinner.

Mom was different. Mom listened to her every plan for the future, her every detail about every date with Adam, her every little daydream about the life they'd lead together. Everything with the assumption that Amy would follow the teachings that good girls of their church were expected to follow—no sex before marriage. Most of them did "everything but," and were too shy to define what "everything but" meant. Most of their mothers knew, and none of them did anything about it. It was a the dirty secret that kept Tripp Creek's teen hormones quelled and its good Christian image upheld at the same time.

So that late fall afternoon, right before Adam's eighteenth birthday party, when he'd let his hands wander under her shirt and over her breasts—under her bra—Amy had had no idea whether this fell into the 'everything but' category or the 'sex before marriage' category. She knew what sex was, parts-wise, but when Adam's mouth had grazed her nipple, then sucked there, it felt more intimate than anything she'd ever imagined doing before being married to someone.

It had also felt really, really good. And that had terrified her.

So, when mom had asked how their date was, she'd frozen up. For the first time ever, she hadn't known whether she could talk to Mom about something without getting her disapproval, without making her freak out, without initiating a CIA-level watch on her at all times. So she'd said it was fine, talked about the wildflower bouquet Adam had brought her, then stewed in her own turmoil about the whole issue for a week. A week later, as the family walked to church, Amy had finally gotten the nerve to ask Mom the question. Amy figured that if the conversation got really uncomfortable, it would have to stop when they reached church no matter what. Mom had looked at Amy like she'd asked whether bread needed yeast to rise.

"What do you mean, what counts as sex? What makes you even wonder that? You and Adam haven't ever done anything further than kissing. I know that," Mom had said when Amy had opened her mouth, cutting her off, "because Adam is a pastor's son and you are a good Christian girl and you've made a commitment, before the entire congregation at your baptism, to live your life for nothing but His glory." Amy had fought to keep from rolling her eyes. God's glory was fine, but she wanted to talk to her mom, not a theology professor. "And you've promised your father—and me—that you will keep

The Broken Hearts Society of Suite 17C

yourself pure until marriage."

Mom had nodded at her own words, trying to reassure herself of her daughter's chastity, and looked back to the path. Amy thought her steps quickened, but she couldn't really tell. She was focusing too hard on holding back tears.

From that day on, it had been hard to know what she could tell Mom and what she couldn't. One thing she knew for sure was that the only thing she could say about her time with Adam was, "It was a great date, he was a perfect gentleman." Then, at Christmas, when Adam's hands had ventured below her waistband, had pushed inside her body, she was too afraid to even ask her sister. Bridget was closer to Mom than Amy was, and that one walk to church had scared Amy off the topic of s-e-x forever.

So much so that when things got ten times worse in the Spring, she was too afraid to do anything but hide in her room.

So she'd managed to bite back most of her tears when she told mom about the breakup, and made sure to paint the details of perfectly obedient Amy doing the major that everyone agreed would be great for Amy. She loved working in the church nursery so much, and she planned to move back home. Probably, mom said, this would all blow over, and she'd marry Adam anyway.

Early Childhood Education, Mom had said, was a perfect career for a girl like her. She could take a break from working to have babies, and go back to work when they went to school. Most people didn't want to teach preschool anyway, especially not in their little town. Amy never told mom that she only liked working in the church nursery because the growl in Pastor Mason's voice when he gave his sermons scared the heck out of her. Especially when she worried so much that she and Adam may or may not have been guilty of the very sins he preached against every week.

So she'd started in her Intro to Early Childhood Education class, numb from Adam's betrayal and desperately clinging to something from her old life that she thought she was sure of. But by now, the first week of November, she'd lost track of how many times she'd fallen asleep doing the assigned reading, how many phone calls she'd ignored from the local Head Start office trying to put her in a field placement, how many times she'd daydreamed in class instead of paying attention to the subject material that was supposed to fascinate her.

She had no idea what to tell Mom as she stood outside the ECE class building with her graded midterm in hand, staring at the red marks and scathing comments, wondering how she could fail so spectacularly at the one thing everyone expected her to be perfect for.

A single tear ran down her cheek, and she swiped it away. Her phone, tucked away in the side pocket of her purse, buzzed against her. She knew it was Mom, who, in her empty-nesting, had taped both Amy and Bridget's schedules to her fridge, calling them every day after their afternoon class.

She also knew she couldn't answer Mom's call. Ever since she'd felt shamed by their one and only sex talk, Amy hadn't walked into a single conversation with Mom without a contingency plan. And now she had none.

Amy forced her legs to walk toward Francis, where she used to walk in search of coffee, and now walked in search of Matt. They never planned to meet, but he was always there when she walked in. In fact, she'd lost track of how many times they'd met there, lost track of how many times he'd guessed just the kind of drink she wanted and already had it on order for her. Matt's Jesus t-shirts had started to grow on her, and he claimed that her presence helped him focus on his school work. "It's one thing to be a slacker in the super comfortable company of your own bad self," he'd said, "but when there's someone you respect sitting right across the table from you, it's a lot harder to spend the whole afternoon watching cheesy reality shows on YouTube."

She knew it wasn't true. Not the part about wasting time on YouTube—Matt was always doing that—but about the productivity. They never got very much work done when they were together, because they talked the whole time. Matt was passionate in a way that would have had him labeled crazy back home. If there was a topic that interested him, or something that tugged at his heartstrings, he would obsessively learn everything about it, and then report back to her. Once, he had said something about non-traditional Christianity, and Amy had challenged him.

"There's only one kind of Christianity," she'd said. "You either believe or you don't."

"So you're telling me that Jesus' followers were the same kind of Christians that ransacked Muslim and Jewish settlements in the name of Christ?"

"I..." a blush had come to her face. "I honestly am not sure what you're talking about. We never learned much about that in history classes."

"You never learned about the Crusades?"

"A little. I learned about King Richard. How he fought for what he believed in, civilized a lot of towns, gained land for England. But I didn't think it was a big deal. Definitely not a bad thing."

"History is written by the people who won," Matt had said, shaking his head. "And they never want to look bad."

Amy wouldn't lie—the whole exchange had made her feel pretty stupid and a little uncomfortable. But somehow, she'd felt comfortable enough with Matt to tell him so. And his response had floored her. "Good," he'd said. "If we don't feel uncomfortable, we're not learning. Now, you tell me something that makes *me* feel all squirmy."

Matt had given her his full attention then, and she'd felt whatever confidence she'd lost to her ignorance of the Crusades come flooding back.

The Broken Hearts Society of Suite 17C

That day, she'd just come from her introduction to urban planning class—one that had been suggested by her advisor to bolster the Early Childhood Education major Amy had been planning on. And the advisor had been right. In short order, she'd learned buckets of things that tied city layouts to educating the littlest minds in the country.

Quality of education was closely tied to socioeconomic status of the local environment, and kids who didn't go to a good preschool and kids who were poor were usually one in the same. Those kids didn't do well in Kindergarten. To Amy, that information had felt like a gut-punch. For one, she had never known that, and for another, any ideas she'd had about helping children learn in her cozy community back home would do nothing to help the fact that there were kids whose lives were determined by how much money was put into their education at the age of three.

Matt had watched her solemnly for a few sips, and then sat back, shaking his head. It was the most incredible feeling to Amy who, up until that moment, had never had the feeling that anyone had really, truly listened to her, let alone understood her. "This world, Amy. What are we going to do?"

That just infused more significance—and more purpose—into every word she'd just said. Matt was taking her thoughts, her concerns, and considering them for himself. Maybe she'd change his mind, open it to a new path, however small. If she could affect Matt in that way, who else could she reach? It was encouraging and terrifying all at once.

"You know," Matt had said after a few moments of long thought, "sometimes I think things are never going to change. Sometimes I lose faith in us."

Amy's heart had started. Her friendship with Matt was easy, unladen with expectation. Something that felt like a breath of fresh air to her. "*Us?*" she stuttered.

"You know. Humanity. What are we even *doing*? We're letting everything go to hell, and for what? A little extra money? A sense of moral superiority?"

Amy looked at him, her eyes wide.

Matt shook his head. "And, yeah. *Us* us, too."

"Us?" she asked again.

"Us. Christians. We say we want to be like Him, but what are we actually doing about it? Jesus knocked down the money changers' tables, and it's like we're all picking them back up again. We're doing the opposite of what He wanted. I mean, can you even wrap your head around that? We say we're following Him when all we're really doing is walking away from Him."

It was something startling, to see Matt there in his "Body piercing saved my life" t-shirt, hackles up, legs fidgeting, all-but-blaspheming in the middle of a coffee shop. But more startling was the fact that Amy wasn't embarrassed at all. In fact, she felt what he was saying, deep in her heart. Not only because she'd agreed with him, but because she knew she had been one of those people who had done absolutely nothing about it.

Amy was pretty sure she hadn't walked away from Jesus, but maybe she hadn't been trying that hard to follow Him, either.

So she'd leaned forward, placed her hand gently over his, and caught his eyes. They softened immediately when they looked into hers. "You're right," she'd said simply.

And he'd replied simply. "Thank you." Their work for the rest of the afternoon was quiet, comfortable, but Amy knew something had shifted. Some of the lightness in their conversation had darkened, but so much had deepened with a new, calming strength. It was a certainty that warmed Amy whenever she thought about seeing him again.

Standing in the middle of the sidewalk clutching the paper with the ugly red "71" scrawled at the top, Amy wondered if there had been a higher purpose to that little exchange between them. When Matt had revealed a part of himself that made her see him as more than the goofy, lighthearted guy that most of the world saw, and Amy had shown that she had understood. The fact that he had shown her something so deep maybe, just maybe, meant that she could share something deep with him, too.

So she wiped back her tears, just because she probably looked horrible, and walked into the cafe, plunking her stuff down on the floor beside the chair that Matt always saved for her, just like she always did.

The signature lopsided smile Matt always flashed her when she sat down quickly turned down when he caught a glimpse of her face. "Amy. Are you okay?"

She shrugged, and made a split second decision. She reached into her bag and pulled out the test, and handed it to him across the table.

Almost instantly, her fingers itched to grab it back. What would he think of a girl who couldn't get a decent grade on an entry-level test, the first step in what would be a very long road to her degree?

"Aw, crap," Matt said, scanning the front page of the test, then quickly flipping through the others. "The first bad grade of college always sucks. What did this come to?"

"A C minus," Amy mumbled. "No curve. It's just…I don't know how I'm going to get through the rest of these classes. I have three more years full of them."

A look of confusion swept over Matt's face. "What do you mean? This is about two- and three-year-old kids. You're not majoring in stay-at-home momming, are you?"

"Yeah. Haven't you been listening to anything I've said?" A flash of anger went through Amy. "Sorry, I just—my major is Early Childhood Education. I'm going to be a preschool teacher, remember?"

"Nope. No." Matt shook his head back and forth vehemently. "I promise you, Amy Bauer, I have been listening intently to every word you've said. You've told me how ridiculous you and Arielle are in biology lab, and

The Broken Hearts Society of Suite 17C

you've told me every marginally interesting thing about your Urban Planning class. I know more about the evolution of downtown Indianapolis than I ever thought I would know."

Amy smiled, looking down at her hands, which she'd folded in her lap. "Okay, but that is fascinating. Of course you remember what I said."

"No, the way you talk about it *makes* it fascinating. Which is exactly why I thought you were in the City Planning program. One of the best in the country? You're an academic rock star?"

"Did I say that?" Amy asked, blushing and checking his eyes to see if he was teasing.

"No, you'd never boast like that. But I put the pieces together. Anyway, this whole Early Childhood Kindergarten major thing? There's no way. You like buildings and cities and the way they affect society way too much for anything else to be your focus."

As he said the words, she ran through her memories to see if they matched his. She realized he was right. Of course he was. Suddenly, every solid feeling about studying here at Northern became splintered, mixed up, and muddled together.

"The thing is," she said in response to that quiet watchfulness of his that told her he was willing to wait for a response, "I'm supposed to be a preschool teacher. I'm supposed to go home, work in my old school, and—" the end of that sentence had always been 'marry Adam.' But she knew, deep down, that was off the table now. He'd changed so much. And now, she realized as she looked at Matt's waiting posture, so had she.

"Who says?" Matt asked, and Amy scoffed. "No, seriously. Who tells anyone, at the age of seventeen, what the rest of her life will look like?"

"I did," Amy said quietly, trying to work out whether she was ashamed, embarrassed, sad, or just as confused as Matt seemed to think she was, after all. "I wanted that to be my life. I'm the one who said that."

"Okay, even if that's one hundred percent true…you're not allowed to change your mind? You're not allowed to fall in love and let that change the course of your life?"

Amy's eyes snapped to Matt's and her heart dropped into her stomach. "I…I thought…I mean, the whole thing with Adam…I haven't even considered…"

"I'm not talking about falling in love with a person!" Matt's fist pounded the table, and Amy jumped. "Sorry, I just…you love something, you're good at something, you should let that guide you. Not anything else. That was, like, the most important thing I learned last year."

"What do you mean?"

"Well, you know I just declared my major."

She nodded. She'd bought him a Francis Bean special recipe magic bar to celebrate. "Nonprofit management." She knew what a strong Christian he was, and imagined that he would one day be the guy on the commercials, asking viewers to sponsor a suffering child in Guatemala for eight dollars a month.

"Guess what my moms wanted me to do?"

"I...really have no idea." She thought of everything Matt was to her—enthusiastic, passionate, positive, supportive. Nonprofit management had seemed perfect for him.

"Well, for starters, something lucrative. We never had a ton of money and they wanted me to have an easier time. But if not that, at least to pour my love for Christ into leading a congregation."

"So why didn't you?"

"It just wasn't right for me. Not big enough, maybe. Too constricted, to set in stone as just one path. And I wanted—I *want*—so much more."

Amy's breath caught. His words shot straight to her heart, because they articulated everything she'd been thinking about the difference between the life everyone expected her to have, and the one she'd been rudely jostled out of the day that Adam had ripped it away from her.

This was the first time she realized that she wasn't all that sad about it. Her heart had been broken, certainly. But that was all about having a plan, about safety, and security. It had turned out that, when all that hinged on one person, when that person was gone, the rest of the dream fell apart.

And maybe Matt was right. Maybe that meant she was

cut out for something else, after all.

"So what changed your mind? What was the final push?"

"I've never really told anyone that before," he said, his cheeks flushing just as hers had a few minutes earlier, when he'd called everything about her future plans into question.

"Would you tell me? Since, you know, it might be crucial for me making this life decision?"

"It's...kind of a long story. With a simple message. But, long story short, it was a volunteer gig that really changed my heart." He stopped there.

Amy just watched him, trying so hard to be patient, kind, and open as he'd been for her.

"I'm actually heading there now. Would you...I mean, you definitely don't have to, and it's pretty unconventional...and I know for a fact that most people don't want to get involved in this kind of thing..."

"I think I just discovered that I'm not most people," Amy interrupted, speaking slowly enough that he'd understand how sincere she was. "I'd love to come along."

Matt sighed and shook his head back and forth slowly, a look of wonder in his eyes. "Are you sure?"

"As sure as I can be," Amy had said, suddenly unable to tear her gaze from his. "Surer than I've been of anything for a long time." She didn't really mean the gig—she had no idea what kind of volunteer work it was. But what surged through her now was clearer and purer than anything she'd ever felt—it was a belief in Matt, in his goodness. A trust that she'd never felt for anyone before, besides her mom and dad when she was little. Even that had long since crumbled.

The two of them packed up silently, and when Matt stood, he held his hand down for her, even though she didn't need the help getting up. She took it, and followed him out.

They drove quietly for about ten minutes, and in settled a strange peace. For the first time in a very long time, Amy felt like she was in the right place, with the right person, doing the right thing—even though she had no idea where she was going.

Soon, after they got off a highway exit and wound through the streets behind a nondescript white-walled office park, it became clear that that feeling had been completely and totally wrong.

The building, square and stark with windows high off the ground and a solid metal door, could have housed anything. It was only the complete lack of any signage that set Amy on edge. That, and the fact that at 2:00 in the afternoon there were only two cars in the parking lot. Outside of one stood a girl with a long, blond French braid, not much younger than Amy, wearing worn blue jeans and a long button down shirt. She looked out past the building where cars whizzed down the highway, blinking the harsh wind out of red-rimmed eyes. She looked alone, resigned as she leaned against her rusting car. She was the picture of hopelessness.

Amy's heart broke for her even before the third car got there. Three people piled out—a younger teenager from the back, a man in jeans and a black suit jacket, and a woman in a turtleneck sweater from the front. The woman reached in the back seat and pulled out two posterboards, the man clutched a stack of thin leaflets and a small leather-bound book.

Amy's mounting sense of dread was confirmed when the boy flipped around his sign and it read, "In God's court abortion is murder."

The other sign, held by the woman Amy presumed to be his mom, read the slightly milder, "Abortion harms women." Amy braced herself for the gruesome images she'd first seen when her shaking fingers had searched "abortion" on the computer six months ago—she'd later found out that they were computer manipulated, but that hadn't scrubbed her brain of the image of raw, bleeding miniature humans, murdered by selfish girls.

Girls like her.

"Dammit!" Matt swore, throwing the car into park and wrenching his door open. "We tried to feed them a fake schedule, but it looks like they're getting smarter. Dammit," he repeated before hoisting himself out of his seat, slamming the door shut, and doing a quick jog to the

The Broken Hearts Society of Suite 17C

front of the clinic.

Amy's mouth gaped in horror as she watched. This wasn't Matt. He wouldn't hurt someone so vulnerable on purpose, would he? He hadn't even brought a sign, but people like this probably had an extra in the trunk. Had he decided not to waste time and just follow the girl to the front door instead? She shook her head back and forth, silently praying that this wouldn't be too horrible to watch, wondering what in the world she had gotten into by dating another guy who was so very, very religious.

But then Matt did something nothing short of miraculous, something that sent one fat tear cascading down Amy's cheek. Mid-stride, he shrugged out of his jacket, swung it around the arms of the girl, and started to walk her into the building.

The three protesters swarmed her, shouting things that Amy couldn't decipher through the car window she didn't dare roll down. It didn't matter. All she could hear was the sounds of her memories, anyway. Memories of parishoners from the church about twenty miles away from the clinic, which, thank God, was another hundred miles away from her house. The fact that she'd dressed so differently than usual, her fiery hair stuffed in a knit cap, so that nobody would recognize her, didn't take the sting out of the words that bombarded her as she quick-stepped into the clinic. "Don't kill your baby! Abortion is murder! Mommy, mommy, don't hurt me!"

Matt pulled the jacket in closer, pushed the girl to

move a little faster, using his own body to shield her from the people brandishing signs at her, so wild-eyed they looked about ready to foam at the mouth.

Amy barely saw the woman nudge the boy, and he pulled a small silver square out of his pocket, then held it up to his eye. Quick as lightning, Matt stopped in his tracks, pulled his jacket over the girl's head, spun her around, and put her at his back. Between being able to see the movement of his mouth and his voice being louder than all of them, Amy heard the words he shouted—"NOT TODAY." And he shoved his hand in front of what, it was now clear, was a camera phone.

What a nightmare.

Amy had read about cameras, that some people used them to record and publicize the identities of all the girls who had killed their poor innocent babies. Even though Dad rarely went online, and Mom barely knew how to use a computer, she hadn't doubted for a second that word would get back quickly if her face showed up on the Internet. She had stupidly hoped the heavy makeup she'd put on, plus the tucked-away hair and sunglasses, would be enough to disguise her.

Luckily, there had been no cameras on the day Amy walked into the abortion clinic. But there had been the posters, which would haunt her memories just as long as her image online would have haunted her reputation, at least in Tripp Creek, forever.

Her mascara had bled down her face in mean black

streaks when she'd sat in the abortion counselor's office, weeping and repeating that there was no other option, that if she carried the baby she wouldn't be able to go to college, that her father would kill her. Even though she knew he wouldn't *literally* kill her, the shame she knew would be on her would feel worse than death, anyway.

For her, on that day, there had been no Matt, appearing seemingly out of nowhere to take her into the scariest, most sorrowful, shameful place on earth. As though her suffering weren't bad enough. But watching him do the same thing for this girl, it was like something aligned between his spirit and her heartache, like pins in a combination lock connecting at the perfect point. He may not have been there for Amy on that terrible day months ago, but his heart had done something no boy from home, not even Adam, would have done for her in that dark, dark moment.

When Matt saved that girl from some small measure of pain and humiliation, he became Amy's champion.

The door shut behind him, and she watched the girl's silhouette fade into shadow as the heavy door sealed them safely inside. Amy leaned her head against the car's sweaty window, watching the raindrops roll lazily down the outside, each taking its own slightly varied path.

Some scatterbrained searching on her phone's browser confirmed that they were, in fact, at an abortion clinic—or, rather, the Carmichael County Womens' Services Center. Her tears picked up, each one carrying another ounce of the weight of everything she'd been ashamed of for the last six months. The only stronger feeling was the realization that Matt, this friend who had grown more important to her than she ever would have expected, wouldn't think she was a horrible person if he found out.

After another minute, her tears started to plop on her phone, so she let her vision drift outside again. Somehow, she missed the wavy outline of Matt returning to the car. The door opened with a hard whoosh, sucking the steamy air out and blasting her with a chill that took her breath away.

"I'm so glad I caught her. I wasn't late, I swear, she was early."

Amy's mouth gaped, shocked at his seeming apology toward her.

"I…"

"I know, it's horrible, I'm sorry I didn't explain to you what was going to happen. I thought we'd have more time," he said, shoving the heel of his hand against the steering wheel on the last word, almost growling when he said it. "It just didn't feel like something I wanted to have my attention divided on when we were driving. Maybe I shouldn't have taken you today, I just wanted to show you…you don't have to be like everyone else. You can follow your gut, and still do good things. Still *be* good. You know? "

Only then did he see the tears streaming down her

The Broken Hearts Society of Suite 17C

face. "Oh no. Amy. What did I do? Whatever I did or said or didn't say, I'm really sorry. Geez, I seriously screwed up here." The heartbroken look that curved his eyes down and the whoosh of breath that lowered his chest and slumped his shoulders pushed her to take a deep breath. Now it was her turn to explain.

"No no no. Matt. No. I'm not upset." He raised his eyebrows at her, waiting patiently to hear her out, like always. "I mean, I *am* upset, but not with you. For any reason." He leaned in further and raised his eyebrows again. "Okay, maybe you're right about the whole 'briefing me' part. That would have been good, probably. But still." Amy raised her eyes to his, looking for something. Reassurance that what she was about to tell him would be alright, even though she already knew it was. First, one more question.

"Why did you do that? I mean, why do you do this? I assume it's not your first time. It seemed like you knew what you were doing."

Matt dipped his head into a nod. "Obviously." He ran his hand over the top of his head, then looked out his dashboard, watching the protestors tuck themselves back into their car. A cold standoff, where each knew neither would win. "I took a women's studies class my first semester at Northern. Same one your roommate is taking, I think. Anyway, the professor was completely nuts, but she did make me realize just how really, really difficult it is to be a girl. I never really knew. I mean, obviously. I'm a guy. But especially growing up with my moms…well, feminism was always kind of how things went in our house, you know? I didn't really realize just how involved our society thinks it can be in individual women's health care.

"And that's one thing, you know? To have your own beliefs, to make choices based on your faith. That's great. But it's totally another to stand outside a medical care facility and yell at the girls going inside. Anyway, in class we saw a documentary about these guys who spent their weekends helping women's clinic patients get through the doors without totally losing it. It was just what I needed, because it made me feel like there was something I could do to help. So I went through training, and now I do it. At least two days a week."

"Isn't it dangerous?"

"Sometimes," he said in a quieter voice. "Usually it's more scary than anything. I've never been hurt or anything, but the protestors will get in your face. I've only heard of one guy getting hit. The most important thing is not to touch a protester, at all, because then legally they can claim battery, and then you'd get mixed up in lawsuits and stuff."

One fat tear rolled down Amy's cheek every couple seconds as she nodded, and bit her lip against speaking. Finally, she got some words out that didn't threaten to twist her words into a flood of tears. "I just know you're such a strong Christian. And where I grew up…abortion is not okay with Christians. You know?"

Matt nodded. "I know. But there are a couple other things I know, too. I know that this—" he motioned out to the parking lot, still calm for the moment "is not about abortion. They're not here because they want to save babies. They're here because their self-righteousness and absolute arrogance that their beliefs are the one truth have overshadowed the number one thing that is supposed to make us Christians—acting as Jesus would have."

"And you think Jesus would be okay with abortion? You think he would protect those girls, encourage them to do what they're doing? Killing babies?" Now her lip trembled as she repeated what she had heard, in one form or another, since she was small girl.

"I think Jesus saw people, and He saw their pain, and He loved them, and whether or not He would have done what they had done, would have made the decisions they made, wasn't even part of the thought process. He took care of them, and He takes care of us, no matter what. He was perfect because He didn't let anything get in the way of that. And I believe that that's what Christians are charged to do. No more, no less. It's so simple, but for so many people, it's impossible. I don't want to be like everyone else. I want to do what I know is right."

Every single word rang clear, not just to her ears, but to her heart. It was like Matt had scanned Amy's soul, figured out exactly what she needed to hear to finally feel better, and said it to her in the most straightforward, wonderful way possible.

"And," Matt continued, "I don't think they're killing their babies. I think they're making a tough medical decision to keep themselves alive, in one way or another. I think they're doing what they have to do. And I think most of them do it after deep thought, and with great sorrow, but with nowhere else to turn. I want them to know that there are people out there that they can turn to, *and* I think it's very important that some of those people are doing it with the inspiration of Jesus." He shot a glance at Amy, who still bit her bottom lip, trying to keep it at least appearing steady. "And that's all I'm going to talk about theology, because as you can see, there is lots of work to do on this front. And if I keep talking I'm going to sound like a greeting card, and I know you don't want to hang out with a sappy poem of a guy. And also, if we don't hurry to get back I'm going to miss Naked and Afraid and you know how I feel about that show."

The purposeful quirk in his lip, testing her to see if everything he said was okay, made her giggle, then laugh, then start seriously, full-on crying. Tears poured down her face, snot filled her nose, and she felt unbearably awkward and one hundred percent at home all at once.

"Seriously, Amy. Are you okay?" Matt reached out and brushed a damp bang back from her face, and then something utterly otherworldly happened—his touch was electrifying, setting every part of her on edge.

"I'm okay," she nodded, trying to figure out how she

The Broken Hearts Society of Suite 17C

could ever tell Matt everything that just went through her head, had just twisted her heart. He still watched her, questioning, watchful and caring.

"Will she be okay in there?" Amy asked, blowing her nose.

"Yeah, she'll be in there for another couple of hours, and there will be another escort here to get her home. She came alone," he finished softly.

"Well," Amy said, with a whooshing sigh of relief as she watched the protesters pack up in their car and pull out of their spot, "I know how she feels. I was there, six months ago."

Matt's mouth dropped open a bit, but he quickly closed it. Clearly putting his skills as an abortion clinic expert to work. For a split second, Amy froze, terror that she may have just ruined whatever it was she'd just felt between her and Matt with that bit of information seizing her words and her breath. But in the next moment, she watched his fingers reach for hers, wrap around the back of her hand, squeeze. Warmth coursed through her as she took in a shuddering breath and started to tell her story.

She told him everything, reminding him that Adam had been the pastor's kid, and her family had been lifelong church members. They'd been together for four years, and planned to be together forever. Which was why she'd finally agreed to lose her virginity to him on prom night.

"I'd thought about it for a while," Amy said, looking down at her hand, which had stopped shaking, but had started to grow sweaty, under Matt's. She didn't care. His touch was grounding. "I'd wanted to, you know, have sex. But they'd always said it was my job to keep myself pure. For my future husband, to guard my heart and to save myself for him. But Adam had been pushing to go farther, saying that we were going to get married anyway, so what was the difference if we did it a little sooner?" She sniffed. "If I didn't really want to, I wouldn't have—I'm not weak, and I don't let other people boss me around. That doesn't mean I wasn't afraid." She shot Matt a hard look, and he nodded.

"I know," he said softly, leaving the space for her to continue.

"But, you know, it was prom. And he'd asked me, and I'd had a drink. And we knew each other so well…I loved being with him. I loved him. So we did it."

Amy thought she saw Matt's jaw twitch as he stared out the windshield, thought she saw the start of a head shake. But it was like the two of them remembered what he'd said about being judgmental at the same time, and he swallowed. "I see. So you're worried about…what? That I'll think you're a bad person for having sex? Because you shouldn't…"

"No," Amy interrupted, feeling her own hand twitch under Matt's, watching as his posture took on an edge, one that told Amy he'd heard her warning. That he needed to listen, to calm some of his own jumpiness for her sake. A sense of relief that he had almost perfectly read her signals sunk in.

"No. That's not my...issue. Not the main one." She took another deep breath, commanding her stomach to settle for the next part. She'd melted down in Matt's car. She owed him an explanation, at least. Not only that, but she wanted to give it to him.

"Well, uh...three weeks later, I was feeling a little off." She'd had cramps, lots of them, when she never had them before or during her period. And then her period hadn't come. "I'd been stressed with cheerleading and end-of-the-year stuff...getting ready for college, planning my summer. You know."

Matt nodded.

"Anyway, it was like an out of body experience. A little voice in my head kept telling me to take a pregnancy test. And it was positive."

Matt pressed his lips together and nodded, like he'd known it was coming but hated to hear it at the same time. Again, she squashed down the fear that this would change the way he looked at her, the way he felt about her. She'd started her story, and she was going to own the end of it.

"So I called Adam, and I told him. He wasn't horrible or anything—he didn't accuse me of sleeping around, or get angry—he was just really quiet for a really long time."

"Didn't you guys use a condom? I mean, I don't want to pry, but..."

"We did. But we were just guessing at how to use it,

really. We thought we'd done it right, but nobody had ever taught us, and it was late, and we'd had things to drink. Anyway." She swallowed, hard. "He said that the best thing to do would be to end it. The pregnancy," Amy explained, even though she didn't have to. "That it was so early, that it wouldn't hurt anything, but if we had the baby, he'd have to stay home and work instead of going to college. That his mom and dad would want us to get married right away, and he'd give up his scholarship, his spot on the team, our future. He's going to the NFL, you know."

Matt scoffed and stared intently out the windshield again.

"He said that if we got an abortion, we'd be protecting our future. And that we'd have a house full of babies later, and it would all be okay. That we'd make up for it." The tears started again, even though Amy had begun to numb, all over, inside and out. "I couldn't talk to my mom—I knew she'd freak out. Knowing my dad, he'd make me confess the whole thing in front of the church. There's a home in Nebraska a few girls from our church went to so they could have their babies, then give them up. I knew that's where I would end up. Either that, or in a shotgun wedding, with a miserable, resentful husband." Just the idea of Adam as a husband, after everything he'd done, made her roll her eyes. "There was just…nothing for me. No options."

"Amy, I'm…that's really awful. I'm just really sorry."

The Broken Hearts Society of Suite 17C

"That's not the worst part," she said, the tears starting to come harder. This was it—her confession. Just like always, Matt waited for it patiently. And for the last time, she worried that he'd hate her. "The worst part was that I didn't want the baby either. I felt so sick. I'd heard people say that you felt so much love, the minute you got pregnant. I just felt like something horrible had taken over my body, and was taking away my choices."

She paused to breathe for a few seconds. "Adam didn't come with me to my intake appointment at the clinic. He gave me half the money, at least. But then on the morning I had scheduled, he called and said he was sick. I don't know if he really was," she said, shrugging. "Anyway, I didn't even cry. I didn't feel anything except that I knew I was doing the right thing. Until the protesters came."

"Let me guess. There was no escort where you went."

Amy pursed her lips together, shaking her head back and forth slowly, methodically, trying to come up with the words for the end of the story. "They eased up on me when I came out after fifteen minutes. The girls having the abortions are in there for a couple hours," Amy finished softly. "That night—I don't know if it was the stress or the guilt or if I didn't love the baby and somehow, it knew. Or God knew. But I miscarried, and I never ended up going in. I tore up the papers from my intake, and after that it was like the whole thing never happened. Just like Adam said it would be. Nothing to prove what a horrible person I am."

"Amy. Ames," Matt said, sliding his hand up and around her shoulders. "Please tell me you don't believe that. Please tell me you don't think *I* believe that."

She spent several long seconds looking out the window, then said, "I don't know what I believe, not about myself. Sometimes, not even about God. But," she said as she turned to him, "now I know that we can be friends. Real friends. And I can't tell you what that means to me." The tears freshly flowed when she gave in to Matt's pulling her to him, fit her forehead in the crook of his neck, and breathed in his warmth, felt the strength of him holding her.

Eventually, the tears stopped, and she felt Matt's hold loosen. "It's dinnertime," he murmured. "Let me feed you something." She nodded, and before she could pull away, Matt buried his lips in her hair. It caught her off guard, arrested her thoughts. It wasn't something a guy who was just a friend would do, but, she decided as she slowly pulled back, it was definitely something Matt would do. Right now, that was all that mattered. She managed to pull herself from him and fall against the seat behind her, and let the rhythm of Matt's car rumbling back down the highway carry her into a deep sleep.

The Broken Hearts Society of Suite 17C

My first love broke up with me because he thought he was going to lose me to his best friend.

Jeremy was the charismatic one. He was tall and charming. He could sing. He was smart and loved to act. He played basketball and could grow facial hair. Everyone loved him. Everyone except me.

I loved Josh, Jeremy's best friend. Josh was short and funny. He could turn anything into a joke. He was sarcastic and irreverent. He loved his baby sister with a passion. He looked like his daddy. He had eyes that scrunched at the corners and hands that engulfed mine, and he made me feel so so safe and special. He told me he wanted to marry me. He even gave me his mother's engagement ring as a promise ring.

After college, he promised.

But Josh had always felt inferior to Jeremy. Jeremy was popular and Josh was too, in his own right. But he didn't have girls fawning over him. He had me. Just me. I wasn't popular. I was small with big hair and too-pale skin and poor parents. But Josh loved me and that was okay.

I was friends with Jeremy purely because he was friends with Josh. Jeremy was friendly to me. He lived nearby so he occasionally gave me rides to school. I don't think he would have if I hadn't been Josh's girlfriend. Jeremy was a bit stuck-up. His daddy made me feel uncomfortable. When I told my teachers he'd made me feel weird, they told me to ignore it. He's like that with all the females.

One afternoon, Jeremy told me he was going to pick me up early for school because our choir was going to a competition. He wanted breakfast so he was going to drive through McDonalds and figured it'd be easier to get me and we'd both go. Josh, who wasn't in the choir, interpreted this to mean Jeremy was trying to steal me. Josh showed up at my house that night and asked me if I was going to leave him for Jeremy. I said no.

He didn't believe me.

So he left first. He asked for the ring back and left me first so I couldn't hurt him.

He was my first boyfriend. He was the first boy I ever loved. And the first one I ever cried myself to sleep over.

~Tristina Wright

Chapter 15

Arielle

It had been the longest week of Arielle's life. Technically it had only been four days and fourteen hours. Not that she was counting. She'd gone through a brutal cycle every 24 hours or so since she'd last seen Lauren, one that started with relative cheeriness and coffee, usually involved some moony doodling or daydreaming at inappropriate times during class, and ended with her laying on the floor of the dorm, trying to focus on some stupid reality show, *Naked and Afraid*, which Amy had inexplicably started watching, trying to distract herself.

The weekend had made things complicated. For one, Arielle had way too much free time, since she hadn't ever actually signed up for any of those things she'd collected fliers for all the way back at the involvement fair. Probably because she'd been too consumed by crushing grief.

This morning, that sadness was nothing more than an annoying twinge. Funny how the deep, desperate pain of getting dumped by Rachel had been largely numbed by making out with a beautiful girl in the rain.

For another, Arielle's main mission was to catch sight of Lauren over the weekend, and not to admit how pathetic her plan was to her roommates. She'd declared to her roommates that she wouldn't turn into a crazy Lauren-stalker over the agonizing five-day wait, and they'd sworn to hold her to that promise. Now, of course, all Arielle wanted to do was lay eyes on Lauren again, be close to her for even just a minute. But she'd look totally pathetic if she just sat in different locations all around campus by herself, and she didn't have any friends at this godforsaken school other than Amy and Rion.

Rion had to work Saturday afternoon, but agreed to hang out with Arielle for brunch. "How did you know this existed?" Arielle asked, sliding into a shining red melamine booth across from Rion, who looked strange without her usual pounds of eye makeup.

Rion yawned. "Came here with Crash."

"This is where he took you?" Arielle's eyebrow flicked up. Rion had told her Crash had taken her out, but she hadn't said he'd taken her to such a normal place. From what Arielle and Amy had been able to tell, not very much about Crash was normal, including the one thing that meant that Rion would date him—he was totally, one hundred percent clean. In fact, Rion had been largely

The Broken Hearts Society of Suite 17C

stony-faced in the last Society meeting, and had skipped the part about the restaurant to tell them how amazing Crash's art was, his romantic gesture with the picture painting, and how she'd ended up in bed with him on the first date. She'd ended by telling them how he'd made fun of her, and how mortified she'd been.

Because of this, Arielle had no real clue whether to put the guy on her shit list or on her "thank God she met you" list. Rion had been unsettled since then, distractible and cranky. It was all adding up to something, Arielle just couldn't figure out what.

Nevertheless, she would not have imagined Crash, with tattoos up to his ears and down to his fingertips, stretched ear holes, and a job in a head shop, to take a girl out for a first date to a pancake place. But all those thoughts moved to the backburner when Arielle saw the incredible array of pancake flavor choices on the menu. A plate full of carbs drenched in liquid sugar was the siren song of any good, solid Midwestern girl, and Arielle was no exception. She ordered a stack of three, don't bother with the eggs, please, and another cup of coffee when the waitress had a chance.

When she and Rion grinned at each other and shoved the first bites into their mouths, Arielle closed her eyes and, for the first time in days, felt relaxed. She couldn't help but wonder if Rion had taken her to this place simply because it was on Francis, and away from campus. They'd gotten close enough that Arielle thought she could call her on it. "So," Arielle mumbled with a half-full mouth, "Spill. Did you bring me here because you figured there was no way she'd be off campus?"

"Who?" Rion said, smiling and batting her eyes innocently.

Arielle grinned and took a swig of lukewarm coffee. For as fluffy and rich as the pancakes were, the coffee could use a little bit of work to get near to mediocre. "You know perfectly well who," Arielle said. And then, out the plate-glass window of The Hole in the Wall Diner, passed a group of three people. There was a man with salt-and-pepper hair and a polo shirt tucked into his pants, and a woman two heads shorter than him with pearls and a matching cardigan and shell—pretty much exactly what she would have expected to see Mom wearing. And, walking between them, those absolutely unmistakable tall, curves and shining black hair. "Lauren," she breathed, and before Rion could finish her sentence of "Of course I know who you were talking about, you idiot, you only—" she was out of her seat, hurrying the twenty steps to the door, and pressing her palms against the cool metal handlebar to open it. Then, again, the name came out into the crisp, clear air—"Lauren!"

God, the swing of her hair. She was like a goddamn Pantene commercial, and looking at her now, Arielle was ready to buy stock in the stuff. Even though, with her mess of curls, washing her hair more than twice a week was like asking to be a social pariah. It didn't matter. Any potential embarrassment at shouting down the street to a girl she'd barely known a few weeks and barely kissed once was erased as Lauren's smile pulled out the dimple that told Arielle it was genuine.

"Arielle! Hey!" Lauren's feet stayed planted on the sidewalk, and realizing just how quickly this could turn awkward, Arielle hurried to erase the distance between them by trotting up to her. The smiles on the two other people's faces were not as glowy as Lauren's, though still there. Within a second and half, Arielle took in their still-slightly-summery outfits, remembered that Lauren was not only from California, where such clothing would be typical this time of year, but also adopted, and realized who they were.

"Mom and Dad?" Arielle asked Lauren, smiling nervously between the three of them.

"Yeah," Lauren smiled, her voice sounding a little breathy and distracted, even though she wasn't the one who had just trotted down two storefronts' worth of concrete in super cute, but unbelievably uncomfortable, flats.

The smile stayed on Lauren's face for a couple seconds of eye-locking with Arielle. The excited, happy, make-you-walk-on-a-cloud butterflies rioted in Arielle's stomach. She felt like she was on edge and floating on air at the same time. How could she have been stupid enough to try to push these feelings away? And, just like that, the reality switch flipped.

"Mom, Dad...this is Arielle."

Another weird half-second pause, then Lauren's dad offered her a solid, friendly handshake. Then her mom. But something was off in their smiles, and as Lauren's mom shot her a side glance, Arielle knew what it was. Lauren hadn't mentioned her. In the nine weeks they'd already been in class, having lunch together at least once a week, flirting, touching, and kissing, Lauren hadn't said a word about her. And she'd probably already introduced her parents to her friends, the ones who worked with her at the rec center or were in her other classes. Maybe there was a boy in her residence hall that Lauren had already introduced to them to. Maybe her parents assumed that they were dating. Maybe...

"We met in women's studies class, and we have the same lunch break. So we've been spending a lot of time together."

Arielle snapped back to attention. Lauren had taken the lead. That was something, wasn't it?

"Good thing, too," Arielle said, "because I am not going back to that kickboxing class. It was good, but I'm not going back."

"You're teaching kickboxing?" Lauren's mom pushed an eyebrow up. "I thought it was karate. Or at least Muay thai."

"Mom, you know that was never my thing. I—whatever. It doesn't matter. I'm a freshman, and I'm lucky they let me teach *any* class." There was a certain finality to

The Broken Hearts Society of Suite 17C

Lauren's words, a way she nodded her head curtly and looked to the ground, that seemed to communicate to her parents that the conversation was over. At least for now. "Anyway," she said, "Arielle's kidding. She *is* coming back to my kickboxing class."

"No way," Arielle laughed, her heart beating a mile a minute. "I was hopeless. A total wreck. It's not as easy as Lauren makes it look, learning where to put your feet and when and how to turn your belly button to the floor, and where to start your punch. Way too much for me to remember. Not to mention that anything remotely related to exercise is a recipe for total disaster to me. Regardless, it means Lauren is genuinely a wonderful teacher for her to have gotten the position. She's really amazing."

Arielle couldn't help it. When she said the last sentence, her eyes drifted to Lauren's, filled with a hundred thoughts, emotions, and most of all, questions. Watching Lauren's eyes flare, her smile grow to a grin, and her chin tuck to her chest until she could get it back under control, was all the encouragement she needed. This was something more than a kiss in the rain, than hands sliding down hips when they had a good excuse. It had to be.

Suddenly Lauren looked up at her mom. "Didn't you guys need to stop at the bank? There's one right there," she said, brushing her dad's forearm and smiling up at him with the most obvious 'Daddy's little girl' expression that Arielle had ever seen. But, damn her, she found it absolutely adorable. Maybe it was the curve of Lauren's butt under her long skirt, maybe it was the dimple that looked like she'd pulled it out just for her dad. And it totally worked, too. "I'll wait for you here. I have some plans to figure out with Arielle for tomorrow anyway."

Had she just admitted that they were going out? *Were* they going out? Would Lauren say the same thing about her friends? Arielle would, but her parents knew everything about her friends, including which of them she liked more than friends.

Back home they had, anyway.

But Arielle knew one thing for sure. Lauren's parents crossed the street to the ATM and she became enchanted by the way Lauren's perfectly straight teeth bit her smooth, glossed bottom lip. She couldn't let this girl slip away from her because she was assuming the worst. She wasn't going to let Rachel, or the memory of how badly Rachel had mangled her every emotion, take something new, something so potentially amazing, away from her.

"They're in this weekend because they're going to be out of town for Thanksgiving," Lauren explained. "They won't get to see me then, so they said they wanted to see me now. I think it's been good for them. Especially Dad."

Arielle soaked up every word. Lauren was close to her dad, much more than her mom. They were out of town for Thanksgiving, which meant Lauren wouldn't be in California for Thanksgiving. Where would she be? Would she stay here, like Harry Potter at Hogwarts for

The Broken Hearts Society of Suite 17C

Christmas? She looked so pretty with a pea coat on. How would she react if Arielle touched her hair? So many disjointed thoughts flew around in her head, but added up to nothing. So Arielle just said the first coherent thing she could manage: "Can I see you tonight? I…I've been hoping I'd see you. I mean…ever since…you know…I didn't want to wait until class to see you again."

Lauren's mouth crinkled up, turned down in one corner. "They're here till tomorrow morning. I'm supposed to give them a tour of campus, and then they're taking me out to dinner."

Everything in Arielle screamed "I could come too! I love dinner! Let me be part of your life!" but then the memory of how quickly and how hard she'd fallen head over heels for Rachel arrested her thoughts. Hanging out at Rachel's house, letting her mom see how in love she was. Making plans—big plans. Meeting parents, hanging out with parents, was something that happened after like three months in most normal relationships. Three months of normal-relationship stuff, which included, but was certainly not limited to, making out pressed up against the brick wall of your dorm room. Hopefully many more times.

So she gave an understanding smile and said, "Okay. Well, it was good to—"

"But Sunday," Lauren rushed in. "Sunday, I could…I mean, we could…hang out, or whatever. If you wanted to."

"Sunday as in tomorrow," Arielle said.

Lauren shot a glance over her shoulder. Her parents were making their way back across the street. "Tomorrow," she said, stepping forward and crushing Arielle in a hug without warning. She was so warm, so soft. Smelled so damn good. "I don't want to wait until next week either," Lauren said low in her ear, tickling Arielle's ear with her breath and sending her heart into a tailspin of palpitations again.

Then, as quickly as she hugged her, Lauren stepped back.

"Everything set, girls?" Lauren's mom said, clearly trying to be casual, but looking between them for information at the same time.

"Yep," they said at the same time, and Lauren giggled when they did. God, she was so freaking adorable.

But Arielle knew that she couldn't keep staring, because this could get really awkward really fast. She forced her feet to move, one at a time, turning away from Lauren and heading back down to the cafe, where, thank God, at least she could talk to a Society member about the worlds of important things that had just happened in the last two minutes.

"See you then," Arielle called back over her shoulder, remembering at the last second to add, "Great to meet you!" and a short, totally lame wave to Lauren's parents. She forced herself to focus on not letting her feet step on each other, so she wouldn't fall on her face, make Lauren rush over, and start the whole goodbye awkwardness all over again.

Arielle hadn't even realized how cold it was outside until she got back into the warmth of the cafe, and slumped into the booth. Rion's eyes turned into saucers as she leaned back to take Arielle in. "Whoa there, lady. What is this Lauren person doing to you?"

A huge breath whooshed, letting relief in. "She's just…I mean she's so…" There was the goofy grin again. "If you met her, you'd get it."

Rion snorted. "Okay. Whatever you say."

"You would! She's so gorgeous, and she's funny, she's so smart, and it's like she gets me, you know?"

"And she has a hot ass, I assume?"

"And she smells amazing," Arielle concluded, slumping moonily to the side and leaning her head against the wall.

"Jesus Christ, you have it bad," Rion said, shaking her head.

"We'll see," Arielle replied, still in a dreamland where she was imagining feeling Lauren's lips against hers again, almost felt her hands clutch at the soft curve of her waist.

"Remember your promise, okay? I mean, Jesus, Ari. After what that bitch Rachel did to you, you just really need to make sure…"

"Lauren's not in the closet." But even as Arielle said it, snippets of the last two times they'd spoken replayed in her mind. Lauren might not be in the closet, but between having a recent relationship with a guy, not kissing Arielle hello when she'd just seen her, and a couple of other, minuscule, almost not worth mentioning things? She definitely wasn't out, either. "Well, not totally in. And high school is, like, half a country away."

"Yeah, and less than half a year away," Rion said, turning a serious look on Arielle. "If she was fucking a guy mere months ago…I don't know. It makes me nervous."

"I don't know how long ago she did…you know…all of that." Arielle sat upright again, her buzz effectively killed, and started stacking silverware on their empty dishes. "Whatever. It's just the beginning. It's not like we're getting married or anything." *Not yet.*

"Exactly. It's still early. So let me be your parachute, okay Casanova? It's a Society duty. You helped me, I helped you."

"Helped you how? Serving as an audience while you publicly humiliated your boyfriend?"

Rion smirked and shook her head. "Literally nothing is true about that sentence. But yes. You are looking out for me with Crash, so I'm looking out for you with Miss Pretty Perfume Shop. Okay? I trust you one hundred percent to tell me if you see Crash getting trashed, with beer, pot, or otherwise. Or see any sign of it. Or, hell, even *smell* it."

"Yeah, yeah. I get it."

"So I want you to trust me to tell you if I see you getting in over your head with a girl who isn't even sure if

The Broken Hearts Society of Suite 17C

she likes girls. And I know she made out with you, and I know she's sweet, but it was the same story with that fucking bitch Rachel. That's all I'm saying. If your heart gets broken, it's my fault. Society Rules."

Arielle grabbed her bag and stood up. "Society Rules," she repeated, nodding a genuine smile at Rion. "But I really think it'll be okay." She threw down a twenty for the bill and tip, and headed for the door.

"Are you going to do *anything* to figure her out? Or are you just going to fall so deeply into the tar pit of love with a maybe-lesbian before you figure out just how sure she is?"

Arielle held the door and Rion ducked under her arm. Maybe her abrasiveness helped make up for her utterly teeny size.

"When I figure out the certified lesbian screening process, I'll let you know," Arielle mumbled as she walked against the kicking-up wind, head bowed down, back to Harrison. If only it were that easy.

"Well, that's easy," Amy said, her mouth distorted in that gaping frown that girls seemed to universally get when applying eyeliner. "Take her out on a date. Like, in public."

Arielle stared at Amy in the bathroom mirror, where the three girls stood together late Sunday morning, with her eyebrow up.

"No, that won't work," Rion countered, smearing pink eyeshadow, which seemed to only look good on Rion, over her eyelids. "Because, whatever. Girls go out together all the time, friends or otherwise. That won't tell her anything about Lauren's pride status or whatever."

"I wasn't finished," Amy said, starting in on the mascara. Arielle grinned. Maybe Amy didn't notice that she'd become more assertive in the two months they'd been here, but it was obvious to anyone who spent enough time with her. There was a world of difference between the scared, innocent freshman who arrived at the door of empty Suite 17C and the girl getting ready for church, which was really a date, with a completely different guy than she'd imagined spending her college free time with.

"When you're out with her, hold hands with her."

Arielle raised an eyebrow. "So you want me to make the first move."

Amy nodded. "Yes. Well, no. I mean, she kind of already did. She's the one who kissed you, right?"

Arielle smiled. "Yeah."

"Not only that," Rion said, reaching for a tube of lipstick on the other side of their counter, "She chased after you. So maybe that's like a mega first move."

"Not in public, though," Arielle whined, backing against the cool painted cinderblock that made up every wall in this place, it seemed. "She ran after me, but in a courtyard where nobody could see."

"You're overthinking it," Amy said, leaning against the wall and crossing her arms over her chest.

"Yeah, Amy's right. Besides, this is your test. You're the one who's Miss *all lesbian all the time and whoever I date has to be too*. It's kind of your duty," Rion said, pressing her lips together and doing a duck face in the mirror.

Rion had a point. Arielle had never seen anyone take more initiative with pre-screening guys to date than Rion. It was kind of admirable—and definitely something that would totally freak out a polite, non-confrontational Midwestern girl. How did they feel about confrontation in California? Did that even matter in this context? "God, why do I know nothing about dating?" Arielle growled, pushing her fingers back through her hair and catching the curls on her fingers. "Goddamn hair."

"It looks good," Amy said, picking up some of her ruddy, stick straight strands between the tips of her fingers and glaring at them. "Mine is so flat it makes me crazy."

"It looks like a rat's nest. But thanks."

"Just cut it off," Rion mused. "It's changed my life." Rion had chopped all her hair off a few days ago, not seeming to think any more about it than she thought about brushing her teeth at night.

"Yeah, in that you look like more of a lesbian than I do."

"Well maybe you wouldn't get yourself in so deep with gorgeous, charming California girls if you looked more dykey. Just saying," Rion said, swiping on lip gloss and tossing it back into Amy's bag. She moved behind Ari and squeezed her shoulders like a boxing coach does before a fight.

"Point taken," Arielle muttered. "Where are you going?"

"Work!" Rion sang, practically skipping out of the bathroom.

"Well tone it down, Mary Sunshine. You don't want Crash thinking you were body snatched."

One of Rion's flip flops came flying back into the bathroom, narrowly missing Arielle's ear. She shook her head, smiling, and ran a toothbrush through her mouth. She had some planning work to do.

Arielle stood outside Harrison, shuffling her feet, more to quell her nervousness than to stave off the cold that whipped through the corridor of uniform dorms like it was a wind tunnel. She'd spent about three hours scrolling through online reviews and menus, trying to figure out the perfect place for a first date, and settled on a trendy Thai place on Francis. It was a tough balance

The Broken Hearts Society of Suite 17C

between too basic and too fancy, too trendy and too typical. Things like messy burger joints were for later in the relationship, and super fancy places were for first anniversaries. Especially when you were only eighteen.

Jesus, Ari. Rion was right. Tone it the hell down. You made out with a girl, and it was amazing, and then she gave you a flirty smile and agreed to go out with you. It doesn't mean anything except exactly what it means.

Somewhere in the whole intense research process, Lauren had texted her. Lauren. Had texted her. She still glanced at that first contact like it was a gold medal. "We still on for tonight?" With a rose beside it. What did that even mean? Roses weren't just for friends, right?

Okay. She was going to make herself crazy like this.

Arielle finally picked up her phone and replied—she didn't want to look too desperate—and said, "Sure. Meet in the courtyard? 6?" Just thinking about standing in that spot with Lauren again made Arielle shiver. She pulled on her coat, checked her hair, which Amy had helped her tame into smoother curls, and headed out the door.

Lauren stood in the middle of the courtyard, her long legs fidgeting in dark jeans under a cream colored pea coat. That she looked absolutely stunning was no surprise, and her humungous smile at seeing Arielle set her heart at ease. Arielle stretched up on tiptoes to give Lauren a hug, consciously letting Lauren's movements dictate how long and hard they would hug. Again, it was sweet, just long enough for Arielle to feel Lauren's chest press into hers.

But when she pulled back down, Lauren drew her arms up to gently cup Arielle's face, and before Arielle could even think about how her feet were positioned, who was taking the lead, or what it all meant, Lauren's lips pressed so softly against hers it made her want to cry. This girl was sweet in every way, and standing in a dorm courtyard with her, and holding her. A soft 'mmm" came from Arielle's throat, and she forced herself to drop back down, breaking the kiss.

Arielle bit her lip and smiled up at Lauren. "Okay," she said, breathing out and grinning up at her. "I have plans. I mean, I made plans."

Lauren cocked her head. "You did? Really?"

"Yeah, is that okay?" A little hint of nervousness crept onto the cloud Arielle was floating on.

A slow smile curved Lauren's lips. "Sure," she said, nodding and shoving her hands into her pockets. Dammit, that would make it hard to try to hold her hand. "Where to?"

"Um, just...up on Francis."

"I'll follow you," Lauren said. It was so hard not to hear the double entendre there. Could it be that Lauren really was waiting for her to set the tone and pace of their relationship? Did she want a relationship at all? She had to, if she had been the first one to kiss her. Right?

The girls made small talk as they hiked the sidewalk's steep slope, bending their heads to minimize the wind whipping back against their faces. Arielle watched

The Broken Hearts Society of Suite 17C

Lauren's long strands flying up and around her with every step, even into her mouth. Every time Lauren reached up to pull one out, it took Arielle an extra second to force herself to focus on something other than Lauren's lips. Thank God Francis was really only a block and a half away.

Finally, they turned onto the street, which had a fair amount of college students milling around. Probably trying to postpone the end of the weekend as long as possible, even if it wasn't a great time to be drinking. The ice cream parlor was full despite the near-freezing temperatures, and even the obscure art galleries were full of patrons.

"I can't believe they started decorating for Christmas already," Lauren said, pointing at the string lights that roped around the light poles and the shining chrome ornaments that hung from the tops. "Oh, hey. Does that bother you? Because, you know…"

"Because I'm Jewish?" Arielle smiled. "Nah, not really. I mean, I know everyone around here is Christian. The fact that I don't really see all the shiny holiday stuff as mine doesn't mean I can't think it's pretty. You know?"

"I can't believe you said that," Lauren said, shaking her head. "That is literally how I always felt. Like it wasn't mine."

"Christmas? Don't you guys do Christmas?"

"Yeah, just like all Americans do. But growing up without very much religion…I don't know. The holiday just seemed to sort of be about cheesy songs and shiny ornaments, and tacky sweaters and parties. And spending too much money on presents and food and alcohol nobody needed. You know?"

"Sort of, I guess. But people are nicer to each other during the holidays, right? That's cheery. I suppose."

Lauren shrugged. "The fact that there was no snow in California didn't exactly help the holiday spirit. And the commercialism...it just felt foreign. There are, like, no Asian people in any of those ads. It sounds stupid, but it always felt like I was an outsider, even when like all of America was coming together to do something. Is that ridiculous?"

"It's like, the opposite of ridiculous," Arielle laughed. "You just described my whole life. Nothing applies to me. Like, I'm an outsider in every possible way. Not even regular dating rules apply to me."

She hadn't meant to say it, but it perfectly described every single frustration of the last 24 hours. Which felt a lot longer than that, for what it was worth. She snuck a glance up at Lauren. Had she caught Arielle's meaning? What would she say back?

Lauren caught her bottom lip between her teeth and gave a half-bob of her head. "I guess. I...well, I'm still trying to figure all that out too. For what it's worth."

Well, that wasn't a total loss. Arielle tried to distract herself from the conversation that she had started by looking for the restaurant. "So, I found this place..."

Arielle looked down at her phone, realizing she had no clue how to pronounce the name of it. "It's Thai, it looked good, and it should be…"

"Um. Is it the one with the ridiculous line stretching halfway back to campus?"

Arielle looked up and checked the sign. "Holy shit," she breathed. Lauren hadn't been exaggerating. "What the hell is going on?"

"It's okay," Lauren laughed. "Let's go check it out."

Over half the people standing in line were students. What the hell had she missed?

"Excuse me," Lauren said to one of the people near the end of the line. "What are we all waiting for? Is Elvis in there or something?"

"Better," the tall guy she'd asked said. "It's Bahn Li from Chop Your Heart Out, you know, that reality show? Anyone who makes it in before eleven gets a spring roll he made himself."

"Before *eleven*?" Arielle choked. It was six now, and even though she was excited to spend time with Lauren, she had fully planned on being crashed out by eleven. Next morning's eight-thirty class was hard enough to get out of bed for as it was.

Arielle craned her neck at the line, trying to figure for herself how long it would take to get in. Pointless, she knew. She'd envisioned a quiet night, sitting and talking over noodles she would probably end up slurping. And it would be okay. No matter how much she'd embarrassed herself so far, Lauren hadn't seemed to care.

But she'd been letting that daydream run through her head ever since they'd made plans, and now it wasn't going to happen.

"What do you think?" Arielle asked Lauren. "Do you want to wait?"

"Well, you picked the place. Are you going to be upset if we go?"

"I didn't even...I mean, I don't really know much about the place," Arielle admitted with a chuckle, staring at her feet. She was pretty sure, but not completely certain, that this was a date. How much to admit to her nervous date planning? "I sort of...well, honestly?"

"Honestly is good," Lauren said, watching her.

"I wanted it to be nice. I wanted to impress you. You know?"

Lauren bit her bottom lip, smiling a little. "That's sweet," she said, nudging her shoulder into Arielle's.

"But?" Arielle asked, watching as Lauren kept fidgeting, feeling the extra warmth from her being a couple inches closer. A little body heat against hers made her realize just how cold it really was.

"But it's freaking freezing out here," Lauren said, checking Arielle's eyes. More a statement than a question. She nudged closer to Arielle and Arielle did the same back. Now they stood, arm to arm, and Arielle felt an unmistakable surge of bravery.

The Broken Hearts Society of Suite 17C

"Can we still hang out even if we leave? I still want to spend time with you."

"Me too," Lauren said softly, moving her head a fraction of an inch closer to Arielle's. Then, suddenly, she stopped, her eyes darting around the crowd.

Arielle could taste the almost-kiss—not just how much she would love it, but what it would mean—Lauren, the maybe-lesbian, kissing a girl in front of everyone. It was a test, and when Lauren stopped, she had failed.

But, over Arielle's disappointment was layered something else. It was a little voice at the back of her mind, telling her she could walk away from Lauren, from all the stress and confusion, if she wanted. Of course she could. But if she did, she would really, really regret it.

So she decided to open herself up. Put it out there. She couldn't possibly be more heartbroken than she'd been when Rachel had left her less than two months ago, could she?

Sure she could, if the girl who had given her a little hope, had brought something unexpected and fun and amazing into what, by all accounts, should have been a shitty year, turned her down for a kiss in front of hundreds of their peers.

But maybe Lauren needed space to do it. Maybe Lauren needed this date just as much as Arielle needed to know just how gay Lauren was.

So Arielle craned her neck down the street again, this time the opposite direction. Sunday night, and this sleepy town had mostly shut down. Well, except for the two places that never shut down—McDonald's, and Starbucks.

"Looks like those are our choices," Arielle said, gesturing at the two.

Lauren made sure to speak the next words looking directly into Arielle's eyes "I'm starving. You told me not to eat."

"Me too," Arielle said, disappointed. She'd been envisioning a dark, quiet corner of Starbucks, not too different from the Thai restaurant which had so annoyingly insisted on hosting what's-his-name on the one night she'd gotten brave enough to ask Lauren out. But she was hungry. "McDonald's it is."

Lauren laughed and shook her head as she stepped out onto the sidewalk, waiting for Arielle to get to her side before starting to walk. "I'm totally going for a bacon double cheeseburger. I mean, if you're going to eat at McDonald's, you should do it right."

Arielle bobbed her head. "Whatever you say. I'm getting the usual."

"As if I know what that is."

Arielle smiled to herself.

"You're not gonna tell me?"

By then, they'd arrived. "Here, you'll see." Arielle stepped up to the counter, wincing in the bright fluorescent lights. She'd done her eye makeup for this date, for dim, subdued lighting. She didn't even know how to do eye makeup for McDonald's, because nobody would

The Broken Hearts Society of Suite 17C

ever go on a date to McDonald's, and oh holy shit, this was so ridiculous.

"What can I get for you girls?" the bored worker asked, clearly overloaded from a long weekend of loitering college kids. Her eyes flashed to the clock on the wall.

"Are you closing soon?" Lauren asked.

"An hour. You have plenty of time."

Arielle's heart sank. An hour at McDonald's wasn't a date, it was a study break. Still, she ordered for Lauren and her, shooting Lauren a surprised smile when she added an extra order of fries and a vanilla milkshake to her order. "How do you keep your body in such amazing shape when you eat like that?" Arielle asked, motioning to the tray full of junk food. Lauren scooted into a booth, her long legs jutting out on either side of the pole that held the shining melamine tabletop in place. First thing, she pulled the plastic top off her vanilla milkshake, grabbed five fries, pinched them together with her fingertips, and plunged them into the milkshake like a giant straw.

Arielle was mesmerized, as usual with Lauren, by so many things at once. The way her fingers moved against her lips, the way her eyes fluttered closed with a particularly delicious bite, all of it was the most fascinating thing Arielle had ever seen.

Then Lauren focused on Arielle again. "Huh?" she said, as though the milkshake and fries had been so amazing that she literally hadn't been able to think about anything else while the food was in her mouth. And then Arielle just started thinking about her mouth again.

But she laughed, utterly contented to be in Lauren's company, in this spot. "I asked how you keep that body when you eat like this?"

Lauren shrugged. "Genes? I don't know. I'm already a freak of nature. I'm five eight. I'm like a giant among the Chinese."

"I guess your height is kind of a white person thing," Arielle said absentmindedly.

Lauren scowled. "Yep. Just one more addition to the anomaly that is me."

"Hey," Arielle said, sensing the mood becoming serious. "Don't do that. You're…you. And that's really good."

"Yeah? Even if I can't, like, settle down anywhere? Fit into one single mold that I'm supposed to?"

"Not true," Arielle said, faking an air of superiority. "You're an Asian medical student. Bam. Stereotype fulfilled."

Lauren laughed. God, that smile could keep Arielle going through miles of doubt about most stuff. Wasn't that how she'd gotten herself into this situation? Being so bewitched by Lauren's stupid flashing smile and gorgeous hair that she just did stupid things like planning dates for girls that weren't even gay? *Focus, Ari.* "But seriously, what do you mean?"

The Broken Hearts Society of Suite 17C

"Oh, just what I said before," Lauren said as she took a huge bite of her double bacon cheeseburger. "It never used to bother me that much, you know? I mean the Chinese kid not fitting into being white, really, but not being Chinese either. I always knew something was off about me. But it's like being here at Northern amplifies it." She paused, like she was about to say something else, then dug into her fries again.

Arielle used the excuse of needing to chew and swallow to give her time to think. "What does that mean? You're happy here, right?"

"Well, you know how I feel about women's studies class," Lauren laughed. They spent the next several minutes re-hashing the events of that week's class, which had been entirely composed of discussion on the politics of breasts.

"So, obviously, yes. I feel the same way. About women's studies," Arielle said. But what do you mean, that there's something off about you? Or that Northern amplifies it?"

"Well, you know. There are just a lot of…questions. About where I fit in. Chinese, American, feminist, doctor…. And it's like I feel all this pressure to make a choice, like I'll lose something if I don't. You know? But I don't know how to make that choice, or even to figure out what the choice is." Lauren's face twisted in something like uncertainty and something like pain. And the overwhelming need to make it better washed over Arielle, a sensation she'd never felt before.

Maybe because she knew Lauren was talking about her, too.

"Are you talking about what I asked you the other night?" Of course she was. Part of Arielle wanted her to declare a change of heart, wanted her to be a full-on lesbian, ready for a committed relationship and a lifestyle declaration, a coming-out ceremony to her parents over Thanksgiving, and maybe some grand gesture of love in the middle of the quad when Springtime finally hit.

Yeah. Arielle was getting way ahead of herself.

"Sort of. There's, like…a lot I want to say. A lot I'm feeling, after that night, and I don't know what I can say or how I should say it."

"Why not?" Arielle asked softly, already partly knowing the answer.

"Because I really like spending time with you. I really like *you*," Lauren said, casting her eyes down and crumpling up an unsuspecting napkin that lingered on the table.

"So?" A swell of emotion forced Arielle's hand across the table to cover Lauren's. Lauren flinched against her touch, but in a split second, her hand softened, and she gently squeezed back.

"So I don't want to ruin it…whatever 'it' is…but I don't want to lie to you, Ari." Her easy use of the nickname warmed Arielle's heart.

The Broken Hearts Society of Suite 17C

"So don't. Tell me what you're thinking." The words rushed out of Ari's mouth before she could even think about the courage it took to say them. She didn't want to know what Lauren was thinking. She wanted Lauren to be a copy of Rachel.

Which, she realized as she thought it, was really freaking unfair. And, besides, she didn't want to be with any girl who thought it was okay to break up with her like Rachel had, or to act like that, ever again.

"I had a boyfriend in high school."

"I know. You told me."

"Yeah, and then you ran away from me." Lauren looked at their hands, still joined on the top of the cheap plastic table. "So obviously that's not okay."

"I mean, it's…"

"I get it, okay? You had your heart broken, and…I don't want to make you feel like she did. Ever again."

"I'm okay," Arielle said, and for the first time, she really believed those words. "I'm okay," she repeated. "And I'm here at McDonalds, the crappiest restaurant in town, with you because I just want to hang out with you, and I didn't want to wait until after class. It was too long."

Lauren smiled, then looked down at their hands again. "I had sex with him," she said quietly. "A lot. We…just had a lot of sex."

Something stung at Arielle's chest, spreading numbness throughout her body. She swallowed, somehow feeling like that would force her creeping tears back. She'd figured they'd had sex, even told Rion she was almost certain they had, but hearing it from Lauren made it so much more real.

"Arielle," Lauren said with a sharp edge to her voice, forcing Arielle to look up. "I want to be honest with you, okay?" she blew out a breath, and before waiting for Arielle's response, said, "I liked it. A lot."

Arielle gave a sharp laugh. "Well, I guess that's why you did it so much. So what the hell are you doing…here? I mean, what are *we* doing?" Arielle forced some kindness into her voice, despite the fact that the words were accusing. Paranoid, maybe.

Lauren leaned forward, reaching her hand out and brushing her fingers gently down Arielle's jawline. Arielle shivered. "Like I said. I like you. And I know you've been hurt, and I respect that. But I couldn't just let you go. When you kissed me…when I kissed you back…I felt something that I'd never felt. Like you'd reached into some part of me that nobody had even ever seen before. That nobody had ever tried to see."

Arielle raised her eyes to Lauren's, so close to hers now, so beautiful, that she could have cried. "And?"

"And I want more."

That was it. Arielle pushed forward, pressing her lips into Lauren's. A small whimper that sounded like surprise and relief all at once came from Lauren, and if Arielle hadn't been using her arm to push herself across the table, she would have pushed her fingers through Lauren's hair, letting them tangle there and then slip through, like she'd daydreamed almost constantly since the last time. God, Lauren was so soft and so perfect, so completely wonderful that this should be a dream.

Maybe it was. That's what she had been trying to tell Arielle, wasn't it? Maybe Lauren didn't even have an ounce of lesbian in her, and maybe she couldn't really ever love Arielle like Arielle wanted to love someone—madly and deeply enough to be not just smitten, but devoted, for a lifetime. But then Lauren's tongue flicked out along her bottom lip, giving Arielle just a taste of something even more intense, and every stray thought left Arielle's head again.

Until seconds later, when a rough, rasping throat broke through the haze. Arielle pulled away, trying to steady her breathing and memorize the feeling of Lauren's lips against hers, never wanting to forget how one touch could take her away from everything.

One problem with Lauren—Arielle never knew whether there would be a next time. Would she ever?

Lauren had already sat fully back in her seat, and when Arielle snapped out of her daze, she realized why. Some skinny, pimply kid stood there at their table, shuffling from foot to foot, sneaking glances at them. "Can we help you?" Arielle asked.

"Ah…I'm sorry to disturb you. It's just that…"

"You don't want to see that kind of thing in here? Is that it?" Arielle was in attack mode now. She'd been brave enough to set this date up, brave enough to kiss a girl who wasn't even really hers in public. Brave enough to try to convince Lauren that Arielle was what she wanted, fast food restaurant be damned.

"No, Ari." Lauren leaned her head into the restaurant, empty except for a couple of workers, one turning out lights behind the ordering counter and the other wiping down tables in the main eating area. "They're closing up."

"Just because it's Sunday, we're closing at seven...ah...I'm sorry about that." Arielle's eyes flicked down the to the guy's pants, which weren't too far below her face, the awkward way he was standing. Poor kid. He had a boner the size of Texas. She smirked, satisfied that she and Lauren at least looked damn hot when they were making out.

When Lauren stood to take her tray to the trash, Arielle started to collect her things. Arielle shoved her arms in her jacket sleeves, slung her bag over her shoulder, pushed in her chair, and grabbed Lauren's bag for her. When Lauren walked back to the table from dumping their trash into the bin, she reached out to Arielle for her bag with gentle fingers and a plain smile, the light in her eyes purely electric.

It transferred to the space between the two of them so strongly that Arielle felt like if she didn't touch Lauren again, soon, she'd burst. As so she did, reaching out to grab her hand, her heart swelling when Lauren grabbed

The Broken Hearts Society of Suite 17C

hers back, squeezing with that hand while pushing the door open with the other.

The wind whipped down Francis Street, especially cold on this early November night. Winter would be here soon, and the semester was almost over. Arielle would have to answer a million questions when she went home for Thanksgiving—*if* she went home for Thanksgiving. She knew all this, and she also knew that the girl she was rapidly falling in love with was probably completely and totally wrong for her. But when Lauren looped her long arm around Arielle's waist, pulled her close, and kissed her again, Arielle didn't care about anything else in the universe—not even the things that should have stopped her from kissing Lauren in the first place.

"What do you want to do now?" she managed when the soft press of Lauren's lips finally eased from hers. She meant what did Lauren want out of this relationship, what would happen next? Was the date over now, and if it was, would there be another one? Should they talk about this or act like it never happened. At this point, Arielle would have been ready to convince herself that making out, and eventually having sex, in secret would be just fine, as long as she never had to stop tasting Lauren, never had to stop feeling the soft warmth of Lauren's skin against her body.

"My place. I want to…I don't know exactly what, but I don't want to stop. I want to kiss you again. I want to kiss you more, and harder, and…" Lauren's words were breathy, feverish and fast. Arielle had trouble finding her breath. She wanted that too, and so much more. She wanted this all to end perfectly. Which meant she didn't want it to end at all.

"Okay," she whispered, letting her forehead touch Lauren's, watching their breath make clouds and mingle together in the frigid air.

Lauren smiled, biting her lip. "My room is all mine. Do you want to...I mean, I could make you a cup of tea or something. Help you warm up."

Arielle nodded, trying to keep her breaths even. "I want to." This time, she left the statement open-ended on purpose. She wanted so many things, and the only thing she didn't want, right at this moment, was for this to end.

"Come on," Lauren said with a smile in her eyes as she nudged open the heavy main door to Lauren's residence hall, motioning for Arielle to go in first.

"Isn't there a thing with visitors?" Arielle asked when she caught sight of the desk worker.

"There is," Lauren said under her breath, "But Phil is more interested in beating the next level of his video game than how many people are coming in. Just stay by my side and stay quiet. His peripheral vision is not stellar."

Arielle nodded, and did as Lauren asked. When they passed by the desk, Phil, a lanky kid in a hipster plaid shirt and thick orange glasses, flicked his gaze over to them for

The Broken Hearts Society of Suite 17C

a fraction of a second. "Hey Lauren," he mumbled, already engrossed in his game again.

"Hey yourself," she said. "Kill those zombies before they eat your brains."

"All the zombies want my brains," Phil said absentmindedly, and Arielle stifled a giggle.

When the elevator doors slid open, Arielle was nervous all over again. The only real relationship she'd ever had was based on closed doors, on keeping careful track of who knew, and who didn't. Who saw, what they thought. Even though Lauren had kissed her in public, now—twice–it was a reflex Arielle just couldn't shake.

Inside the elevator stood two girls, dressed to go out, which was idiotic given the frigid whipping wind. Their tight skirts could have been tube tops for all Arielle knew, and they tottered on four-inch stilettos, leaning on the walls for support. Arielle gave them the once over and fought to keep from wrinkling her nose. She'd never understood why girls did this. Did guys actually like girls who wore mere scraps of fabric in the frigid cold and strapped spikes onto their heels that made it impossible for them to move?

"Heading in early, Lauren? Or are you girls pre-gaming?"

Lauren gave a disingenuous laugh. "Obviously you already have been pre-gaming. You're lucky Phil's at the desk tonight."

"It's not my first day in the dorm. We checked the schedule before we decided to stay in a few extra hours tonight." This girl had long blond curls, too perfect and inflexible to be natural, and lips painted a wet-looking red, like if someone breathed on her the wrong way they would smear irreparably. "Why aren't you coming out with us? I thought you wanted to check out the houses before recruitment officially starts."

Lauren shrugged, like she hadn't even thought about going out with these two before this moment, even though their words suggested otherwise. "Another time. We've already been out tonight."

The other girl, another blond, but with straight, wispy layers, shrugged. "Your loss. Sig Eps are the hottest guys on campus."

"I'm sure they are," Lauren said, with not a hint of interest in her voice.

"Well, enjoy your girls' night in or whatever," the shorter girl called as they wobbled on their heels out of the elevator. Damn, wearing those outfits out tonight was a mixture of stupid and brave. The door slid shut, and Arielle murmured, "I can't tell whether you're friends or enemies with those girls."

"Aw, they're harmless. Just a little drunk."

Arielle raised an eyebrow. She'd found that simple conversation with them exhausting, but then again, that was how she felt about most normal social interactions. It was no secret to anyone who had known Arielle more

The Broken Hearts Society of Suite 17C

than a few weeks that she was an introvert—a character trait that Rachel had taken full advantage of.

Had Arielle enabled the whole horrible breakup to begin with? Had she made Rachel think that she *wanted* to be kept a fun little secret?

Dammit, she had to get Rachel out of her head. Whatever was about to happen here with Lauren, Arielle had to just...let it happen. She had to appreciate it for what it was, be happy for whatever good things came out of it, and, for once in her life, deal with the implications of something after it happened, rather than before.

Lauren fidgeted opposite her on the elevator, her fingers playing with the zipper tab on her jacket, her knees moving ever so slightly while her feet stayed in place. And Arielle remembered that, as much as her feelings for Lauren scared her, this might be even scarier for Lauren. This was all new to her.

"Thanks for bringing me up," Arielle murmured as the elevator lurched to a stop and the doors slid open. The seventh floor lay quiet outside the doors, not a sound to be heard on the honors-designated floor. Something small in the back of Arielle's mind wanted to ask a hundred questions about how Lauren fit into this world—ached to know every detail of her life, to find out more about her, as soon as possible.

"Thanks for coming up." Lauren's mouth twitched up in the corner as she reached for Arielle's hand and pulled her silently out of the elevator.

The key rasped into the lock, and Arielle swore she could hear every turn of the pins inside. Lauren moved into the room so quickly that Arielle reached back to save the keys from dangling outside the door all night. Maybe she turned away from Lauren on purpose, just to break the intensity that had been building between them, because, dear Lord, she didn't know if she could say one more word while looking into her eyes without lunging for her and pulling her onto the bed.

So she started to ramble. "So I think I remember which movies were online for streaming, and if you want, we could…"

Arielle watched the door slide against the jamb, heavy and final. What happened in the next few moments would change everything, one way or another. She held her breath and turned to look at Lauren, then let it out in one full whoosh when she realized that Lauren stood inches from her, as though she'd had a plan for something to do, something to say, and let something stop her. But then Lauren's eyes darted to Arielle's lips, and then Lauren's tongue ran along her bottom lip.

"I have to know," Arielle said, looking into her eyes. "What are we…I mean, what do you want to…" her breath stopped short in her throat when Lauren moved one step closer to her, then another. Then Lauren's hands moved to Arielle's hips, and Arielle's world spun.

"I don't know for sure," Lauren said. "But I know I don't want to stop."

The Broken Hearts Society of Suite 17C

That was enough for Arielle, who closed the distance between them in a single step, let her fingers rest gently on the sides of Lauren's face, looked into her eyes. There was no more room for "Are you sure?" or worry. There was hunger in Lauren's eyes that mirrored her own. And, finally, Arielle gave herself permission to satisfy it.

Lauren's room was still dark, outlined in pale blue shadows from the scant lights coming in from the courtyard. The whisper of her hair against Arielle's shoulder as she moved in, closer and closer, made Arielle's eyes flutter closed, and then, all at once and completely wonderfully, what she wanted—the warm, soft press of Lauren's lips against hers. Lauren's hands never left the sides of her face, but didn't grab her and seize her, either. When Arielle's lips parted, Lauren's tongue sensed the welcome, and came in quietly, patiently. Like she thought this kiss deserved all the time in the world.

Arielle's arms snaked up over Lauren's shoulders, and she clasped her own wrist behind her head, telling Lauren that every inch of her body was in this. But the kisses stayed soft, fluttery, questioning. Teasing, almost. Standing with every inch of their bodies pressed together, alone in Lauren's bedroom, Arielle was done with questions. She wanted answers.

Arielle's fingers danced over Lauren's ribs as she slid them up Lauren's shirt, electrified by the perfect smoothness of her skin. Her hands gripped Lauren's sides, strong, as she turned her around, pressing her back against the door and standing on tiptoes to deepen the kiss. A small moan rumbled up through Lauren's throat, and Arielle thought she would die right there on the spot if she couldn't have more of Lauren's perfect skin under her hands.

It was almost as if Lauren had heard her thoughts, because her long, beautiful fingers skimmed Ari's waist and rested on her butt, thumbs hooking into her belt loops. It was so sexy, so possessive, that Arielle couldn't help herself. She moved her hands up, and when Lauren's breasts rested heavy on her palms, she just about melted into a frenzy of lust.

Hands weren't enough anymore. She had to have her mouth, her tongue, on every inch of Lauren. Every worry that had plagued her melted away at that one strong, simple need.

When Lauren's head bent forward and she sucked at Arielle's neck, the last shreds of her concern melted away. Lauren wanted this too. Arielle let her head fall back and gasped, inviting Lauren in, asking her to show her just how much she wanted to taste Arielle, too. Lauren's hands skimmed around to Arielle's waist, squeezing so that her thumbs dug into the bottom of Arielle's ribs. So close to Arielle's breasts that she thought she might die.

Arielle wanted more, but she wasn't going to be the first to take off clothing. Except…maybe her bag. It fell to the floor, and tugged the sleeve of her jacket down, too. So Arielle wiggled her arms out of that, stepping back from

The Broken Hearts Society of Suite 17C

Lauren for the briefest of seconds, just to let it fall on the floor. When Lauren grabbed for her and tugged her close again, diving in and devouring her mouth like she was starved for it, Arielle moaned and gave in, arching her back as if to tell Lauren to take her, if she wanted to.

And thank God, she did. Still clutching at Arielle's waist, Lauren took one step back, then paused. The wait for more was excruciating, and Arielle started to wonder if Lauren was changing her mind. Lauren let go, and took two steps more away from Arielle. Just as Ari's heart began to sink, Lauren pulled her cotton long-sleeved tee off in one motion, then stood there, waiting for Arielle. The static cling in her hair framed her swollen lips and flushed cheeks like a halo. Her breasts sat full and flawless in a nude lace bra that matched her skin perfectly.

Arielle stood there, frozen, taking her in, barely able to move and dying to touch her again all at once.

"Is…is this okay?" Lauren whispered, looking down to her shirt, crumpled on the floor, like maybe she'd made some mistake. She checked Arielle's eyes.

"This is perfect. I said it once, and I'll say it again. And again and again. *You* are perfect." As she said it, Arielle felt just how much fear bled into every word. Because every time she thought how perfect Lauren was, she fell more in love with her, without really knowing whether Lauren would ever—*could* ever—really love her back.

Arielle was throwing herself into this girl's arms, letting Lauren into her heart, without ever knowing whether Lauren would be the girlfriend she wanted, the one she needed.

Lauren shook her head. "I'm a mess. I don't know what I want. I don't know if I can say what I want," she corrected. "I mean, from you." Then, bravery flashed in her eyes. "Except I know I want you."

Arielle made a snap decision. For now, even if it turned out to be for only one night, that was enough. In one smooth step, her hands slid up Lauren's back, grabbing at the clasp of her bra, halfheartedly trying to unhook it before just yanking one strap down. If Lauren's breasts had looked perfect in lingerie, they were freaking unbelievable without it. Arielle gasped at the feel of one, heavy in her hand, at the perfect hard bud of a nipple under her fingertips. Lauren arched her back, and Arielle bent her head, flicking her tongue against it, her lips circling and sucking and tasting.

There was no guessing anymore, not a single worry left as Lauren's fingers tangled in her hair, then started to tug at Arielle's shirt. Arielle thanked God and Jesus and the Buddha and any other gods that anyone had ever believed in that she'd checked that her black shelf bra was reasonably cute and matched her panties before she'd gotten dressed.

Lauren pulled Arielle back up for another kiss, tugging her back to the bed by her belt loops as she went. Lauren sat back on it easily, but when she tried to bring Arielle along with her, her knees met the solid wooden frame with a thud and a flash of pain. She cried out, but realizing how much the sound of pain reminded her of the sound of pleasure made her want Lauren that much more.

"Oh, Jesus!" Lauren sat up, pressing one arm against her chest and reaching for Arielle with the other.

Arielle grimaced at the lingering pain, but then whispered, "I'm fine." Gingerly, she climbed up on the bed, kneeling at the end of it, tightening her core and feeling strong and beautiful for the first time in a very long time as Lauren's eyes raked over her. "Are you? I mean, are you sure this is okay?"

"Not touching you is not okay," Lauren murmured, running her fingers along Arielle's jaw again. She leaned in, and lowered her voice to a whisper. "Not kissing you is worse."

Lauren's sheets were so soft, and smelled exactly like her—coconut and slightly floral, absolutely feminine and delicious. Arielle breathed them in, letting her head tip back as Lauren kissed her there again, savored the feel of her teeth grazing just above her collarbone. She growled lightly, gripping at the belt loops of Lauren's jeans. The thrust of Lauren's hips into Arielle's thigh spoke to just how much she meant what she'd said about wanting Arielle, tonight. The rounded tips of Lauren's nails scraped gently at the small of Arielle's back, and then lower, lower, until they were under Arielle's waistband.

Arielle couldn't take it anymore. She pulled back, and in an instant, Lauren was looking into her eyes. "Are you okay? Is this okay? I don't know what's…too far."

"That's kind of what I'm asking you," Arielle laughed, burying her head into Lauren's neck, then pulling it up again when the thought of sucking Lauren's nipple again crowded out all coherent thoughts. Arielle moved her hands slowly down Lauren's smooth stomach, feeling goosebumps pop up as she did. Lauren shivered when Arielle's fingers hooked into the top of her jeans, her thumb pads playing at the button. "Can I?"

Lauren pulled in a shuddering breath and nodded. Arielle smiled, pressing a kiss to Lauren's breastbone, almost getting lost in the firm warmth under her lips and the soft gasps that made Lauren's chest rise and fall so quickly. Arielle fluttered her lips in a straight line down to her navel. She pulled Lauren's zipper down and started at the sight of her white cotton panties, a stark contrast to the gorgeously grown-up bra she'd had on. And…what was that little picture there on the front of them?

The second it hit her, she grinned up at Lauren. "Wonder Woman? Seriously?"

"Oh, God," Lauren half-moaned, half-laughed, as she crossed her arm over her breasts in that maddeningly sexy way again. "I haven't done laundry in weeks, and I didn't think that you'd…I mean, that we'd be…Oh, God," she repeated, but Arielle just laughed, brushing a light kiss against Lauren's hip bone and feeling her shiver. "I love it," she said as she slid up to kiss her on the lips again, this time biting the bottom one lightly as she pulled away. "They're perfect. Definitely memorable," she said, grinning into another kiss while sliding one finger, then two, under the band of the cartoon character panties.

Lauren whimpered, and Arielle's head spun. This was a big deal, a big decision, she knew that. If she made Lauren come undone in her arms, it would create something between them that neither could deny. Certainly not Lauren, without shattering Arielle's heart into a thousand pieces for the second time in one semester.

The realization that this one moment held so much potential for pain or pleasure crashed over Arielle like a wave. She knew she had a choice to make—let it drown her, or ride it as best she could. Her fingers moved farther down, and Lauren's eyes tipped back while her eyes fluttered closed. Arielle nipped at her throat, then her collarbone, then the inside curve of her breast, until her fingers brushed soft curls, then the hot, wet seam below. Lauren's hips raised up, and she gasped when Arielle pushed inside her.

"More," Lauren rasped out in the moment before Arielle's tongue tangled with hers again, and she let the cool, blue room, and the soft, warm, delicious girl squirming under her touch crowd out every worry that had plagued her for far too long.

Chapter 16

Rion

"I think I have a problem," Rion said, burying her head in her hands at the next Society meeting.

"Oh, really?" Amy asked. "Because I'd say you have a hot new boyfriend."

"Hello, Miss Outspoken," Arielle said, grinning at Amy. "That's new. But seriously, Rion. I know you like to be all emo and shit—"

Rion raised her head halfway so she could glare at Arielle.

"Sorry, but it's true. He seems really decent. What's the problem?"

"He violates my rules."

"How? He works at a shop that sells bongs? Who cares? So do you," Arielle pointed out, shooting a glance at Amy, who looked concerned. Amy got it. Even though Rion didn't really even know what "it" was.

"He also paints things. Illegally." Rion pulled her knees to her chest and let her forehead rest against her arms. She'd spent a good hour determining that, yes, it was illegal to cover a brick wall with your painting in the middle of the night, even if you didn't permanently damage anything and the painting was partly a love letter to a girl you'd just met. Rion sighed. Even she was finding it difficult to argue with this. She knew she was grasping

"Okay. Do you have any indication that he is doing anything from your list from our very first meeting? Pot? Alcohol? Cigarettes?"

"He smokes one a week," Rion said. "One cigarette," she qualified. "But he said he'd stop if it bothered me."

"Does it?"

"No. I kind of want one, too. I think that's maybe what kills me. He does one or two slightly non-perfect things, works in a head shop, and nobody bothers him. I hang out with a bunch of losers and I'm the one who loses."

"You've been kind of miserable lately," Amy offered quietly.

Rion glared.

"I mean, not like Rion-miserable," she rushed to explain. "Like, melancholy. Emo. Whatever. Like you're mooning over this guy. Why don't you just go for it? Seal the deal with him?"

"I'll tell you why," Arielle said. "Because even if he's not doing any shit, he looks like the kind of kid who would, just like she does. And she knows that's the kind of kid who gets in trouble, eventually."

"No, dammit!" Rion yelled, pulling her head up and looking at both of her roommates, endlessly patient like always but looking a little concerned now, "It's because I think I really like him, but…when I got together with Tate, he wasn't really into anything heavy. Nothing that could get him into any trouble. And by the time it got worse, I was already in so deep…I let that overshadow everything. I don't want falling for a guy to make me blind. Not again. Not ever again."

"Aww!" Amy said, pressing her palms together and touching her lips with her fingertips. "You really are falling for him! I like him, if that helps."

"Because Miss Turbo Christian's judgment is better than anyone else's," Rion snapped.

"Hey. Uncool," Arielle said softly, but loud enough for Amy to hear. "She's just saying it's our job to look out for you. Same thing you said to me last week," Ari said. "Your heart gets broken, it's my fault. And I think he's great, too."

Rion bristled at the feeling of actually wanting Amy and Arielle to approve of Crash, and then at the realization that their approval made him even more irresistible. "So what are you saying?"

The Broken Hearts Society of Suite 17C

"I'm going to give you an assignment just like I gave Arielle," Amy said, pushing for a smile. "Give a little more. I know you two made out and you were, like, in bed naked with him," she said, pink streaks rising to tinge her cheekbones. "But that's just your body. How much does he know about you? Like, how much have you really shared with him?"

That sent Rion's hackles up. She didn't deal very well with being judged.

Arielle noticed, and shot her a nervous glance. "Maybe that's all she wants from him, Ames," Arielle said. "Although…he did paint a picture of you in the alley mural he's never shown anyone else." Arielle hazarded a half-smile at Rion, and it took everything Rion had not to growl in response.

"See?" Amy continued. "And that was a big thing, on his part. Just try letting him in a little bit. He gave you something. Maybe you should give him something. See how it feels to trust someone, just a little bit."

"I don't know what you're smoking, Amy, but most guys are not attracted to girls who got arrested for possession. And who get calls from their moms in jail."

"I don't think that's what she meant. It's not all or nothing," Arielle said softly. "I know you don't want him to watch you mix your music, but maybe record something for him."

Oh. Music, she could do. She might be able to give him the music without giving him the memories and emotions that went along with it. Nobody had to share her memories of learning about rhythms and styles and how they mixed together, how they could elicit so many emotions, so many memories of all those lazy weekends in Dad's studio.

"So you're saying you want me to make him a mix tape."

Amy grinned and nodded wildly. "Yes! Oh, that would be so cute."

"I don't do cute," Rion grumbled. "Absolutely fucking not. No. Never gonna happen."

"Okay, why not? I would love to hear you tell me why you can't sit your pretty blond little ass down at your computer for twenty minutes to make an awesome mix for him."

"Because it's more than that," Rion said, half-rolling her eyes at Arielle's comment about her hair. The more she thought about mixing something for Crash, the more stupid it seemed. "The music is…it's more than that. Nobody even knows about it except…"

"Except the people you care about. Share it with him. Then you'll figure it out."

"Figure what out?"

"If he can take it. If he can take *you*, with all your baggage or whatever you're so afraid of sharing with him. And if you're ready to trust him with more than your vag."

The Broken Hearts Society of Suite 17C

"Seriously, Arielle," Amy said, pressing the back of her hand to her freshly-pinkened cheek.

"Well, you know what I'm saying," Arielle finished lamely.

Yeah, she did know what Arielle was talking about. So much so that her chest started feeling tight, twisting and fucking killing her with each breath. She raised her head, a single tear already starting to spill from her lower lid.

"No, no. No," Arielle said, hoisting up and collapsing back on the floor right next to Rion. Her chest got even tighter, and when Arielle touched her she involuntarily flinched away. "Sorry," Arielle said quietly.

"No, it's just…I really thought Tate would be there for me. After everything else that had happened…Dad, then Mom…I didn't think he was my soul mate or anything, but we met in the group home. He'd dealt with shit in his life, too. And I think he knew that, knew that I trusted him, that I needed to be able to trust one person. I expected him to have my back, even though I don't think I really loved him, and I'm pretty damn sure he didn't love me, either. So I guess it's hard to trust a guy again. With anything. I mean, I just started to trust you two. Even though you haven't really left me a choice." Rion smiled.

"Especially because you like him so much."

"Especially because I know he's not lying. He passed the one condition I put down for him. The only excuse I have left is being fucking terrified."

Now, here were the tears. She'd promised herself she wouldn't be a fucking pussy about her feelings, and here they were. Damn it. Damn her, damn everything.

"Okay, come on. You're doing it. Right now." Arielle stood up and reached a hand down to Rion.

Rion looked up at Arielle like she was on crack, then looked at Amy, who shrugged. "You said it last week. If your heart gets broken, it's our fault. Everyone and their mom knows you like this guy. Everyone knows he's clean."

She looked up at Arielle again. "Either call him and tell him you want to see him again, or make a gesture. But you have to do something. I'm not going to be responsible for your emo heartache." Then she winked.

Goddamn this annoying girly kindhearted teasing. Goddamn her annoying roommates. Most of all, goddamn them being right.

She took Arielle's hand and let Ari hoist her up.

"Do I need to supervise you?"

Rion rolled her eyes. "No. I can do it." Now that she was done feeling sorry for herself, Rion had to admit that it was a damn good idea. She could put something together, something that really made her happy, that she loved, and give it to Crash. Just like he'd done with her, except she wouldn't have to be there for it.

Amy was grinning, standing next to them now and practically bouncing in her good-girl flats. "How are you going to do it? Email? Send him a playlist?"

"The files are too big," Rion grumbled, "And playlists are so platform-specific, and I'd want to mix it into one long track anyway, because you can't really communicate anything with one song all on its own…whatever. It's going to have to be a flash drive or CD. I have a shift tonight anyway, I'll just give it to him then."

Putting together a playlist sounded so simple to Rion's roommates, but to her it was nothing short of a therapy session wrapped in memoir-writing and sprinkled with a thousand tiny tugs and pinpricks at her most fragile emotions. Music had been so woven into Dad's life, and at moments like these, Rion had wished that he hadn't made it the same way for her. If he hadn't sat in their basement letting her sit and think and feel through every album he'd ever loved, he wouldn't have left anything behind, and there would be nothing left to make her hurt quite this much.

She'd also probably be in a catatonic state, since she would have felt completely and totally abandoned after Mom went to jail. At least now she had Jim Morrison, Joni Mitchell, Chris Martin, and a thousand other tortured artists to help her feel less like a fucking freak, drowning in a swamp of anger and resentment and fear.

In the last few weeks, Rion had taken cooler sound engineering classes than she even had thought were possible. She'd thought she'd known everything about equalizing, dynamics, compression—she'd known enough to mash songs together, but it was like every piece of homework sent her down a rabbit hole of mixing way more songs than she actually was required to. In fact, it had been the number one way she had distracted herself from thinking of Crash—both at home and at work.

She plopped into her desk chair, slamming the door behind her and listening to the vague chatter of her roommates behind the door. Damn them, it was like they knew her better than they possibly could with that suggestion. Even though Rion hadn't mentioned the alley art thing since the day after it happened, the girls must have seen how much it meant to her, how it let Crash wriggle under her skin in a way that pretty much nothing and no one else had managed to do. Damn him.

Her mixing program sat open on her desk, from where she'd left it that morning. In her coffee-fueling haze, she'd pulled up two songs that she would never have thought of putting together, one country-pop and another R&B. The genre of a song hardly mattered—if you had real talent, you could find connections between two songs regardless of their exact key, tempo, and lyrics. Slow one down, speed another up, and suddenly you had a cohesive unit that was better than the original. But these two songs, when she meshed them together—it was like they found the tiniest blood vessel in her nearly-dead, hardened heart, and tugged on it until it pulsed with hot blood, and she couldn't ignore it. Something in the songs sounded like heartache and joy all at once, something that she had to share with someone or she would burst.

The Broken Hearts Society of Suite 17C

Now that her roommates had forced her to think about it, there was only one other person she'd ever met who was willing to take the art that was inside him and take a huge risk showing it to someone who he really liked, but may or may not get it. Crash. And if she was going to figure out whether or not she could trust him with all of her, not just the physical that he loved or the snark that seemed to turn him on, she had to pull every blood-thumping feeling out of those songs and send it his way. And then see what he did with it.

In the lyrics, there were words floating around that scared her, but that, strangely, she hoped wouldn't scare him, too. "Dreams" and "perfect" and "take me." It didn't matter—they took a back seat to how the two songs blended together—so different from one another, but with a little work, blending seamlessly.

Rion put herself in a trance, ignoring everything but the chords, beats, and melodies, hoping that by focusing on the maybe-but-not-definitely hopefulness she felt about Crash maybe actually being right for her, she could magically make the music sound how she felt.

How was that, exactly? Scared shitless, but desperately wanting more of the thing that scared her.

Inside, it felt like her organs were slowly but steadily shaking down to nothing, her stomach growing queasier and her heart pounding a little more with each change she made to the file. When she had made every edit that she wanted, she closed her eyes, forced her hands to steady, and cupped her headphones tight over her ears, so she could drown out everything else but the music she had created.

When the 23-minute track was over, tears dripped off Rion's chin. They wrote a sloppy signature on the dorm-provided, cheap-as-shit laminate desk.

"Get your shit together, Rion Burke. Nobody else is going to do it for you now." Her fingers shook as she converted the file to a playable format, stuck the flash drive in her laptop, and clicked "save."

Then, after the computer had finished grumbling at the transfer but before she could change her mind, she yanked it out, stuffed it in her pocket, shoved her feet into shoes, and shouldered her way out her door.

By now, Amy had already left to do something with Little Red, and Arielle's freakishly tall and gorgeous girlfriend was chilling on the couch with her calves resting on Arielle's thighs while Ari squeezed her knee.

When she saw Rion, Arielle got that damn shit-eating grin back again. "Did you do it, like, just now? I wasn't sure because it took so long. But you look determined."

Rion shot her a glare. "Shut up." Then, to the girl, "Sorry, uh…"

"Lauren." At least she wasn't grinning, but her dark eyes, sparkling with mischief, were almost as annoying.

"Sorry, Lauren. Arielle's been on my case about this and I'm about to get her off."

Arielle snorted. "Nice word choice there, Cranky."

The Broken Hearts Society of Suite 17C

Rion grabbed her coat from the peg beside the door. Jesus, Amy had thought of everything. It was like her teeny boondocks town infused the water with a homemaker gene. Whatever. Today, Rion was grateful for a coat in easy reach, because if she didn't get out of here with this goddamn flash drive containing all her feelings soon, she might never do it.

"I'll be back. I need to pick up my paycheck."
"Okay. Take your tiiiiime!" Arielle sang as Rion listened to the door thwack shut.

The second week of November at Indiana Northern meant some serious weather. Not snow—worse. It was a frigid wind that bit through almost any coat, and laughed in the face of anyone who hadn't thought to wear a scarf, hat, and gloves. Rion clenched her jaw tight and put her head down, feeling the top layer of her hair practically mess itself up. It was a good thing the color at least looked good. She'd managed to bleach again and get an even purer blond out of it. Where most girls would get pissed off at the stubborn dark roots, which seemed to grow out in a few days no matter what Rion did, she remembered how Crash had admired her hair, and smiled.

Yeah, so apparently in addition to being smoking hot, incredibly considerate, clean as a whistle, a great kisser, and the most polite guy she'd ever met, he also transformed her into an eighth grade girl. Goddamn sexy bastard.

She couldn't even completely calm her smile as she pushed into the Studio. Olivia stood in the back, having a quiet conversation with Stephanie, who looked upset about something. The place was dead, except for one girl getting her nose pierced, which Jack was taking care of while hitting on said girl. Rion rolled her eyes at how obvious he was, running his hand down her back and helping her lie down. Next time she'd have to tell him to wait until after the stud was actually in a girl's nose before telling her how hot she looked.

She tilted her head up at Olivia. "Be right back down," she called. It was the day that Studio employees could pick up their checks, and Rion had a whole $172 after taxes coming to her. It was better than nothing.

But if she didn't keep her feet moving toward Crash, she'd never make it. At this point, she couldn't figure out what would make her into a bigger emotional pussy—chickening out of doing this, or going through with it in the first place. Because, seriously, who gave a fucking music mix to someone they'd hassled to hell and back and still wasn't even their boyfriend?

Either a bitch or a pussy. The only thing worse than being one would be both.

So Rion pushed through the door that led to the tiny "lobby" of the building, and, stair by stair, up to Crash's. Five stairs up, she realized she hadn't been breathing, and

The Broken Hearts Society of Suite 17C

forced a deep breath into her lungs. Goddammit, there was Crash's scent—some combination of his aftershave and laundry detergent, and maybe some man-lotion. Comforting and sexy at the same time. So many things at once, just like he was, and a little confusing, which she wished he was. Then she'd be able to deal with him better.

She stared at the door, heavy metal with pings in it, covered in dulling and slightly chipped red paint. There wasn't even a number—there was only one apartment here. Rion glanced under the door—just like a stupid scared girl stalking her crush. She took a deep breath in, blew it out, yanked the drive from her back pocket, and flicked it under the door. No note. If he was watching for some communication from her, some sign that she wanted him just as much as he wanted her, he'd at least guess it was from her. If he'd been listening to her about her passion for music, he would know it was from her. And then she could trust him.

An immense stress lifted from her shoulders as she backed up, slowly. She'd put herself out there—or, into Crash's life—and now it was his turn to respond.

But then, the unmistakable sound of a shower turning off floated out into the hall. Wet footsteps splashed and slipped a little on a hard floor. A light directly on the other side of the door switched on.

Rion said a silent prayer that the stairwell was carpeted, because otherwise the noise as she scrambled down the stairs would have been louder than a herd of elephants.

There was no way she could look him in the eye now. Not until he listened. Not until she knew.

She growled. If all the Society was going to do for her was convince her to do stupid things without thinking them through, maybe she needed to rethink her reliance on the Society. Now Crash was going to think she was a total psychopath, and never talk to her again. She definitely deserved it, since only girls with a unique combination of batshit crazy and utterly stupid made mix tapes, put them on flash drives, and slid them under the door of an apartment they'd never been to before.

Yeah. It was time to abort this mission and go back to blowing Crash off even though that was the exact opposite of what she really wanted to do.

The door to Crash's apartment was opening. She stood paralyzed in the stairwell as she listened, trance-like, to the sound of the door swinging on its hinges, Crash's steps on the carpet, coming toward her. She couldn't move. She couldn't *not* move. God-fucking-dammit, he was here. And he smelled delicious.

"Rion! Hey! Is this—did you bring this by?"

Godfucking*dammit*, that scent of slightly damp skin and boy-smelling freshly shampooed hair was killing her, in that she was going to combust from the heat running through her. She turned her eyes to Crash and pressed her lips together.

The Broken Hearts Society of Suite 17C

Move, you stupid bitch.

"Yeah, actually, it was...a mistake. Sorry." She held her hand out, giving him the chance to get rid of the flash drive, trying to focus on anything but his ice blue eyes that killed her every fucking time she looked at them. Crash narrowed his eyes at her. "I don't think so. Seriously, Rion. What is this?"

Rion turned her eyes down, examining the carpet. Office grade, dots of blue and burgundy woven in through a boring medium tan. And, dear God, Crash in only jeans and bare feet. Had Rion even realized how sexy a tattooed guy in bare feet was? Or was it just Crash?

"I...it's stupid," she said, thrusting her hand out further, wiggling her fingers. "I made it and I thought for a sec I wanted you to listen to it. But I'm good, you don't have to."

"Oh. It's music. *Your* music," Crash said, a smile tugging at his lips.

Rion had never thought those words could sound so sexy, but she couldn't imagine anything being more of a turn-on after Crash said them in that low, slow voice.

His fingers curled around the drive and he pulled it close to him. "Yep. This is definitely the most important thing in the universe right now. Come on." He held his other hand out to Rion, and she took it without even thinking. When his fingers weaved with hers, she snapped out of it.

"Wait, what? Why? No no. I'm just fine right here, thanks." He still didn't drop her hand, just looked at her with a smug look like he knew what was going through her head better than she did. "Or, you know, I could just leave. In fact, call me when you're done. If you want to. I mean, if you like it. I mean, you could just tell me when you see me at the Studio. Actually, don't worry about it. You don't even have to—"

And then, he was tugging her toward him so fast her bangs blew off her forehead, pulling her tight to him, bending his head to hers. His lips grazed her ear, the same way they had done the first time they'd been alone together in that that damn alley, and whispered, "Shut up." They stood there like that, pressed together, Rion's back against the wall, for a few heartbeats. She listened to his breathing, patient and waiting, for her. So slowly, she turned her head to his, so their breaths mingled together, and then his lips were on hers, moving so tenderly that she wanted to cry.

He pulled away, keeping his forehead against hers. "I want to," he whispered, low and gravelly, and Rion got the distinct impression that he was talking about something more than listening to her mixes.

"If you're sure," she said. She wasn't talking about music either, not with the feeling of his thigh pressing against hers, the twitch of his forearm as he adjusted his fingers. The unexpectedly sexy sight of his bare feet under jeans.

He moved away from her and she felt the absence of him like a shock, cold on her face. Her body wanted to be against his again, screamed it at her as he led her back to his apartment. *His apartment.* Inside, was a couch, a small cart with a TV in the corner, and a small kitchen with two burners built into the countertop. An unopened bill on the floor sat near his shoes, which Rion imagined him kicking off at the end of a long shift at the studio. How did such a normal guy, one who stepped out of his shoes and made an indent with his butt in what looked to be a secondhand couch, who cooked for himself and slept in a normal bed with normal sheets, get under her skin so badly?

"Sorry it's a mess," he mumbled, giving her a lopsided smile as his eyes flicked up and down her body. "That's a good look for you," he said. "Sweats. You look comfortable."

"Oh, Jesus Christ on a cracker," Rion said, forcing even more irritation at herself into the background of her mind. "I look like a slob," she grumbled, tugging at her loose heather gray sweatpants, her off-the-shoulder black long-sleeved shirt with a thick-strapped mustard yellow tank underneath. She looked like shit in yellow, but her motivation to do her laundry had been shockingly low since she got to college. She completed the outfit with the jean jacket she wore practically every day.

"You look like you."

Rion raised an eyebrow.

"Which is amazing." His grin was lopsided, and his head cocked to the side like a damn puppy dog.

She couldn't suppress a smile now. She turned her eyes to the carpet again. "So, are you going to listen?"

"Definitely. Computer's in the bedroom. Uh…the corner." After checking to make sure she was following him, Crash walked over to the bed, plopped down, and pulled an ancient looking laptop onto his lap, flipped open the lid, and tapped at the trackpad as it clicked and roared to life.

"Mine sounds like that," Rion said, nodding at the ancient beast of a machine. "Well, maybe a little worse."

"I just put it in, right?" Crash's eyes flashed to hers, and a heat shot through her. She nodded at him and pressed her back against the wall right next to the bed, trying to steady herself. Everything about this guy made her feel so awkward, so off-guard and pliable. She hadn't trusted anyone in a very long time. But she trusted him.

It took Crash a few more clicks to get the music started. When the first chords came through the speakers, as sharp and clear as they could be for a laptop, she let her eyes drift closed. She'd gotten better at mixing, that much she knew. Each class helped her tweak some small part of her mixing, helped her learn about the nuances of the music in a new way, so that weaving the songs together had begun to feel more like working out and less like breathing. Harder, but in a good way, full of concentration, focus, and purpose.

The Broken Hearts Society of Suite 17C

When you felt the music like Rion did, being able to work hard and get a specific result felt more like an endless possibility than a struggle.

Crash had been the only thing on her mind the whole time she'd worked on the music, slowing one song down and speeding another up, starting with a slow, minor key. It sounded dark to her, suspicious, and for the first time it occurred to her that music could be colors and moods and art in a million different ways than she'd imagined.

The music started to pick up, a little brighter in tone, and the singer's voice weaved through the chords, skipping once, then repeating over and over, digging deep into the notes, sometimes harmonizing, sometimes matching them. Her voice dipped and skated along the words, light but with a depth that meant there was a possibility of something more. Another song began to dip in, this one sung by a gravely baritone. Rion, eyes still closed, felt a smile drift onto her face. This singing voice was Crash, taking over the song, filling in the gaps of the girl's voice, coaxing out her best notes as they harmonized, twisting long after hers through the quickening beat, then fading away. Now the notes were electronic and intense, pulling each other along like they all dangled and danced chaotically from a wire line, clashing and teasing, drawing out the clearest parts of each other.

Rion's heart jumped as she realized just how closely her mix followed her memory of every single interaction with Crash since the moment she'd met him. Every single emotion, tug on a heartstring, rush of attraction, urge to tear his clothes off, was somewhere in this song. And then, poking through the jumpy, tinny tones of the electronic beats came a languid strum of a guitar, along with subdued but driven vocals. The voice in the song could have been male or female, or both harmonizing together. It could have been going anywhere, could have ramped up or faded away, and each would make equal sense. She felt the song coming to an end, remembered the feeling of wanting to find a stopping point still deep in her bones.

If anyone had asked her this morning, she would have said Crash was an annoyance, someone she wished would leave her alone so she wasn't in danger of attaching to anyone or anything. Maybe someone she wanted to fuck, and then never see again. Obviously, this creation of hers was a better indication of her emotions than any of her actual conscious thoughts.

A storm of tension brewed inside her, making her feel hot and anxious, but absolutely stuck to the wall. Her eyes would open, watching how he would react to this barest of offerings of her emotions since she had lost her shit at Dad's funeral. That had terrified everyone, including her. Her own tears and wailing and rushing to the bathroom to yak up whatever stupid funeral finger food had been sitting around the house had made everyone around her, and most of all herself, so disgusted and uncomfortable that she vowed to never ever let that happen again.

The Broken Hearts Society of Suite 17C

That was when her music had started to get really good.

Crash's eyes connected with hers, just as open, but not hopeful. Not pleased. Just slightly surprised, and most of all, sad. "I'm sorry. I didn't know...I mean, I get what you're saying, but I didn't know I'd done that to you. I'm sorry." He dropped his head. "I'll let you go now. I'll help you get home," he corrected himself, sliding his laptop from his legs to the bed.

It took a moment to register. "What? What do you mean? I...no. I don't know what you heard but that's not what I was trying...I mean, I wasn't trying to do anything, but I don't feel that way."

"Don't feel what way?"

"Like...I want to go home? Like I want to get away from you?"

"Oh," Crash said, crinkling his eyebrows down, swallowing hard. "Then why...I mean, it was pretty clear."

"What was clear? That mix...that was everything I've been feeling, you know, for you. It wasn't good?"

"It sounded great, until they started singing."

Rion stared at him blankly.

"The lyrics?"

"What lyrics?"

"Lyrics are the words to the songs. Artists typically use words to add meaning to a song."

"I know what lyrics *are*, I just…didn't listen to them I guess." Rion's hand flew to her cheek. "What did they say?"

"You can't touch me—could never get the heart of me—we're different breeds, spinning on the same ball of dirt. This is the last time you'll see my face."

"I…um…what?"

"That last song. The Blinking Innocents."

"That's what they were singing? I could have sworn…Jesus fuck, I…can I just see your computer?" Whatever emotional maelstrom had been grabbing Rion thirty seconds ago increased tenfold, and desperation commanded her body. She knelt next to Crash and reached over him, grabbing for the computer, fingers itching to click back and listen for herself.

"I mean, it's fine. I get it. I can take a hint," he said, closing the laptop and grabbing her hands. Looking in her eyes. She knew this was going to be what Crash took with him. This was her chance to make a decision.

"Shut up, Crash. Shut. Up. There was no hint. I mean, there was, but you had to listen to everything. Didn't you hear it? I wanted you to hear…how the songs all worked together. How they complemented each other. This is what I do." She took a deep breath. "This is my alleyway painting, okay?"

He still looked confused as hell, and Rion's heart sank. This was the test, and he had failed. Or maybe she had failed, and the test was shit. Her shoulders slumped, and her eyes with them, looking at their joined hands. Something about the way he touched her—it was never forceful, never hard. He didn't squeeze or force or push. Still, she never felt that she could pull away.

"Okay…and it's just some songs? No message?"

"No. Well, yes. I mean, there is a message, but the message is in the music, the tones, the tempo. I never notice the words, I'm so obsessed with where the song is going, how it'll play out, how I can make it different or more awesome. Anyway, I thought it was beautiful. Hopeful." She looked in his eyes again.

"Let me listen again," he said. "Please."

Disappointment turned to soaring hope, and Rion fought to keep it in check. "If you want to. Just…hold my hands. I can feel it. Maybe I can make you feel it too."

Crash's eyes flicked to her lips, and his own parted. "Can I kiss you?"

She wanted him to, so badly. But she had done something stupid, put herself on display, had begged for some guy she was inexplicably drawn to, to understand her. She had to know if he could.

Slowly, almost reverently, Crash opened the computer again. Clicked play again. Waited.

"Close your eyes," Rion whispered, more begging than commanding. He did, and then held his hands out for hers. She weaved hers into his, admiring how strong his fingers were, watching the tattoo around his right wrist move when his fingers wove pliant through hers.

This time, when the song played, Rion watched Crash carefully. When the first song change approached, his body tensed, his back straightened, and a soft sigh lowered his shoulders gradually. A seed of happiness lodged itself in Rion's throat, and grew when she watched his reaction to the male voice joining in, his eyebrows twitching when they harmonized. And at the end, when the relaxed, persistent, sure voice sang the words he'd heard as all wrong carried along a tune that sounded nothing but beautiful to Rion, a small smile twitched the corners of his lips. And as the song faded out, Rion knew. He couldn't read her mind, but when they were on the same wavelength, Crash got her. Completely.

His eyes opened and she searched them. He knew he'd passed, too. After a few steady breaths, he said, "So you don't want me to go away and never talk to you again."

Rion bit her lip. Every sentence that flashed into her mind at that moment sounded stupid, sappy, or worse, sounded insufficient. So she just shook her head, begging him with her eyes to see what she was trying to say.

"Do you want me to…?"

And then she couldn't stand it anymore. Just like the song, words didn't matter. Just actions, just feelings. Just touching him, feeling him, and being lost in him. She leaned forward, opening her lips just enough before she pressed them to Crash's that she could taste him when she did. He sucked in a surprised breath, and his arms went from the laptop to the sides of her face in an instant, sending the black hunk of wires and plastic thudding on the floor. His fingers moved, sure but gentle, over her skin, making her feel like something desired and precious for the first time in a very long time. She felt promises traced over her scalp, hardly caring that he was sending her hair standing up every which way. In fact, she was fairly certain that she looked damn sexy right at this moment, a feeling that sent her chest pressing into his, powered by an electricity that could only be calmed when his skin touched hers. Her nipples hardened, calling the electricity out again, and she knew, so suddenly and so clearly, that just kissing wasn't nearly enough.

Something sent her fingers seeking under his shirt, translated the smooth feel of his skin, the hard ridges of his muscle running alongside bone into a tug deep inside her. Yet, she wasn't anxious, wasn't desperate.

This felt like it was a long time coming.

His shirt coming off, and hers shortly after, had been written in whatever crazy story this was since the first time they'd locked eyes. Crash's mouth opened, devouring hers, and she felt the hard edge of that irresistible lip ring pressing sideways into her skin, all the way down to her shoulder, warming a bit with each touch. And then Crash biting at her collarbone, making her arch her back and gasp. He pulled back, still gripping at her sides, like he was willing to stop but certainly not let her go. "Are you okay? Is it okay?"

For once, she said exactly the words she was thinking. "Don't stop," she gasped, pulling his mouth to hers again, biting at the opposite corner of his lip, grinning into his mouth when that made him moan.

"I love this bra," he said against her neck as he traced his finger under the strap, then nudged it down, making it flop down her upper arm, tickling the skin there and making her nipples bud with wanting more of his lips against more of her.

It was a thin fabric, nude, bare bones. An underwire and not even enough padding to conceal her nipples when it got cold.

"Can I take it off?" he asked, even though he didn't have to.

"Please. I want you to." She wanted so many things. She wanted to feel his hot mouth covering her, sucking on her. She wanted to lick his lip ring, to feel it smooth under her tongue. She wanted to do this, and be here, and not worry about anything. The emotion slammed into her all at once—she wanted him to take care of her. In this way, for now. Maybe more ways later.

So she pushed against him harder, arching her back and silently begging him to take that next step. Thank God, his lips traveled lower, and she moaned when they reached the high round curve of her breast.

"I have to tell you something, Rion," his voice ground out, hungry and sparse.

"Now?" she panted.

"It's important." He looked up at her with the start of a cocky smile. "I'm a boob man."

Rion grinned. "I think mine are pretty nice."

"Mmmm." His strong hands glided down and gripped just below her rib cage, his thumbs teasing up along her underwire. "Nice is the biggest understatement I've ever heard. But if you let me have yours, I will go insane. I will really, really, really not want to stop. It's like flipping a switch."

"I will go insane if you don't," she sighed, letting her head loll back and closing her eyes as she gave herself over to the sweet, insistent softness of his mouth covering every inch of her breasts. When the lip ring flicked against her nipple, she almost lost it, moaning and pushing her hands into his waistband.

"We don't have to rush," he murmured before lowering his head and sucking hard. Rion whimpered.

"I want you," she whined, fully aware of, and not giving a single fuck about, how pathetic she sounded.

He raised his eyes to hers, suddenly one hundred percent serious. "You want…"

"Yes. I want you to fuck me. I want you to make me scream your name and forget my own."

Under her right thigh, she felt what was already hard get even harder and twitch against her, and Crash growled. She grinned, satisfied and hungry. Crash moved his hands down her sides, got a strong grip, and flipped her over so that she tumbled onto his sheets.

Almost instantly, he was licking the underside of her breasts, smoothing a hot trail down to her belly button, notching his thumbs into her waistband and tugging her sweatpants down. "So sexy," he growled, peppering the insides of her thighs with rough kisses as she squirmed and tried to keep from coming before he even touched her. When his hands crept under her ass, then hooked up over her thighs and gently tugged them apart, she started to tense.

"No, no, you don't have to—"

He looked up at her, eyebrows raised in alarm. "You don't want me to?"

"I just…I know guys don't like to, and…"

"What guys don't like to? Idiot guys," he answered his own question. "You have the most beautiful fucking pussy on the planet, as far as I'm concerned," he said, kissing her thighs again.

Rion blushed and gasped. He was damn lucky she liked dirty talk. She was damn lucky he'd guessed.

"Please," he mumbled into her leg, and she scooted down half an inch and opened her legs a bit more. Within half a second, his tongue was inside her, then one finger, then two, moving in and out and hitting some amazing spot on her upper wall that quickly wound a coil inside her tighter and tighter until she was so high she couldn't sense the ground beneath her. And he hand't even licked her clit yet. When he did, the hard curve of his lip ring wiggling against the sensitive skin there, and she came

The Broken Hearts Society of Suite 17C

crashing down, everything dark and spiraling and thrillingly twisting inside her. Her scream was like a cry, a beg for mercy, the need for him to be inside her, for her to see his face and feel his tongue twisting with hers again.

He seemed to understand, because as her body spasmed, clenching over and over again like it never had before, not even when she got herself off, he didn't pull his body away from hers. He held her to him, strong but not tight, covering her with his warmth, making her feel safe and secure in the midst of coming completely undone.

His mouth was on her neck again, kissing softly, like he could wait there forever for her to take the lead again. For the first time in as long as she could remember, she wasn't worrying about the next class or the next bill, wasn't flinging angry thoughts at a professor or her mother. Definitely not at Crash.

Crash, for this one moment, had saved her from her own exhausting brain.

As Rion came down from the waves that had utterly taken her breath away, she began to notice him more and more. The strong, smooth curve of his back. the way that his hand wrapped around her side, how his thumb played over her skin, like they had all the time in the world, like he never wanted to stop. "Thank you," she breathed, and she felt his cheeks push into a smile against her skin.

"It's my pleasure," Crash said. "You are…delicious."

"Oh my God," Rion said, smiling as she bent to kiss his forehead, then his cheek, then finally his mouth, so tenderly it was like they'd done this a hundred times before. Tate had never gone down on her—said it felt weird when he was high, which he almost always was—and she had assumed that no guy wanted to. The way Crash was acting, she would have thought he had just had an amazing orgasm, too. Except for his cock, so hard against her thigh that it was starting to make her uncomfortable. God knew what it was doing to him.

She let her hand trail down his side, practically giddy at the feel of the ridges of his abs. She made a mental note to ask him what he did to work out, but it wasn't important now. The few guys she'd slept with had all been ripped—Rion was the kind of girl to not settle for anything less than what she wanted, and she was as red blooded an American girl as any. Lickable abs were important to her.

"I meant...thank you for...you know. That was incredible." She let her hand wander to the front of his pants. Rion liked to give dirty talk as well as she could receive it—it sort of came naturally when you had the everyday mouth of a sailor. But Jesus, she couldn't find two brain cells to rub together to dole it out right now. Her head still spun, but her hand knew what to do.

Crash slid up her body so she didn't need to reach. The only answer he gave was a rough "Unh," but that was all she needed. Wedging her hands into his waistband, she tugged his jeans down, then gave her own grunt of

The Broken Hearts Society of Suite 17C

frustration when the unexpected boxer briefs, instead of boxers, didn't come right down with them.

She felt a rush of excitement when she wrapped her hand around him, knowing that she was about to get more of what her body so desperately wanted. Typically at this point, guys tried to push her down so that she would suck it, because that's what always showed up on porn videos—the girl going after a guy's dick like it was a fucking ice cream cone. Rion had always thought the damn things were ugly, and didn't really ever have the desire to put her mouth around one and suck. Especially when she knew they were useful for so much more.

That was especially true right now, because, compared to the handful of guys she had been with, Crash was endowed. Seriously endowed. No wonder his head lolled back and he gave a lazy sigh when she ran her hand up and down his length—the poor thing had been trapped behind two heavy layers of cotton.

"Okay," she laughed, kissing him again, strangely loving the taste of herself on his lips, "This is…impressive."

He laughed roughly, lazily shifting his weight on top of her, then propping up slightly on his elbows. "I haven't heard any complaints."

It was like his body auto-adjusted to hers, and his dick was no exception. She wanted it, and her urge grew stronger every second.

The lingering orgasm pulsed through her slowly now, matching the tempo of his breathing, making her feel like she could handle things faster again. A lot faster. But first, she had to keep her goddamn head on straight. "Are you…checked out?"

She'd always hated using the word "clean" for sexual status, but how else did you responsibly ask a guy if he had syphilis before you let him fuck you?

He dipped his head to the other side of her neck, nipping and licking as he went. In a few seconds, she wouldn't give a shit if he was clean. She'd be begging for it even if he was crawling with crabs. She squirmed beneath him. "Yeah," he growled. "There's only been one other girl, and I was her first. You?"

Relief flooded her, chased by a need to have him in the next five seconds, maximum. "It's been more than one for me, but I checked out in my last physical before I left high school." Rion bit her lip. Had she seriously just reminded this guy how young she actually was? She didn't care.

"I know I told you it would be hard for me to stop, and that was true," Crash murmured, running his palm up her belly, cupping her breast, making her squirm to have him touching her inside as well as out. "But I can. I told you, I like you. For more than your fucking incredible body." He bent his head to lick her nipple again, tugging lightly with his teeth as he pulled away, and stars flooded her vision again. "Of course I want you, but not if it means I won't see you again. You've already tried running

The Broken Hearts Society of Suite 17C

away from me too many times for me to chance it again. I don't want you to feel forced. At all."

"The only thing that's going to be forced is your dick inside me if you don't make it happen soon," she gasped as his hand made it back down between her legs, thrusting two fingers inside her, his thumb flicking her sensitive clit and making her clench. Wanting him even more.

She almost growled in frustration when he shifted away from her, until she realized he was stretching his arm over to a bedside table, rummaging in a drawer.

Oh, God. He had condoms, and she didn't have to ask him to use them. Had she dreamed this guy? Seriously, had some obscure god looked inside her brain and created the perfect guy for her, then dropped him on the sidewalk outside the Studio?

When he pressed into her, bit by maddening bit, she knew the answer—he *was* perfect, and the size of his dick confirmed it. When he finally held himself all the way in, panting into the crook of her neck like he had just sprinted a mile, some part of him fit against some part of her that sent her head spinning and the whole rest of the world, the whole rest of life, to the background. She groaned, hooking her arms under his and clawing at his back, squeezing her legs against him in some subconscious attempt to keep him closer to her while feeling like she was going to fly away with pleasure. When he moved inside her, she thought she'd lose her mind, and the only way to keep it from happening was to move along with him.

As she rocked against him, she fell into a hypnotic rhythm, like a girl possessed. She'd never realized it before, but this—her naked body, her unguarded cries, her willingness to cling to another person—these were all the beginnings of a trust that had been so soundly violated the last time.

Crash was the first one to make her even consider going down that road again. She'd thought it was a miracle she was even letting any guy in, bit by little bit, but in that last minute before the hot press of his skin against hers and the building explosion inside her, she knew—he was the only one she could let in.

Chapter 17

Amy

Matt had asked Amy about her plans for Winter Break three times. Each time, she told him she was going home. From his reaction, she knew her dread seeped into every word. There were about a million things she wanted to do more than sit in her parents' living room as if everything was the same, even though nothing was. She definitely didn't want to answer questions about Adam that she didn't have answers to.

Matt already knew what she was thinking. He always seemed to be listening for things to fill in the gaps between her words. And so he offered to take her home with him, trying to entice her with the promise of a fireplace and a comfortable guest room and all the pie she could want. His mom baked four kinds, but nobody ever ate more than one slice.

A small, insistent part of her felt like she would fit so easily into that picture that she couldn't *not* go home with Matt. Matt was comfort and acceptance. Home was many things, but not those.

But they weren't together, she kept telling herself on every afternoon coffee date, which seemed to go later and later as sunset got earlier and earlier. She told herself a lot of things—he wasn't really interested in her in that way, he was just walking her home because it was dark. She liked hanging out with him because he was funny, and something about the way he looked at her made her feel brilliant and important. Sometimes she wanted to hug him, then panicked a little when she thought about how it would feel to have his skin touch hers. She couldn't name the feeling—she only knew that she didn't know what would happen if she felt it.

Matt always kept a respectable distance. Day to day, she couldn't tell whether she was relieved by that or frustrated beyond belief.

Arielle wanted Amy to go home with Matt, reminding her that Harrison was one of the few dorms that stayed open over winter break, so she would really only have to stay for a three-day weekend. Rion acted like she didn't care what Amy did, but Amy could tell she felt the same way as Arielle.

Amy explained that she didn't really have a choice. Mom had been going on for weeks about how excited she was for Amy to spend time with the family and old

The Broken Hearts Society of Suite 17C

friends. Yes, Mom was still convinced she and Adam would be getting back together any day now. Every time she mentioned it, Amy felt the chains linking her to Tripp Creek and the life she was supposed to have there pull tighter against her. The only thing that tug toward home made her want to do was break them to pieces.

"Well," Arielle replied, considering. "I mean, yeah, it will suck to have everyone asking you about Adam. Saying it's such a shame, asking if you're seeing anyone else, blah blah blah. But then you can eat pie, go hide in your room, and be reasonably certain that you will have a boy-stress-free weekend. Because you know what you'll do?"

Amy set her lips in a hard line. "What?"

"You'll tell them that you're done with Adam. D-O-N-E. And then there will be no more questions, no more gossip. Just one firm sentence from you, and it'll all be over. Like tearing off a Band-Aid."

"Yeah, right. Do you have any idea how small my town is?" Amy grumbled, picking at a bubble on her pizza crust. Mom had always said pizza-dough bubbles were lucky, but between the dining hall and Society meetings, she must have eaten hundreds, and her luck hadn't budged.

Her early childhood education classes were more mind-numbingly boring than she'd imagined anything could ever be. Worse than that, when she'd actually observed in a daycare setting, so many of the little boogers had touched her face that she'd wanted to run away screaming. She'd even arrived late, and with wet hair, to coffee with Matt that day so that she could fit in a scorching, germ-killing shower beforehand. Anyone who knew Amy from home knew she wanted to be a preschool teacher. While the idea of a New and Improved Amy had started to grow on her in the last three months, that Amy didn't exist yet to the people of Tripp Creek. The sad result was that there was only the shadow of what Old Amy had always said she was going to be, filled with nothing.

"Oh, believe me," Rion groused. "I know. Can't go back there without everyone and their mom talking about you at the one janky bar that same night. That's why I'm arriving in the dead of night, wrapping myself in a blanket, and sitting in bed with my laptop the entire time."

"I told you to come home with me," Arielle said, half-rolling her eyes.

"And I told you that I think girl-on-girl action is pretty hot, just like anyone else, but I don't want to be in the car with it for two hours. Especially when I'm not invited."

"You *are* invited! I invited you! Just now. It's not like we can make out while I'm driving," Arielle said, blushing.

"Oh, you'd be surprised what you can do while you're driving," Amy mused, feeling a pang of memory for teasing Adam's neck with kisses while he was behind the wheel. His neck was more solid and muscled than sinewy

The Broken Hearts Society of Suite 17C

and defined, like Matt's. She'd done it mostly because he'd told her how much he loved it.

"Hey hey, hold on there, Ames. Save your wet daydreams for when you're actually with the guy. He'll thank you, and so will we."

"I wasn't daydreaming, I...anyway. I just don't know if I can go back there. In fact...maybe I should come with you."

"Oh no. No no no. You are not coming with me, little miss Strawberry Sunshine," Rion said. "First, I'm pretty sure your parents would lose their shit. Second, I just...don't think you want to deal with going back to my house. Shit, *I* don't even want to deal with going back there. Third, I don't go to church."

Amy frowned. That was important to her—going to her church. She'd dreaded going to Sunday services over Thanksgiving break, cringed at the feeling of Adam's eyes boring into the back of her head when she refused to look his way during Fellowship Greeting. But Christmas Eve was different. Something about the combination of the choir singing "O Holy Night" and flames passed from candle to candle in the still December dark made her feel safe, and held. It made her feel peace, which she needed very much right now. "Maybe you should come with me, then, Rion."

"Nah," Rion replied offhandedly. "I should...I really need to go see her. Christmas. You know. And I am definitely not bringing you to prison."

Amy swallowed any words she might have had. She loved Rion, in her way, but she was right about that. Amy really didn't know if she could handle going to prison. Or dealing with whatever wreckage Rion would be turned into in its wake. She was the kind of girl who was accustomed to wrapping herself up in a comforter and taking care of herself.

Amy? Not so much. She'd never been left to deal with problems alone. Ever. Well, not until the two pink lines showed up on that pee stick. Even then, Adam had been there. Sort of.

Well, she probably should learn to deal with her problems sometime. And doing it alone in your room while the guy who had broken your heart after fundamentally changing your life forever was having dinner a few doors down was probably a pretty good start. Everyone else would be in a food coma. It was an easy fix. Her roommates were right.

"Yeah. You gonna be okay?" Amy asked, reaching over to squeeze Rion's hand. Rion tensed up, but nodded. Amy knew she was carrying a lot—she had a feeling that the conversation they'd just had about Christmas was a repeat of the one she'd had with Crash, who'd wanted to go home with her too. Rion had come a long way, letting Crash into her life, trusting a guy again, but it seemed like this part of her life was unbreachable.

Amy sighed. "And I can tell you're just dying to get out of here," she said, turning to Arielle.

The Broken Hearts Society of Suite 17C

Arielle laughed. "I guess. We still haven't had the 'what should we call us?' conversation, though. Like, what I should tell my parents. But we did talk about the fact that we don't actually celebrate Christmas, and she said she didn't care—that being with me was more important."

Amy gave her a knowing smile. "Hmm. Well, keep me posted. Okay?"

Arielle nodded and patted Amy's knee. "Are *you* going to be okay, *Mom?*"

Amy bristled. "Shut up," she murmured, returning Arielle's smile, showing her she knew it was a joke. She may have been teasing, but the truth was, Amy was no longer feeling the appeal of mothering anyone, little preschool kids and roommates alike. If there was one thing she'd discovered over the past couple months, it was that she may have been good at taking care of other people, but first she should probably learn to take care of herself.

"You've got a ride, right?" Rion asked.

Amy nodded. A senior she barely remembered from back home was the daughter of her aunt's best friend. CarrieAnn would be delighted to give Amy a lift for a little gas money, Mom had said in that soothing voice that could right a ship in a storm. Amy had relied on that voice for so long, then gone without it for so many days on end, that it had a hypnotic effect on her.

So Amy had arranged a spot and time to meet with CarrieAnn, and figured that if she decided not to go home, she could pull out at the last minute, no harm, no foul. No consequences, either, because it wasn't like her mom was going to drive out to Indiana Northern from their sleepy little lake town off of 225 with a turkey in the oven. God knew Dad couldn't handle the turkey to save his life.

Amy eyed her suitcase. She'd packed more with her heart than her head, knowing deep down that she wanted to do exactly as Rion had instructed, and hide in her room with a book or mindless YouTube videos. Her favorite sweatpants, nearly threadbare at the knees; a huge cowlneck sweater that she practically swam in; fuzzy socks and the softest t-shirts she owned. No makeup. She wouldn't be going out anyway. "I'm going, then."

"Text me," Arielle said. "Promise." For all she made fun of Amy's mothering, Arielle was like a bordering-on-overbearing older sister.

"Only if you promise to tear your eyes away from Lauren long enough to text back."

Arielle dipped her head and grinned. "It's not even a thing," she mumbled. "Not really."

"Yeah, okay," Rion said with a grunt from her throat. "You can text me too, you know. It won't be sunshine and cuddles, but that shit gets fucking annoying after a while anyway. Consider me the antidote."

"Aww, I love you too, Rion," Amy said, a genuine smile cracking through the fog of dread that hung over the impending drive. She'd ridden with CarrieAnn on the way home for Thanksgiving, and she wasn't boring or snobby or braggy or any of the million other things college seniors could be. Most of all, it was good that CarrieAnn didn't have a boyfriend, so she didn't have to listen to her talk about men. Amy loved Rion and Arielle, but seeing them wandering around in a fog of relative happiness for the past month was starting to make Amy twitchy.

Amy stood and rolled her suitcase to the heavy metal door and pointed at the bulletin board on the wall as a last gesture. They'd recently added pictures of Crash and Lauren and Amy had doodled floating hearts around their heads, which produced a chorus of laughter. "Society meeting right when we get back. A special one. I need to hear about all of it in person."

Amy forced a smile.

Adam breaking up with her had destroyed her in the beginning, but the pain had quickly faded, leaving an empty space in so many ways—how to relate to church, how to make a plan for a life that was no longer, well, *planned*. She loved hanging out with Matt, and heard her roommates' teasing about him loud and clear. Over the past couple weeks, there had even been one or two times she'd looked at him in the waning light or mid-laugh and thought he was cute.

Attracted or not, there was definitely something there that made her want to be near Matt on even the worst days. But nothing had happened between them, and nothing would happen. Any time they made eye contact that felt electric, any time he came close to touching her and she felt a shiver run down her spine, every time he said something sweet and her heart sped up, she pulled away again. She reminded herself that she needed to be alone, not attached to anyone emotionally or otherwise, to figure out what she really wanted to do with herself, who she really was. Or she would regret it later.

That was a Society promise.

Matt had kept his promise that he wouldn't try to kiss her, or do anything with her, unless he knew for sure she felt the same way. The only problem was that Amy kind of hoped he would try something. Because maybe if he did, she'd find herself ready.

Arielle and Rion swore he was in love with her, and Rion had even thrown out the phrase "blue balled to hell" a few times, which made Amy wince. She noticed Matt distract himself on purpose, but he was easily distractible anyway. Everything seemed to energize him—from his volunteer work to his classes to the kind of latte he was going to try that day.

Amy knew one thing—she wanted that kind of energy. Maybe if she hung out with Matt long enough, some of it would rub off on her.

Getting away from campus, where Amy had caught a glimpse of Adam with a new girl every couple of weeks, true to his declared mission when he broke up with her, probably would help clear her head. But it would also take

The Broken Hearts Society of Suite 17C

her away from the three anchors that had settled into place for her on that first week. It had been incredibly lucky, and the two girls and Matt had taken her away from the stress of being at home, confronting a past and a future that no longer felt like hers.

It didn't really help that Mom and Dad were convinced she and Adam would be getting back together. "Just a phase" and "he'll come around" and "normal for boys when they leave home" were phrases that got thrown around a lot on her weekly phone calls home, in that dreaded moment when Mom asked if she was seeing Adam again. Mom and Dad had been convinced of her destiny right along with her since she first went to homecoming with Adam. She'd been convinced of it too.

But it wasn't like she could tell Mom in graphic detail exactly what she heard about Adam's activities on campus. Word traveled fast back home, she didn't want to be the one to plant the seed of badmouthing him, and besides—Adam might have been a jerk, but. Badmouthing the only son of the long-standing pastor of the only church in town was the fastest way to bring drama down on your house. Even though Amy would be at Northern most of the year, May would be here before she knew it.

She couldn't endure a summer back home being gossiped about as the jealous, lying ex.

She sighed as those thoughts circled through her head on the way to the bench in the courtyard outside

Harrison, where she said she'd meet CarrieAnn. Matt had an uncanny way of knowing where he could find her, so she'd stayed inside until the last minute. If he asked her one more time to come home with him for Christmas, she would probably accept.

CarrieAnn drove a red SUV, and Amy kept her eyes trained on the closest intersection, waiting for her to turn the corner any second. Cold bled through Amy's jeans within seconds, and the wind seemed to kick up more every minute that she sat there, watching cars roll by. Most Indiana Northern students weren't rich, and the beat-up old sedans and station wagons rolled by in a tired parade, full of students dispersing to their nearby towns to eat turkey by day and get drunk with high school friends by night.

When the outside chill sent a shiver from Amy's shoulders to her shoes, she checked her phone. This was annoying. CarrieAnn must have wanted to get home as soon as possible, so why was she almost fifteen minutes late? But when Amy glanced up again and saw a bright blue pickup rolling down the street toward her, a pit of dread formed in her stomach. There were lots of cars on campus. That pickup could be anyone's, right?

Except, when it pulled up in front of the bench, and the window rolled down, Amy's worst fears were confirmed—it wasn't anyone's. Amy wanted to stare at the ground and cry when she saw him, but she forced herself to look into Adam's eyes instead. *Be brave, Ames.*

"Hey. Headed home?" she asked.

"Yep. And so are you."

It didn't sound like a question. Amy's brows knit together. "Yes…"

"No, I mean, with me. I called your mom, and she told me you were riding home with CarrieAnn Thompson. Which seemed kind of silly since we're both going to the same place."

"We're *all* going to the same place, Adam." She said his name clearly, with as much emphasis as she could muster. "Tripp Creek is a pretty small town."

The smirk on his face grew wider as he shook his head at Amy. His neck looked even thicker, she noticed. They must have been working him hard at practice, even though he'd been relegated to third string. He'd cut his hair short, too, leaving sharp cheekbone lines that had been framed by his shaggy style back home. The kind eyes she'd once loved so much now looked hard and out of place in his new bulky figure. She shook her head and blinked hard. How had she ever found him attractive?

"No," he said, taking the tone of someone speaking to a third grader. "Our families are having Christmas dinner together. Your mom arranged it. So I messaged CarrieAnn and told her she could head home after her last class, instead of waiting for yours. I wanted to drive you. I even called your mom, to let her know I'd be happy to drive you. She thought it might be a nice idea to give us a chance to spend some time together. And, Ames," he said with his voice suddenly softer, "I think so too. I miss you."

Amy's eyes narrowed, and she reflexively stood up, feeling the need to stand eye to eye with him. She may have been broken, and she may be a serious work in progress, but one thing the Society had made her promise was not to get caught in any kind of dependent relationship again. And that definitely included taking a ride home for Christmas with Adam.

"I don't' think you do." She shook her head and winced. It was irrelevant whether he missed her, because she didn't—*refused* to—miss him. For a while, she'd thought she had. But soon she realized she'd just been lonely. Seeing him in person only solidified that instinct.

"Come on, baby. Get in."

"Baby? Don't you even think of calling me that. Ever again." A soft snarl rose in the back of her throat, and she had to suppress a smile of satisfaction that Rion and Arielle would totally approve of that answer. That tone that showed she was going to stand her ground, not be pushed around anymore no matter what.

"How are you going to get home if you don't ride with me? CarrieAnn headed home last night after I called her and let her know I was taking you. You don't have any other friends from back home here."

Again, not a question. A dig, designed to knock her down and then emphasize how she needed him. Had Adam always spoken to her like this, and she'd just never

The Broken Hearts Society of Suite 17C

noticed? Amy said a silent prayer of thanks to college for helping her to understand that, out of all the things she was, she wasn't helpless.

"I'll take her home."

Amy's heart wrenched when she heard Matt's voice, and twisted up tight when she spun around and saw him, walking briskly toward them. In the distance, his maroon Civic sat idling in the parking lot in front of Harrison, and for a second Amy wondered if he'd been coming to say goodbye.

Next to Adam, Matt looked even more wiry than usual. And much more attractive than usual. One of the colors in his plaid shirt perfectly offset his eyes, so that even with his glasses on, they jumped out at Amy, making her pace her breaths. His brown oxfords planted firmly on the ground beside her as he clenched his fists and locked eyes with Adam, his jaw hard and his body tense, like he was ready to spring on Adam if he kept pushing.

"I'm going to take her," Matt said firmly. "Amy just called me to say her ride ditched her, so she's coming with me."

"A simple misunderstanding. It makes sense for her to ride home with me. You're not even from anywhere near us, are you buddy?"

"Doesn't matter." Matt didn't show an ounce of fear or a flinch of reaction to Adam's condescending nickname, despite the fact that, even from this distance,

Adam was significantly larger than he was. "Amy said she doesn't want to get in the car with you."

"Oh, please. Of course she's okay riding with me. We've known each other for years. We were together for years." Adam emphasized 'together' with a flick of his eyebrow and a tilt of his head, so that there could be no mistake about exactly how close they'd been. Another testy smile. "I'm harmless. Right, babe?"

Matt didn't need to glance at Amy for more than half a second before stepping even closer to Adam's truck. "Okay, Gaston. That stuff is just not going to work out here. Not sure if you didn't understand me the first time, so I'll say it again. *She doesn't want to go with you.* She's been very clear about that, and now so have I."

"How are *you* going to get home then, champ?" Adam sneered, that self-satisfied grin seemingly plastered on his face. Amy had never had an urge to hit someone, not in her entire life. But now she would like nothing better than to slap that smile right off.

From the looks of Matt's clenched fist, he was thinking the same thing. "She's my friend, so I'm happy to drive her home. We already talked about it."

That wasn't a lie, and that only added to the warmth Amy felt when she looked at Matt's calm, but determined, face.

Now Adam turned his attention to Amy. "What am I supposed to say to your mom?"

The Broken Hearts Society of Suite 17C

"Tell her that I didn't want to ride for two hours in a car with my ex-boyfriend." She didn't mention how many times they'd made out, how many times Adam had felt her up, in the seat she was supposed to sit in with him again. "And tell her…" now the rage was beginning to build. Mom hadn't told her anything about Christmas dinner with Adam's family, and the more she thought about it, the more she realized that must have been on purpose. All the comments Mom had been making about boys being boys, and what she had with Adam being stronger than that…of course she'd arranged this dinner, and known that Amy wouldn't have come if she knew Adam would be there. "Tell her that if she wanted me home for Christmas, she would have been honest with me about her plans. And if she wants to see me at Spring Break, she won't pull anything like this again."

Amy could feel the heat building behind her eyes, the one that meant that tears would soon follow. Matt looked at her, and the expression on his face changed almost immediately, saying that he'd seen what was about to happen. He pulled his cell phone out of his pocket, and almost instinctively, Amy did the same.

"I'm on Student Government. I have a very close, friendly relationship with Campus Police. I'm sure they'd be happy to tell you exactly the same thing I've been telling you—if a girl doesn't want to ride with you, leave her alone. They'll make sure you get on your way without any trouble." Amy slowly punched in the three-digit code that would summon the flashing blue police lights.

The not-so-thinly veiled threat only deepened the redness rising up Adam's neck and over the tips of his ears, while his knuckles turned white from clutching the steering wheel. But, at the same time, he didn't move. He just let his mouth drop open, glancing quickly between Amy, Matt, and Amy's phone. Then he looked Amy hard in the eyes, muttered a barely audible, "Whatever, bitch," and sped off, squealing the tires of his overpriced, over-polished pickup behind him.

Amy stood there, shaking, but not from the cold. The trembling came from deep inside her, radiating out to her limbs and making her completely unsteady. After taking a moment to breathe deep in her belly and force the shaking back inside, she looked up at the empty space on the road where Adam's truck had idled, forcing down the memory of him trying to reclaim her, like a sweatshirt he'd left in the lost and found bin and only thought about retrieving when it would be useful again.

But she wasn't a sweatshirt. She wasn't a decoration, and she wasn't a utilitarian something that you wrapped around you only when the air got a little chilly.

"I can drive you home," Matt said softly, his words perfectly matching the space where her thoughts dissipated into raw, incoherent anger.

"No," she said harshly, whipping around to look at him. He flinched and took half a step back, but then stood his ground and waited for more. How did he know she just hadn't gone full bitch on him? What in the world was making him stay?

It was his faith in her, that was what. Damn him, he trusted her like she had trusted Adam. But she didn't want to be like Adam, cutting Matt down for no reason. Because there *was* no reason.

"I mean," she started again, "no, thanks. I can't go home. Did you hear what my mom tried to do to me? Blindsiding me with a dinner with…with…*him*?" Betrayal planted a stinging slap on her soul, the one that had always believed that Mom was there to love and support her, not to push her back into a relationship that had almost destroyed her. And more than once at that.

"Arranged a dinner between you and Adam. And your families."

"Not just a dinner. Christmas dinner. The dinner that families do together. This is…I mean, now I know it's kind of sick, but when we were dating, it felt normal. I was supposed to marry Adam. It wasn't like they would kill me if I didn't, and it wasn't like we were engaged or anything."

"So…" Matt's face twisted in confusion. "So who cares if you broke up?"

"We were the perfect couple. Every single person in that town expected us to get married. According to life in Tripp Creek, we were the perfect couple. He played football on my daddy's team. He's the pastor's kid, so he would be a strong spiritual leader for me. I was the good Christian girl who agreed that teaching preschool would be a great career to wait and prepare for motherhood. So, that means that if we broke up that we were the stupid ones. Adam wanting to drive me home means that he's acknowledged that, but I refuse to. Because none of that's the same anymore. I'm not that girl anymore, and he never was that guy."

"You were pretty upset," Matt offered, moving a step closer. "You know, when it happened. When he dumped you." His voice dropped, and so did his eyes. When he turned them to her again, they looked up through long, thick eyelashes. How had she never noticed those before? Probably his glasses had been in the way. But now that he was so close to her…

"I was," Amy acknowledged, slowly working through the ridiculousness of what had just happened. "But the more I thought about his reasons, the more I felt like at some time down the line he'd turned into the wrong guy. A guy that I *wouldn't* spend forever with. So I guess I'm not upset anymore, even though…yeah, the memory of it is bad, it was like getting the rug pulled from under me. I fell on my butt and I didn't even see it coming. Worse, I had nobody to help me back up."

"You had your roommates," Matt said. "And you have me."

Amy's heart soared, and all of a sudden she wanted so badly to find the words for what Matt meant to her. If she

The Broken Hearts Society of Suite 17C

had been able to define it for herself, she might have been able to say something meaningful. Instead, she just said, "Yeah. You were there."

The smile Matt gave her at those words was pure warmth. "So you're saying you don't love him anymore? That's why you don't want to go home?" Confusion and hopefulness mingled in Matt's voice.

"No, I don't love him," Amy said, feeling the frustration slap at the edges of her patience. "I don't want to be with him, and I don't want to sit around a Christmas tree for three hours listening to my mom, Dad, and my ex-boyfriend tell me what's best for me and my future. I want…"

The wind kicked up, whipping her fiery hair into a cloud around her and even catching Matt off guard as he scrunched up his face and bent his head down to meet it. "Let's get inside. We'll figure this out inside."

"Matt, if you were headed home, you should keep going," Amy said, knowing the edge of her voice was hard, not really caring. She was pretty done being taken care of. Even though shakiness still surrounded every cell of her body, she'd survived. She was alone, the day before Christmas, with nowhere she naturally fit. It wasn't an awesome feeling, but she could survive it. These past fifteen weeks, the wind had tried to knock her down, and she'd won. Her shoulders trembled as she shook violently. "Seriously, I'm fine. I can figure this out."

"Geez, Amy, I know, okay? Of course you *can*. Everyone knows you're strong."

Was he reading her mind? Amy couldn't decide if she was frustrated or relieved at this, and the two feelings mixed together, making the hairs on the back of her neck bristle, newly sensitive to what Matt would say or do next.

And then his arm was around her shoulders, warm and comforting and strong. Not holding her up, but encouraging her to relax into his support.

"I know you're strong," he continued. "And that's why I want to help you figure out what to do. I don't feel sorry for you. I respect you, and I want to be good to you," he said, his voice softening at the end. "I want to be a good friend to you. Friends don't leave their friends alone in a dorm room on Christmas."

Amy's heart sank on that word. *Friend*. She felt angry with herself for that feeling almost as soon as it struck her. She was the one who wanted to be friends, and only friends. Matt was respecting her wishes. Did she *want* him to force herself on her? Did she want someone who felt entitled to touch, kiss, possess her, like Adam did?

She shook her head roughly, biting her lip to try to wake herself up from whatever downward spiral of confusion she felt herself sinking into. Like it or not, Christmas was happening, and the dorm would be a ghost town. If she didn't want to be all alone eating ramen noodles on the day of Christ's birth, she had to make a plan. Matt was asking to stand next to her while she did.

The Broken Hearts Society of Suite 17C

Friends. There was nothing wrong with that. Nothing to be afraid of.

And just like that, the possibility of having him standing beside her made her feel stronger, not weaker.

Matt dropped his arm from around her shoulders as soon as they started walking back toward the dorm. Again, with the sinking heart. Finally, the blast of relatively warm air when they stepped into the Harrison lobby let her breathe again.

Amy collapsed into one of the office-upholstered lobby chairs and sighed. She raked both hands back through her hair, realizing only after she did it that it was a habit she'd picked up from Matt. He plopped down in the chair opposite hers, staring at the cheap particle board lobby table that was probably cool five years ago, but just looked sad now.

"What were you still doing here? I thought you were planning to leave this morning."

"I picked up a gift card to Francis Beans. You said you were coming back on Saturday night but I need to stay with my moms for church on Sunday morning. Didn't want you to miss our Sunday morning coffee, so I was going to slide it under your door. A surprise."

He glanced up at her and shrugged, like it was no big deal. Like it wasn't the sweetest thing a guy had ever done for her—sweeter than the flowers Adam got her at homecoming, the Valentine's Day chocolates, and certainly that prom night when everything started going so wrong. Amy had wondered what was wrong with her, that she didn't melt at all Adam's gestures—this was the first time she had considered that those things hadn't really been romantic at all. Because they had proven that Adam didn't know much about what made her happy at all. Or maybe didn't care.

Then the dreaded redhead blush flooded her cheeks. She had to get it together and figure out what she was going to do, because eventually, Matt would have to leave. She buried her face in her hands.

"I really can take you home. It's no problem. What is it, two hours?"

"Four hours round trip, since you're in the opposite direction," Amy groaned, surprised that she even knew where Matt was from, had a concept of how far it was. "Plus however long it takes to get to your house."

"It's no problem. We have dinner late anyway," Matt said, still staring at the table. Weird. He usually had no problem looking at her, smiling at her, acting like there was nothing horrible going on in the world when he was with her. The usual.

"No, no, that's crazy."

"You don't want to go home, do you?" Matt asked, staring at her now, boldly. Like if he was afraid of anything before, he certainly wasn't anymore. "Come home with me," he continued, with Amy's mouth hanging open, before she could get an answer in. "Offer still stands. My moms would love to have you. And not," he said when she started to protest again, "because they're waiting for me to bring home a girl, or anything. They know that we're just friends."

Amy scoffed. "How can they possibly know anything about me?"

"I've told them. A lot. You're important to me, Ames." Eyes dropped to the table again, and this time, when Amy heard her nickname, she didn't feel sick.

What she did feel was a pang of guilt. Because if Matt was telling the truth—and why wouldn't he be—she had spoken to her parents 100% less about him than he had about her.

"And they know where I'm from?"

"I...think so? How is that even relevant? We're going to church and watching It's a Wonderful Life and eating homemade French toast on Christmas morning."

"Oh no," Amy said. "Presents. I didn't get anything for your moms. I didn't get anything for you." This was just getting worse and worse. No matter how awkward this was, though, it couldn't be worse than sitting at a Christmas dinner table with the two people she was most angry at in the entire world.

"We don't do presents, not since I was in junior high. We donate to charity instead."

Amy's eyes snapped to Matt's. "You're serious?"

"Dead serious, like Jesus on the cross."

Amy snorted out a laugh and clapped a hand over her mouth. She shook her head, slowly lowering it. "Of course you donate to charity. Of course."

"What do you mean by that?" Matt asked with a bemused smile.

"Just that, you know, of course you would be perfect in that way, too." Now Amy's cheeks flushed bright red. Apparently the encounter with Adam had completely removed any filter she'd had between her thoughts and speech. "I mean…uh…"

Again, Matt came to her rescue. "Whatever. You can meet some of my friends and we'll go to church and hear my mom preach. Relaxed and chill."

It did sound really, really nice. The only thing nicer would be going home, but only if nobody was meddling in her love life, judging her, or insisting that Adam was still the perfect guy for her. Because after seeing him today, Amy was more sure than ever that she never wanted to see him again. She just had to convince everyone else of that next.

"And they have room for me?"

Matt dipped his head down. "We've always had a guest room. Mom is meticulous about it because once the Bishop was in town, and we only found out he was staying with us at the last minute. Ever since then she lives ready for drop-in guests of extreme importance."

Amy scoffed. "Which I am not."

The Broken Hearts Society of Suite 17C

"You're important to me. So you're important to them. So you're coming, then? And I assume you're all packed?" he asked, rising and grabbing the handle of her rolling suitcase.

Amy sighed. "I guess you're right. As usual. If you're sure they won't mind," Amy said, checking his expression again for any signs of doubt. Even though Christmas at Matt's house sounded cozy and happy, she wouldn't have been completely opposed to putting her new skills of independence to the test. For the most part.

Amy's rolling bag in one hand, Matt stuck the other one down for her to grab. It was warm and soft, and for the first time, Amy noticed how strong his fingers were when they wrapped around hers. He wasn't a humungous muscled athlete like Adam, but Amy saw all the measures of his strength knitting together before her eyes now—friendship, morals, faith. Plus, the actual literal muscles.

"Come on," he said, that vague smile sending sparks of light into his eyes, "we need to get going if we're going to make it for 2:00 dinner."

Amy stopped in her tracks, pursed her lips together, and shook her head. "You said Christmas Eve dinner was late at your house," she said.

"Two *is* late, compared to eleven."

She glared at him, trying very hard to keep the smile that was trying to wiggle its way out tamped down. "What? Some people eat dinner at eleven o'clock."

"Sure, somewhere. Maybe. Not in Indiana." Now her grin was unstoppable, though. As annoyed as she was that Matt had been about to miss his own family's Christmas Eve dinner just to take her home, at least they were joking about it now, and the awkward tension surrounding the whole issue had dissipated.

"I guess they're the same people that stay on campus 'til Christmas Eve," Matt said.

"Nah, you have an excuse. You needed to escort at the clinic yesterday when everyone else bailed. Even CarrieAnn had some service project to do for her sorority. I was just…waiting." Amy frowned. That sounded pathetic. That *was* pathetic.

If they hadn't been about to get in the car and head to the house he grew up in—a reality that felt strangely inevitable at this moment—they would have been having just another conversation over coffee. One where jokes and half-insults rolled off their tongues, but the smiles told them they were full of friendship, where they finished each other's sentences and could keep companionable silence with equal ease. But somehow, this felt bigger. Heavier. Matt smiled. "Come on. I'll be lonely without you."

Matt's car was old and rattly, roaring down the freeway just a little over the speed limit, with a distinctive draft blowing in through the floor or under the door. It was strange to be sitting next to him shoulder-to-shoulder; she was used to being able to look straight at

The Broken Hearts Society of Suite 17C

him, to watch his animated talking, to laugh about his t-shirt or make fun of his sugary latte.

But the flat Indiana countryside, occasionally interspersed with cornfields, which had already been flattened by the fall harvest, and clumps of trees that had lost the last of their brightly-colored leaves weeks ago, gave them nothing to do but talk. And they did. Whatever it was about being in the car together forced a quieter, deeper conversation, and by the time they pulled off the highway, Amy had heard about every single one of Matt's childhood pets, including the current black Labrador rescue who acted like a cat, and Matt had heard about Amy's most embarrassing high school moments, including the time the pyramid flyer kicked her in the face at homecoming freshman year.

"Holy wow," Matt said, shaking his head and flicking his eyes over to her. "I can't believe they let a new cheerleader do that."

"That's just the thing. I wasn't a new one. I'd been doing it competitively since the fourth grade, because that's what my mother did, so that's what she signed me up for. I usually was really good about being the base, you know, because I've always been kind of…big."

Matt raised his eyebrow and made a show of looking over the length of her body, the first time she could ever remember realizing he was actually looking. At her body. "Now, come on. You cannot be serious."

"At my school, yeah. Size 8 and five foot seven in the ninth grade was sturdy. To say the least."

Matt lowered his head even more, exaggerating his eyebrows and flicking his glance at her every few seconds to keep his eye on the road.

"Anyway," Amy continued, trying to distract herself from her quickening heart rate, "I was unconscious for, like, ninety seconds. Apparently the girls tried to get me to wake up, and Adam was the first football player to arrive on the scene. He gave me mouth to mouth without checking if I was breathing first. Which I was."

"Genius," Matt muttered.

"I know. But at the time…I don't know. I thought it was sweet," Amy admitted, a small part of her longing for some younger, dumber form of herself that could live in blissful ignorance of how imperfect Adam had actually been for her. Her parents would certainly be happier. "Anyway, now I know that he bragged to his friends about how he got me to kiss him when I wasn't even awake, and it's all kind of creepy."

"To say the least," Matt filled in.

"Yeah, but you know what? Nobody had ever paid attention to me before, between my braces and my big butt and my red hair, which…it takes a lot of effort to make a redhead look good, you know?"

Matt shot her a puzzled look.

Amy shook her head, blowing him off. "But all of a sudden people were calling me Sleeping Beauty, and talking about how my prince had rescued me, and how it was fate and meant to be. I got really popular really fast, because he was really popular. And high school me kind of got really carried away with all that. Brainwashed, almost."

"You're not the kind of girl who cares about being popular, though," Matt said. "You're so *real*. Not like you're a freak or a degenerate or something," he rushed to correct, "but you're just you. I've been on this campus for over a year and I've never met anyone like you. In the best of ways."

Amy turned her face to her shoulder, trying to keep from saying something stupid. For a few long minutes, they said nothing, which was mostly as comfortable as usual. Then Matt turned on his blinker and slowed onto an exit.

Amy's eyes flicked to the big green sign over their heads. "University City?"

Matt shrugged. "My moms liked it because it's pretty much the only place in the Midwest where they could settle down and most people wouldn't hassle them. Also one of the few places that didn't think aerobics classes were for whores and black Episcopal pastors were something to be afraid of." His jaw clenched when he said that last bit.

"Your mom is black?" Amy asked, sitting up a little straighter. "I mean, one of your moms."

"Is that an issue?" Matt asked. All of a sudden his voice was guarded, sharp.

"No, no…I mean, definitely not. I just didn't know."

By now, they had pulled down a mile of suburban road and into a neighborhood. Matt turned slowly into a concrete driveway, put the car into park, and looked at her with eyes full of dread.

"I guess I was just so focused on the fact that you have, you know, two moms, that I hadn't stopped to think that they weren't both white. But it doesn't matter to me," she said softly, her voice full of apology. "I mean, it doesn't bother me. Not that it should bother anyone." Amy stumbled through words, trying to access anything appropriate to say and obviously coming up short. "I don't care," she repeated. "There was only, like, one black kid in our entire high school, but it was a small school. Small town."

"Would it bother your parents?"

"What, that the guy I hang out with all the time has a black mom?"

Matt nodded. "And that I have two moms."

"Maybe," she answered honestly before she could check herself. His face fell, and she instinctively reached out to grab his hand. "But remember, I don't really care what they think. I care so little about what my parents think about what I do that I ditched them for Christmas and came home with you." With that, the full force of what she'd done hit her. Her words hung in the air,

The Broken Hearts Society of Suite 17C

waiting for Matt to take them, make them mean whatever he wanted. Amy wasn't really sure what she wanted, but she knew that she was holding his hands in hers, and that she absolutely didn't want to let go.

"You're right, you did." Matt smiled, the same smile he gave her when they were half-teasing, and Amy took a breath again. He popped open his door with his free hand, and when he slid the one beneath Amy's fingers out so he could climb out of the car, the space it left felt empty in a way that she didn't like. Not at all.

Dinner with Matt's moms and a few people from the church was pretty much the same as holiday meals back home. They started with a prayer from Tamara, Matt's mom, and each person had to say what they were thankful for as her eyes moved around the table. There was a little bit of good-natured ribbing, plenty of Harriet, Matt's other mom, buzzing around the table urging everyone to eat more, and a lot of talking shop. Except here, everyone was a college professor, and talked about paper-grading instead of cow-milking. Normally, Amy would check out of conversations around the table, thinking instead about the next school dance, what movie she could go see with Adam and her friends the next day, occasionally an art project or a book she'd only gotten to glance longingly at because she'd been helping mom clean the house top to bottom for days.

The way this conversation, this group of people, fit her just right was like a warm blanket over her skin. Not only were they talking about interesting things, but they included her, and were actually interested in what she had to say. Before she knew it she was talking to the urban planning professor about how she hadn't been able to stop thinking about sustainable building practices, and why they couldn't be implemented in the United States for the poor.

"This is why it's such a blessing that election day is a few weeks before Thanksgiving," Tamara said. "We start to think about turkey and sweet potatoes when we should be thinking about how we can help the people who don't have any of the things we are so thankful for. And Jesus knows if we don't talk about those things, if we don't lead the charge to provide them, nobody will. Even when we vote for the right people, still nothing gets done. Still we're handing out blankets to people sleeping on the streets."

Harriet bent over Tamara and gently kissed her head. "We have guests, my love, and church isn't until tomorrow. Save it for the sermon."

"Luckily for all of you," Tamara replied, "Christmas is about challenging ourselves to look at the world in a new way. So *all* of my sermon will be new to you."

Good-hearted chuckles filled the room as Tamara stabbed her fork into another bite of turkey, a gloating grin spread across her face.

The next day, Christmas, was filled with a trip to the soup kitchen and lazy movie-watching, as promised. But all of that Christmas comfort and joy was overshadowed by the tense text conversations with Mom.

Matt wasn't nosy when Amy ducked into the guest room, twice between dessert and again when both of his moms had fallen asleep in recliners, so she could deal with Mom in private. Her texts were becoming more and more panicked-sounding throughout dinner, but the one that finally made Amy's heart stop was the one that came through in all caps:

THIS IS YOUR FATHER.

A giggle rose up in Amy's throat. But she knew it was a hysterical one when fear squeezed her chest the next second:

GET YOURSELF HOME RIGHT NOW. YOUR MOTHER IS WORRIED SICK.

and then:

I AM VERY DISAPPOINTED.

Finally, she strung a few words together.

I'm safe and sound at a friend's house. We're going to church tonight.

That started the phone vibrating in Amy's hand. She jumped and tossed it on the bed, steeling herself to stare at it until the ringing stopped. She bit her lip and forced her feet to stay stuck to the ground. *Don't let him scare you.* When it went silent, she let out a slow breath, then jumped when it lit up with another text message.

YOU DO NOT GET TO CHOOSE WHERE TO CELEBRATE CHRISTMAS YOUNG LADY.

She held the phone in two hands in front of her, trying to read and re-read Dad's words despite her shaking fingers and the fury casting everything in her vision dark and blurry. Dad was so horribly oblivious to the truth that had been creeping up on Amy since the day Adam had broken her heart—she'd hardly ever gotten to choose anything. Every single thing in her life, from what she would wear to who she would be, had been chosen for her.

Well, now she was going to choose for herself.

The strength that conviction brought her only lasted for a second, until the phone rang. Mom's name on the incoming call screen had almost always made her smile in the past few months. Now it nearly made her pass out.

She shouldn't have answered—she knew that. She should have ignored the call, shoved her phone in her purse, and focused on feeling as contented for the rest of the trip as she had during dinner. And tamping down the building feeling of resentful jealousy that Matt seemed to have these parents that loved him no matter what he majored in or what t-shirt he wore or what kind of slightly inappropriate jokes he made. There were no strikes against him, there were no expectations on who or what he would grow to be. He was just there, and they just loved him.

But she did pick up, held the phone to her ear. Let hope bleed into the one word she managed to get out. "Mom?"

"No. I told her to call. But she's crying too much to dial your number." Dad's voice was hard, short. Unforgiving.

The guilt surged inside Amy and squeezed her chest even harder. She was speechless.

"Well? Don't you have anything to say for yourself?"

"I…" she really didn't. She knew she was supposed to say, "I'm sorry, Daddy. I'll come home." But she hadn't forgotten the way Dad had made her feel, however indirectly, when he ranted about how dirty girls who'd had sex before marriage were. Ten times fresher than that sting was the betrayal of Mom, who'd basically tried to trap her into getting back together with Adam, on one of the most peaceful days of the whole year.

Even though she hadn't verified it, either Mom or Dad had helped Adam surprise her with his unwanted pickup, an interaction that still rattled her down to her last nerve.

"I don't have any way of getting back there. I'll see you at Spring Break." She let her voice go on auto pilot, giving him an answer that, while it wasn't the one she wanted, kept her from either breaking down in tears or dissolving into rage-filled screams. As robotic as her words felt and sounded, she was proud of herself for choking back the "I'm sorry."

"Young lady," Dad said, low in the phone, a growl rumbling from his throat. "I don't care what you have to do. I don't care if you have to pay this girlfriend who took you home or if you have to hitchhike, but…"

"Boy," Amy blurted out before she could hold back. Seizing on the strength coming through her words that she hadn't really expected, she kept going. "My friend who brought my home is a guy. And honestly, he treats me ten times better than Adam ever did. And nobody tried to force me to me to spend Christmas with him, either."

"Amy. Are you telling me that you're dating a boy I've never met?"

"I..." Again. Speechless. Amy had slowly been realizing since she got to college how little she had ever talked to Dad, and having this totally bizarre conversation drove it home even more. "You never told me I had to...I didn't know...Is this some new rule of yours?"

"It is not new. This has been a rule since your sister was born, Amy Elizabeth Bauer. You do not date a boy that I haven't met and approved."

She would have made a mental list of boys she had dated, to see if they really did all fit the criteria, if there had been more than one to list. But of course, Dad knew Adam. The whole town knew Adam. Not only that, but Adam was as good as a saint for having led the high school team to State, then getting a football scholarship to Northern. Of course Dad approved of him, wordlessly and every single time he saw the guy. He was their town's crown prince, fit for Dad's princess. What had they ever had to talk about? Dad had given his approval of Adam before Amy ever looked at him with stars in her eyes.

The Broken Hearts Society of Suite 17C

How had she never realized how completely and totally that assumption of Dad's pervaded her every life decision?

One thing she was definitely grateful for—she was realizing it now—was that now that she was away from home, she was free to make her own decisions.

"Are you listening to me, young lady? Are you dating some boy I've never met?" Dad slowed down his words, enunciating them as though stupidly trying to communicate with someone who was hard of hearing or didn't speak English.

And that was enough to unleash every ounce of frustration and sass and anger and indignation that had ever lived inside her, all at once. She felt it. She was about to get brave. "It's none of your business."

She could have simply said no, told Dad that she'd talked to him later, hung up the phone, and collapsed on the bed with exhaustion, and maybe some tears. Although she was getting really, really tired of crying. Whether it was because she knew that leaving Dad in the dark with his own crazy, misogynistic assumptions would force him to acknowledge her independence, however little he liked it, or for some other reason, refusing to clearly answer the question about whether she was dating Matt felt like the right thing to do.

After all, they were friends, but weren't they a little more than that? People who were just friends didn't spend every afternoon studying together, make each other laugh effortlessly, challenge each other to think about their religion and spend Christmas together without it being weird in any way. No, they'd never kissed. They'd never been on a date and they'd never even held hands. Not like that, anyway.

But something about going through her first semester at Northern with Matt had changed her whole world.

This realization hit her so hard, this friends-but-more truth, that she hardly noticed when Dad started talking again. Some angry mumbling, then, "And I won't come out there to get you. Wherever there is." The implicit threat hung in the air. She was in some serious trouble. "But we will be addressing this when you come home for Spring Break. Until then, we'll be praying for you."

The outrage in Dad's voice had faded a bit to include a tinge of anguish. But Amy's matched his. "We'll be praying for you" meant "You've screwed up so badly that only God can help you now." Amy couldn't bring herself to believe that. Not anymore.

"Tell Mom I'm sorry." That, at least, felt sincere, even if she couldn't say it to Dad. She'd have to ask Mom why she'd planned to push her and Adam back together on Christmas. Maybe it hadn't been her decision after all, Amy realized, now that she understood how few decisions had ever been hers, and hers alone, to make. Maybe Dad controlled Mom just as much as he controlled his daughters.

The Broken Hearts Society of Suite 17C

"You're going to owe your mother a lot more than that," Dad said, the growl fully present again.

"Okay, Dad, I—" She stopped short, her better judgment to apologize warring with her deep, irrefutable knowledge that she was right. She was an adult, and her family was trying to manipulate her, and she wouldn't take it. Couldn't take it.

"What?" Dad snapped.

Amy sighed. "Nothing."

Another long pause, this time on Dad's end. Of what? Disappointment? Anger? Then, in soft, controlled tones, "I'll pray for you, Amy." Then a click and a dial tone as he hung up. Whatever he was feeling on the other end, Amy knew what it meant when Dad said that. He thought she was too far gone to be helped. He would pray for her, sure. But the only people he ever said that about was sinners, too far off the rails to ever be close to him or his family.

With that one sentence, Dad had called her an outsider.

That was when the tears began to fall.

Amy didn't know how long she would have sat there, taking staccato gasps in and out, trying to stay quiet and ward off an even bigger meltdown, if Matt hadn't knocked on the door a few moments later.

"Ames, you awake in there?" The thoughtfulness of just his voice, loud enough so she could hear but not so loud it would wake her from a deep sleep, made the tears flow heavier. "It's about time for candlelight services."

"Yeah," she choked out, trying to keep her voice under control and failing miserably.

"Hey. Are you okay?"

She could picture him, leaning his head closer to the door, wanting to respect her privacy but seriously worried now.

That image alone was enough to make her stand up and walk the few paces to the door, swing it open, and let Matt see her face in all its puffy, red-eyed messiness. What did she care? For the past fifteen weeks, nothing had been easier than talking to Matt. This wasn't any different.

Thank God she wasn't snotting yet.

"Oh, Ames." He barely had a chance to open his arms before she fell into them. She'd always sort of known he was strong despite his reedy-thinness, but having his arms so solid around her, like a force field nothing could break through, made it that much more apparent. Her forehead tucked against his shoulder automatically, and his chin notched on top of her head. After her breathing became steadier, Amy finally felt her body loosen a little. He must have too, because it was then that he spoke.

"I'm gonna guess that pie won't fix this."

She laughed for a few sweet seconds before pushing back a new round of tears that threatened to start again. *Be strong, Amy. Name the problem and he'll be able to help you carry the burden.*

Just that thought, so sweet and true, pushed the words out.

"He's really, really mad," Amy said, just loudly enough that she was sure Matt would hear it. Enough that she knew she wouldn't have to repeat it.

"Your Dad called? You said you guys never talk."

"Exactly. I...I wouldn't apologize. I refused to." She pulled back, making Matt's hand slide from the back of her head to her shoulder. Maybe looking at him would keep the tears back. "He said he'd pray for me."

Matt's eyes went wide. He understood. "Oh, man."

That was enough to start the big tears rolling out again, and to make Matt tug her head gently back to his shoulder. "If it's that big of a deal, I can take you back home. You could make it in time for your church. I could go with you."

A laugh bubbled up through the tears. "I don't think that would be a good idea," Amy said. "I think half of what was making him angry was...well...you."

Matt pulled back again. "I don't get it. Why does a nice sophomore guy from Northern bringing you home to his pastor mom for Christmas piss him off? I mean, any more than the obvious blatant disobedience of his wishes?" Then his eyes went wide again. "Is it the pastor mom thing? Or the gay moms thing?"

Amy grinned. "You would think that would be it, wouldn't you? But no, he doesn't know anything about them. Or you. That's what bothered him, I think. He thinks I'm dating a guy he's never met—never *approved* —which is apparently against the rules."

"But you told him we're not dating, right?"

"No." Then Amy's gaze connected with Matt's, and confused, jittery realization slammed her in the chest. "No, I didn't."

Matt's eyebrows tented up, but he didn't break eye contact for a second. "Oh. Okay."

Amy could have jumped in, and clarified a million different ways—the conversation was going too fast, she'd needed an excuse for not seeing Adam, she had wanted to piss Dad off. But some deep voice inside told her none of those things were true. Not only that, but she couldn't even think of a good reason to make excuses at all.

"Whatever. Don't worry about it. I'm fine."

"You are so far from fine." The soft smile in his eyes drifted to the bedside table, and he walked a few steps to retrieve the tissue box that sat there, offering her one.

Amy smiled. "Thanks. I guess I should clean myself up before services."

Matt shrugged. "It doesn't matter what you look like. Might be better to go all tear-streaked. Jesus came for the brokenhearted."

Amy knew that psalm like the back of her hand. But she could play that game.

"We're supposed to praise Him with a joyful heart, and nobody could be happy sitting next to these mascara streaks."

Matt laughed. "Whatever you say."

The Broken Hearts Society of Suite 17C

Amy thought she knew what the peace of Christmas felt like, with the solemn ritual of the Tripp City Baptist Church Christmas Eve candlelight service. Maybe if things had gone differently, she wouldn't have ever thought anything was better than that.

But St. George's Episcopal Church felt like exactly the place she needed to be that Christmas. Matt's mom spoke about challenging oneself to pour more love into the world, because if God trusted humanity with His only son, the rest of them could certainly trust more people and things with the devotion of their hearts. When the lights dimmed and Matt passed her a candle, the silence was thick and rich. If someone had told Amy it would last forever, she might have believed them, and even been okay with it.

But Tamara's deep alto rang out, pure and clear, seconds later, singing the first notes of "Silent Night." The first candle was lit and the first flame was passed, and as each person received a flame, she joined in the song.

Matt's voice was just like him—calming in its familiarity, soothing and steady. Amy never had been a great singer, and when the words "redeeming grace" passed her lips, a lump rose in her throat that blocked much sound from coming out at all. Tears fell again, but these were slow, cleansing, and welcome.

This was the kind of feeling she wanted to belong to. This felt like home.

The song wound down, and the lights slowly went up enough for the worshipers to find their way out.

Matt saw the tracks the tears had made. Of course he did. He saw everything. "Are you okay?" he asked, considering her with a tilt of the head before reaching up to wipe one tear away with his thumb.

"I'm wonderful," Amy said, simply.

Matt nodded, because he understood.

The morning after Christmas at Matt's house was exactly as he had described it—cinnamon rolls, board games, more lazy reading. Just as they had the day before, Amy and Matt moved in a steady, quiet orbit around one another. The difference now was that Amy watched him with a sense of hope that was stronger than ever—hope for what, she still didn't exactly know. But he seemed to sense that, as well.

They'd eaten deli sandwiches for Christmas dinner, a throwback to when Tamara was exhausted from leading hours of Church activities and Harriet was overwhelmed with taking care of Matt. The practice had stuck, and now it was a tradition. The idea that one day she would be an adult making traditions of her own sent a shiver down Amy's spine. She looked over at Matt and smiled, and the same peace she'd felt in Church the night before washed over her again.

After the dishes had been cleared, Amy settled on the couch in front of a fire Tamara built in the old wood-burning stove that served as a fireplace and pulled out a

The Broken Hearts Society of Suite 17C

book. She thanked God for an e-reader, so it wouldn't be quite so obvious that she was reading a fluffy romance novel. She'd read two paragraphs and already started to become lost in the story, so Matt plopping down next to her on the couch startled her.

"Sorry!" He laughed. "I didn't mean to interrupt your digestion of dinner and War and Peace."

Amy smacked him playfully with the back of her hand. "You're not sorry at all."

"Probably true. Anyway," Matt said, tugging his phone out of his pocket, "I came to see if you were up for meeting my friends from high school. I just got a text. Tonight, when everyone is coming down from Christmas family stuff. I know I promised you movies and pie, and this is not your kind of scene anyway…not even mine, to be honest…"

"What does that mean?" Amy asked, shutting her reader and tucking it between her leg and the arm of the couch. "Not my kind of scene?"

Matt looked at her as if it was obvious. "You know, they'll be drinking. No drugs, but that doesn't prevent them from acting like idiots when they get together. And I know you don't drink, so…"

"It's not like some irrefutable truth. Is there some law that says I can't have a beer or something? Isn't that what normal college kids do?"

"Yes," Matt said, "but you are not normal college kids. And neither am I. Remember? That's why we hang out so much?"

"Well, maybe for the next few days, I am. Or at least want to see what it's like."

Matt just pushed his eyebrows up again, showing her exactly how ridiculous this all sounded. "So maybe I won't drink. It doesn't matter. I want to do whatever you would do if I hadn't crashed your Christmas."

"I don't think—"

But Amy cut him off before he could say anymore. "You should get to do the things you'd be doing if I hadn't butted in on your holiday. Let me clean up my face a little and we'll go." And before he could say anything to protest or she could think much more about it, she'd ducked into the bathroom, splashed some water on her face, brushed on some more mascara over the fading layer of waterproof she'd swiped on that morning, swiped some bronzer over her cheekbones, and smoothed some colored balm on her lips. She could only think two things: Matt was right, what she was doing was completely out of character. But if being away from home for Christmas had felt not only okay, but amazing, maybe she should try changing a couple other things, too.

What could go wrong? She was with Matt.

She took a deep breath and one more look in the mirror with that thought—changing herself on purpose. It was a crazy thought, but it felt good. Maybe Dad was

The Broken Hearts Society of Suite 17C

right. Maybe she did need to be prayed for. What she needed even more than prayers was to figure out who in the world she really was when she wasn't living under someone else's guilt-filled expectations.

Amy let the bathroom door swing open and found Matt, standing in the exact same place he had been when she went in there, looking at her doubtfully. And he still didn't have his shoes on.

"Are you sure you're okay? With going tonight?"

"Are *you* okay? You still don't have your shoes on. They probably won't wait forever." Not that Amy had any idea who these friends were or what their plans involved outside of a few beers. She felt like a train barreling down a track. If anything tried to stop her, she could just run off the rails.

"I don't care. I just...I mean, it's totally fine if you want to stay in. I can see them next time I come home."

"But I can't. What, are you embarrassed of me? Don't want them to know who you're hanging out with at Northern?"

"Don't be ridiculous, Amy."

"So what's the problem?" She forced a grin, and from the way he still stood there, leaning against the banister, he knew how fake it was.

The thing that absolutely killed her was how right he was. She did want to stay in, cuddle up under a blanket, watch a movie, fall asleep too early, maybe after eating another slice of pie. But that was the pathetic Amy, the one who had been trained to want to stay at home, fly under the radar, do what everyone expected her to do. Just once, she wanted to try something new.

The fact that Matt would be with her meant she'd be safe. The fact that she was in a brand new town with people who'd never met her was irrelevant.

"Nothing. I'll get your coat," Matt said, finally letting a small smile creep onto his face and turning to go downstairs.

"Thanks," she murmured, following him.

"Friends over church, huh?" Harriet called after them.

"You mean hanging out with the kids I haven't seen for two months over sitting with half the geriatric population of University City for a second service in two days?"

"I mean supporting your mom while she leads services," Harriet said in a quieter voice, tenting her eyebrows up in exactly the same way as Matt did.

Amy's stomach twisted. "I mean, if we should be there for—"

"It's not Matt's fault that the members asked for a service tonight. Ironically, it's because most of their kids are in college and wanted to go back before Sunday's services. I guess they have friends and their own lives on campus or something." There was a twinkle in her eye that made Amy smile.

The Broken Hearts Society of Suite 17C

"I guess that means I'm staying for Sunday services," Matt said wryly as Tamara stood on tiptoes to kiss his head.

"Guess so," she said, smiling. "You driving tonight?"

"Yep. You've got nothing to worry about."

"Okay. Call us if you need to," Harriet said, slipping her arm around Tamara's waist and watching as Matt handed Amy her coat. Matt smiled, slipped into his shoes, and tugged Amy after him to the garage door.

After she clicked her seatbelt on, Amy stared at Matt, shaking her head.

"What?" he asked, opening the garage door and pulling his clanking car out of the driveway.

"Did they really just tell their nineteen-year-old—"

"Almost twenty," Matt interrupted.

"Whatever. In four months is not 'almost.' But did they really just tell you they knew we'd be drinking?"

"Yeah," Matt said. They've been saying the exact same thing since I was sixteen. Annoying, really, when you consider that I have never once driven drunk. Never even came home drunk, come to think of it." He snuck a glance at Amy. "Maybe they think I'll do something stupid because you're here."

"I don't' think you could do something stupid if you tried," Amy said, only realizing how worshipful her voice sounded once the words hung in the air between them.

"I really, really hope not," he said, giving her one final look before they pulled out of the subdivision and onto a main road studded with strip malls and chain restaurants. In just a few minutes, they were pulling into the driveway of another, much larger house with a manicured lawn and a dozen beater cars lining the street in front of it.

"Anything I need to know before I go in?"

"Nah. These are all school and church friends. Mostly guys, a few girls. Half of those girls are trying to get together with at least one of the guys. None of those guys are interested in them, even though all but one is single."

"So...?"

"So I recommend you stick with me. I trust my friends...I guess. But you are the hot girl from Northern they've never met, and they've been drinking at least a little..."

"The hot girl," Amy scoffed. "Okay."

"Stop that. You're gorgeous and you know it."

"Sure. From my orange hair and spotted face all the way down to my size 8 butt." As soon as she said it, she was embarrassed by her honesty. But Matt didn't seem too embarrassed by his compliment, and she'd been trained to be embarrassed about anything she ever said. She looked at him, willing fearlessness to take hold. Willing herself

"Sure. My gorgeous curvy redheaded best friend from Northern."

Friend. There was that word again. That was the word she'd wanted to be one hundred percent clear between them. So why did it feel like a slap in the face tonight?

"Hey," he said, patting her knee, sending a jolt she couldn't explain through her body. "Come on. The sooner I introduce you the sooner I can get you back home. You've had a long couple of days."

"I'm *fine*," Amy said, feeling an edge creep into her words. "Seriously. Fine." She didn't need Dad telling her what she needed, how she felt, how she should be acting, what she should want. She silently begged Matt to understand that she didn't need those things from him, either.

She felt nothing but relief when he nodded and smiled, genuinely and openly. "Okay. Whatever you want."

That was right. Whatever she wanted. Tonight, at least, she needed to prove that she could want things, and that she could do them, and it would be her decision alone.

Within the first twenty minutes, Amy had decided she wanted a drink, and Jason, a friend of Matt's with big, wide shoulders and a neck almost as thick as his head brought her something he called sangria. "It's just fruit punch with a little kick," he explained, handing her a red plastic cup. Some type of giddiness bubbled up in her as she took a sip, and found he was right—it was a sticky-sweet red concoction with only the slightest burn going down her throat.

"Perfect," she said, then proceeded to watch Matt greet his friends, taking a bigger gulp when she met one, two, three, four absolutely stunning girls, more than one of whom touched Matt's arm with a lingering familiarity that made her wonder about exactly how close they were. By the sixth time she listened to Matt explain that they were 'just friends,' the red drink was gone, and she was nodding at Jason for a refill.

Matt introduced her to another guy, explaining that he was an architecture major at Purdue, and she managed some questions about what his classes were like before the fuzziness transferred to her head and Matt asked if she wanted to sit down. She forced out a normal "sure!" before saying a silent prayer of thanks for an empty seat on the couch and slumping into it. Matt wasn't far behind, and despite the fact that she was more relaxed than she remembered being in, well, ever, she was hyper aware of every place his body touched hers. Hip, thigh, almost-knee. She'd only sat beside him a handful of times—on that bench the night he'd rescued her, in the car, in church just last night. But instead of feeling wrong, the closeness prompted one word flashing like a neon sign in her brain—*more*.

Someone handed Matt a guitar. He'd never told her he played, and watching him handle it so easily, cradling the instrument with such care, was like looking at entirely new person. Amy enjoyed the warm, fuzzy feeling that crept over her shoulders and buzzed at the edges of her lips as his long fingers picked over the strings. She stayed close to him as she waited for him to hand it back to the girl with the long blond bob who watched him play with puppydog eyes. The neck of the guitar stretched over her lap, the vibrations of his voice as he sang some song by the Weeping Marys about pure beauty and faith transferring to every inch of her skin.

Amy shivered, but not from cold. In fact, the sensation made her feel warmer, more at peace with everything. Like she was finally part of something all her own, not handed down to her by anyone, but extended to her for the taking. For a second, when Jason wordlessly asked if she needed another refill from across the room, she thought about what her parents, even her sister, would think. But, no. That was the good girl auto-pilot, the one that had made her feel so worthless when one piece of it fell away and left a wreckage of everything else. When Jason brought the refill, she thanked him with a big smile, and was only slightly confused when he chuckled and shook his head as he walked away.

Matt's fingers were so beautiful as they moved over the strings, so precise and smooth at the same time. Amy closed her eyes and remembered the last time they'd held hands, how comforting the touch of his skin against hers had been, how natural it had felt to be close to him in that way.

How much she wanted to be close to him in other ways. Suddenly, the memories of his hands in hers, his arms around her, his lips pressed to her head, combined into one absolutely certain, overwhelming thought.

Amy wanted to be with Matt. She wanted his breath to mingle with hers, she wanted to feel his hand strong on her waist. Something about coming home with him for Christmas, or her Dad yelling at her, or that indescribable feeling at his church, or the sweet pink drink in the red cup, had removed any complications and barriers and worries, any things she'd ever felt she needed to prove. Now she saw the only thing that really mattered—Matt, and how beautiful he was, inside and out. How very rarely anyone had ever taken care of her the way he did, with no conditions, no pretenses, no demands on how she would act, look, or what she would want. She wanted him so much, and she realized it so strong and clearly, that any other goals she'd had for tonight faded away. Nothing mattered but telling him what she wanted, and finding out, once and for all, whether he still wanted it too.

For the first time in months, a clear prayer rang through her heart. *Let him still want to be with me, too.*

A couple drinks within half an hour made Amy feel warm, fuzzy, very aware of her feelings and not caring at all about her worries. After another half hour, though, her eyelids grew heavy and seemed to drag her head down with them. She felt it loll against the back of the couch, then slump onto Matt's shoulder. The voices all around her, telling stories from the last few months and trading good-natured ribbing about whatever sports, subjects, and relationships Matt's friends were in at their various far-flung colleges, became thick, slow in her ears. The last thing she heard was, "Hey Matty, I think your girl's ready to get to bed," before her eyes closed all the way. Matt's shoulder under her cheek felt solid, and his friend was right—she did want to get home—but she was also newly aware of exactly how much she liked touching him. If he took her home, they'd be in the car, and then he'd help her in the house, and then she'd see him tomorrow morning, and be totally embarrassed that she'd draped herself all over him.

And possibly never have the chance to be so close to him again.

If he took her home, she'd fall asleep, and tomorrow morning she would have lost all the bravery she'd somehow found tonight. So, she managed to say something. "No, I'm good. I'm very comfortable, right here."

"That's exactly right, Ames. And if you get any more comfortable, you're going to fall asleep on Alex's couch, and there's no way I'm going to be able to carry you out of here." His arm nudged at her back, so firm and steady. How had she not realized how strong he was?

"You could," she mumbled, fighting to keep her eyes open, struggling to lift her head off his shoulder, given that she really, really didn't want to. "You're a lot stronger than I thought you were." Finally, her head came up, and she was looking right into his warm brown-green eyes, which danced with amusement.

"Okay," he said with a chuckle. "You definitely need to get home, if you're giving me compliments like that."

In the background, or maybe it was right beside her, one girl whispered to another—"I told you he was taken."

"Neither of them said anything!" the other responded.

A smile crept onto Amy's face and she shook her head lazily. She wanted to tell the girls that no, Matt wasn't taken, but they still couldn't have him. That he was hers, hers to kiss, hers to say yes to, even though he wasn't her boyfriend. For the first time in her entire life, Amy knew, with absolute certainty, that she belonged to Matt just as Matt belonged to her. She also knew that when they left this party, he would kiss her, and she would kiss him back, and everything would be perfect, because he was gorgeous and this night was beautiful and she was so glad that she had come home with him and stood her ground against her parents. Yes, everything was perfect. Or would be, once she got out of here.

Matt's arm nudged up and in on her back, giving her the support she needed to stand. The dizziness that swept her head was gone in a few seconds, and she smiled indulgently at Matt's friends, these beautiful people who had given her an adult beverage for the first time in her life. She wasn't a little girl, and she didn't have to follow rules, and she could choose her own friends. They'd reinforced all these things tonight, and she loved them all for it. Loved them so much.

"Thank you so much," she managed, despite her thick tongue and fuzzy lips, as Matt led her to the door. He held her coat out for her, but she didn't want to move her arm from around his shoulders, so she only slipped one arm in.

"See you soon, Matty boy!" one of the guys yelled as they stepped out the door, and it was followed by whoops, claps, and giggles from the rest of them. Amy didn't really understand what was so funny, but she beamed back at them, because she wanted to be part of the joke too.

"Idiots," Matt muttered as he waved over his shoulder at his friends. The cool air wrapped around Amy as they walked, pricking into her skin and leaving goose bumps behind. She shivered and turned into Matt, slowing him down for the rest of the short walk to his car, loving the feel of being held up by him. After all, he'd been holding her up since she met him. This was just a natural end to the process.

Amy shivered against the car's chilled upholstery, and curled in on herself as Matt shut her door and then started the engine once he'd ducked into his. He looked over at her, put the car in drive, and reached over to pat her knee. More warm electricity bled up Amy's leg, and she surprised herself by darting her hand out to keep Matt from pulling his back to the shifter.

The ten-minute ride back to his house was a beautiful mosaic of street lights and headlights streaking against the cool, slightly damp dark. Amy pressed her forehead to the glass and watched the colors bleed into each other, trying to hold on to some of the warm, fuzzy sleepiness that had already started to leave her.

They pulled into the garage and the automatic lights made her wince. Her eyes pressed shut, she turned to Matt. "Where are your moms?"

"Oh, they have a dessert reception after the services. They said the church ladies wanted to express their gratitude, but I know for a fact that Mrs. Schnuck is trying to show up Mrs. Haffner for the best pumpkin pie."

Amy laughed lazily as she let her eyes open a little. "You are so funny. Have I told you that? So…" she trailed off as his hand cupped her face and he looked into her eyes again. "So great. You're great for bringing me to that party. For bringing me home. For being my friend."

Matt shook his head and smiled at her. "And you're drunk. Let's get you up to bed."

She wanted to protest—she wasn't drunk, exactly. Sure, she was falling asleep, and everything looked and felt and sounded so delicious, so perfect, but she was thinking clearly. More clearly than she maybe ever had before. But before she could even get a fraction of those thoughts in

The Broken Hearts Society of Suite 17C

any cohesive order, Matt had already come to open her door and was offering her his hand.

"I'm not drunk," she protested as he slid his arm around her back again, making her close her eyes with how absolutely perfect his body felt against hers.

"Okay," Matt replied as he guided her to the stairs. "Then why do you need me to hold you up?"

"I don't need you to," Amy said, making sure to turn her own blue-green eyes to his at that moment. She meant every word, now, and she didn't just want him to hear it. She wanted him to feel it, and to know that she felt it, too. "I want you to, though."

Matt swallowed, hard, and blinked once, slowly. He barely broke contact as he shrugged out of his jacket, leaving it on a hook just inside the front door. Matt's grip drifted fractions of an inch lower with every step, until they reached the top of the stairs and his fingers wrapped around her hip. A sliver of extra-intense warmth told Amy his hand was touching her skin, just a tiny bit, and her head swirled all over again. How had she possibly gone this long, knowing him and not touching him like this? How had she never noticed how gorgeous he was?

"Help me to bed," she said, hearing that her words were already clearer, feeling a small pang of awareness that what she said wasn't exactly the kind of thing that would typically pass between a girl and a guy who were just friends. Her heart twisted—was she going to ruin something before it even started? How did you get one of your best friends to kiss you without losing his friendship?

"You're serious," Matt said, and Amy just nodded, taking advantage of the fearlessness the spiked sticky drink had left coursing through her body, making sure her eyes never left his. In the guest room, with the dim light from the bathroom across the hall slanting onto the bed, Matt led Amy to sit down on her bed, then helped her pull her own puffy coat off, letting it drop to the floor. He had to feel her shiver as his fingers brushed down the length of her arm, slower than they had to. He had to want to touch her, too.

"I'll get you a glass of water," he said, half question, half statement.

"Shoes?" she answered.

He swallowed again, and a deep satisfaction settled in Amy's core as he knelt in front of her, his face inches from hers, and silently unzipped her boots, pulled them off, and set them right in front of her nightstand. His fingers brushing down her calves was almost too much, and from the intense look in his eyes as he asked her in a whisper, "what else?" it affected him too.

Be brave, Amy Bauer. You have never told anyone what you want. You have never really known for sure what you wanted, until this minute. Say it. Tell him. You have to.

She may have had a little too much alcohol in her system, but her thoughts had never been clearer. "Kiss me."

He sucked in a breath. "Amy, I—"

"Please. You have to." Fear started to wrap around her, the purest kind of terror that maybe, just maybe, he didn't feel the same way.

He leaned in closer to her, planted his hand beside her on the bed, made knees go down and her shoulders go forward. They were centimeters apart, and his breath mingled with hers, a feeling so intimate and so perfect she could hardly stand it. Her eyes fluttered closed. "Please," she repeated in the barest of whispers.

And then, thank God and Jesus and all the angels, his lips were on hers. Every bit of heat she'd felt when his skin touched hers combined and exploded inside her, only quelled the slightest bit when his fingers brushed the back of her neck, bringing her back to herself. Her hands lifted to the sides of his face, her fingers shaking as they found his hairline, then drifted down his neck.

She desperately wanted that feeling of his body against hers again, and she didn't care how she got it. Instinct took over, and she leaned back, begging him to follow with the slight flick of her tongue against his. Her arms went around him, pulling him down on top of her, and her entire body sang with relief at the pressure his body on top of hers. Her hands slid up under his shirt, and she was acutely aware of every single sharply defined muscle on his back, his sides, and, as her thumbs swept down, his stomach and ridge of his hip.

She sighed happily into his mouth, and he responded with a soft moan and an even harder kiss as his fingers tangled in her hair and his legs tangled with hers. She felt the quick movements as he kicked his shoes off, heard the thud as they landed to the floor. One more big scoot back and her head sunk into the pillow as Matt's lips moved, hot and hungry, to her throat. She tipped her head back, aware she was about to taste victory, and took the risk of moving her hands from under Matt's shirt to grasp at the bottom of her own. In an instant, it was over her head, and her copper waves spread around her head on the pillow.

Matt, having been interrupted, looked at her in awe, shaking his head. "Amy, I thought—I mean, you told me you didn't—"

"I didn't want to date," she said, biting her lip, the sensation coming back to it bit by bit. "But I realized something. I want you. I want this," she finished, edging her hands under his shirt, too, trying to keep control of herself when she finally saw what she'd only just now felt. He may have been thin, but his muscles were clearly defined and absolute perfection. His lips were full, and now that she knew how amazing they felt against her own, all she wanted to do was touch them, kiss him again. And he still had his glasses on, which somehow added to the intensity of his eyes as they stared into hers. She'd never

The Broken Hearts Society of Suite 17C

thought guys looked good in glasses—not until she met him.

She raised herself up and gingerly pulled the wire frames off with one hand while cupping the back of his neck with the other, pulling him back down to her and finally, finally getting what she wanted. His skin against hers. Her breasts looking so sexy pressed up against his chest, and even better when his lips trailed down her shoulder, his strong hand slid up her back and under her bra strap, and his other hand slid down her stomach, his little finger grazing the waistband of her panties.

And then he moved back up her stomach again, then rested on her hip again. His lips back on hers, he kissed her softly, patiently, like they had all the time in the world.

But through the fuzz and fog of the lingering alcohol, Amy knew one thing for sure—they *didn't* have all the time in the world.

They only had tonight.

If Amy threw herself into a relationship with Matt, she'd never, ever be able to drag herself back out. What she felt for him was ten times stronger than the strongest thing she'd ever felt for Adam, and he'd nearly ruined her.

The only way she was going to be brave enough to show him was if she was drunk. Maybe she'd known it all along, or maybe it was just becoming crystal clear now. Matt was perfect for her, and that was exactly why she couldn't fall for him. Drunk sex was the closest she could let herself get.

So she wedged her hand down between them, straight down the front of his jeans. He was hard as a rock, which only ignited something even more desperate inside her. She smiled against his lips, then swept her tongue along his, savoring the taste of him. But as she pulled her hand back out and grasped for his zipper, he grabbed her wrist, tugged it away, and rolled off of her with a grunt.

"What's the matter?" Amy asked, her voice breathy and her head spinning.

Matt stared at the ceiling, his jaw clenched hard. The muscle just above it jumped as he tugged his hand back through his hair.

Amy turned to him, propping herself up on one arm, but when her head spun out of control again, she had to stare at the ceiling too. And then the tears started to come.

"What did I do wrong?" She whispered, the swimming-drunk feeling in her head intensifying every twinge of embarrassment and rejection. Apparently alcohol amplified every emotion—even the horrible, soul-crushing ones.

Matt blew a long breath out through pursed lips, then sat up and grabbed her shirt from where it had landed at the end of the bed.

"Ames, please," he said when he handed it to her and pulled her up to sitting with the other hand. The tears started to roll down her cheeks, fat and heavy.

She couldn't say a word for the giant lump in her throat, couldn't look Matt in the eyes as she pulled the stretchy cotton tee back over her head. Matt did the same with his shirt, then sat cross-legged on the bed, looking helpless. It took him forever to say something else.

"We can't do this. I mean, I *want* to do this. But we can't do this while you're…after you've been drinking. I can't do this," he repeated, his voice trailing off as he stared at his hands, strategically folded on his lap. "I *won't* do this while you're drunk. I'm sorry," he said, hoisting himself off the bed, stalking to the door, and letting it fall shut behind him.

Pain flooded Amy, from too many things for her to count—embarrassment, rejection, disappointment, the realization that she'd fallen in love with someone who had probably fallen out of love with her. Or—oh, God—maybe he'd never been in love with her in the first place. Maybe she'd just been so utterly pathetic and desperate for any guy to love her that she'd imagined everything. Her lips, her arms, her entire body felt too numb to move, too stunned to cry. Eventually, the dark edged out the pain, and she fell asleep.

Even though the sun didn't rise until eight o'clock, it was well up before Amy's eyelids cracked open. The only feeling less pleasant than the bright orange light piercing through the crack in the curtains was the thick, stale taste of her mouth. She groaned and made a quarter turn on her side, coming face to face with a glass of water and two small white pills.

It only took a few seconds of her head pounding in protest to her movements that she realized what those were for.

Just as she'd swallowed the second aspirin, there was a knock at the door that sounded more like pounding.

She half-groaned, "Yeah?" and Matt stuck his head in.

"Can I come in?"

Amy almost told him to wait for her in the kitchen, but then remembered that his moms were probably down there, eating grapefruit and laughing like normal people. She also wasn't entirely sure that she could lift her head up.

"I guess." Amy cupped her hands over her face, just then realizing that she probably looked like mascara-smeared death in last night's jeans. That's how she felt, anyway.

Matt stood a few feet from the bed, shifting from foot to foot and watching Amy. It took a lot of effort to wedge her elbows against the bed and push herself to sitting, then to breathe through her throbbing temples once she did. Matt eased onto the opposite corner of the mattress and let out a heavy breath.

"I brought coffee, too," Matt said, pushing his glasses up on his nose, something he never did. Looking closer, Amy realized they were silver wire-rimmed, not the rounded dark frames he always wore.

"Did you get new glasses?"

The Broken Hearts Society of Suite 17C

"No, um...these are old. When you pulled off my other ones last night, they, um...well, I couldn't wear them this morning."

Amy closed her eyes and held back a whimper. "You're kidding me. Matt, I am so, so sorry."

"I brought you coffee," he said, still not looking at her. "Are you feeling better?"

Amy took it and held the hot cup in her hands, not daring to put it down. It was keeping her trembling hands from shaking.

"I'm feeling less fuzzy. Less dizzy." *Less impulsive.*

"Do you remember what happened last night?" Matt asked cautiously, only meeting Amy's eyes for the barest second.

Amy begged herself to pull forth the same bravery the alcohol had given her last night. Those stupid drinks may have taken away her inhibitions, but she'd loved that feeling—of being herself, of saying what she meant. She needed to do that every day. Even when she wasn't drunk.

"I remember that you kissed me."

"Do you remember asking me to?"

Amy nodded, watching him with wide eyes.

"Do you remember what happened after?" Matt's voice had become low, shaky.

"Do I remember being dropped like a used Kleenex by yet another guy since I started college? What do you think, Matt?"

Matt's eyes went wide and he shook his head, like he had just realized he was in a freaky alternate universe. "Amy, that is not at all what—"

"Except that it absolutely is. You kissed me. You touched me, and I trusted you. And then you decided, what? You didn't want me because I was a little out of it? Because I wasn't picture perfect at that exact moment?"

Matt held up his hands, palms out. "Hold on. No. Amy, I stopped out of respect for you. Out of respect for us."

She scoffed, hoping that calling forth some anger would keep more tears from pouring out. "Yeah, okay. Because I didn't tell you that I wanted to."

"There is absolutely no way you could have made that decision last night, Amy. Not the way you should have, anyway, and I wasn't about to let you. No matter how badly I wanted to." He swallowed and looked at her, his eyes blazing.

"I'm sorry," Amy said, bitterness swirling in her stomach. "I thought I was in charge of my own body. I thought it was mine to control, not someone else's. Definitely not yours. I thought you were the one who told me all that. Guess it's different when you're involved personally. You guys just can't resist telling a girl what decisions she is or is not allowed to make, can you?"

Matt winced like he'd been stung. "That's not what I'm saying, and you know it. Just…last I knew, you didn't even want to let me take you to dinner, and now you want to go all the way in my parents' guest room after you had three cups of jungle juice in two hours? The first drinks of your whole life?"

Amy swallowed hard and shook her head, refusing to look at him. He scooted forward and tipped her chin to him. "Maybe you don't know what you want to happen between us, and that's okay. You know? But if we're going to do this, there has to be more behind it than disappearing inhibitions and convenience."

The fuzz in Amy's brain seemed to have returned full force. His words didn't quite make sense, didn't really connect into an argument she could make sense of. One thought kept running through her mind—she tried to have sex with a guy, something Adam had begged her to do for months, and Matt had turned her down like it didn't affect him at all.

He'd turned her down.

She couldn't think of a response, could only wish it was possible to rewind to two minutes ago and do or say something, anything, differently. "I thought...I don't...I'm sorry, I thought you liked me."

Matt let out another growl and shot to his feet, then started pacing at the end of the bed. "You don't get it, Amy, do you? I don't like you. I mean, I do like you. Every single little thing about you."

"But not like that," Amy said, not even trying to swipe at the tears that plopped off her cheeks and dotted her jeans. "Not enough to want to...you know. *Be* with me." Everything felt so heavy, from her head to her heart. Even the words tumbling out over her cotton-coated tongue were thick, labored.

"Yes! Yes, like that. Okay? More than that." He moved to her side of the bed, and just as quickly as he'd stood, he was down on his knees beside her, grasping her hands, like he was begging for something she couldn't understand.

"I don't like you. I *love* you, Amy. I love your smile, I love your passion for something in life you haven't even found yet. I love how you laugh at my stupid jokes, and haven't ever, not once, questioned meeting me for coffee every single day, even when you didn't order any half the time. I love your faith, that you still have it even though so much has gone wrong for you in the last few months. I love how I can't stop thinking about you. And I hate it, too, because it means that I love you. Even though I know you don't love me back. That's why I can't do this. That's why I know that you don't really want to do this."

"I can decide what I want for myself. I was drunk, but I wasn't so drunk that I didn't know what I wanted. What I still want."

Matt's jaw flexed and he looked down at the ground again. "What about what *I* want? Does that matter to you at all?"

Amy threw her hands in the air. "Of course it does, Matt. You're my best friend. Of course I care about what you want." He stared at the wall, his jaw clenched, and somehow he looked even more injured now than he had when he first walked in. Amy reached out to grab his hand, but he pulled away and stood up, pacing at the end of the bed.

"I don't know what to say to you, Amy. I don't know how to make this okay for both of us." His steps got faster, and he watched them flash over the carpet.

"Matt. Matt, stop it." Amy shot to her feet too, and stood in his path. She didn't know what possessed her, but her hands reached up and grabbed his upper arms. "Just…stop." When she felt him still, her fingers brushed down, grazing the muscle on the inside of his forearms, then finally rested, tip to tip, with his. Matt's head fell forward to rest against Amy's, which tipped up slightly, begging for contact.

Finally, she added, "This is okay. Right here. Right now." She pushed up on her tiptoes to make their lips meet, not thinking twice about morning breath or the coffee that most likely still lingered on his tongue. She didn't care about anything but showing him how she felt about him, right here, right now, so he would understand how serious she was. The rough noise that came from the back of his throat and rumbled against her lips, then his long fingers pushing through her hair, holding her close to him, made her heart soar.

"I love you," he said when he pulled away from her a moment later. His fingers drifted down to her neck, pressing in the tiniest bit in time with his heartbeat.

Amy's heart thudded painfully. "I love you." Her voice was simple, quiet. Honest. Begging him to understand.

Matt's eyes closed, too tightly to be from happiness. The pain squeezed through his voice when he replied. "Then be mine. Not, like, I would own you, or whatever. But be with me. Promise me you're planning on tomorrow. Share your days with me. Let me be yours."

"I can't." Amy's arms wrapped around Matt's waist. "I can't be in a relationship with you, I can't share my everyday life with you until I've figured out what I want it to be." She squeezed him close, held on for dear life.

"Isn't that what you've been doing since you got to Northern?"

Amy tucked her head into Matt's chest, hugged him closer, even as she felt his hold on her starting to weaken. *Please understand.* "I've been spending all this time learning who I could be, what my life could be like, yes. But you've been right by my side the whole time. I'm grateful for that, but I've never been on my own." The force and depth of that truth threatened to drag her down into a deep, dark hole, but she fought to stay on the surface.

"I understand," he said, letting his arms drop so that all that was left of their embrace was Amy, clinging to him where he stood. An emptiness sunk into her heart and bloomed through her chest—the realization that this thing between them, whatever it was, was ending. "I understand, but that means we can't do this."

The Broken Hearts Society of Suite 17C

Hearing it the second time didn't make it any easier. She loosened her grip on him, pulled away, backed up a step. How was it possible that this felt like the dream and last night felt like the only thing that was real? How could something that felt so right to her feel so wrong to him?

She barely realized that she'd started to cry, and when tears dripped down her cheeks, she didn't move to find a tissue. She didn't want to move, didn't want to be the one to walk away. The fear of never being this close to him, never touching him like this again, was so real that it terrified her.

Matt was right. She didn't know what she really wanted. She only knew her feelings were real—the feelings of wanting, and of fear. Sorting them out was becoming more difficult by the second.

When Matt stepped past her to reach for the tissue box on the nightstand, the tears came harder. He handed her a few tissues, then motioned for her to sit beside him on the bed. "You have to understand that this kills me, Amy." His words were choked. She believed him. "There's nobody else," he continued. "Right now, I can't imagine anyone else being as perfect for me as you are. And there's nothing I want more than to be with you—in all the ways. If you figure out who you are, and that's what you want too…you know where to find me."

"But I do," Amy said, and she caught a flash of hopefulness in his eyes. "I told you. I want…this. I've never been surer of anything than I was the moment I asked you to kiss me." That kiss felt so close and so far away at the same time, it seized her heart.

"I know you said you love me. But that's not enough. Not enough for us to do this, Ames." He gestured to the bed and she felt a flash of shame for how she'd put herself out there, what she'd exposed. "Tell me you want to *be* with me, that you want us to be together."

Amy's mouth dropped open, full of excuses about heartbreak and independence that, while real, didn't come close to being enough for Matt, right here, right now.

"Amy, we could even be working toward the next date. I don't care how small it is. I'm not saying we have to get married or anything. College kids have sex. Humans have sex, even when they're not married, and that doesn't make them bad people. That's not a bad thing. But I have to know that you'll still want to be mine the next morning over coffee, or at Easter services three months from now, just as much as you said you did that one time you accidentally drank way too much with my stupid high school friends."

How could she possibly know that? How could she possibly promise to imagine a future with Matt when that exact thing had ended so disastrously before?

She couldn't. How could she let another guy become her everything, a guy she loved even more than she'd ever loved Adam? She couldn't. Not if she didn't want to be totally crushed once again.

The Broken Hearts Society of Suite 17C

Amy forced her body to attention. Pulled her hands away, wiped at her eyes with the pads of her fingers. Then, commanding a stony face, looked at Matt again. "Okay. You're right."

He pressed his lips together in a hard line and blinked fast, twice, three times. Then nodded, getting to his feet again. "You get some rest, okay? I'll take you back to Northern later on."

"No, that's…I don't think that's a good idea," Amy mumbled. "I'll call Rion." She didn't know what Rion was doing, or even where exactly she was, but the idea of sitting beside Matt for two hours after what had just happened was unbearable. "She's only like an hour from here," Amy lied.

Matt sighed. "Just…okay." Amy could hear that he was holding back his concern, and his downcast eyes spoke to just how much defeat was pushing it aside. The swirling fuzziness in Amy's head started to thicken into a heavy ache, probably made a million times worse by the tears that started up all over again, taking hold of her heart and her core and yanking them back and forth so that it was all she could do to muffle her sobs in her pillow.

Chapter 18

Rion

Christmas was shit. Well, at first. She'd gone back to the house, awoken the furnace from a long slumber, and sat under an electric blanket until the living room warmed up enough for her to move her fingers. She hadn't gone grocery shopping, and now that she was bundled up, watching the day's snow start to fall, she really didn't think she would. The box of granola bars and jar of applesauce she'd found in the pantry would do just fine for today.

She'd promised Mom a visit, and tried to psych herself up for it in every possible way. But when the sky darkened on Christmas Eve, she still hadn't driven up to the tall chain-link gates across town, hadn't been able to imagine what she would say, or how she'd even be able to look Mom in the eye.

The Broken Hearts Society of Suite 17C

Christmas morning, when there was a knock at the door, she'd ducked down further on the couch, cursing herself for not parking her car a couple blocks away. She didn't want to answer questions about how her mom was doing, didn't want to look into well-meaning neighbors' pitying eyes when they asked how she was doing. Honestly, she didn't even want to sign for a fucking package. She had a prison visit to psych herself up for.

One more series of knocks on the door, and along with sinking into the blanket, she'd started to sink into a depression. She berated herself. *At least you have a fucking roof over your head, bitch. At least one of your parents is still alive. There are other kids that have it so much worse.*

It was true. She knew kids in the group home whose parents were addicted to crack, or serving life in prison, or who basically lived at the local bar and slept in their own vomit half the time. Compared to that, a father dead in a car crash and a mother in minimum-security prison looked downright cushy. But none of the platitudes she recited at herself made any difference. She was sad, and she was lonely, and there was no fucking way she was going to go out of her way to see Crash again before school started.

As much as she enjoyed spending time with him—hell, as much as she was falling in love with him, an issue she was more aware of each and every day—she wouldn't push herself into his life. She'd already let her emotions lead her to do stupid things that she'd lived to regret. She felt herself falling for him. It was like a dream where she watched herself tumble headlong over a cliff—with a mixture of interest and vague terror.

Yet the experience of being so warm and comfortable and deep with him was too good for her to leave willingly.

Finally, the knocking stopped, and her shoulders relaxed. And then, her phone buzzed in her hand, lit up with a green text bubble and six beautiful, thrilling words: "Hey Miss Hermit. Answer the door."

Rion had squealed and jumped out of her cocoon of blankets like there was a fire under her ass, then sprinted to the door. She was in old sweatpants, no bra, and three layers of old shirts—her hair was standing up on end and she hadn't even bothered to put eye shadow on that morning. But she only thought about those things long after she let Crash in, wrapped her legs around his waist, and let him carry her back to the couch and strip every layer of clothing off of her with his chilled fingers and his teeth.

There was a specialty art store he wanted to check out close by, he'd explained in the afterglow, when they'd halfheartedly fought over the electric blanket—it wasn't big enough to cover both their asses. Rion had finally gotten him to admit that "close by" was almost an hour away, but she only complained for a little bit before he used his mouth to shut her up. Later, when he'd been looking for food in the kitchen and found only her grandmother's old recipe box, he'd gone to the store and come back with armfuls of grocery bags.

It turned out that Crash was an amazing cook, too. He made sweet potatoes with marshmallows on top, a classic roast, mashed potatoes, and, unbelievably, pumpkin pie. It all filled her stomach when she fell asleep wrapped around him on the couch to *A Christmas Story*.

That night, she'd dreamed that she and Crash had moved in together, into this house, the one she'd grown up in, lived almost every happy moment of her life in. He set up a mixing studio for her in the spare bedroom and brought her homemade dinner while she worked late into the night.

The day after Christmas, she'd woken up with his tongue between her legs. After the most amazing two minutes of her life to date, she'd screamed his name, and melted into his laughing chest when he came up for air a few seconds later. "You know what's fucking stupid? You still don't know my real name," he said, dipping his head to suck at her neck just below her ear.

Waves of lingering pleasure coursed through her, and she forgot for that moment that she didn't really want to know his name. "Mmm. Stupid."

"I mean," he said, shifting on top of her, pressing his hard cock between her legs, hitting the exact spot that still throbbed from what he'd just done. "It's fucking unbelievable that you've fallen in love with a guy named Colin."

"What?" she moaned as he pressed in.

"Yep," he growled. "Head over heels in love. Which, you know," he grunted, starting to move slowly in and out, pulling unbelievable friction through her and making her head spin, "I should get a lot of credit for, considering I had to piss in a cup before you'd let me take you out for pancakes." He bent his head to suck one of her nipples into his mouth, and she gasped, the words 'Colin' and 'love' swirling around her brain and refusing to land anywhere solid.

Until afterwards, when they lay in the still early morning quiet, wrapped up in each other, like they'd done every time for the past couple months. Habits, comforts. Rion was developing them with Crash—*Colin*—without thinking twice about them.

So there, with warmth radiating through every cell of her body, Rion made a choice. Instead of watching herself fall for him and fighting every inch of the way, she was going to go along for the ride. She tucked her head into his shoulder and murmured, "You were so right." She felt the breath catch in his chest, cherished the tension she imagined buzzing against her cheek.

Finally, he said, "About not knowing my name?"

"About the love thing," she answered, letting the words come out strong and sure before she could stop herself. "Head over heels. Definitely right. *Colin.*"

Then he dug his fingers into the spot right under her ribs where he knew it killed her every time, and she tucked in on herself, consumed with laughter. She barely noticed her phone buzzing on the nightstand, until it stopped and started, stopped and started again. A total of five times.

"If that is my mom in jail, fuck her," Rion said, trying to hide in Crash's strong, warm side even more.

"You're going to hermit town again, babe." Crash pulled "I will not let you. You have so much life left to live." He rolled over and grabbed her phone, leaving her cold. She moaned into the sheets. "Oh, fuck. It's Amy."

Rion sat bolt upright, pulling the sheet over her chest. "Is she okay? She texted me she went home with Copperhead for Christmas because of her dick ex. But I didn't hear from her after that…" Rion grabbed the phone and scrolled through Amy's messages.

"You know, you could call him by his name. We had a beer once. He's a good guy."

"Oh, fuck." Rion said, pushing a half-black hunk of hair away from her eye. She was trying to grow it out since she'd chopped it off, half because she didn't want to pay to have it done, half because she liked it when he grabbed and tugged while he was fucking her.

Amy's texts read exactly like she talked. "I know you're busy, and if it's not too much trouble, would you mind coming to get me? It's not an emergency but I can't stay here. I'll take you to dinner to make up for it…"

All this was broken up into several texts and before she even finished reading them, some otherwordly reflex had Rion out of bed and pulling on sweatpants before she gave it a second thought. "I have to go."

"What's going on? Is she okay? Family emergency?" Rion's heart did a little flip at Crash's concern for her roommate, a girl he cared about strictly because of her association with Rion. Maybe when her poor dead hermity heart thawed out a little bit, and she made sure her roommate was okay, she'd sit down with Crash—while they had clothes on—and tell him how she felt. But right now, she had to leave.

Crash turned lazily into the sheets. "What do you want me to do about the house? I'm gonna sleep in. I have to drive my car back anyway."

"Key underneath the iron frog in the garden around back," Rion called as she grabbed her purse and shoved some clothes into a duffel. Where the hell were her shoes?

"Hey, Ri?" Crash called when she was nearly out the door. She ran back to her bedroom, still decorated in broody purple and a small collection of stuffed animals she'd decided to keep past 9th grade. The last normal year.

"Yeah?"

"You're a good friend."

Rion's heart swelled, and she scolded herself to keep her emotions in check. Not that that would help her overwhelming need to touch him again, just one more time. She got in close, pressed her hips to his, gave him a long, soft kiss. He smacked her ass when she pulled away, and she grinned.

Just as she crossed the threshold of her bedroom door, staring at the dusty living room and thinking maybe she and Crash would clean it up next time they were here, he called to her again. More softly this time. "Babe?"

"Yeah?"

"I love you."

He'd done it on purpose. When she was running out, and couldn't do anything about it, couldn't have any hard conversations, couldn't keep her emotions from spilling into her smile. And for the first time in a very, very long time, she decided not to fight it.

"Love you too."

Then she was gone.

"You're damn lucky my hometown is only half an hour from Mister Ginger's," Rion said, smiling as Amy hustled from the converted farmhouse into the car. It was only when she took a seat and sucked a truckload of snot back that Rion took a good look at her and saw her green eyes on fire, ringed with red. "Oh, shit," Rion said. "What did he do to you?"

She sniffled again, brushing her fire-orange waves away from her face only to have them drape back. "More like what did I do to *him*. Can we just get out of here?"

Rion felt a surge of love for Amy. Poor girl had been trashed by one boyfriend already this year. She didn't really need any more shit from another one. "Did he piss you off? Sleep with someone else?"

Amy pulled a half-used Kleenex out of her sleeve and Rion nearly gagged. "Girl, I love you, but use a new tissue, okay?"

Amy nodded, rummaging in her purse for another. "Don't you have any of that insane music you mix or whatever?"

"I don't have any sad lady tunes, if that's what you mean."

"What do you have?"

"Pissed off, mostly."

"That'll work just fine," Amy answered, sniffling again.

Rion pulled up one of her most recent mixes, a dark electronic with a driving beat layered over it, morphing into an electric guitar that spun off into long, languid chord progressions before ebbing away. Amy stared out the window until the song had gone quiet. Rion listened. Something about mixing music and listening for the subtle cues, that exact moment in the song when it was ready to change into something new, higher, better, had made her a better listener to people, too. Amy's sniffles had nearly stopped and her breaths had become more even.

Now she just looked out the window, letting her forehead rest against it as Rion's beater car roared down the highway toward school.

The Broken Hearts Society of Suite 17C

"I feel bad taking you away from Crash," Amy said, her voice measured and low. Probably trying to keep herself from crying again.

"Nothing to feel bad about. He's picking up some art stuff at a specialty shop half a mile from campus today. Day after Christmas sales, I guess. I'll have plenty of time with him when I get back. Besides, we're not like that. You know that."

"You mean not attached at the hip. Not like me and Matt," she said, evenly, barely an inflection to make Rion think whether that was something she wanted or not.

Regardless, Rion was damn glad Amy had said his name because she'd called him Ginger or Marmalade or Fire Crotch so many times it was hard for her to remember what his real name was. "Right."

Another half-gasping shuddering breath inward, and Amy's forehead was back on the windshield.

"Do you wanna talk about it?"

This wasn't a Society meeting, which was where Rion had learned to talk about guys and emotions and hopes this past year. But it was also where she'd realized that Amy was in love with Matt, and where she thought she and Arielle would get to watch Amy deliver the news that the two of them had finally, finally gotten together.

Amy sighed. "I don't know."

"You don't have to, but you can."

"He told me he loved me," Amy blurted.

"Jesus fuck," Rion said, nearly swerving the car off the road. She almost did it again when Amy turned her wide, scolding eyes on her at the words. "Sorry, sorry. It's easy to forget when I hear something like that." But then Rion realized that something didn't compute. Amy was in love with Ginger, and he'd told her he was in love with her too. So, yay, the do-gooding Christian kids with raging emotion-boners for each other had finally let it all out. Shouldn't Amy be happy?

"So what's the problem?" Rion blurted.

"That I love him, too," Amy whispered, turning her head back to the window.

"Again, still not understanding the problem."

That brought on a fresh new wave of tears. "He kissed me."

"Yeah?" Rion tried to keep from wiggling with an 'I knew it' dance in her seat. "That's good, right?"

"It was good. So good I tried to get him to sleep with me."

"Holy crap, Amy! I didn't think you had it in you. I thought you were…you know. Waiting. Again."

Amy buried her face in her hands. "Yeah. I mean, no. I mean, I guess not. But, like I said. I *tried* to get him to sleep with me. He didn't."

"Oh. *Oh*." Now it was a little clearer, and Rion's spirits started to sink to catch up with Amy's.

"I was drunk," Amy groaned, twisting a little to slump back in her car seat. "But I was just drunk enough, you know? Like, everything seemed clearer, and everything I'd ever worried about fell away. And I saw how really, really attractive he is. And then when he kissed me, and we got into it, I *felt* how attractive he is."

Rion laughed. "Well damn. I'm still not understanding the issue. Does good ol' Rusty Nuts actually have rusty nuts?"

"We were so close, and then he stopped. Said he couldn't do this. I had no idea what he meant until this morning, when I tried to remember, and I still wanted to be with him. And I told him."

"And let me guess. He's confused, because he's been trying to be your boyfriend for months, but you've been telling him you didn't want one, and he loves you too much to fuck you if you're not together the rest of the time. Am I right?"

"Well he didn't use the F word. But yeah, pretty much."

"So why not be together, Ames?" Rion softened her voice to tell Amy that she really could be honest.

"Because that's not the *point*." Amy slammed her hand on the door's hand rest, making Rion jump a little. This girl never yelled. Maybe the fact that she was raising her voice a little now was a good sign. Healthy to get her frustrations out, maybe for the first time ever. "I have been *with* a guy basically since it was possible. I have always been defined in relationship to one. Yeah, it was bad being Adam's future wife for so many reasons.

Obviously, Matt is a much, much better guy than Adam is. Better for me."

Rion didn't know exactly what was driving this stunning burst of clarity, but she wasn't about to interrupt it. She let the rumble of her old trusty Accord down the highway fill the space where Amy was working out her shitstorm of a Christmas. After what felt like an eternity but was really only a minute, she said, "What are you going to do about it?"

Amy breathed in deeply. "I'm going to get him back. But first I'm going to figure out who I am without him. Without anyone."

Rion's heart ached. She'd been there, when Dad had left unintentionally, and Mom had abandoned her. She had figured out who she was, alright, but it wasn't anyone she wanted to spend the rest of her life with, alone. How she'd gotten lucky enough to find Crash, she'd never know.

The rest of the drive back to school was pretty quiet. Amy asked a few questions about Rion's break, and Rion told her everything, even about Crash making her dinner. Well, everything except the rough and dirty Christmas sex they'd had. Amy may have been newly determined to be her own person, but that didn't mean she could deal with hearing about blow jobs and finger fucking after a breakup with her not-quite-boyfriend she didn't even realize she'd had. And right after celebrating the birthday of her Savior or whatever.

The Broken Hearts Society of Suite 17C

"Hey," Rion said as they sat in the Northern Slice, the only place that seemed to be open on Francis over break. "Do you need to go to Church or whatever?"

Amy looked at her blankly, her eyes still bearing a red tinge. "Christmas was yesterday."

"Oh. Right. Yeah, of course."

"Did you ever go, growing up?"

Rion shook her head. "I literally have no idea how church works. Actually, I kind of always wanted to go check it out, because the big dark sanctuaries and stained glass windows always seemed so creepy-cool to me. I always thought that even if they were empty and quiet, there was still always a lot going on there."

Amy tilted her head, considering that. "I guess that makes sense. I don't know. I didn't grow up going to those kinds of churches. Ours were always bright and loud and in-your-face and honestly kind of scary in a different way. Because of the pastor yelling at us about hell and stuff." Amy tore a hunk of crust off and chewed quietly. "Do you want to go? To one of the old churches? I went to a more traditional one with Matt but never for services. It didn't even have that much stained glass though."

"Well…" Rion took a second to chew too, trying to sort out the weird swirl of conflicts flying around her brain. "I don't, like, believe in God or anything."

Amy shrugged. "It's just a building. You might find something you like, even if it's not God."

"So it sounds like maybe I can help you on this quest to be your own person. Take me to a weird old church with darkness and maybe velvet seats."

The corner of Amy's mouth quirked up in a smile, and then she pushed out a heavy sigh. "I'm trying to remember which one Matt took me to." She whipped her phone out of her pocket and Rion stretched across the table to snatch it out of her hand. "You are NOT calling him, Amy."

"I wasn't going to!" Amy insisted.

"Yeah, right." Rion peered at the phone. Amy really hadn't been pulling up his texts or anything. "Do you think you might, later?"

"I wouldn't call him," Amy mumbled.

"But you might obsess over his texts from the last four months?"

Amy rolled her eyes up to the side.

"That's what I thought." Rion pulled out her own phone, searched for Matt's number in the contacts page, and copied the information into her own contacts. Then deleted Matt from Amy's phone. All of him, even his texts.

"I'm doing this because I love you," Rion informed Amy as she passed the phone back, while Rion smiled to herself that she'd freely and easily used the l-word for the second time in one day without her heart freezing up or the world stopping spinning.

Amy took the phone back and started typing away on it.

The Broken Hearts Society of Suite 17C

"What are you doing now?"

"I'm texting Arielle. I think I need a Society meeting, and I can't wait a week."

All of a sudden, Arielle's face popped up on the screen, and then soon after, Lauren's over her shoulder.

"Hey Ames, what's up? How was Christmas with Matt?" Lauren made a kissy noise in the background, puckering her lips, and Arielle turned to lay a kiss on them.

Amy and Rion groaned. "Seriously, Ari, PDA."

"We're not in public," Arielle said, laughing. But then Lauren disengaged from her waist and perched on a full bed several feet behind Arielle.

"Hey, Pretty Lauren, do you think you could duck out for a few minutes?" Rion looked pointedly at the camera.

"Rion," Amy complained, turning red. "Sorry, Lauren, I'm happy to see you, I swear. It's just that Christmas actually wasn't so good, and…and…" tears choked off her words.

"And we could use a Society meeting. An emergency one."

"Oh, yeah, of course," Arielle said, her voice dipping into a pitying rhythm. "Society meetings are private," Arielle explained to Lauren, but she didn't need direction. Lauren was already gathering up her things.

"I promised your mom I'd crush her in Monopoly anyway," Lauren said on the way out. Arielle's grin was so bright it could warm up the frigid, blustery afternoon.

Another weird feeling—Rion was happy for Arielle. Really, seriously happy.

"Okay, Ames, what's wrong?" Arielle's voice softened and her eyebrows pulled together. Rion watched Amy's pained smile in response, and shook her head at the memory that the two girls had ever been anything but close. "We're not supposed to have a meeting for another week. And you're supposed to be taking it easy at Matt's."

Amy's face crumpled and she squeezed her eyes shut. Rion's hand automatically lifted to rub her back. "I didn't even know how I felt about him. You know?"

"Oh, God. But now you do?" Arielle asked, a hint of hope in her voice.

"Yeah, but it didn't really turn out so well," Rion said as the tears started to run down Amy's cheeks all over again. She squeezed Amy's shoulder. "Do you want to tell her, or should I?"

Amy stumbled into the start of the story, letting Rion pick up when she had to take a break.

"Well, shit," Arielle said when they were finished. "Obviously this is our fault. I'm so, so sorry."

"What do you mean, *your* fault? It's my fault! I was so obsessed with just staying friends with him that we became the best of friends, which I guess in this case is falling in love too. And he saw it, and I didn't, and now I screwed everything up." The tears were finally starting to slow, and Rion handed her a rough brown napkin. Amy winced as she wiped her eyes with it.

The Broken Hearts Society of Suite 17C

"No, it is our fault. Because we knew. We knew from the beginning there was something between you two. And we never said anything."

Rion hung her head and twisted her lips back and forth. Arielle was right, but that didn't change the fact that Amy was backed into a really shitty place with this whole thing. Within ten minutes, Arielle had helped Amy write a self-discovery to-do list—a phrase that only made sense in Arielle's crazy type-A universe—then promised to come back as soon as she could, and hung up.

"It sneaks up on you, doesn't it?" Rion asked, quietly eyeing Amy's list, which had normal things like "major" and weird things like "ice skating."

"What's that? The mortification of having a crush on someone and it being mutual and then getting dumped by your non-boyfriend anyway?"

"Sort of? Really I just mean falling in love." Rion shook her head. "Jesus, that's cheesy."

The sunshine of Amy's grin broke through what had been a ridiculously gloomy atmosphere. "So you finally realized you love Crash, huh?"

Rion shrugged. "It's whatever."

"It's a big deal. I don't suppose he told you his real name, did he?"

"I guess he never told me because I never asked. Anyway, it's Colin."

Amy nodded. "Makes sense."

"Okay, how? How could a *name* make sense?"

"Well, for starters, it's one of the few names I can think of that really doesn't have like a tough-sounding nickname. He seems like someone who wants to hide behind that. If he told you, it means you're special to him."

Rion shrugged like she didn't care. But that didn't make too much sense. Crash had always been the one who was trying to get her to let him in, not the other way around.

"I mean, it's taken you a little while to see him as anything but a guy you sleep with. Not that I'm judging you," she rushed to explain.

"That's not true!"

"But it is. That's not bad. I've been through enough stuff myself and paid plenty of attention in Womens' Studies, so I know. Nobody can fault you for…you know…enjoying yourself with him. But the connection has changed, no doubt. You talk about him more, you know, like a person."

"I wasn't talking about him like a person before?"

Amy laughed. "You know what I mean."

"No, I don't."

"Well it's the same way you've been with the Society. At first, our meetings were just a thing on your schedule, but now it's like…you like hanging out with us. It's kind of sweet."

Rion grumbled. "Okay. Well, I do like you. For what it's worth."

"Yeah, and Crash too. Does he know?"

"He kind of told me he loved me? Right when I was about to come get you?"

Amy's eyes opened so wide Rion could have wedged coasters under her lids. "What?" she screeched. "You didn't tell me that!"

"It's not a big deal. Not like you're not busy enough with your own stuff."

"It is a big deal, and it's Society news! I'm never too busy. Really." Amy's face turned serious. "You guys have helped me so much that I really don't know what I would be doing without you right now. Wait," she said, her eyes going wide again. "Did you say it back?"

"Um, yeah. Well, kind of. I mean, I kind of…yelled it on my way out?"

"Rion! And you haven't talked to him since?"

Rion shrugged, trying to tamp down the weird crazy fluttering in her stomach. "No."

"Well, you should!"

"I don't know, isn't this the kind of thing you're supposed to talk about in person? You know, so you can see his expression and everything? And he can throw you into bed right after?"

Amy's cheeks blazed and Rion smirked. "You're welcome. Anyway, he'll be back in a couple days. They're going to pay him overtime to staff the shop when all the other students who work there are still on break. I can wait."

Amy just grinned at her. Clearly she could tell just how far of a reach that last sentence was.

Two days of waiting for Crash to come back felt much longer than Rion would have expected. A lot of things had changed, and she couldn't pinpoint exactly what it was that made the connection stronger. She wasn't planning a wedding or even making a stupid Pinterest board with diamonds so big she'd be embarrassed to wear them, like she'd definitely seen Arielle doing. She wasn't mentally decorating their first apartment together, or even thinking about how they'd spend Spring Break.

But for the first time ever, Rion wasn't on guard, wasn't stressed about falling—maybe because she had a parachute. Her roommates were awesome, and even though Amy had spent days frantically making addenda to her Arielle-assigned lists and crying in the spaces in between, Rion knew that they were cool and that they had each other's backs, at least when it came to relationships.

Now she had a relationship, a real relationship, that she was part of. An idea she was still getting used to during her usual text check-ins with Crash. Always about what they were listening to or what they were watching. Sometimes she would ask him which song to mix with another. Sometimes he'd actually be familiar with all of the choices. His was always the last text before she fell

The Broken Hearts Society of Suite 17C

asleep. They talked once, but didn't say the L-word again. Maybe he sensed the same thing she did—maybe he knew how important it was to really look at him the next time she said it, to make sure that he knew and that it was real.

Crash's first shift back was a Thursday afternoon. He'd told her when they first met that when college girls were bored, they drank, and when they were bored and drinking, they came to get tattoos. It was a Thursday night, which was probably why it was so quiet—a weird day for most people to come back to campus, and too late for any of the girls left standing to be sober enough for a tattoo. Rion daydreamed as she drove from the off-campus lot where freshmen had to keep their cars and up toward Francis. She'd come and sit with him, thumbing through the same book of tattoo patterns to see if there was one she hadn't seen before, and she'd listen to him make her promise, for the hundredth time, that if she got a tattoo she would let him design it. Maybe, this time, she'd ask him to go ahead and do it.

But every warm, fuzzy, relaxed feeling she'd allowed to flood her during that two-minute daydreaming drive blew apart into a cold, panicked emptiness when she pulled up to the Studio on High and saw two police cars in front, one with a K-9 unit designation. There was only one reason police would bring a dog in the middle of business hours—drugs.

Shit. Shit shit shit. Shit.

Who the hell would have brought drugs into Olivia's studio? She took care of every one of her workers like they were family—who would fuck with someone who took care of them that well, would do anything to ruin the integrity of her business? Maybe that asshole sophomore who'd come from one of the top fraternities on campus, trying to disguise the fact that he'd lost his bank teller job from his parents? Maybe the old rasta guy who swept up at night, and didn't seem to give a shit about much of anything? Rion peered into the front desk area of the Studio and saw Olivia talking to an officer, one hand ghosting at her throat, as if she was trying to keep her head attached to her body, and another on her hip. She half answered the officer's questions, half looked around the studio like she was hoping the scene would magically change any minute now.

When Rion walked in, Olivia's head snapped to the door. "Rion. Are you scheduled?"

"No, but I came to see—"

Olivia shook her head sharply, once in each direction. "You should go home, Ri. I'll call you in a little bit, okay?"

Rion's stomach bottomed out when she heard the click of handcuffs and the undertone reading of rights. Shit. Shit shit *shit*. The cops had found enough drugs for it to be considered a felony, so there had to be an arrest. Olivia just prayed no dumb-shit freshmen were around to tweet about this and bring the name of the whole studio down.

The Broken Hearts Society of Suite 17C

A shadow approached the doorway, and Rion's heart stopped. Stephanie's unmistakable spiraled mop peeked out the doorway, then the rest of her, her dark skin looking somehow grayer, her expression a mixture of shock and sorrow as she shuffled out of the back room.

But she wasn't the one in cuffs.

Rion wanted to throw up when she heard his voice, softly assenting to everything the cop said. No way. There was no fucking way she had fallen in love with a guy who not only carried, but probably sold, pot—then lied, over and over again, about the fact that he did.

Crash's Adam's apple bobbed with a hard swallow as a cop on either side of him escorted him to the front door. He looked up at her and squeezed his eyes shut, shaking his head as if he couldn't believe she'd actually shown up. Or that he'd actually been caught. Either way, the bastard had the balls to look her in the eyes, and if she hadn't been in such complete and total shock, she would have reached down and torn them off.

She wanted to cry, wanted to scream, wanted to beat the everloving shit out of him for wanting her bad enough to chase after her, to spend so much time with her, to be the first person to care about who she was and what she did, to make her fall in love with him, goddamn him, only to have been a motherfucking liar.

Maybe it shouldn't have been a shock. Maybe she should have known better, and maybe she actually had. Maybe she should have taken his lip ring and his tattoos and on-again, off-again student status and his over-21 drivers' license into account and seen how it all added up to a guy who had to be trouble, couldn't possibly stay out of trouble. Maybe that was on her.

The lying, however, was on him. She knew exactly one thing was true as she watched the cops lead him to their car, help him into the back, and drive away, with no sirens, thank God for Olivia—she had absolutely nothing left to say to Crash. Not now, and not ever again.

It didn't matter how much she hated him, how much the burning rage in her chest should have eradicated any emotion—by the time she made it back to Harrison, hot tears were streaming down her cheeks, and she couldn't get her coat off her body fast enough. She burst through the door of 17C and tossed her jacket and bag on the floor. Arielle and Amy were on the futon, Amy watching something—*Kill Bill*, Rion recognized from the music—and Arielle on her laptop, typing like a madwoman and occasionally pounding on a sticky key.

"You could use the coat hooks I put up, Rion."

That was it. Just those words, Arielle nagging her about the neatness of their Suite like her entire world hadn't just turned upside down, sent Rion sobbing. She slumped against the door, just like she remembered Arielle doing so many weeks ago, when she'd thought she was such a pathetic loser. Well, now Rion was the pathetic loser. And it was all Crash's fault.

The Broken Hearts Society of Suite 17C

Just thinking his name started a fresh wave of pain, and she pulled her knees to her chest, trying to hold something—anything—together.

Rion heard the thunk of Arielle's laptop, noticed that the telltale fight sounds from the movie had stopped. She felt two hands on her back, opened her eyes to see a girl crouching on either side of her. "What did he do to you?" Amy asked in a quiet growl, the first time Rion had ever heard that girl sound remotely dangerous. "I should have seen it. I should have fucking guessed." Rion lifted her head and smoothed her palms down over her eyes, feeling the greasy resistance of the eye makeup she'd so carefully painted on. Crash liked smoky eyes on her—said they brought out the blue of her irises. Fucking shit. Another jolt of pain, just thinking about him telling her that.

"Shit," Arielle said. "Is it another girl?"

"What? No. No, it's not another girl. At least, he'd better not be fucking anyone else. No, it was drugs. Fucking marijuana, probably in little plastic Ziploc baggies. Just like last time. Except this time, it wasn't me who got caught with it, which he'll probably regret, because if I ever see him again I might actually kill him."

"No. That's...are you sure? It was his? You're absolutely certain," Amy said, shaking her head.

"Yeah. With fucking intent to sell." With one tight fist, she smashed into her own calf, having nothing else close by to hit. "Pretty straightforward. The cops somehow got a tip, or maybe they were waiting for it in the Studio, who the fuck knows? They came in with dogs, pried open a few break room lockers. Next thing I knew I was listening to them read him his rights."

"That just doesn't sound like him. And I asked Matt, when you first met him. I know it's weird, but with his student government stuff, he knows a lot of the campus police—and they said he's never even been suspected in a case. Not once."

"You did a background check on my boyfriend?" *Ex-boyfriend.*

Amy looked sheepish, tucking her chin down. "It's in the charter. If your heart gets broken, it's my fault. I was just doing everything I could."

Rion laughed shortly. "Well, my heart's fucking broken. It's not your fault, though."

Arielle raised a single eyebrow, tentatively raised a hand to touch Rion's shoulder, then let it fall when Rion glared at her. "Rion, I…"

"Doesn't matter," Rion continued. "I don't give a shit. I told him right from the beginning, if he smoked, bought weed, was friends with weed growers, any of that shit, I wouldn't see him. That's my line. More than alcohol or parties or cigarettes, pot was the line I drew. He knew that. I was very clear about that. And he liked me enough to take a fucking piss test, but didn't love me enough to be honest with me. Goddammit! What *is* it about me, guys? Do I seem so fucking fragile that everyone has to lie to me about everything, or do I just look stupid? Or—maybe this is it—am I just doomed to have everyone I love and trust be total fuck-ups, and lose them?"

"Hey now," Arielle said, reaching out to gently rub her back again. "I'm not a total fuckup. Only mostly a fuck up."

Rion laughed, managing to choke out the sound between tears.

That was when her phone rang. Once, twice, and she didn't bother to answer. The only person who ever called her anyway was her mom, and Rion would rather talk to fucking Putin right now than her mother. But after two long rings and all three girls staring at the phone, Arielle bent forward to grab it and hit 'answer,' putting it on speaker at the same time.

A bored, nasal voice droned, "You are receiving a phone call from the Francis county jail, will you accept it?"

Mom was in a state prison, and there was really only one other person who had her number and would be in jail. Fucking Crash. She leaned forward to yell into the speaker. "No I most certainly do—"

"Yes!" Amy said, cutting her off and grabbing the phone from Ari. "Yes, put him on."

If looks could obliterate someone on the spot, Rion's to Amy would have done just that. "I have nothing to say to him," Rion growled. "There's nothing he can say to me. No matter what, we're fucking finished."

"Rion?" Crash's voice was crackly and tired, and her heart twisted at the thought that maybe he'd heard something she just said. Like she should fucking care. She didn't. She didn't care about him at all. She imagined little bricks being laid at the foundation of the wall around her heart. Fucking asshole made her start from scratch.

But all she could manage to say was, "Why are you calling me?"

"Why am I—baby, you're my one jailhouse phone call. I need you to come get me out of here. I'll explain everything after we—"

"Two words in what you just said are a huge problem for me right now, you nutclutching douchebag. Calling me baby and the word 'we.' You don't get to call me that anymore, because there is no 'we.'"

"Rion, I know this is killing you. I promise you, I will tell you literally everything as soon as I'm out and you'll understand, but right now my two minutes are almost up and I need you to come post bail for me. I have some cash at the apartment, in the back of the pantry inside—

"It's not killing me, actually. I have zero fucks to give about you or anything your sorry lying ass has been involved in for the last four months. The only thing that slightly bothers me is that I was dumb enough not to realize what a fucking liar you were for this long."

"Ri, please, I'm—"

"I'll tell you what you are. Fucked. Have a nice life." And then she threw the phone across the room, where it mercifully landed in the corner of the futon with all the throw pillows Amy had meticulously arranged on their first day in 17C, and every day thereafter.

Thank God at least she and Arielle were still here. Looking at those girls, their mixed expressions of shock and pity, the way they watched her, frozen, Rion glimpsed the tiniest bit of faith that maybe someone in this backwards, fucked-up world really loved her. That maybe she could trust these girls.

So she cried until she couldn't cry anymore, until the heavy buzzing of rage and confusion and shock in her chest poured out. Though the lightness that followed was a slight improvement, it still sucked because now all she felt was empty.

"I should have done what Amy did," Rion said into the peaceful quiet of the 17C common room when the tears finally stopped flowing. "I should have said no dating, under any circumstances."

"Yeah, because look how well that worked out for me," Amy snorted.

"Besides," Arielle said quietly, "you still would have slept with him."

Rion laughed and smacked her on the shoulder lightly. "Shut the fuck up." And then, a few seconds later, "Yeah, you're right." And then to Amy, "and you are too. I still would have fallen in love with him." She buried her face in her hands. "Ugh, just saying that makes me feel pathetic. Falling in love. Like I'm some kind of swooning hyperromantic pussy."

"Well, you did!" Amy said, "You did fall in love, and it happens to the best of us."

"No. I was stupid. I was stupid and wrecked from the last two years and I think I wanted to trust someone."

"Well I'm sorry. He was a damn decent person to trust. Good job, nice place, gets along with everyone."

"Clear pee test," Amy interrupted.

"There was no way you could have figured out that he's…what? A drug dealer?"

Rion sniffed. "I don't know. I don't even fucking know anymore. I just know I'm done."

"I just don't get it," Arielle murmured. "Even Matt, Mr. Standup Citizen, said he was a really good guy. You have to talk to him. Get your answer as to why, how he thought it was a good idea to lie to you about the one thing he promised not to lie to you about. You've gained too much by being with him to walk away quietly like it never happened. You're in love, Rion. That doesn't come easily."

Rion rolled her eyes.

"Besides," Amy finished, "If you don't get his explanation, you'll never trust anyone again."

"So maybe I won't. Maybe I'm just fine on my own, thank you very much, and probably even better, because apparently the only people I can attract are high-caliber fuck-ups."

Arielle sighed. "Well, I guess it's good we don't have class for a few more days."

"No class, yes shifts at the Studio."

Arielle wrinkled her nose.

"At least he won't be there, I guess. Since he burned his one call on me. Even though I kind of wish I had just gone to get him." The tears started all over again.

With a last look of sad understanding from the roommates, they shifted their seating arrangement to fit Rion and her sporadic weeping. She watched the rest of *Kill Bill*, occasionally adding commentary on the brilliance of its weird mashup of a soundtrack and its Zen Buddhist themes that most people tried to ignore in favor of savoring the gore.

Yeah, Crash had managed to tear out her heart and smear it all over her visions of her own future, leaving her weak and empty. But at least, for this one little moment, she had two really, really good girls willing to hold her up.

Rion barely slept that night, tossing and turning and hating the memory of being able to reach out and touch Crash. Yeah, he had a ridiculously hot body, but damn him, he'd turned into so much more for her. A symbol that things she thought were impossible could turn into reality. That is, until that reality turned out to be one huge lie.

She stared in the mirror and winced at her rumpled shirt, her eyes, still slightly puffy and burning from last night, and her tangled hair with roots probably one week past due for a dye. She shuffled around the room, trying to find some combination of clothes that were sort of clean and sort of went together. She couldn't remember a time when she cared so little about her appearance, actually, and cursed her past self for scheduling any shifts during break.

Jesus, what had Crash done to her? Setbacks had always just pissed Rion off, made her push harder against whatever had knocked her down, had her figuring out how to get back on her feet as soon as possible. Now her whole body was just on strike, dragging itself through every movement like it would rather not have shown up to work today.

Probably because Crash hadn't just knocked her down—he'd smashed her to smithereens. Was there a way to come back from it? Sure, but it would be a hell of a lot harder than holding up her fists and fighting back.

Rion's shift started at one in the afternoon, and as she walked in, Kelly, a girl with a bleach-blond pixie cut who had taught her some great tips for getting a perfect post-bleach tone, was just taking a girl back to get her nose or navel or tongue pierced. Maybe even her nipple, but from the look of her—trendy jeans and a pea coat, it was a tiny stud in her nose.

The Broken Hearts Society of Suite 17C

Rion forced a teeth-showing smile at Kelly before she disappeared into one of the piercing rooms, and forced her legs to walk over to the curving desk, then her arms to hoist her bag onto it. She collapsed into the chair and lazily pulled up the mixing software, already mentally searching for the songs she could blend together, and found a slow Imogen heap track, dark and soothing, and let the tinny chords flood her ears.

So a few seconds later, when a slight figure with long, dark waves plopped into the chair next to her, she was caught completely off guard.

"Holy shit, Olivia, you scared me!" Rion's heart thudded, an unwanted reminder of how much it had ached since yesterday.

"Rion! Oh my God, are you okay? I've been calling you and I was seriously just about to send somebody to your dorm."

"Of course I'm okay! Are *you* okay? You're the one who had a drug bust go down in your studio yesterday."

Olivia sat up straight, and she stared at Rion with a confused look on her face. "We need to back up here. When I finally got to Crash last night, he said he hadn't been able to get a hold of you, that he didn't know where you'd run to. And if he didn't know where you were…well, that worried me. That's all."

"Wait a minute. What do you mean you got to Crash?" Suddenly, every nerve in her body was a live wire.

"I bailed him out. Thank God it was only five hundred, because we hadn't cashed out the register yet and—"

"Well, aren't you pissed at him?" Rion's voice had risen at least two levels. The girl getting pierced by Kelly squealed in the piercing room, and Olivia shushed her.

"No. Kind of pissed at Steph, because I can't keep her on now, and she was one of my best piercers. Not to mention she really needed the money."

"Hold on," Rion said, biting her tongue from inserting a mother curse word. "Now you need to back up. What does Steph have to do with this?"

"Rion, the pot was hers. Fell out of her damn locker. So fucking careless."

Suddenly, Rion felt like all the air had been sucked out of the room. A tiny part of her hoped this wasn't a horrific alternate reality, and what she thought was happening was just a dream. "But, Crash...he got arrested, so..." Rion managed to stutter.

"Rion, no." Olivia looked sad, disappointed. "Crash just took the fall for her. I don't think he realized how much she actually had in there, but still. It was cool of him."

"What the...?" Numbness smacked Rion in the chest and spread over her whole body. "Why would—I mean, how could—I mean, I had no idea. God, why would he *do* that?" Her voice was back to hysterical pussy levels again, and as the piercing room door swung open, Olivia gave her another glare.

While nose ring girl—Rion had been right about that one—checked out, she whirled on Olivia. "But seriously, what the fuck? Why would—"

"Are you talking about Steph?" Kelly butted in. "Yeah, that sucks. Crash is amazing."

Rion blinked. So Steph was the one selling pot, and the boyfriend she'd written off completely was actually a marijuana knight in shining armor. Goddammit.

"Rion, you know Steph has been going through a lot. Her husband had to have another surgery, and they didn't have much savings to begin with. It's a real shit storm. She can't take another job because she can't get good child care at weird hours."

Rion swallowed and nodded.

"She told me used to sell a little on the side when she was in college, just to help pay her tuition, which I knew, but I hired her with the understanding that she was done with that," Olivia explained.

Rion let a short, shocked laugh escape. Olivia and she weren't too different, after all.

"I guess she dug up new contacts when things got really rough. Anyway, I don't know who the tip was from, but getting arrested would have ruined her whole family, basically, because of her past record. Definitely jail time. So Crash stepped in."

"Because he has no record," Rion said, guilt and mortification blooming through her stomach. Dammit. He had no record. Just like he'd promised her.

Olivia nodded. "And he's white. And he has some spare cash to fund bail. And he's seen Steph going through a lot. Anyway, the worst he'll get is community service and a fine, which I'll help with because I love the fuck out of both him and Steph. And also because my big brother bailed me out more than once, and I really do need to pay it forward, for karma purposes."

Olivia glanced at a framed picture of her, a guy two heads taller with a near-identical face to hers, and a woman a little shorter than her with bouncy blond curls standing under a sign that read, *Joey and Hawk's Bar and Restaurant.* "I worked for him. He and his wife started the Joey and Hawk's chain in Philly. Figure I can do my part for a kid struggling like I was."

"Oh my God, why do you look so mortified?" Kelly asked, her eyebrows wrinkling up. "I thought you and Crash were a thing. And how did you not know all this?"

Even Rion's lips felt numb, but she forced them to move. "Because I...oh God," she moaned, putting her face in her hands, smudging her eyeliner even more. "I told him I wouldn't speak to him. I've had...some really bad experiences with guys who were users. We only started dating when he swore he wasn't. And I thought he'd been lying to me, and now...oh fucking fuck fuck fuck."

The Broken Hearts Society of Suite 17C

Rion had never believed herself to be one hundred percent wrong about anything. Until now.

"Hold on," Olivia said, narrowing her eyes. "You're telling me he called you and you told him to rot in that jail cell?"

"Oh my *God*," Rion moaned, pushing her fingers back through her hair. The air had gotten so thin in the room, and her heart physically ached.

"Well, you'd better get up to his place, then," Kelly said, wide-eyed. "Olivia doesn't really need you. Still winter break. Right, O?"

"Yeah, get out of here. Come back if you can but otherwise, don't worry about it."

"But, I—"

"Don't *worry* about it. Paid. Okay?"

Rion stood up, swiped her coat off the arm of her chair, and slung her bag over her shoulder. She squeezed Olivia and tripped over the rolling chair when she tried to walk out from behind the desk. Olivia and Kelly dissolved into laughter, and Rion silently swore to glare at them for it later. Right now, they were saints, even if it was just for making her realize what a complete and total idiot she was. When she was halfway out the door, Olivia called, "And don't kill yourself on the way up!"

She couldn't get to Crash's place fast enough. She ran out the door, then through another outside door that the key to his apartment fit in. Rion thanked every deity out there that he'd given it to her. She dashed up the stairs, dying to see his face, trying to figure out the words she'd say to apologize, to try to fix things, to ask him why he didn't just tell her what he'd done?

She banged on the door, her heart galloping a mile a minute. He had to be awake. After thirty seconds, she knocked again, passing the seemingly endless moments by visualizing the layout of his apartment. She couldn't hear the shower running, so that wasn't it. Finally, she heard the creak of footsteps on the old wooden floor.

"Crash?" she said, begging her voice not to get all crazy. Not with him. Not when she had to get him to hopefully forgive her for all the shit she'd screamed at him last night. When he was in jail.

The footsteps padded to the door, and she steeled herself. Should she touch him? Hug him? Kiss him? The peephole darkened, and she waited for him to pull the door open and let her fall into a hug. She'd never looked forward to apologizing so much in her life.

The door slowly, torturously, opened a crack, and Crash rested his head against the doorjamb, looking at her with one eye open. "What do you want, Ri? Did you come to take your shit home?"

"I…um…" Immediately, she was deflated. He didn't smile, and his eyes didn't sparkle. He wasn't standing with square shoulders and arms crossed, ready to tease her for her horrible mistake.

Probably because none of this was funny. *Dammit, Rion.*

The Broken Hearts Society of Suite 17C

The hallway was suddenly beyond awkward. Nowhere to lean, nowhere to sit, no place to ground herself. "Can I come in?" she asked, her voice suddenly turning meek.

Crash scoffed. "Suit yourself," he said, flicking the door open with his fingertips and then turning to go inside.

"Okay…" she said as he stalked to the kitchenette in the corner. "Should I sit?"

"Like I said. Suit yourself." Crash filled up the coffee pot and spooned in some grounds—not nearly enough, which apparently he hadn't learned from the dozen times she'd tried to teach him. The moments where he set the coffee to brewing and walked, looking exhausted, to the big mismatched chair opposite Rion were excruciating. He looked at her with tired, red eyes ringed in purple.

"Are you okay?" Again, that quiet, careful voice. Something she never thought she'd use, never thought she'd want to use. Never planned on being sorry, wanting to give someone else consideration.

"Well, I had a fucking shitty night, as you can probably guess. Obviously you don't care, but don't tell me you don't know that it took for fucking ever for Olivia to get done with her police interviews and come check on me at the jail."

"I didn't know," Rion said, quietly, watching her shoes.

In the two years since she'd been on her own, Rion never backed down from any confrontation. She prided herself on looking conflict directly in the eyes, stating her opinion, standing up for herself, not feeling sorry for a single damn bit of it.

Now all she wanted to do was rewind the clock 24 hours and start over again. She wanted to be the kind of person who could trust someone she loved, even though she knew that would take every ounce of strength she had.

"Of course you knew!" Crash said, slamming his coffee cup down. Rion counted the sloshes, one side to the other, as they spilled out each side of his mug. Seven, before they stayed inside. It was the only thing she could do, to focus on the coffee, because everything else around her fuzzed and blurred into something unrecognizable, something she couldn't even begin to touch.

"You know what happens when you get hauled into jail. It was bad enough, with the drunk off his ass kid throwing up in the corner of the cell and the officer glaring at my tattoos like they automatically mean I'm some delinquent. But then to have to wait for my boss to come and find me? To have to stuff a handful of condoms back in my pocket from the giant plastic bag they put all my shit in? Jesus, Rion. What the hell?"

By then, his voice had softened, like being angry with her had taken everything out of him. He slumped back in his chair, shaking his head back and forth, refusing to look at her.

The combination of an instinct of self-preservation, standoffishness, and stubbornness was not serving Rion

The Broken Hearts Society of Suite 17C

well. After all, he had still lied to her, even if it wasn't in the way she'd originally thought. "I mean, I didn't know you covered for Stephanie. You didn't tell me she was selling, and..."

Crash finally looked at her with narrowed eyes, and Rion suddenly regretted wishing he would. His voice was low, steady, measured. "You mean you actually thought that was my pot?"

Rion pressed her lips together, shook her head. Yes, she regretted the assumption. But she wouldn't apologize for trying to protect herself. "You surrendered! It happened before I could even look at you. What the hell was I supposed to think?"

"I'll tell you what you were supposed to think. This is Crash, the guy I've shared everything with for the past three months, the guy who spent Christmas with me, the guy I love. If you still do."

Rion's heart twisted, the pain of it taking her breath away.

"You were supposed to think, 'Wow, this is the one thing Crash promised me, absolutely and positively, he had nothing to do with. So I trust that he wasn't lying to me.'"

"You know what that is, Crash? That's the way to get burned. I've been through it once, and I'm not going to let it happen again."

Crash pressed his lips together and started nodding sort of manically, like a storm was brewing behind his eyes and he was just trying to figure out the best way to let it out. "It would never have happened with me. Because I wouldn't lie to you. Because I love you, Rion. But obviously you don't love me enough to believe me when I tell you I don't do that shit."

Rion didn't have an answer to that. "It's not you, Crash, it's me. I would have that reaction with anyone, because look how one asshole's stash of pot, one time, totally fucked over my life! An asshole I totally trusted. I don't have anyone left to have my back, so I have to look out for myself."

Crash stood and shook his head, staring at the floor. Rion stood, too, a reflex she'd probably developed from spending so much time with him. The realities of the moment swirled into a terrifying mix she couldn't grab hold of, couldn't predict.

"I wanted to be the one to have your back, Rion. I thought that's who I was. But obviously I'm not good enough. And I'm sorry for that, I really am. Because you are the first person I thought was able to look past my job and my appearance and see me—a stand-up guy just trying to make it. Guess you're just like every other shallow bitch out there."

Rion's shoulders tensed against the sudden and violent urge to sob. She looked him square in the eye, wishing she could apologize, knowing she'd hate herself if she did. Crash reached down, wrenched open the door, and stared at the hallway outside.

The Broken Hearts Society of Suite 17C

All at once, Rion realized—he was kicking her out. Pushing her out on her own, saying goodbye without a second thought. That wasn't love. Love gave second chances. Love understood past hurts and forgave them. Didn't it?

Whatever. She didn't fucking need him and his sanctimonious anti-stereotype bullshit anyway. What a fucking douchebag, making her feel bad for trying to protect herself. As she picked up her hoodie from the chair, still wrinkled and warm from her pathetic ass crushing it just seconds ago, she pushed down the confusing, whispering feeling that she was the wrong one, that she was throwing a hell of a lot away by walking out right now. That maybe her pride wasn't worth it if this was the price.

Fuck that. She was nothing if not strong. It was the girls who broke down in tears, who apologized and groveled, who needed a guy in order to breathe, who were setting themselves up for a world of hurt later. She slung her bag over her shoulder and stalked out the door. "What the fuck ever," she said, pushing past Crash, regrettably bumping his shoulder on the way.

The entire four-block walk back to Harrison was filled with the thought that she'd never feel that shoulder against hers again, but not a single tear rolled down her cheek on this walk back.

Being alone was better anyway. Okay, so maybe Crash hadn't been selling drugs this time. But if someone they worked with was, and he was willing to take that fall for her, what else would he do? Someone who was complicit was almost as bad as someone who was actually dealing, actually using, wasn't it?

The warm blast of air in the Harrison lobby alerted her to the fact that she'd swiped her card and walked through the door—actions she barely noticed because the loop of rationalizations running through her head was so loud. The eerie quiet of the Harrison lobby on Winter Break barely registered with her, except in a vague feeling of gratitude that nobody would have to see her like this.

Like what, though? She wasn't crying, wasn't raging, wasn't losing control. She was perfectly calm and stoic, like stone. Frozen, rigid, and strong. Dying on the inside, steady and functional on the outside. It could be worse. She could be losing her shit, like the night Dad died or the day Mom went to jail.

Now if only she could get through life like this.

Suite 17C was empty and dark, but the door to Amy's room was ajar, casting a triangle of light on the rest of the room. She'd either gone to get something to eat or gone to shower, and that girl deserved both. Getting dumped by a non-boyfriend was almost as bad as getting thrown out by a real boyfriend. Or maybe just equally bad.

It was better for Rion, too. If she tried to lean on anyone else right now, she would learn to always expect someone to be there for her to catch her when she fell. As she was learning now, that was a dangerous expectation indeed. She'd almost gotten there with Crash. Almost.

The silent blue-black of the Suite's common room felt like the perfect place for Rion to be now, so she settled onto the futon, trying so very hard to feel like she was in her body and not out of it, like she was okay, like she was whole with or without Crash, with or without someone who matched her so well.

Even though Rion knew that wholeness shouldn't feel like a desperate battle to hold all the pieces of yourself together, she sat there, wrapped her arms around herself, and told herself, over and over, that she was just fine.

I had a guy break up with me for being Jewish. No joke. We had been dating for a couple of months. I thought it was going great and we were getting ready to introduce each other to our families. Then one night he comes over and says that he doesn't think we are moving forward on the same path. I was absolutely dumbfounded. So I asked why. He said, "Well, I'm pretty religious and you seem pretty religious. So I just don't think it would work out." Keep in mind that I told him I was Jewish the night we met.

~Taylor Vydra

Chapter 19

Arielle

"You're going to do *what*?" Arielle stared at Lauren like she'd lost her mind. Lauren continued shuffling through stacks of papers, cross-legged in maddeningly short shorts on the edge of Arielle's bed.

"Ari. Baby."

Arielle still blushed like mad any time Lauren called her that, even though they'd been using the name for each other since Lauren had introduced herself as Arielle's girlfriend at Arielle's parents' house, right before they lit the damn menorah. Ari swore her mom almost cried. Lauren loved Chanukah so much that even the fantasies Ari'd had of her converting to Judaism and them having a wedding under a chuppah didn't seem that crazy anymore.

"Yes. I'm listening. I swear."

The Broken Hearts Society of Suite 17C

"My face is up here," Lauren teased, but then turned serious again. "Sororities are, like, a thing in California. My mom did it, and all her friends and their sisters, and their daughters rushed. I never had a sister in real life. You can't blame me for at least wanting to check it out."

"You shouldn't have to pay for sisters. Real ones or fake ones."

Lauren shrugged. "Hundreds of girls on this campus don't have to. But they decide to anyway."

"It's just so…mainstream," Arielle grumbled.

"What, and you're not?"

Arielle's eyes flew wide open and she dropped her jaw, feigning shock. "Absolutely not. I'm, like, the opposite of mainstream."

"Oh really. Long layers in your hair, a crush on Taylor Swift, this season's hottest jeans and an obsession with Starbucks lattes? Yes, Arielle, you're so unique."

Arielle scrunched her lips together and pulled them to the side. "I'll give you that. But I'm…you know…"

"Gay? Yes, I know. Probably better than anyone."

Arielle grinned. She'd gotten damn lucky when she met Lauren, that was for sure. No, Lauren wasn't Jewish, but everything else about her was absolutely perfect. Best of all, even though Arielle discovered Lauren was uncomfortable with serious PDA, she showed just how aware she was of Ari's relationship fears by linking fingers with her when they walked across campus, or giving her a quick kiss when they parted to go to their respective classes. Who cared if Lauren wasn't a card-carrying lesbian when she spent all her free time with Ari and wasn't afraid to kiss her right in the middle of Northern's humungous student body, at the busiest time of day?

"Whatever. Gay girls rush. More importantly, girls who don't have any other extracurriculars rush. You can't just go four years here doing nothing but studying."

Arielle knew too well that gay girls rushed. She also knew that, at least in Rachel's sorority, gay girls were not something they exactly got excited about being part of the sisterhood. "I don't know. What if Rachel is doing recruitment shit for her sorority?"

They hadn't talked about Rachel much—Arielle figured Lauren really didn't want to hear about her ex, especially when she was on campus. Plus, even though Arielle was happy with Lauren, there was no way she could hide how pinched and twisted her insides still got at the memory of Rachel smearing her heart all over the quad.

Lauren brushed her lips down Arielle's nose, a move that always threatened to completely undo her. "Then she'll see how completely and totally okay you are without her. And then she'll see me and be crazy jealous and pissed at herself that she lost her chance with you."

Arielle tried to pout, fighting against the stupid head-in-the-clouds smile that tugged relentlessly at the corners of her lips. "That's true. But I won't rush a sorority as revenge on an ex." As sweet as the devastated look on

The Broken Hearts Society of Suite 17C

Rachel's face may turn out to be. "Besides, I don't need an extracurricular. I'm not even bored." Arielle already knew her argument didn't hold water. She wasn't interested in very much at all—couldn't even think about deciding on a major without having a panic attack, and her classes were the opposite of challenging. Now that she thought about it, she realized just how bored she really was.

"Yeah, because we're, you know…new." Lauren stood up from the bed and walked slowly over to Arielle's desk chair, then settled on her lap, roping her arms around Arielle's neck. Arielle grunted and gave her a begrudging smile when Lauren propped her forehead against hers. "Shut up," Lauren murmured before kissing her softly. "I'm not that heavy."

"Not for a Chinese giant," Arielle said, leaning her head against Lauren's shoulder. She debated whether to keep kissing Lauren, maybe sneak a hand up her shirt, or control herself and kill this conversation once and for all. "Besides, you really don't need anything else to do. You have kickboxing, and soon I'm going to make you come to yoga with me."

Arielle spent more time daydreaming and dozing in yoga class than actually working out, but she noticed a little bit more flexibility in her legs since she started downward-dogging twice weekly. She might have even seen an ab muscle the other day, when she turned just the right way.

Now it was Lauren's turn to grunt. "You know that shit drives me crazy. It's so slow. I almost fell asleep the last time you made me go."

"Which is why *you* should totally do the sorority thing. You always want to be moving, want to be doing something. I always want to be home. In my pajamas. Preferably with you."

"Right. Which you can still do if you join a sorority. I'll come to your house."

Arielle narrowed her eyes at Lauren. "You're not going to let up on this, are you? I didn't even know you cared about sororities."

"I don't know. I still feel like I'm floundering here at Northern, you know? Except for you, I don't really have anything besides my classes. And my mom keeps asking me what the best thing about school is…"

"Seriously? So you tell her it's me, right?"

Lauren groaned and kissed Arielle lightly again, melting her from the inside out. "She knows about you, but not *all* about you."

Arielle raised her eyebrows. "Say more." She could feel her hackles starting to rise, and begged the sick feeling in her stomach to ease.

"Not because I don't want to tell her we're together. She wouldn't even care. Well, she would care—too much. She'd be desperate to meet you. You know, I'm an only child, and she's not that young—she's like sixty, Ari."

Arielle nodded. Lauren had told her about how desperately her mom and dad had wanted a child, how hard they'd tried, until her doctor had basically told her she was too old to keep going. Lauren's mom had been 42 years old when she'd flown to China to bring Lauren home. "She'd fly both of us home right away, and you'd see how overbearing she is, and she'd start asking you how soon you want to have babies because she doesn't have grandchildren, and you'd freak out and leave me."

"Never," Arielle said right away, pulling back so that Lauren could see the look in her eyes. She stopped herself before she could tell Lauren about the feeling that had been creeping into the edges of her consciousness for the past few weeks. She just wasn't willing to risk it when there were so many unknowns, and when there were more than three years left for the two of them to figure things out.

"If it would make you happy, I'll tell her the next time I talk to her. How I met you, how long we've been together, how I'd rather be with you than anywhere else. You can even stick your head in the camera next to mine."

Just the offer calmed Arielle. "There's really no rush. You're away from home, and you guys aren't that close anyway, right? Don't worry about it. This, right here, is what matters most to me," she said, squeezing Lauren's waist.

"Well, you know what matters to me?" Lauren said with a smile and one more light kiss, standing up again to go back to the bed. She held up a glossy folder. "Checking out this recruitment thing."

Arielle groaned and let her head fall back, rolling her eyes at the ceiling.

"I'm serious. I've just heard a lot of really great stuff about sorority life, and, you know, it might be for us. For me, or for you. I've heard so many good things, Ari. Like how so many girls join a sorority and find their home away from home. I could use that, here."

"You don't feel at home?"

"With you? Yes. With the rest of Indiana Northern? Not yet."

Arielle sighed and leaned her head on Lauren's shoulder. But Lauren was not giving up.

"At least it would be something different to do for the next few weeks, right?" That soft whispery lilt in her voice was going to be Arielle's undoing one of these days. Maybe today.

"It's just a few weeks?" Arielle asked.

As soon as Lauren turned her laptop around to display the schedule, the pressure in her stomach eased. "It's only two weekends."

"Yes! Two weekends. And your classes are easy, you don't have a job, so why not?" Lauren practically bounced.

"Because it's cold?"

"Come on, baby," Lauren said, leaning over so her chest touched the bed, and grabbing Arielle's hand. Arielle was mostly distracted by her cleavage. Again. "Just four days. Then it'll be over and everything will go back to normal."

"What if you join?" Arielle whined. "Then you'll be too busy with sorority stuff to see me."

Lauren tented an eyebrow up. "Seriously? Do you seriously think I would rather be busy with something other than you?"

"I don't know," Arielle said, picking at some fuzz on her sweatpants. "What if you meet someone else?"

"There is nobody else," Lauren said, her tone completely serious. "Have you not noticed how I always want to hang out with you? I even ate two lunches the other day just so I could see you between classes!"

"You didn't have to eat," Arielle pointed out. But it was true. Lauren had agreed to lunch with her even though she was drowning in premed coursework already.

"And I'm here almost every night."

"And that won't change?"

"No, especially since you're so sure the sorority thing's not for you. Even if I move into a house next year, I'll just spend the night with you in your dorm or apartment or wherever. No problem. Your roommates already love me."

Next year. Lauren was talking about next year, and the hopefulness that Arielle had pushed down time and time again grew a little more.

"What if I have different roommates?"

Lauren scoffed. "Yeah, right. You're almost as attached to Amy as you are to me. And if there's anyone who can put up with Rion better than you, well, I haven't met them."

Arielle shrugged. It was true that the girls were astonishingly close for three random roommates. But living together for another year, on purpose? That was a whole different level of friendship.

"Okay, I'll register. If it'll make you so happy," Arielle grumbled, not even trying to hide her indulgent smile this time.

"Thank you!" Lauren's grin almost made this whole ridiculousness worth it. She held her laptop out to Arielle. "Here. You first."

Arielle had imagined that she'd be pissed off about the $75 sorority recruitment fee, having to wear something other than sweatpants on a Saturday night, and her cheeks hurting from fake smiling so much. But over the past several weeks with Lauren, she'd discovered that doing things to make Lauren happy was even better than doing things that Arielle wanted to do for herself. The fire in Lauren's eyes as she walked up to a group of girls welcoming her to that first night of recruitment was electric, contagious.

The Broken Hearts Society of Suite 17C

At that first meeting, they learned that they'd be divided into groups by their Rho Gams, which was the generic sorority sister name for the girls from each sorority on campus who'd volunteered to lead the wide-eyed freshmen through the two weekends of recruitment events and answer all their questions in the week between.

A part of Arielle had wanted to walk out of the room right then. Lauren had promised her that going through recruitment together would give them some couple time, but the group divisions erased any promise of that.

But Lauren hadn't seemed fazed by the separations, still squeezing Arielle's hand between their chairs and sneaking her winks. Something remarkable had happened, a feeling that Arielle had only ever experienced when it applied to herself—Lauren's utter joy was making her happier, too. The girl yammering on about sorority procedure faded to the background as Arielle looked at Lauren taking it all in. The way she fit in so well, the way her hair shone in the weird recessed multiple lights in the student union conference room.

She could do this for two weekends. She could do this for Lauren.

As the meeting went on, Arielle was shocked that sorority life actually didn't sound that horrible. Until the girl talking about recruitment dos and don'ts started in on the don'ts.

"Always remember the 3 Bs,—things you should not ever talk about during sorority recruitment," she said, her expression grave. "We teach this every single year and we are dead serious. The girls in the houses know this rule so well that if you do mention one, we'll probably take it as a hint that you're trying to drop out of the recruitment process. Got it?"

Okay, this was ridiculous. Now even their small talk was being censored? But Arielle glanced at Lauren to see her watching and waiting for the info, completely serious.

"First B—Bucks. Nobody cares if your daddy owns a private jet or your mom is an heiress. I mean, that would be kind of fun, don't get me wrong," she said with a wink. "But if you insist on working money into the conversation with us during any of the pref rounds—and trust me, we will not be asking about the size of your bank account—we'll think you're trying to either impress us with your trust fund, or bribe us with it. Each of the houses is looking for new sisters who really belong there, not who are so insecure about who they are that they have to wave their money in all our faces. Rich or poor, let your beauty shine through."

Again, Arielle would have rolled her eyes if it wasn't for the expression of wholehearted agreement on Lauren's face.

Okayyyyy.

"Next is B for..." The RhoGam stared at them all like she was waiting for them to complete the sentence. To Arielle's utter shock, some of them actually did, chiming in "Booze!" Oh for the love. These girls were such ass kissers. Wasn't it enough to just show up to the info session? Was she actually supposed to do research?

"That's right, girls. Your love of alcohol consumption is another thing that doesn't say very much about you and how well you'll fit in to the house. If you love getting hammered that much, then you should just walk out of here right now. The focus of being a Greek woman is not on which parties you'll go to and how much there will be to drink. If that's why you were thinking about going through recruitment, it's best to save your time and head down to the bar right now."

"The last one should be obvious, but I'll say it anyway." Arielle racked her brain. Bs? Were they not supposed to talk about grades? Body? That would make sense. She'd heard about some crazy hazing on other campuses and, especially since she'd been with Lauren, she really had grown to appreciate lots of things about her body. No issue there...

"Boys." The Rho Gam said smugly. "Yes, we know how much you love your boyfriend, and if you don't have one, we know how much everyone hopes they'll meet some frat hottie when they party with us. You might even think that dropping the names of some frat guys you know will get you in with us. Now, all of us appreciate the beautiful abs of a Pi Psi." Giggles rippled through the room and Arielle spun around to look. Maybe it was because Lauren had made her feel so absolutely normal over the last few months, but for the first time since she'd arrived at Northwestern she felt like a sad, strange little lesbian bobbing in a sea of horny straight girls. She looked pointedly at Lauren, who gave her a troubled look but shrugged.

"Pretty simple, right?" The Rho Gam and the Stepford freshmen filling the room bobbed their heads. "See? Nothing to worry about," she said, and then started chattering about dress code and punctuality and some shit that didn't even matter after what Arielle had just heard.

Suddenly, the meeting was over and all the future sorority drones were filtering out of the huge room. Then, as if someone had snapped their fingers and changed the scene, they were alone among the rows of empty folding chairs.

"See? Not too bad, right?" Lauren's eyes still danced. "It'll be cool to see if we really fit in to one of the houses like she said. It happens all the time, I hear. Instant sisters."

"I...you're joking, right?" Arielle blinked at Lauren as though she was about to announce that Arielle was being punked.

"Yeah, I know you're cranky about having to go out and wear heels on sidewalks that'll likely be icy. But I'll look out for you. No worries." Lauren laced her fingers through Arielle's and Arielle said a silent prayer. *Please don't let her actually be this clueless.*

"I just figured that one of the things that Aubrey said up there would maybe...I don't know...convince you not to do this whole thing?"

Lauren scrunched her eyebrows in and turned to Arielle. "I don't...no. Nothing."

"Oh my God, Lauren!" Arielle stood up so fast the chair wobbled. "The three Bs? BOYS? This is the most crazily hetero collection of humans I've ever been a part of."

"I...I guess? Most girls have boyfriends, right? Only ten percent of the population is gay?"

She didn't say something like "only ten percent are like us" or "I really don't think you have a single thing to worry about. I won't talk about boys, because I don't like boys."

"Whatever," Arielle grumbled, picking at her nails. "I just don't see why you want to be part of a group like that so much."

"I don't know. I guess I don't really blame them for assuming we all like boys? Not everyone is as...aware as we are. But I think they're cool. I think they're good people, regardless of their obvious heteronormative attitudes. I don't think that makes them bad people. I like them." Lauren shrugged and reached out her hand for Arielle's, something she knew made Arielle melt.

"I like you," Arielle murmured as Lauren pulled her to standing. "And only you."

Lauren scoffed, but stepped in even closer so their hips pressed together.

"It's true," Arielle said, standing on tiptoes to brush a light kiss against her lips. "I don't like anyone else in the entire world. Not like you. But you know what I'll do because I like you so much?"

"What?" Lauren whispered, returning Arielle's brush of the lips with one of her own.

"I'll do sorority recruitment. We both will, so that then the question over whether we—you—are missing out on anything wasting your weekends in bed with me and a pizza will finally be answered for you. Because you're important to me, and I don't want you to feel like I'm making you miss out on anything."

The absence of the 'I love you' Arielle so badly wanted to say felt tangible to her, like a blanket folded at the ready. She had to pick the right moment, between when the blanket would smother Lauren and when Lauren couldn't live without it. Without her.

Unfortunately, Arielle had the strong sense that that moment was buried deep somewhere in these four rounds of recruitment. And the only way to find it was to go along for the ride.

It was freaking freezing outside, but Lauren had insisted that Arielle's legs were too gorgeous to hide inside

The Broken Hearts Society of Suite 17C

the fleece-lined leggings she really wanted to wear to the first recruitment round—the open house. Standing in front of the cheap full-length mirror bolted to the inside of her closet, Arielle turned to the side and surveyed the damage of trying to squeeze her butt into this stretchy black skirt that hugged every curve.

Her concentration was interrupted, happily, by Lauren's manicured hand running down her hip and squeezing her butt for a brief second.

"Hey," Arielle said as she turned into Lauren's arms, tipping her chin up to beg her for a kiss. Arielle was such a whore for Lauren's kisses. Lauren's lips could send her head spinning and make her forget where she was or why she was doing whatever she was in the middle of.

Tonight, Arielle could use the distraction.

"Hey, gorgeous. Have you seen my girlfriend? She's really hot and I'm pretty sure she lives here but she promised me she wouldn't be caught dead in a skirt under any circumstances."

"Very funny," Arielle said, standing on her tiptoes to grab a kiss for herself. Lauren responded by squeezing Arielle's hips and pulling them tight to her own, sending pleasure through every inch of her.

"Now, about the shoes…" Lauren said as she rummaged through Ari's closet.

"What's wrong with my shoes?" Arielle had stepped into black leather ballet flats, because they were cute, broken-in, and hopefully would deal with the walk from house to house to house pretty well.

"There's no point in wearing that skirt if you're not going to maximize those calves. Get in heels."

Arielle laughed. "Yeah, right. Not happening, baby. Maybe later tonight."

Lauren's eyebrow flicked up. "Is that a promise?"

"I don't know. We'll see how much I loathe walking to sixteen different sorority houses in two and a half hours, and being enthusiastic for all of them. Without you there with me, which, by the way, I'm still mad about. You owe me four weekend nights of just you and me to make up for the ones that were robbed from us by the evil sorority overlords. Overladies. Whatever."

"Oh, they're not that bad," Lauren said, smiling absently as she checked her small purse for her cell phone and keys. "The worst part will be not being able to mention you."

Her soft smile told Arielle those words made sense to Lauren, but they bounced around in Arielle's ears, disjointed and senseless. "What do you mean?"

"Well, you know. They said we shouldn't talk about our boyfriends, and I assume that's even more true when you have a girlfriend that you absolutely adore, and if you talk about her it could make everyone lose their focus on, you know, you."

"But hold on. Don't you think they should know? What if it bothered them that you were gay? Wouldn't

The Broken Hearts Society of Suite 17C

you want to know that before you got yourself into a really bad situation?"

Lauren approached Arielle again, holding out her arms. Even worried and stressed and totally amped up as Arielle was, she couldn't resist melting into Lauren's arms. "Baby. I would know that, okay? All the houses are so nice. Times are different. You heard them—they talk to every chapter about discrimination based on all sorts of things. And nobody even cares anymore."

"I just don't see how you would know without telling them," Arielle whispered, keeping her voice quiet so the tears pricking at her eyelids wouldn't be able to escape. Not with all the time she spent making her mascara perfect.

Lauren pressed a light kiss to Arielle's forehead. "I will figure it out. I promise you, I will love you just as much after this whole thing is over as I do right now. The only difference is that my new sisters will love you too."

Something caught in Arielle's throat and she raised her head, slowly, to look into Lauren's eyes. She begged her heart to stay steady, not to get too excited at what she thought she just heard. At what she didn't even trust herself to confirm with words. So she just stared at Lauren like an idiot and bit her lower lip.

Lauren leaned down and planted a lingering kiss right where Ari's teeth had pulled in her lip. Pulling back just enough so that she could get the words out, she said, "You heard me. I love you. I've never felt this way about anyone, and I've never been happier. My mom even loves you."

Arielle's eyes fluttered closed, remembering the Skype call just a few days ago where Lauren had put her arm around Ari, kissed her cheek, told her mom and dad how they'd met outside of women's studies class. Lauren was so calm, collected, and she told the story just like Arielle had heard straight couples tell similar stories dozens of times. The relief and reassurance that had come from that had kept Arielle's hopes up every moment since then.

Maybe this was something real. Maybe this was something that wouldn't be destroyed by worrying about what other people would think.

"You know I love you too," Arielle's voice ground out, still fighting valiantly to keep back tears.

"I know," Lauren said, cupping Ari's jaw and making her look into her eyes again. "We both know, and the sororities will know too, as soon as we get through recruitment."

"You don't know what I know about these girls. I think we have to tell them. If they know that you and I are together, we'll be able to see how they really feel. Lesbians are just fine with these Greek girls in theory, until they have to see girl-on-girl romance every day. Then, things are different."

"Ari, why are you making this into such a big deal?"

Arielle's stomach twisted, sour and sick. Why did such a beautiful declaration have to be framed by so much worry? But she had to say her piece. "How can you NOT make this into a big deal? This is who we are."

"This is who *you* are."

"What are you saying?" Arielle recoiled, pulling back like Lauren had stabbed her in the gut.

Lauren sighed heavily and tried to close the gap Arielle had put between them. Arielle pulled back more. "That sounded bad. I didn't mean that I'm not gay, or whatever. Just that being a lesbian is such a big part of your identity, Ari. I'm different. I'm so happy we're together, but there are so many things that the girls need to know about me, that say more about me, just *me*, than the fact that I'm head over heels with a girl. Another girl who's going through recruitment, I should add."

"God, who cares if I'm going through recruitment? I don't even care about this sorority bullshit!"

Lauren's mouth twisted. "You don't have to do it if you don't want to. I just wanted someone to give me the push to do it, to come along with me. Because I really do care about it, a lot. And I think if you check out the houses, you might too. But if you don't, there are two options. Go tonight, and when you don't like any of the houses, drop. Or drop now. I'll be okay."

The look in Lauren's eyes said something different, though. There was also the sinking feeling that if Arielle put an end to her involvement in sorority recruitment, it would be the beginning of the end of much more than that. She simply wasn't ready to think about giving Lauren up. She couldn't bear two heartbreaks in one year.

"Okay," Arielle said softly. "I'll come. No girlfriend talk," she added begrudgingly. The gut punch stayed inside, twisting and forming a ball that seemed to get tighter by the minute. She didn't like this, not at all. It felt like lying.

It felt like the beginning of Rachel leaving her all over again.

"Baby, listen," Lauren said. "We're going to be late, which will ruin this whole thing whether you decide to stay in or not. And I really really want to stay in. I know you're upset, but please, for me—just go through this round and we'll talk about it tonight. I promise. We'll work everything out." Lauren tipped Arielle's chin up again. "You are too important to me not to work everything out. I promise you that. Do you trust me?"

Keep it together, Ari. "I…yeah, okay." She knew what Lauren wanted her to say—that she trusted her, that she knew everything would be just fine.

But saying 'I trust you' was too big of a leap for Ari when she didn't even trust herself.

The second block of Benedict Avenue, affectionately referred to as sorority row, was a tree-lined street just off Francis, and it looked festive in the frost-covered twilight.

The Broken Hearts Society of Suite 17C

Banners of welcome hung on the front of each house, and there were folding tables along the sidewalks where smiling, pretty, dolled-up girls handed out paper cups of steaming hot chocolate. When Ari and Lauren passed the first one, a girl with bouncing blond curls handed them each a pink one with green polka dots and "Kappa Kappa Beta" in big swirl-tipped letters. "Hope you'll consider KKB!" she chirped, more to Lauren then to Arielle. Lauren grinned back at her. "Thanks!" Ari mumbled something into her cup.

They walked a couple steps farther, then Lauren stopped. "I think we need to head to our first houses. Do you know where yours is?"

Arielle didn't. She nodded anyway, and watched the slight frothing swirl around the surface of her hot cocoa. The paper telling everyone from Harrison Tower where to go was folded in quarters in her pocket. She knew studying it while she was actually on Benedict Street would make her look like a loser. She didn't really care.

"Listen, Ari. It's just one night. We'll talk when we get home."

Home. God, How did Lauren know exactly how to twist her heart around when she was trying to keep it still. "Your place?"

"Whatever you want." She touched Ari's elbow. "We're going to be talking to a lot of girls tonight."

"Yeah, what did that Rho Gam say? Five hundred something?"

"Something like that. But listen. You are the only one I'm even remotely interested in coming home with. Okay?"

Arielle's eyes shifted to all the banners and cheerful girls. What had Rachel thought about when she was standing in this exact position one year ago? Did she know that what her sisters thought of her would become more important than the girl waiting for her back home, who she said she loved?

Rion's words from earlier that day rang clear in her memory. "Lauren is not Rachel. You might be hurt, but you still have to be fair."

So Arielle took a deep breath, looked into Lauren's eyes, and said, "Okay."

Then Lauren squeezed her hand, kissed her on the cheek, and started walking, calling over her shoulder, "Text me. See you soon."

Arielle sighed and checked her list. "Gamma Delta Chi?" she groused in an undertone. "Yep! You've made it to the right place!" Another bouncy girl, this one with several layers of makeup, flashed her a million-watt smile. She wasn't even wearing gloves, or a scarf. Jesus, was she made of plastic?

"Well, come on in! You're going to love GDC!"

Arielle's cheeks felt stiff as she tried to match the girl's smile, not even coming close.

The Broken Hearts Society of Suite 17C

Open house round of recruitment was a special circle of hell that only the dumbest girls at Indiana Northern subjected themselves to, Arielle quickly learned over the following two and a half hours.

One house looked like a tea party at a retirement home with cardigan-shell sets on all the girls and a slideshow of their philanthropy events playing to classical music in the background. Others included a trivia game and an impressive selection of hot tea—maybe their mothers were sponsoring this event. Another house blared music through dimmed lights and the rank smell of overpriced teen cologne. Yet another house was workout-obsessed, with the girls' various gym and weight training schedules hung on the wall of the dining room. Another emphasized the fellowship and Bible study opportunities they offered at every turn. In Beta Gamma Psi, the sisters greeted the freshmen visitors while dancing to disco music, all wearing identical silver platform heels. The main point of that sorority seemed to be getting as drunk as possible for as many weekends in a row as possible.

An hour and a half in, Arielle had begun to despair of humanity. Or at least female humanity at Indiana Northern. The upside was that she realized how lucky she'd been to find Lauren, not to mention her roommates—bastions of female semi-sanity in a sea of girl idiots.

The saving grace of tonight was that at least, when she got home with Lauren, they could laugh about how stupid sorority recruitment had been and go on with their lives. Arielle actually started to get kind of excited—she'd be proven right, everything would go back to normal, maybe they'd start discussing plans for Spring break.

The only thing worse than the first ten houses she had to drag herself to was Arielle's second to last, Alpha Rho Omega. Those three Greek letters were burned into the back of Arielle's mind. She'd memorized them as she stared at the back of Rachel's t-shirt when she walked away from her for the last time. She hadn't realized they were emblazoned on the door of the house, however, until she stood right in front of it. Too late to run away. Arielle cursed herself for not making a plan to deal with Rachel's house before then, and pulled in a deep breath when the door swung open.

The house was bright and warm, spotless, smelling only the slightest bit of fresh, clean perfume. Dozens of the sisters milled around the first floor, and they were easy to spot. They all wore the same height of boots, the same fit of jeans, and they all had long hair that they'd straightened to shining perfection. Of course they weren't all the same—nobody was—but it was so very clear that they all wanted to be. Yes, Arielle could see why Rachel had chosen this place.

Just as she thought Rachel's name, Arielle spotted her on the other side of the room. Her hair wasn't perfectly straight—that was impossible, with Rachel's curls. The slightly puffy hair framing the perfectly glossed roundness

The Broken Hearts Society of Suite 17C

of her lips and the hearty belly laugh Rachel tried to tone down but never could…they were all still there.

Only one thing was missing. When Arielle used to see Rachel across the room and feel like she was in the presence of a goddess, someone she couldn't wait to be near, to touch, to speak to, now she just saw a girl. A normal girl in a sea of other normal girls, so indistinct that Arielle didn't really feel anything when she saw her. Being in the same room didn't feel scary or traumatic, like Arielle assumed it would—it felt like nothing.

Walking to the last house felt like the longest slog of Arielle's life. Just like half the others, it had an immaculately kept lawn, white pillars, and in the early winter twilight, the Christmas lights were still up and twinkling, despite the holiday being three weeks gone.

Great. Not only was this house a cookie cutter Greek house probably filled with the same giggling girls and the same superficial, meandering conversations, but it was obviously not so Jew-friendly either.

Arielle walked in, shivering, and took a second to roll her ankle against the ache of the balls of her feet in her flats, which had become surprisingly painful somewhere between houses six and seven. On the inside, the house looked…normal. No blaring lights, no gimmicky signs, no picture slideshows or pop music-singing girls in heels. Just a warm, inviting house with a fire roaring in the common room. One girl came out to greet Arielle and the half dozen girls who had trickled in after her, trying to blow some warmth into their fingertips.

"Oh, geez," she said, looking Arielle up and down.

What the hell did she say that for? Arielle didn't even care what these girls thought of her—in theory. But every conversation that included a semi-judgmental reply to a question, or talked way too much about their frat "brothers" despite the girls going through recruitment being forbidden from talking about boys, or were dressed in clothes more trendy than Arielle had ever considered wearing, had worn her down to feeling not really confident in herself, or who she was, at all. This "oh, geez" was the last straw.

"We've got a shoe situation," the girl continued, and Arielle blushed and started to stammer. "I know they're not heels, but I knew we'd be doing a lot of walking, and flats just made more sense to me."

"Of course they did," said another girl who came in to join the first. The first one came behind her and tugged Arielle's coat from her arms as she shrugged out of it. "Honestly, I'm in awe of you girls who wore anything with a heel. I never even attempted it. Which is how I ended up at Alpha Chi."

The second girl smiled at Arielle, and for the first time that night, her smile in response felt genuine. "So what'll it be? Socks or slippers? Both fresh out of the dryer, you can keep either."

The Broken Hearts Society of Suite 17C

"Seriously?" Arielle's mouth dropped open, and by the murmurings of the girls around her, they were just as surprised as she was. She scanned the room. Each and every member of Alpha Chi was wearing some form of stretchy, soft pants, and a warm, comfortable top.

"Yeah," the girl replied with a knowing smile. "Other girls can pay as much as they want for videos and karaoke machines and matching heels. Everyone knows what they all really want is warm slippers and a fire."

"We wanted to get sweatshirts for you all too, but that would have been a little expensive. Plus our main priority was to feed you. Come on in." Another girl in the same yoga pants and zip up hoodie came in.

After accepting a pair of slippers, Arielle settled onto the couch next to the girl with the sleek chestnut ponytail who had greeted her. Apparently she was responsible for the first wave of potential new members, who all the girls kept referring to as 'PNMs.' She invited all of them to find a seat around the huge sectional couch and on floor cushions where she asked about their recruitment experience so far. "We can't talk about it too much, because it's against the rules, but just wanted to make sure everyone was okay. Obviously we are dedicated to warming up your feet, but if you need anything else, like a Tylenol or a tampon, do not hesitate to ask."

The laughter quickly turned from nervous to relaxed when she said that. "I'm Lanie, and if you have any questions about Alpha Chi, you should absolutely ask me.

For now I want to hear about you. Let's do a quick round of best and worst thing about your first semester at Indiana Northern."

Wow, this was super cheesy. But as Lanie went around the circle, Arielle half-listened and half-surveyed the other women in the room. More and more Alpha Chi sisters trickled in wearing their yoga pants and hoodies, asking each PNM who came in whether they needed anything and how they were doing, with genuine concern on their faces. They were actually listening. Everything about them—from their clothes to their jokes to their complete absence of showmanship—felt so real.

As more sisters came into the room, each PNM was paired with one of them. This was nothing new—it had happened at every single house. Unlike the disco house where Ari had felt like she was in the middle of a bar, and the trivia house where she felt like she was reading an academic resume out loud, and the Abercrombie house where the girls' opinion of a PNM seemed to increase with the number of fraternity names she could drop, Alpha Chi felt like a place she could relax, speak her mind, maybe even find a friend. Or a whole house full of them.

Any knots of worry that Arielle still had started to unwind when Lanie plopped down on the couch next to next to her. "What do you think?" she asked with just enough energy that Arielle believed she really was interested in the answer, but just enough softness that she

The Broken Hearts Society of Suite 17C

didn't feel like she was under the glare of a microscope, or interviewing for a high-stakes job.

"About...?"

"Anything." Lanie said with a gentle smile. "It's a trick they taught us. If you answer what you think about the different houses, you're in interview mode. If you answer with a question, it'll show us that you're actually interested in having a conversation. It's supposed to teach us something about who you really are, but honestly none of this process can really show us that anyway."

Arielle laughed for the first time all night. "Are you seriously telling me that you joined a sorority whose recruitment process is pointless?"

Lanie shrugged. "Nah, it's not pointless. I'm a sociology major. Humans need structure, rules, and boundaries to function successfully in groups. But what I am saying is that, almost hands-down, the best way to learn about a girl is not through structured conversations that carefully avoid forbidden topics."

"The Three Bs," Arielle said, nodding.

"Yeah. Not that money and drinking and who you're dating is actually important to us, but this is my fourth year in college. I know those things color all the other things in your life. If they were smart, they would have told us specifically to ask about those things, and judge a sister based on how she talks about them. But, you know, humans are stupid." Lanie laughed, and her statement struck Arielle as so ridiculous and so true at the same time that Arielle laughed with her.

"You know? You're right. I've gotten really close to my roommates, who were totally random, and I consider myself so lucky. In fact they're two out of three people on this campus that I've gotten close to so far, and I didn't know any of them in my life before this."

"Right? And you never would have seen them walking across campus and thought, wow, that girl and I would so be amazing friends."

"Definitely not," Arielle laughed. "In fact I probably would have avoided them like the plague. One of them was a cheerleader church girl, and the other one has a nose piercing, bleach-blond streaks, and mixes hard rock, pop, and electronic music in her spare time. I'm Jewish and not a cheerleader and I only have one hole in each ear. And I mostly like to read, lay around in yoga class, and go to the occasional concert, so…yeah. I'm really glad they're my roommates though."

Lanie's eyes opened wide. "You're Jewish? What synagogue did you grow up in?"

They filled the next several minutes with Jewish geography—rapid-fire questions about youth group acquaintances and second cousins and rabbis each of them knew. There was at least one youth group conference they'd both attended.

"Well, I'm really glad you told me about your roommates, because Alpha Chi is kind of like that. We're

The Broken Hearts Society of Suite 17C

all pretty different—see, Bella over there loves to wear makeup, and I don't think Dani has ever tried any in her life." Lanie motioned to both girls, and it was clear that, yes, Bella had spent a lot more time getting dolled up in her yoga pants and sweatshirt, and looked pristine, where Dani looked like she'd just rolled out of bed. Both looked equally happy and relaxed to be doing this whole crazy recruitment thing, though. There were very few moments in Arielle's life when she'd felt one hundred percent happy and relaxed, but when she tried to envision herself in this room, a year from now, doing the exact same thing— welcoming freshmen with warm slippers, a comfy couch, and totally inclusive conversation—she could see herself fitting in here, too.

That was something that rarely happened.

A handbell rang, and Lanie groaned. "Dammit. I actually like talking to you. We've got five minutes to go. Anything else?"

"Oh, I..." Arielle stammered. It was crazy, but she was actually sad about this recruitment round ending, too. The thought of being cut from this house in the next round made her fidget, and the idea of never coming back to Alpha Chi made her heart sink. Damn her, Lauren had been right.

Oh, shit. Lauren. She'd agreed not to say anything to anyone, but last week, it had only been principle. Now Arielle had gone and done the thing she would have sworn up and down she'd never do—fallen in love with a sorority. If Alpha Chi hated gay girls, it would kill her. And that was why she had to find out, now, before she fell even more in love with it.

"Oh! You never told me about the third girl. The one you liked even though you didn't expect to." Lanie smiled, apparently having no idea that she'd just opened the one can of worms that Arielle had promised not to open. Jittery terror bloomed in her chest, skittering down her arms and twisting in her stomach.

"Yeah. She's…um…I'm going to be honest right now, okay?"

"Okay…" Lanie said. "Are you going to tell me she's like an axe murderer or a prostitute or something?"

Just the idea of beautiful, sweet Lauren being either of those things sent Ari into a fit of giggles. "No no. No. It's just…she's my girlfriend."

"Right. You said she was a friend of yours."

"No, like my girlfriend. Like, I'm gay."

"Oh. And?" The look of bored confusion at this revelation on Lanie's face almost gave Arielle another giggling fit.

"Well, I know we're not supposed to talk about dating, but…"

"No, you're not supposed to talk about the sorority as straight path to hooking up, or make us think your entire life revolves around the person you're dating. Our president last year was a lesbian. Her girlfriend was here all the time."

The Broken Hearts Society of Suite 17C

"Seriously?"

"Yeah," Lanie scoffed. "Seriously, it's like the opposite of a big deal. No offense, but whether the person you're making out with has a dick or tits is like one of the least interesting things about you. You know?"

Lanie's face was so open, so easy. It made Ari feel stupid for thinking this would ever be a big deal to anyone at Northern. "My ex is in Alpha Rho. She made it sound like it would not be good for her if they knew she was dating a girl. That's actually why…well, never mind. It's not important."

"No, it's not. Especially past relationships. Sorority recruitment is the beginning of your next three and a half years here, not about what happened before. But that's weird. I'd never heard of Alpha Rho hating on lesbians."

"Oh," Arielle said as a thousand new questions cropped up in her mind. "Well…then I guess I was wrong."

"You have nothing to worry about here. Seriously, no stress. As long as you and your girlfriend don't end up in the same sorority, nobody should even give it a second thought. And if they do, they're a total bitch and you don't want to be in that sorority anyway. And we don't let bitches like that in Alpha Chi anyway. Okay?"

And there was the kicker. The sentence that echoed in Arielle's mind. "As long as you don't end up in the same sorority."

Lauren wanted to be in a sorority, to be part of something bigger, so badly. What would happen if she showed up at Alpha Chi and felt the same comfort and connection that Arielle had? It seemed almost inevitable now, because Lauren and Arielle got along so well. How could they *not* love the same group of girls?

Just as Arielle was changing back into her flats, her phone buzzed, and she grinned at the message there.

<3 : AT STARBUCKS. YOU'RE LATE! HAVING MORE FUN THEN EXPECTED?

Arielle shook her head and swallowed hard. Lanie came up behind her and slung and arm around her shoulder. "See you tomorrow for philanthropy, right?"

"I can't wait," Arielle answered. The best and the worst part of that small sentence, and the smile that accompanied it, was how genuinely she meant both.

Lauren got to her feet the minute Arielle walked into the coffee shop to meet her. She grinned so wide it looked like her cheeks would crack open. "You liked it, huh?" Arielle said, smiling. Once again, seeing Lauren so happy was making her heart nearly burst.

"Yes. I shouldn't have been worried about it at all. I'm so sorry I made you go through with it. I can't believe I was so nervous. Ari, these girls are amazing!"

"All of them?"

The Broken Hearts Society of Suite 17C

"Well, obviously, some of them were insane."

"Like, the mirrored shoes?"

Lauren laughed, never breaking her grin. "Yeah. But the gym rats were so sweet, and then—" And then Lauren checked herself, like she'd just realized something. "Wait a minute. You don't look totally miserable. You liked one of the houses, didn't you?"

Arielle shrugged. "Whatever. It's not important."

"Is it not important enough for this to be your last night? Or are you going back for philanthropy tomorrow?"

"Well, I…"

"Oh my God, you are! I can't believe this! My girlfriend is going to be a sorority girl!" Lauren wiggled in her seat, seemingly even happier now.

But the pit in Arielle's stomach that had started there only got heavier and heavier. "Yeah, it's great. Listen, though, I feel really bad about this."

"Wait, why?"

"Well, I really only liked one, and I told them about you. And the girl—I really, really liked this house, Lauren—she said that it would only be a problem if we ended up in the same house."

"Wait. You told her about me? I thought we weren't going to mention each other. The three Bs, remember?"

The shock of seeing Lauren's face, anything but happy or loving, made the ball in Arielle's stomach wind even tighter. "Well, I thought I was going to be able to write this whole thing off as something that I did just because I love you. I never thought I would end up actually liking one of them."

"So you told her about me. Did you say my name?"

"No, I don't think so. It was at the end of the session, and I…wait. Why do you care? What are you afraid of?" Arielle knew she shouldn't let her mind go directly to that place, the one of paranoia and fear. But now, it was way too hard to make any more excuses.

"I'm afraid of it hurting my chances. God, Arielle, you know why this is so important to me. There are rules, and you have to follow them. They're there for a reason. What if we end up in the same sorority? Then what are we supposed to do?"

"Well isn't that why we should tell them? So that we don't?"

"No! Don't you get it? You're not supposed to match with a certain sorority so you can keep dating your girlfriend. We're supposed to be focusing on finding the place where we really belong."

"Well there's nothing we can do about it now," Arielle huffed, throwing her hands in the air. "You're not the only one who deserves to find a group of girls you feel comfortable in. You're not the only one who can act normal. I liked one of those houses. It's just that I consider you a big enough part of my life to make sure they know about you before they accept me."

Arielle took a deep breath before she finished her speech. "Look, Lauren. I love you, so much that I consider us a package deal. But I guess finding the right sorority is more important to you than keeping me in your life."

There were too many emotions swirling around Arielle now, and she stood up abruptly, making her chair stutter against the floor when it pushed back.

"Ari, baby, please."

"Don't call me that. You don't get to call me that in private when you won't even talk about my existence in public."

"That is not fair, Ari. I understand why this upsets you, okay? I know Rachel treated you like shit."

"Well then explain to me why you're doing the same thing. Explain to me why you're so determined to keep me a secret, too." One tear fell out of Arielle's eye, and she reached up to swipe it away with her still-gloved hand.

"Explain to me why you have to tell everyone we're together, immediately, even if telling people too soon could ruin my chances. You know how badly I want this."

"Well, if you want to pretend you're someone you're not just to get something you want that badly, then maybe you don't want me enough to keep me." Pain sliced through Arielle's chest as the full impact of the words she'd just let loose rang back in her ears. She stared at Lauren, begging her to do something to fix this whole conversation. But she knew nothing could. She knew they were at odds, and what was worse, she knew both of them were being a little stupid. She also knew, deep down, that neither of them was going to budge.

The worst part was that she loved this girl so damn much that she wouldn't ask her to do the only thing that actually would fix this—tell her to stay away from the sorority that Arielle really, really wanted now. Because what if Lauren loved those girls too?

Then came the craziest realization of her whole life—Arielle wanted Lauren to be happy, even if it meant making herself miserable.

"You know what? I'm not going to ask you to lie. Go ahead and tell them the truth—you don't have a girlfriend. There are no conflicts of interest, nothing to worry about. I understand how bad you want it, and I won't be the person who ruins that for you."

Now tears were streaming down Arielle's cheeks, and she gave herself a small pat on the back for at least refraining from raising her voice. Lauren's eyes were wide, panicked, and she looked like she was going to throw up.

"I don't understand why we can't…I mean, just for the week…Arielle, I love you."

Arielle shook her head, forcing the lump in her throat down far enough to get the words out. "Not enough. And that's okay. I'm done asking people to love me more than they can."

With one last look at Lauren, her frozen posture, and her trembling bottom lip, Arielle headed out into the dark, whipping wind. The sound of Lauren telling her for the last time that she loved her started her heart hardening around the edges.

She should have listened to her gut—once a straight girl, always a straight girl. If Lauren wasn't sure enough of her identity to let her future sorority know, then she wasn't sure enough for Arielle. Period.

She pushed into Suite 17C and dropped her bag, realizing vaguely through her tears, which felt angry instead of devastated this time, that she couldn't feel her face, and there was a vague numbness running through her arms, spreading through her legs, which she had to concentrate on moving one after the other. She collapsed into bed without washing her face or brushing her teeth, unable to feel a single thing except her poor, throbbing heart.

Chapter 20

Arielle

Before Lauren, everything in Arielle's life had felt completely amazing or completely devastating. It sounded simplistic, and maybe Arielle's life had been beyond sheltered and privileged, but there it was.

Before Lauren, going through sorority recruitment with her sights on Alpha Chi would have been completely amazing. She freaking loved that sorority—everything about it, from the girls she had increasingly meaningful conversations with to their damn living room. It had been so long since she felt like she'd brought her whole self, with everything out there, to a place, and been accepted for it.

Well, almost her whole self. For one thing, she couldn't say anything about who her girlfriend was—no matter how upset she was about Lauren refusing to

The Broken Hearts Society of Suite 17C

disclose the fact that they were dating, she wouldn't ruin something like that for any girl—and for another, the words Lauren said and the looks that had twisted her normally relaxed, happy features into confusion and pain wouldn't stop playing on a loop in Arielle's head.

Arielle knew that Alpha Chi was the perfect place for her, just like she thought she'd known Lauren was the perfect girl for her. And so the deep rooted fear set in—was the problem with Lauren, or with Arielle? Was she trading one shaky reality for another? Was she abandoning one thing she desperately wanted, desperately *needed* for the sake of another? And why the hell, for once in her life, couldn't she have both?

So recruitment week was anxious. It was hard enough worrying about whether the group of girls you hoped to call sisters liked you, and furthermore, saw the real you. There was something so warm about the idea of having sisters—Arielle had never had one, and while she loved her mom and her friends dearly, there was nothing like the idea of definitively belonging to a group of friends who carried the bond of family.

Every time she thought about that, she tried to ignore how much she knew Lauren needed that exact same thing. They only had to get through this one week, and then they would each be in a house, or at least know for sure that they wouldn't be in a house, and they'd be able to talk through it. It might be difficult, but they could do it. They'd grown too close, and Arielle had planted Lauren in too many of her daydreams about the future, to abandon what they'd started.

At every single movie night, philanthropy meeting, and mid-week activity planned by the recruitment coordinators, Arielle kept one eye on the sororities that she visited—the list was narrowed with each meeting, and Alpha Chi always remained front and center—and the other on the crowd of girls. If Lauren was there, she'd see her right away—if she didn't catch sight of her shining black hair, she'd hear her laugh, or maybe smell her perfume first. The more Arielle scanned crowds, desperate to catch a glimpse of Lauren, the more she realized how utterly attached to Lauren she'd become. Addicted, even. The hope of seeing Lauren, even if just for a moment, was a tiny carrot at the end of a very twisty-turny stick. At the moment, though, the only thing twisting and turning was Arielle's stomach when she realized just how close this feeling was to what she'd experienced with Rachel. Too damn close.

One thing Arielle couldn't stand about sorority recruitment was how steeped it was in pomp and circumstance. Each girl's list of houses she was interested in narrowed for each round, and when Arielle went through the entire week without seeing Lauren, she started to hope that maybe what Lauren said would turn out to be true. Maybe they'd end up totally loving different sororities and they could keep dating like nothing had ever gone wrong.

The Broken Hearts Society of Suite 17C

Like Arielle hadn't decided she wanted something else just as much as she wanted Lauren.

That, however, was assuming that she could get Lauren to talk to her at all. She was still stewing about it, and she wanted the chance to work through it, convince Lauren to get back together with her. And assuming that Lauren had told her sorority that she was gay, which Arielle wasn't too sure she'd do after all, and assuming that that sorority didn't hate gay girls. Like Rachel's did.

But now that she was in it, she really did feel so at home at Alpha Chi. Obviously, her relationship with Lauren had started with attraction, and the one with her roommates as a Society meeting. As nice as attraction and blind circumstance were, the Alpha Chi girls were looking at Arielle the whole person, and—hopefully—saying they wanted her to be part of their house.

Arielle growled at her stupid curly hair as she tugged some smoother through it with her fingers. At least recruitment in the dead of winter meant that there would be no humidity to puff it out into oblivion. She sighed as she tugged the curve-hugging white dress she'd borrowed from Amy up over her waist. Her hips were about the same size as Amy's, but she was about three inches shorter, making the thick-knit skirt fall mercifully just below her knees.

White dresses were one more ridiculous thing about sorority recruitment. It was a holdover from wearing white during Spring recruitment, or maybe to graduation ceremonies—nobody really knew anymore. Apparently, along with being traditional, white was awesome at accentuating lumps and bumps. Arielle frowned in the mirror, tugged at the way the dress bunched up around her waist, tried to figure out how she could pose in pictures so that the dress looked natural on her instead of looking like the hand-me-down it was. The sleeves only went to her elbows, and it was ass-cold outside, so she pulled on her dressiest sweater, which happened to be purple, with a line of sequins around the hem. Definitely not on the dress code. But she shrugged. Now that she was all in, and she knew her reasons why, she knew she didn't want to be part of any sorority that wouldn't have her if she wore something slightly off-plan—something that made her feel more comfortable in her own skin.

Arielle scrolled through the email about bid day protocol on her phone for the millionth time as she shivered on the short walk to the student union. Rion had called it cultish and Amy had called it weird when she'd told them about the process, and Arielle had found it hard to argue. Each original recruitment group, organized by dorm, was supposed to meet in a different room with their recruitment advisor. The girls who didn't match with a sorority—the main reason people didn't was because they'd suicided, or only listed one acceptable sorority—would get pulled aside before bids were handed out, so they could leave through a back door, embarrassment-free. Most girls were dreading that possibility, of not

The Broken Hearts Society of Suite 17C

finding somewhere to fit in, of nobody accepting them. Arielle was different. She thought 'suiciding' was a stupid term, because not matching with a sorority wouldn't be the end of the world. She certainly wouldn't want to *die* if no sorority wanted her. She'd be sad, because she loved Alpha Chi so much, but she'd find somewhere she fit in. Probably.

She did, however, feel like she might die if she never saw Lauren again.

Arielle settled into a molded plastic chair in the random conference room the Harrison recruitment group had been assigned. She smiled as the last few girls walked in. Everyone had done their hair and makeup, and the buzz of excitement that ran through the group made them all glimmer with excitement. Most of all, it was nice to be excited about pretty much the same thing as a group of girls her age were.

Here, in this moment, she was normal. She fit in. She belonged.

The worst part was that she wasn't really angry at Lauren anymore. Anger would be easier. This uncertain hope and longing might kill her before today was over. If only she could figure out how to talk to Lauren again.

Anita, the Rho Gam for the Harrison Tower recruitment group, stood at the front of the room clutching a stack of white envelopes. She wore one of those conciliatory smiles that made Arielle's stomach twist. She could totally handle the disappointment of not being in Alpha Chi, but that didn't mean she was eager for something else to make her cry just two weeks into what would feel like a very long semester if there were two huge disappointments to start it out.

"Okay, welcome to bid day, girls!" Anita looked stunningly out of place in frigid Indiana, with her nose stud and golden-tanned skin from her winter break to Greece to hang out with her grandparents. "First, I'll need to speak with Kelly Newman, Diana Singh, and Elissa Overholt. And that's it." Her smile looked relieved, even though the three girls—who Arielle vaguely recognized, probably from running into them at the Harrison mailboxes or elevator—looked like they were going to be sick. They filed out after Anita, and as soon as the door shut, the sparkly happy anticipatory energy turned a little more solemn. In high school, they would have gossiped and chatted about the other girls, reveling in their own good luck. Back then, Arielle would have expected sorority girls to do the same. But there was one thing about this recruitment process that had stuck with her—sorority girls, by and large, were really, really good people. Sweet and dedicated, ready to be amazing friends and sisters.

Most of all, Arielle was trying to contain her happy butterflies. She hadn't suicided for Alpha Chi and she hadn't been called out of the room—which meant that Alpha Chi was offering her a bid. When Anita announced it was time to open their envelopes, Arielle was one of the girls who grinned and squealed and wiggled in her chair.

Alpha Chi Beta cordially invites Arielle Duval to become a New Member of Kappa Mu Chapter, Indiana Northern University.

What a rush. What a strange feeling, to feel like she was one of a select few completely and totally happy people in a situation that she would have called bizarre a month ago.

At that realization, it was like everything started unraveling all around her. A month ago. Just thirty days ago, she would have never imagined herself as someone who would join a sorority—in fact, if anyone had suggested it, she would have glared at them and told them to shut their stupid mouths. What did they think she was, a stupid mainstream giggling college girl? But now, she'd fight for her affiliation with Alpha Chi to the death—that was how quickly her viewpoint and feelings had changed.

What if Lauren was just as wishy-washy about dating girls? Arielle had always put so much emphasis on knowing who she was, and only dating girls who knew who they were, too. But what if dating her was the one thing that made those other girls sure? What if Lauren had been with Arielle, and her identity had taken an unexpected turn, too?

Arielle's elation suddenly became coated in panicked regret. Because, now that she knew she was joining Alpha Chi, that it was an undeniable part of who she was, that she loved the sorority so much and felt completely comfortable there, if they'd asked her to shout her commitment from the rooftops the first time she'd walked into the house, she would have balked. The realization of how unfair she'd been to Lauren in essentially asking her to do the same made her face fall and her shoulders slump.

"Since there are only 200 girls rushing, we'll meet in the downstairs lobby. Then they're going to call each girl to their new house individually. So, indicate your acceptance or rejection of the bid on the back of the small card they included and hand it back to me, please. Keep in mind that if you reject, it's likely you won't be offered a bid from another house, at least for this year. I'm ready to talk to anyone who has questions, but please don't discuss bids among yourselves."

The silence in the room was palpable. About half the girls seemed as excited and sure as Arielle, but the other half were lukewarm over whatever they scribbled, or agonizing. She couldn't help thinking of Lauren—whether she'd gotten a bid, where it was, how she felt about it. The bid process was so highly guarded that Arielle didn't want to mess up her chances by asking the Alpha Chi girls inappropriate questions, but she knew it was a possibility that Lauren would want a bid from them, too. A slim one, since she hadn't run into her, but still. Now that they were definitely all in the same building though…maybe…

The Broken Hearts Society of Suite 17C

Arielle's hand shot up. "If I need to go to the bathroom, is that allowed, or...?"

Anita nodded quickly—the girl she was talking to looked like her dog had just died. Arielle ducked out of the room and slunk down the mostly quiet hallway. The student union was newly renovated, and rooms on the third floor were rarely frequented. It still smelled like new carpet. Almost every room was completely closed off to the main hallway behind heavy metal doors but there was one, a triangle-shaped corner room with long mahogany tables, that had windowed walls on all sides, probably because it offered the best view of the rest of the union. Arielle didn't expect it, but there were girls in white in all those chairs, too, and then she caught a glimpse of the sign on the door—CRAWFORD. Lauren's dorm.

Arielle's heart thudded in her chest. The bathroom she was supposed to use was just to her left, but there was another one past that conference room. Nobody would question her walking by it, especially since the purple cardigan was long enough to not make her white dress so totally obvious.

She was dying to see Lauren, just like she'd been all week—but part of her had also hoping Lauren had dropped out. That was the selfish part—the part that imagined that she could have it all, without bending. That she could be a sorority girl and a gay girl, and that it would be okay because her girlfriend wasn't even involved with all that stuff. Didn't even want to be.

But Arielle had spent so much time staring at Lauren's back, her profile, the way she sat in a hard-backed chair, the exact swoop of her hair, and she spotted her instantly, chatting with another girl across the table from her. She didn't look panicked or worried or sad. She seemed happy. Best-case scenario, she'd matched with a sorority she loved, which might be okay. Worst-case scenario, since she and Arielle had fought, or broken up, or whatever they'd done, she had fully embraced lesbianism and was flirting with other sorority girls with complete abandon.

Arielle fought to steady her breath, numbly used the bathroom, and forced her legs to walk back to her recruitment group. She had to focus on the positive. She was about to have a brand new home.

If only she could ignore the sour, twisting feeling in her stomach as she walked away from Lauren, maybe for the last time ever,

Arielle had fallen in love with Alpha Chi for every reason opposite of what was going on right now on the main floor of the student union. Groups of girls, dressed alike—white shirts with denim, mint shirts with black pants, pink shirts with khaki…and tall leather boots as far as the eye could see. Each group stood in a cluster, chanting cheers, doing dances, bouncing around with posterboard signs and streamers in the sorority colors. If aliens descended on the student union at this moment and were presented with this view of humanity, Arielle wouldn't blame them for laser-zapping all two hundred-some squealing girls.

Some of the girls in her group were just as squealy and bouncy. Arielle glimpsed Lauren coming into the room where all the potential new members waited to join the craziness, shouldering in next to another girl. Arielle couldn't tear her eyes away. She had to know how Lauren was doing. Arielle watched the downward flick of Lauren's eyes, the half-smile that showed no teeth or dimples. When she talked with the girl standing next to her, she kept her shoulders facing forward, only said a few short words. Not like Lauren at all.

Clearly she wasn't doing okay, a realization which gave Arielle a jab right in the heart. It didn't matter whether or not Arielle had been the one to cause the upset—even if she hadn't, she'd ruined any chance of being there to comfort Lauren, to help her out. She'd left Lauren all alone at this giant university, where she'd been feeling more homesick and lost by the day. No wonder Lauren was still rushing.

Just as her self-loathing reached its peak for the moment, Lauren raised her eyes, and they connected with Arielle's, so clearly and strongly that it couldn't have been a mistake. Immediately, tears pricked at the borders of Arielle's eyes, and she blinked hard to will them away. She gave Lauren a sad smile, mouthed 'hi.' Lauren's eyes widened, and her cheeks pushed up. She mouthed 'hi,' back. Arielle felt electric with hope. Maybe Lauren didn't hate her. Maybe Arielle would be able to make it up to her. Maybe, even though this week had felt like one horribly wrong turn after another, they could be fixed.

Lauren smiled a bit wider and mouthed, "Good luck." God, that dimple was enough to make Arielle melt into a puddle right there. "You too," Arielle mouthed back.

Then, the head Rho Gam approached the windowed door, waving madly at all the girls. Arielle knew the music was loud, but nothing could have prepared her for the way it boomed through the room, seeming to spin every molecule faster, infusing even more nervous energy into every girl standing there. She flung the door open and squealed. "Are you girls all ready for the best day of your lives?"

Arielle smirked and shook her head. That was definitely overkill, but she'd play along. She wasn't too much of a snob to admit she was excited, too. Every single sorority girl in the room was chanting the same thing about sisterhood and Greek women at Northern being the best of all the rest, which actually didn't make much sense, but Arielle still smiled. She never thought she'd feel like she belonged to anything ever again—she thought she'd left that all behind her when she left youth group back home. This was totally different, but somehow the same.

The Broken Hearts Society of Suite 17C

Then a hard shoulder slammed into hers, and sharp pain shot down her arm. "Holy Shit!" Arielle cried, immediately grateful that her yelling basically had the force of a whisper in all this chaos. She spun around, clutching her shoulder, and stared into the one face that could undo her more than Lauren.

Rachel looked good—her eyes were bright and her cheeks were flushed. Her hair was longer, almost to her waist, and the ridiculous amounts of glitter on her face and in her hair, plus every piece of sorority bling she wore, actually made her look absolutely freaking radiant.

"Ari?" She stepped back, eyes wide, and scanned her head to toe. "Holy shit. What are you doing here?"

Unlike the unexpected Lauren sighting, Arielle's first reaction was to frown. "What do you mean?" Arielle held up her bid card. "I'm a new member."

Rachel blinked like Arielle had just told her she was about to move to Mars and open up an artisan soap shop. A mixture of surprise and pity. "Oh, Alpha Chi. That's perfect for a girl like you."

"What the hell is that supposed to—" Arielle only got a few words out before Rachel grabbed her and smooshed her into a tight hug. Equal parts perfume and stale alcohol bloomed up around her face. Mixed with the bitchiness of Rachel's last comment, Arielle's skin crawled. She stiffened, hoping Rachel would drop her and she'd get away from her without making a scene. But then Rachel's breath blew hot on her ear. "I miss you. Maybe we could—"

Arielle wrenched herself away, anger churning through her. "No, we couldn't. Whatever it is about a 'girl like me' that makes you think I would go for that, you're wrong."

Rachel backed away from her, flicking her hands out when they broke contact, like she was trying to shake dirt off her skin. All of a sudden, the shiny gloss on her lips didn't make her look beautiful—it made her look poisonous. "Whatever," Rachel hissed. "Enjoy yourself in your little geek club."

Pride for Alpha Chi swelled through Arielle. Rachel liked to keep things shiny on the outside and real on the inside. Arielle was only interested in the real. Just real, honest girls, who had each others' backs, no matter what. Girls that didn't care if you fit in, because maybe they didn't fit in themselves. That was where Arielle belonged.

So why had she tried to make Lauren fit in to some lesbian girlfriend box that Arielle had constructed for her based on her one and only relationship with bitchy Rachel, who obviously sucked?

"Welcome to Indiana Northern bid day, PNMs and the sisterhoods who love you!" A particularly chipper Rho Gam crowed into the microphone. Arielle winced at the feedback from the speakers and the Rho Gam giggled. "Sorry. Anyway, the girls knew when they picked me to emcee this shindig that I don't like to waste any time, so

The Broken Hearts Society of Suite 17C

let's get this party started!" The girl was obviously very comfortable on the stage, grinning as she strode across it with sweeping arm gestures and perfectly timed bounces in her steps.

"PNMs, you are no longer POTENTIAL new members...soon you'll be standing with the sisterhood that will carry you through your entire life, from this day on. These are the most important relationships of your life. Maybe even more important than your future husband!" Every girl in the room cracked up, except for Arielle, who winced. The heteronormativity of the Greek life on this campus was something she was definitely going to work to change. Well, maybe. If she found the extra energy.

Arielle smirked again at the thought. Lauren would have called her out on her proto-activist bullshit right away, except she would smile like Arielle was the most adorable girl for getting annoyed by it in the first place. Arielle's heart twisted.

"We're going to announce for each sorority in order of the Greek alphabet, which you all should have memorized by now," the Rho Gam said in her sing-songy voice. So first up is Alpha Chi!"

The butterflies in Ari's stomach started a rager. So much insanity in one day—her bid, Lauren, Rachel, having to get up on stage in front of everyone—meant that her dearest wish right now involved sweatpants and a cup of chamomile tea. Okay, maybe her second-dearest.

Arielle fought the butterflies to scan the crowd one more time, focusing on the back left corner where she'd seen Lauren before. Nothing. She sighed and turned her attention to the positive. Sisterhood, starting in about thirty seconds.

Her new sisters swarmed the stage, looking like very good sports in black tees and very non-fancy jeans, holding up their posterboards and smiling through their chants. Arielle grinned and danced a little on the spot. Yeah, it was cheesy, but they were all being cheesy together. And something felt so good about being carefree, if only for a few moments.

The chant involved stomping of some kind, sung to the tune of "Brown-Eyed Girl," and most of the words were unintelligible except for the periodic "Alpha Chi."

Then, "Now it's time to say goodbye to all those other houses—Don't Cry!—Theta Pi, Delta Tri, sorry, we chose Alpha Chi!"

The Rho Gam screamed, "Come on up, new Alpha Chis!" Arielle grinned even harder. Thank God she was so close to the stage, or she might have been lost in the screaming and jumping that filled the room. She shouldered her way past a couple clusters of girls, tripped onto the steps, and right away was folded into one, two, three hugs. It was the best kind of delirious, a breathless, exhausted, crushing, overwhelming kind of happiness of knowing that fifty other girls on campus now considered her one of their best friends—that they'd picked Arielle

The Broken Hearts Society of Suite 17C

because of exactly who she was, openly and without question.

She quickly picked up on the cheer and joined in. One of the huggers, Cat—Arielle recognized her from the second house visit where they'd geeked out over Harry Potter—let her go a little quickly so that she could go hug another new member. Arielle stumbled against another new member and made her apologies, cracking up. She clutched on to the poor girl's arms to help her stand back up, and as she did, the chant came to an end again. Arielle yelled "Alpha Chi!" right as she raised her eyes directly into Lauren's.

Seriously, this bid day was going to give her a heart attack. Lauren's eyebrows knitted together, pulling deep lines through her perfect skin. "Oh, Ari," she said, almost moaned, her voice loud enough to hear over the yelling masses of girls. Lauren pulled her hands back. For the briefest second, Arielle's palms brushed Lauren's, and everything around them stopped. Then, another soft, sad smile pulled Lauren's lips up, and all Arielle wanted in that moment was to kiss them. "I should have guessed you'd get this bid. Of course you did. Alpha Chi is perfect for you."

"Well obviously it's perfect for you too!" Arielle realized their voices were raised, just to be heard over the chanting, but she didn't care. She didn't want to lose Lauren, not in this moment, and especially not all over again. Didn't want to lose the chance to do everything she could to make things right.

Lauren started to step back again, and Arielle lunged to grab her hands. "Don't go. Please."

"I've already made up my mind!" Lauren yelled, her eyes growing watery.

"So have I! I want you to be happy!"

"Arielle, you know I can't be happy if we're in this house together," Lauren replied, pulling her hands away and heading toward the chapter president, who hugged her tight around the neck. Arielle watched Lauren's face crumple as she pulled away and handed the president her bid card, then ran off the stage.

Arielle was frozen in place and confused beyond belief. Given how well she got along with Lauren, she really should have prepared herself for the possibility that Lauren would get a bid from Alpha Chi too—especially since, apparently, Lauren wasn't telling anyone she was dating any girl, let alone Arielle. But had Lauren just left Alpha Chi because of her? Or for her?

The noise roared on around her, and Arielle vaguely registered the president, Sydney, listing the names of the new members over the microphone, as if her head were an inch underwater. "Ari, you okay?" Cat was back by her side, wrapping an arm around her shoulders and squeezing tight."

"I..." Arielle's head snapped to the other side of the stage, catching the swoop of Lauren's hair running down

The Broken Hearts Society of Suite 17C

the stairs and to the exit. "I'll be right back," Arielle managed, trotting and then running the same path through her new family that Lauren had—except she was planning to come back.

Damn those long legs of Lauren's. She was a shadow winding through the halls of the student union, getting further away from Ari every second. Finally, Arielle saw the big glass doors to the outside slide shut just as she rounded a corner, and went barreling through them.

The frigid January air snapped against her skin, instantly reminding her that she was wearing a dress with very thin hose. She glanced up and a small grainy snowflake drifted into her eye, followed by a dozen more dusting against her face. Then she heard a whimper, and turned behind her to the sidewalk that stretched all the way to her dorm.

Lauren sat in the middle of the sidewalk twenty or so yards away, looking forlorn. Well, that was a little dramatic, especially for Lauren. Arielle's feet carried her to Lauren automatically—she couldn't stay away if she tried. About halfway there, she realized that Lauren was clutching her ankle with one hand, hidden beneath her calf.

"Jesus! What happened?" Arielle started to jog toward her, and Lauren held out a palm. "Stop, it's slipper—"

Before she could finish the word, Arielle's flats slicked against the apparently unsalted path and sent her butt sliding the remaining couple of feet so that she was in arm's reach of Lauren.

"Oh my God, are you okay? Ari, what the hell are you doing out here?" Lauren shakily tried to stand, then apparently decided against it.

"I don't have this curvy ass for no reason," Arielle joked, rubbing her butt anyway. Her tailbone felt fine, thank God, but there would be a big bruise on her behind tomorrow. "I'm gonna help you up, but first you have to get out of those ridiculous shoes."

"Shut up. They're gorgeous, and I didn't plan on making a mid-bid sprint."

Arielle shook her head and tried to keep from smiling too much as she carefully undid the straps of Lauren's shoes and eased her feet out of them. God, even touching the skin of her feet was sending jolts of electricity through her fingertips. The way Lauren was looking at her made Arielle think that maybe, just maybe, Lauren was thinking the same thing.

"Think you can stand?" Arielle said, scanning the courtyard for someone bigger than her to help this crazy, impulsive girl she loved so much limp back into the building.

"Give me a couple minutes," Lauren said, biting her bottom lip.

Arielle forced her breathing to stay even. "I'm sorry," she finally said.

The Broken Hearts Society of Suite 17C

"For what?" Lauren asked. "Doing exactly what I wanted you to do and signing up for sorority recruitment?"

"Well yeah, and—"

"And finding what is obviously the perfect house for you, and finally figuring out what on this campus would make you feel like you belonged somewhere?"

Lauren was right. Damn her, how did she know all that just from a few shared looks in an overcrowded room?

"I'm sorry you felt like you had to give up your bid, though." Even as she said it, she knew how stupid that sounded. The house was relatively small. Would she be able to put up with three and a half years of seeing Lauren across a dining room every day, sitting in chapter meetings every week, taking different girls—or even guys—to formals and socials? No way. It had to be Lauren or Arielle joining Alpha Chi. Not both, or Arielle's heart would be smashed to pieces all over again.

Lauren looked at her steadily, as if she knew everything Arielle was just thinking. Then, she shook her head. "I didn't quit. I made a choice, between something definite and something I hoped for. The thing that was definite would have been good, in a lot of ways, but the thing I hoped for would be so much better."

Arielle's cheeks turned red and she wanted to smile and throw up at the same time. "I mean...I know the sure thing is Alpha Chi, but..." her fingers played at the straps of Lauren's shoes, and she was barely aware of her ass getting wetter and colder by the second as she sat there on the icy sidewalk. She didn't really care. She would have waited forever for Lauren to say the words she wanted to hear.

Then Lauren's fingers brushed hers, picking them up gently, like she was testing something. Arielle looked up at her, reminding herself to breathe. "I'm sorry. Okay? I was stupid."

Arielle scoffed. "No, *I'm* the one who—"

"Sorry, your Mack-truck approach to conversations is not going to fly this time," Lauren said, her face stern but teasing. "I was being a freak about the rules. And, yeah, I was scared. I knew what Rachel did to you, and I knew how that killed you. And I felt bad, but at the same time…I don't know. I thought all the sororities were maybe like that, and I didn't want to ruin my chances before I found out how I really felt."

"About me?" Arielle dared to ask.

"No, stupid. About being in a sorority. Whether it was really for me."

"And now that doesn't even matter, because you gave up your bid."

"Yeah, I gave it up because I didn't think I could stand to look at you every single day without losing my mind."

"Because you hate me," Arielle said, pulling her hand back and sighing. She shakily got to her feet, ready to get

The Broken Hearts Society of Suite 17C

Lauren inside no matter what it took so that she could say her goodbyes.

"Oh my God, you're a steamroller and a numbskull, apparently. Because I love you, you idiot. I should be pissed that you left me without letting me explain myself better, and I should make you apologize."

"I know, I have a lot of work to do, with trusting you better. I'm trying. I mean, I promise to try harder. It just felt so much like what happened before that I couldn't even see clearly. But now I do, I think, and I..."

"Ari. Seriously. Yes, you acted crazy. But I get it. I promise. And there's one thing I know for sure now—there's no way I could join Alpha Chi, because seeing you every single day and not being able to be with you could turn even the most perfect place into hell."

Arielle hadn't even realized the tears were coming until she felt one roll down her cheek and grow frigid against her chin. She bent at the knees and thrust her arms underneath Lauren's, hauling her up with a seriously mighty core effort, relishing the feel of Lauren's body against hers as she gained her footing on her good leg and what seemed like a little pressure on the foot she'd hurt.

Then she looked up at Lauren and saw tears rolling down her cheeks, too. Arielle's mouth opened to speak, but now it was Lauren steamrolling her. "I blew it, didn't I? I mean, you hate me now, right? God, I'm such a bitch, I knew what happened to you at the beginning of the year and I—"

It was all Arielle could do to squeeze Lauren tight, lift her three inches to the right to stand on the non-slippery grass, and lay a big, shivering kiss on those gorgeous lips. Lauren whimpered and pushed her fingers up through Arielle's hair, melting into the kiss and making the fact that it was about fifteen degrees outside completely irrelevant. They were two perfectly fitted puzzle pieces who had found their way back together again.

And, given that the sidewalk Lauren had slipped on was directly outside the long windowed wall of the room where bid day was being held, they were now as public with their display of affection as any two girls at Indiana Northern could possibly be. Finally, Lauren pulled back, her eyes still closed. But for some reason, Arielle glanced to the right, and saw it all. Staring at them, having just come off the stage from their bid announcement, was every single sister of Alpha Chi. And they all had humungous smiles on their faces.

When they started to cheer, Arielle almost burst into big fat sobs.

"God, this sucks," Lauren said, looking up and blinking against the fat flakes that fell and dotted her bangs, her eyelashes, her shirt over the jut of her breasts.

Oh, shit. This was probably exactly what Lauren *hadn't* wanted. What if she wanted to rush again, or claim another bid, or just keep the whole fact that she liked girls quiet for a little while longer? "I'm so sorry, I didn't even realize we were right next to—"

The Broken Hearts Society of Suite 17C

Lauren lifted an index finger to Arielle's lips, and the feel of it made Arielle weak in the knees, stopping her words on her tongue.

"I was just going to say, this snow is not as romantic as the rain was."

Arielle shook her head and grinned. "I guess you're allowed to keep up this new interrupting thing if you're going to say things like that."

Who gave a damn about the cold and the wet and the cheering new sorority girls? They had time for at least one more kiss. And once they got inside, they'd have all the time in the world.

Chapter 21

Amy

Five weeks into Spring semester classes, and it was the first day in months that the temperature went above freezing. That morning on the way to class—Sex and Sexuality in American Cinema—she'd heard a bird singing, and felt something small, but clear, shifting inside her. Now she stood in front of the list she'd made with Arielle the day her heart had been broken again, despite her best efforts. It was a self-discovery to-do list, which, when it was finished, was basically a rundown of everything Amy had ever avoided doing because it had scared the snot out of her.

She'd been waiting for that click, that small shift in thinking, to really look at the list, to assess her progress. After an initial few days of panic over the list itself, she'd started asking Rion and Ari to cross things off it when she'd well and truly done them. "Career prospects," "Church," and "Dad" had been the big ones, the ones she'd been most afraid of, if only because she realized that each of those issues had bunch of subheadings, each one as scary as the last.

It turned out that the little things had subheadings, too. That was harder, because it took her by surprise. "Ice skating" had seemed easy enough until she had to do it alone. She'd started crying before she even fell for the first time. She later realized it was because she'd never fallen from ice skates before, let alone fallen doing anything where there wasn't someone right beside her to help her up again. When she finally did fall, then managed to stand up again all on her own, she felt like her heart would burst out of her chest. That little achievement pushed her to do things like go out for ice cream alone, volunteer for an organization she knew nothing about, doing something she had no experience in. Wearing an outfit she loved yet worried made her stand out too much, to dinner with the Society. She read a book full of swear words that Rion had given her, *Silver Linings Playbook*, and realized she really didn't notice them after awhile because the characters tugged at her heart harder than the profanity punched her in the gut.

For someone who grew up thinking that profanity was one of the worst sins someone could commit, this was a big deal.

The urban planning class she'd signed up for spring semester as an alternative to another history class, in an attempt to avoid the horribly depressing study of wars and genocide, turned out to be the best decision she'd ever made. The truth she thought she'd known her whole life—how poor people were poor and unhealthy because they were lazy and stupid—was challenged from the first class, which focused on social justice. It turned out that if a neighborhood of poor people included things like a preschool and a decent supermarket, their health, and job acquisition and retention, improved dramatically.

The night after that first class, she'd cried at the realization that every child in the country didn't have a safe home, a place to learn colors and letters and sing songs, and fresh fruit and vegetables. The next morning, she'd sat in her advisor's office and mapped out an entire strategy for majoring in urban planning with a focus on nonprofit organizations. The week after that, her professor had gotten her an internship with the Fair Housing Center of Northern Indiana. It had taken her one day of interning at the Fair Housing Center to know that she was head-over-heels in love with the work they did there. Just like it had only taken her one day of volunteering at the university's day care center to know that not only did she not want to be a preschool teacher, but she didn't want to have children of her own for a very long time.

The Broken Hearts Society of Suite 17C

The day after that, Amy called Dad. Arielle had wanted to hold her hand, coach her through, but Amy knew that that conversation would basically be Arielle talking to her dad, and she wanted to be herself. More than that, she wanted her dad to well and truly *know* she was herself. So when she told Dad that she loved him very much, but that she wasn't sorry for freaking out at Mom about Christmas, and that by the way, her major had changed and she no longer aspired to be a pastor's wife and move back home, she was terrified, but she was one hundred percent sure about every word. Including telling him that she'd switched churches.

Amy knew darn well that "Biblical interpretation" was a dirty phrase in her hometown Southern Baptist church, which insisted on reading the Bible literally, and when she told Dad that she was participating in a Bible study class with that same title at the local Episcopal church, she could practically hear the steam shooting from his ears. But she used a calm voice, and reminded him how much she loved him, and heard him breathing deeply instead of yelling.

When Dad told her he expected her home to visit for Easter, she told him she would let him know whether she'd be there, or whether she'd stay on campus. Best of all, she did all of it with a steady, calm voice, staring at the list and promising herself that she'd be able to cross "Dad" off the "big stuff" column very, very soon.

"Music" was the only thing that was left. That conversation with Matt stuck with her—the one where he asked her what kind of music she liked, and she couldn't name anything specific other than "nothing with curse words." Hundreds of songs and dozens of playlists later, many of them built with Rion's help as she mixed her way through her second audio engineering class, and Amy finally had favorites. She could name artists she knew would make her want to dance, and she had an entire playlist for when she wanted to call forth the deepest aching of her heart and sit with it, really feel it. She had discovered artists whose chord progressions and lyrics carried her away to a happy place in a way she never knew music could. Entire genres made her feel swoony and hopeful and in love with nothing in particular, besides the moment she was listening to it.

So, today, as she listened to a smooth male voice crooning old tunes, she grinned at her list and spun around. No matter what happened, or who she had in her life, Amy knew she would be just fine.

Amy got the pizza for that night's society meeting—she secretly loved when it was her turn to do it. She grinned as she ordered an individual pizza for each of the girls with their favorite toppings, so she didn't have to listen to Arielle's complaints about having to pick off the

The Broken Hearts Society of Suite 17C

pepperoni, or Rion comparing the sliced onions to worms again. She threw in breadsticks with extra sauce and a cookie 'pizza' too. And then totally went crazy with a 2-liter of Diet Coke.

The Society meeting was both better and worse than Amy had anticipated. For the past three meetings, at Amy's request, she hadn't talked about relationships, she'd just talked about herself. Which was about relationships, ultimately, she supposed. But Arielle had been happy to include Amy and her dedication to the list in the minutes as "self love," and Rion had been happy because she had something to roll her eyes at and an excuse to swear in Amy's presence, under the excuse of "exposing her to the wider world."

Arielle was over-the-moon happy, even if she was exhausted. She and Lauren were back together, and even though her new sorority was taking up a whole lot of time, she was oddly—even sometimes freakily—chipper. Maybe the lack of sleep would get to her eventually, but for now, she didn't have much to contribute to Society meetings despite how she was getting ready to present something to the PHA on heteronormative Greek culture on campus. Amy even sort of understood what that meant, which she couldn't have said six months ago.

Rion, in contrast, had moved from being sullen and belligerent the previous week to staring blankly into space. When Arielle was done bouncing and grinning and giving her update in between, both girls stared at Amy. "I have something but I want to go last," she said, trying to hold back a smile when she looked at Rion. "Do you have anything?"

Rion sighed. "If being fucking miserable and tortured to hell and back and fucking hating myself for it every time I see him at work, which is EVERY FUCKING TIME, then yes, I have something."

Arielle put on her somber face, so well that Amy almost forgot she'd been joyful a few minutes earlier. "What are you going to do, Ri?"

"Die of sorrow and self-hatred? Or I don't know, maybe become a motherfucking drama queen full time, since I can't focus on anything anyway?"

"Maybe, I don't know, try to talk to him again?" Arielle said, dabbing her mouth with a napkin. "I know, it's crazy."

Rion shot dagger eyes at Arielle, and Arielle's mouth twisted into a half-frown. Ari gave a half-hearted "hmph" before she sat back on her heels, shoved another piece of pizza in her mouth, and gazed broodingly at Rion. Amy knew that she was coming up with some strategy to drag Rion out of her self-professed misery, which was getting more intense and sweary by the day. After Ari finished chewing, she turned her attention to Amy.

"Okay, sweet Amy," Arielle said. She swept her hand, still clutching her half-eaten piece of vegetarian pizza, over the spread. "What did we do to deserve all this?"

"Nothing."

The Broken Hearts Society of Suite 17C

Rion glared again.

"I mean, not what did you guys do. It's something *I* did." She whipped the folded piece of notebook paper with all the stuff crossed off and unfolded it, holding it out in two hands for both girls to see, like a royal proclamation.

"Jesus fucking Christ," Rion whispered, apparently distracted for a moment. "You crossed everything off? I thought that would take you, like, the semester, at least."

"Thank you for your confidence," Amy said with a wry smile. "And thank you for helping me deal with the 'foul language' item in the 'big stuff' category so thoroughly and frequently."

"Have to be fucking good at something," Rion muttered, twisting a blond-streaked lock of hair around her fingers, which just called attention to her badly chipped midnight-blue polish.

"Whoa, Ames. Are you sure? You really are okay with all this stuff?" Arielle grabbed at the list, scanning it.

Amy pulled out a folder, organized by tab, and shoved it toward Arielle, who leafed through it with a grin. The leaflets for her new church home, class plan for the next three semesters, selfie on ice skates, and smudged receipt from the cafe where she now ate alone with ease provided plenty of evidence. "Major, check. Church, check. Ice skating, eating alone, illicit literature, Sexy movies...damn, Amy. You really have tackled it. What about Dad?"

Both Arielle and Rion listened to her update them on her conversation with her father, their jaws dropping a little bit with each sentence.

"Well, I think our little small town girl is all grown up," Arielle said, wiping a fake tear.

Rion pitched half a breadstick at her and Arielle squealed. "Shut the fuck up, you're not her fucking mother. She's not a goddamn baby."

"I appreciate your sweary sentiment, Rion, but it's okay. I think it's sweet." Amy air-kissed Arielle.

"So…have you told him?"

Amy blew out a shuddering breath. "I don't know what I would tell him, even if I could. Or how, or why."

"What do you mean?" Ari asked.

"Rion is still policing his phone number and I haven't been brave enough to steal her phone to get it."

Rion grinned, doing a half-bow.

"And I haven't thought about stalking him as an option. Not really." Amy stared at the ground as she said it. She didn't want to seem pathetic. She wasn't pathetic anymore. She could take care of herself, and if Rion didn't give her Matt's number, she would figure out how to get back in touch with him. If she could talk to Dad, if she could change her life plans, if she could hear a swear-word filled sentence as sweet, she could swallow her pride and find Matt.

If she decided that was a good idea. If she could be brave enough to tell him that she still wanted him, even

The Broken Hearts Society of Suite 17C

though it was highly likely that he didn't want her anymore.

"Do you want to tell him? I'm not trying to push you into anything." Arielle, as always, was patient, listening.

"I don't even know anymore."

Arielle's face grew concerned, but Rion scoffed. "What?" Amy protested.

"Of course you want to. You're even more in love with him than you were before, which I wasn't actually sure was possible, by the way."

"I don't know what you're talking about. I mean, are you being serious?" It was a valid question, considering the deep sticky pit of self-loathing Rion had obviously fallen into headlong.

"I mean, she's right. She hasn't talked to him," Arielle said, reaching out to rub Amy's back. "She has no way to know what he's thinking."

"And obviously you haven't talked to her," Rion said. "I guess there is some benefit to my wallowing…I listen to her talk about the damn list every damn day."

"Of course. That's what I've been doing. And not worrying about Matt," Amy nodded, trying to reassure herself.

Rion snorted. "Not worrying about him, no. But you went to the church he told you about when you did that volunteer thingy. I know because you told me when you were searching for it, and when you said his name your voice went all moony. That one time we ordered Thai, you got the one thing you'd had when you went home with Matt for Christmas. You listen to the bands he recommended, and you read all the books he left here. Consciously or not, it's pretty much like he never left."

Amy glanced down so she wouldn't have to look at Rion and noticed she was wearing a shirt that she'd picked up at one of those movie theater churches Matt had taken her to, featuring a bust of Jesus and text reading "I had followers before Twitter." She'd felt a pang of memory when she'd put it on, but her life had been so insane for the past six weeks that she hadn't had time to do laundry. And this shirt was comfortable. And, okay, it made her think of Matt. Even the pain of missing him was better than forgetting about him altogether.

She felt Rion and Arielle both staring at her. "Okay," Amy sighed, looking at them. "You're right."

"So you might as well make it official." Rion lobbed her phone across the pizza boxes where Amy caught it. She swiped the screen on with shaking fingers.

"I don't even know what to say to him," she said. "I mean, what if he doesn't even want to talk to me? What if he changed his mind?" Her next thought made her gasp and clap a hand over her mouth. "What if he's with another girl?"

"Okay, now you're *really* being ridiculous," Arielle said, sitting up straight and staring down her nose at Amy. "Obviously you don't trust us at all."

"What do you…?"

The Broken Hearts Society of Suite 17C

"If your heart gets broken, it's our fault. Rion and I have eyes all over this campus. Even though there are twenty thousand kids here, word gets around fast. Especially since most of us are from Podunk Indiana. Someone would have told someone who would have told Lauren or me or Rion if they had seen Matt with anyone but you, Amy. Everyone knows there's something between you two."

"If I ever left my room," Rion mumbled.

"You go to class," Arielle said gently.

"Sometimes," Rion smiled.

"He's not with another girl, and considering how hard he loved—*loves*—you, there was no way that was going to change any time soon."

That word—love—opened a floodgate inside Amy. All the hopes and fears she'd been shoring up for the past six weeks came bursting through the tiny crack in the fortifications around her heart, and she gasped with the beginning of a sob. The tears came trickling down her cheeks, and she clapped a hand over her mouth. Her head shook back and forth. She didn't know if she wanted to believe that, or not.

"Oh, for fuck's sake," Rion said, flicking her bangs out of her eyes for the millionth time as she reached for another slice of cookie pizza, "You have nothing to worry about. You shouldn't waste your energy crying until he actually turns you down."

"Rion…" Arielle's tone was all warning.

"I mean, even though Arielle is dishing out some seriously convincing bullshit right now, and I mean straight from her curvy little ass, I'm sure she's right. Gingerbread man was seriously devoted to you. No way that's changed." Something shifted in her tone at the end of her words, and she went back to sad staring into space again.

Amy sniffled and forced herself to sit up straight, commanding her tears to stop. But her hands shook even harder. Her emotions swung back and forth to being sure Matt was seriously done with her to believing her roommates—if he'd felt for her what she felt for him, there had to be something left there. Right?

Amy's stomach twisted and doubled over on itself as she scrolled down the contacts. Nothing there under 'Englin,' and nothing there for 'Matt.' Then a particularly long entry flashed down the screen—'Flaming Cheeto Pubes.'

Amy turned to screen to Rion. "Do I have to ask?"

Rion smirked. "Obviously not."

Amy pulled up the number, then reached for her phone. The heel of her hand must have brushed the screen of Rion's fancy new smartphone when she turned, though, because all of a sudden she heard a dial tone—the weird beeping one that always preceded a video call.

And sweet, trusting Matt, damn him, picked it up, even though he didn't know—couldn't know—whose number it was.

The Broken Hearts Society of Suite 17C

But then he was there, and seeing his face—the familiar curve of his freckled cheekbone, hair that had begun to flop over his eyebrows again—was such a shock and a relief at the same time that tears started to roll down Amy's cheeks all over again. Who cared if they were rational or not? Amy had spent the past six weeks learning that the most joyful things in life lacked rhyme or reason.

"Hey, Rion, what's up?" He wasn't looking at the phone, but obviously he knew it was her. Amy's eyes went wide and she flung an arm out, staring at Rion.

"I told him I had his number. Just in case."

"Just in case WHAT?" Amy managed.

"I don't know. In case you needed him. Or he needed you. Or something."

Apparently, even Rion, the greatest romance buzzkill of all time, had been assuming Amy and Matt's separation would be temporary. Amy must have been the blindest person on the planet to not have seen it herself.

"Rion?" This time, those deep brown-green eyes of Matt's, their color clear even through the phone connection, met hers.

"Amy? AMY. Oh geez. Are you okay? What's going on?"

Even though she still felt a trembling underneath every inch of her skin, Amy smiled, gave a short laugh, swiped a tear from her eye. "I'm so sorry, I didn't mean to call you."

"But are you okay? Why are you crying? And why are you calling me from Rion's phone?"

"I just…I mean…It was…I was just going to text you."

A brief flash of confusion crossed Matt's eyes, but then she saw him get it. She was going to text him. After six weeks.

"Would that work better for you? I mean, do you just want to go ahead and text me?"

"I…maybe?"

Matt nodded and the screen immediately went blank.

Amy quickly added his number back into her phone, and then texted, **Hi.** Her tears had already started up again, and she held her breath when the little dots indicating that Matt was typing showed up on her screen. They stayed there for a long time, several seconds, and he must have been going through his whole "Are you okay?" panic. She'd wait.

But then when his text came back, all it said was **Hi.**

Then, a few seconds later, **It's nice to see your name on my phone again.**

She could barely contain her grin.

I just wanted to text you without seeing 'Cheeto Pubes' at the top of the screen.

Amy couldn't believe she'd just texted the word 'pubes' to a guy she was trying to win back. She bit her lip.

Amy Bauer, did you just type a semi-almost-dirty word?

The Broken Hearts Society of Suite 17C

Amy laughed out loud, swiping the lingering tears away with the back of her hand.

"What? What did he say?" Arielle moved behind her, staring at the phone from over her shoulder. Rion sighed, like it was some big burden, but quickly did the same thing.

Amy: **Texting about body hair in close proximity to sexual organs is not dirty. It's anatomy.**

Matt: **Did you just type 'sexual?' And—oh my God—ANATOMY?**

Rion snorted. "This guy. I knew there was a reason I liked him enough to come up with all those nicknames."

Arielle frowned. "What are you going to say to him now? You have to have a real conversation eventually."

"Yeah, and right after 'pubes' is a perfect place to start it," Rion said, feigning a serious face.

Are you okay? Matt texted again.

Amy: **You already asked me that. I'm fine.**

Matt: **You're not saying much.**

Amy: **I don't know what to say.**

Matt: **It was probably stupid to think we could just pick up where we left off.**

That wasn't stupid. Not at all. It was actually probably the most perfect thing he could have possibly said. More perfect than she had dared to hope for.

This was her chance to start over with Matt. The right way.

Now Amy's hands were noticeably shaking, so she clutched her phone until her knuckles practically glowed white. She had to make sure.

Amy: **Are you saying *you* think that's stupid?**

Amy: **I mean...do you hate me?**

Matt: **Amy Bauer, I don't know what planet you went to for the last six weeks, but there is no way in heaven or on earth I could ever hate you.**

Amy bit her lip and smiled a sad smile. It was so wonderful that he didn't hate her. That didn't change what she'd been hoping, deep down, he'd say—that he still loved her.

Matt: **Wait, you don't *want* me to hate you, do you?**

Amy blew out a long breath. **No. But how much do you not hate me?**

Matt: **It's really hard to put in a text. Give me a few seconds.**

And then the bubble with the dots appeared at the bottom of the screen again, and stayed there for a long time. Too long. Was he composing a novel, or was he just having trouble figuring out what to say next? Amy swore she would have a heart attack waiting, and from the way Rion held her breath and Arielle squeezed her hand, it seemed like her roommates were about to, too.

And then she jumped about five feet off the ground when she heard three knocks on the door.

The Broken Hearts Society of Suite 17C

"Oh my God, that's Lauren," Arielle squeaked, shooting to her feet and practically sprinting to the door. She shot a look over her shoulder and said, "I'm so sorry. I told her we'd be in here for an hour, and even though we haven't been meeting for that long lately, I…"

But when the door swung open, it wasn't Lauren. Looking rumpled, and tired, with one shoe untied and a t-shirt that said "Cool Story, Bro" next to a picture of the Bible, was the most beautiful face that Amy could imagine seeing.

And she was so stunned all she could do was gape at him.

"Oh, shit," Rion murmured, getting to her feet and leaving Amy's side instantly cold. It was amazing how unanchored she felt without those two at her sides. Rion grabbed her coat and her bag from the floor where she had dropped them just after her last class yesterday, which was the last time she'd left the suite, knelt down, plucked her phone from Amy's lap, smacked a kiss on the top of Amy's head, and stood up and was out the door in a flash.

Arielle stood there looking at Matt, then Amy, over and over again, some complicated strategizing obviously going on in her head, making sense of all this and what she was about to do, which probably she didn't even have a handle on yet. Then, like someone flipped on her talking capability, the words tumbled out. "I have a thing. Promised Lauren. Important. Hungry. I…I'll be back." Then she halfheartedly waved her phone at Amy, telling her in the haphazard sign language they'd established in the few short months of the Society that she could text and call if she needed to.

Then the heavy metal door shut all over again, and Amy was standing on shaky legs, not remembering the decision to get off the floor in the first place. Matt's face was open and calm all at once, but he stayed quiet, looking at her. Endlessly patient for her, like always.

Finally, Matt whispered, "I said it was hard to say in text. I guess it's harder to say face to face." He laughed, but the look on his face was pure anguish.

"Why?" Amy choked out.

"Because as much as I hate to admit it, that day you left? I just felt really, really bad. I mean, just…gutted. I know we were never together," he rushed out when Amy opened her mouth to respond, "but that almost made it worse. I don't know. It was like nothing I'd ever felt before, and I guess I just missed you so much that seeing you kind of smacked me in the face. It's like when the sun finally comes out after weeks of cloudy days. You didn't know how much you would miss it, how important it is to just, like, getting through the day, until it comes back."

"I still don't…"

Matt sighed, dragging his fingers back through his hair. "The amount I don't hate you is infinite. I don't know how else to say it. I've tried to be mad at you, I've tried to hate you. I've tried to resent you and demonize you. I've tried to forget you. And all those things are just, like, precursors to hate. And I couldn't even touch them. I'm hopeless."

"I don't hate you, either. I never did. Well, maybe that one minute that you made me feel like the least desirable…"

Matt's ears had already begun to blaze red. "Yeah, I know. I know. I'm still really sorry about that."

"Don't. Don't be. I'm glad you did it. Sort of. That was the moment where I decided that doing whatever I wanted would probably only work if I knew what I wanted. If I knew me."

"Okay."

She commanded her shaking fingers to still. No use. She bent down and picked up the list anyway, and limply handed it to him.

"What is this?" Matt asked, his mouth twitching up at the corners.

"I know most people have stuff figured out when they get to college, but I didn't." Amy took a deep breath. "I was used to other people figuring out my stuff for me, and leaning on them, depending on them. I ditched all that from back home, yeah, but when I got here, I met you. And you are wonderful," she said. "But you just became my new…leader, I guess. We got along so well that I think, after a little while, I was sort of depending on you to tell me who I am. To tell me what to like, what to be interested in, how to relate to my faith. And I had to step back from that. For me, and for you, and…for us." She said the last words in a whisper, but it was okay. He was hanging on her every word.

Matt looked down at the list again. "They're all crossed off. Does that mean you have everything figured out?"

Amy laughed. "I think I figured out the stuff that was bothering me the most. And I'm hoping that'll help me figure everything else out."

Matt's eyebrow arched up in a silent question.

"I don't want to be a preschool teacher. I don't want to be any kind of teacher. I want to help kids, but I want to be an urban planner and help underprivileged kids, and homeless ones. I'm good at strategy and logistics, and a classroom full of kids exhausts me."

"Makes sense."

"I don't like going to movie theater church with guitars. I don't feel spiritual there, I just feel like I'm in a movie theater."

Matt nodded.

"I like Pearl Jam and the Spice Girls and Nickelback."

Matt's mouth quirked up at the edge. "Well, one out of three of those is okay."

"I like watching political thrillers and romantic comedies and, yes, cheesy reality shows."

"Like *Naked and Afraid*?"

"Well, um…no, more like *The Bachelor*."

Matt rolled his eyes and chuckled. "I guess that's okay."

The Broken Hearts Society of Suite 17C

Amy stifled a laugh. "Will you shut up? I don't care if you think it's okay. I don't care what anyone thinks, not anymore. I like what I like and I care about what *I* care about and I love what I love. Nobody tells me what's allowed and what's not."

"I just noticed one thing missing from the list," Matt said, running his finger down the dog-eared edge.

"No. There's nothing missing. I thought of everything."

Another raised eyebrow.

"Are you sure?"

"Yes, Matt. What in the world is missing?"

Matt pressed his lips together and handed the paper back to her. She was afraid to take it, for fear that he'd leave once he'd given it back. "Me. I'm missing."

Relief flooded Amy, and her eyes watered with relieved tears. She took a deep breath and forced herself to look in Matt's eyes. No matter what else happened, she wanted this confession to be clear as day. "You are the one thing I never had to figure out. I always knew, I just needed to see it in the context of everything else. But you, I'm one hundred percent sure about. In fact, even though you still haven't told me how much you don't hate me, I'm still going to say this."

Amy pushed down every emotion swirling into a storm inside her—fear, worry, self-consciousness, and a half-dreading, half-hopeful anticipation. "I'm sorry it took me so long to catch up here. I love you."

Matt's eyes were big, and it was hard to tell whether the emotion behind them was happiness, shock, or maybe—from the glistening that could only have been caused by tears—sadness.

"What? What is it? Did I say something weird?" Amy fought the horrible feeling that he had already made up his mind about her, realized that someone who had his life as together as he did needed a girl who knew she wanted to be with him from the start, not this redheaded mess from Nowhere, Indiana.

Why had she ever let her roommates go? How had she been so confident that his feelings would still be the same?

But at the exact moment that the silence between them and the quiet of his eyes punched her in the gut and forced a sob up through her throat, Matt took two quick steps forward and folded her in his arms, without asking, without any more hesitation. His hand moved up to her head, smoothing over her unruly coarse waves, and he rocked from one foot to the other so slightly that she could have been imagining it. He pulled her head to his shoulder and tucked his face into the bend of her neck and held her there, just like that, for a really long time.

Amy was at once afraid to take a breath and desperate to hear something from him, but above all, happy to just be in his arms again. She couldn't imagine what he wanted to say, and probably neither could he. Standing there, quiet, rocking together, Amy felt the most uncertain she

The Broken Hearts Society of Suite 17C

had felt about anything for weeks, yet there was absolutely no place she would rather be.

That was why she both hated and loved the speeding of her heart when Matt slowly pulled back from her, letting his hands run down the backs of her arms, telling her that he wasn't ready to let her go. Amy hadn't been able to stop her tears, and she supposed it didn't really matter now. They wouldn't change anything. Torturously slowly, Matt lifted his hand to her face and rested it against her jaw, making her close her eyes. The brush of his thumb against her cheekbone made her open them again.

Matt swallowed, hard. "I never left, you know."

"I...what? You're the one who turned me down! After that I figured a lot of things out, but..."

"I mean I never stopped waiting. I did my homework in the dining hall next door, in the computer lab in the basement, sometimes in the lobby downstairs. Just in case you called, I wanted to get to you as soon as I could."

"That's what you did." Amy wanted to laugh and cry at the same time.

"I'm not trying to be cheesy, but I had faith in you, Amy. I knew you were strong enough to get answers to all your own questions."

"And to yours," Amy said, tentatively taking the smallest of steps back toward him. He didn't move away in response. "You asked me if I could promise you tomorrow, and the next day, and the next month. I don't think we can really promise anything, but that's what I want. Tomorrow, and the next day, and the one after that, being yours."

Matt let his hand slide down to grip her waist. When Adam had done that, it had felt possessive, protective. But the soft, solid touch of Matt's palm carried nothing but safety and peace. Amy pressed even closer against him and closed her eyes. Matt's kiss was sweet relief and a spark of desire, so much more meaningful than that insane Christmas night, all rolled into one.

As they stood there, wrapped up together, not intending to move any time soon, Amy finally understood—belonging to a person you loved who really, really loved you back, meant freedom for your heart that wasn't a prison, not even close. It was a safe place to fall, a home to return to no matter where you were.

Finally realizing that made all the times her heart had been so terribly broken more than worth it.

Chapter 22

Rion

Even though she knew there was a security camera, and the possibility of seeing him there was pretty good on any given day, Rion couldn't stop walking back through Crash's alley.

She didn't tell anyone, mostly because her roommates were the Queens of Figuring Things Out and Talking About Feelings. The first thing was impossible and the second was just out of the fucking question. Rion still showed up to Society meetings this semester—five of them, so far. For the third one, Arielle was miserable, and for the entire first four Amy was in tortured emotional limbo. Now her two roommates were sickeningly happy and mooning all over themselves and each other any time they happened to be in the suite.

Between that and the stir-craziness that affected every

resident of Northern Indiana in late February, walking down frigid, winter-bleak Francis Street actually felt like some kind of a relief.

For the first few weeks after Crash's arrest, the wall didn't change. The swirling reds, oranges, and yellows Crash had added in the last four months flowed so beautifully from the bright blues and greens that had been there long before he first showed it to Rion.

Since that first time Crash showed it to her, he'd painted little moments between them here and there in different spots on the wall—pancakes, him listening to her music mix with a smile on his face, their trip to her hometown for Christmas. Each of these pictures had a thick line connecting them, and somewhere along each of those lines was a heart. They weren't cheesy hearts, they were subtle—nestled in the corner of a border, etched into the curve of a cloud. She hadn't seen these, hadn't asked to see the wall, until after the whole incident.

Now, she wished she'd seen it then, wished she'd been able to tell him what she was feeling when she was feeling it, somehow. Wished she'd realized that he'd opened up his heart to her, completely, in thick paint on a cold brick wall. She had just never asked to see it.

After the whole refused-call-from-jail incident, Rion had once again arranged her schedule to avoid Crash. This time around, he hadn't seemed to mind. She'd only seen him in passing, and made eye contact with him exactly once. In the six weeks since, there hadn't been a

The Broken Hearts Society of Suite 17C

single change to the wall. Rion figured that was part of the reason she loved going there so much—it was the one thing that didn't change, that was frozen in time before it all went bad. Before she blew what would probably turn out to be her one and only chance.

Today, though, something had changed. There had been a shift inside her, something that diverged the slightest bit from the autopilot that had been getting her through the day. On her way out the door, almost without realizing what she was doing, she'd picked up a piece of sidewalk chalk Arielle kept in an organizer on their chalkboard wall—the kind she insisted on because it was softer, with bolder colors. She slipped it into her pocket.

There weren't very many blank feet of brick left on the wall, Rion knew that much. Crash had already filled two thirds of it, at least. Even so, the solid color stood in such stark contrast to Crash's heart and soul beside it that she felt even emptier trying to figure out what to do with it.

Rion hadn't felt this antsy in a very long time. With every step, her legs protested a little bit more, telling her to turn back, telling her she didn't have to do this. But she fought that feeling, just like she'd fought everything else in her life—ferociously. Nobody could keep her from doing what she wanted to do, deep down, not even herself.

She clutched the chalk like a child might, in a fist, and wrenched it out of the pocket of her motorcycle jacket. Using the cool hardness of the wall to steady her hand, she wrote, "I MISS YOU," one letter per brick, just a few inches from the last painting.

It wasn't a commitment, and it didn't even come close to scratching what she felt, what she wished she was brave enough and smart enough to say. But hell if she didn't feel every bit of it down to the bone. She blew out a hot breath that had gathered in her chest as she wrote the words, releasing anything intense that could grow toxic later. And then a soft *scritch scritch* in the gravel sent her breath silent and set her body on high alert.

"You know graffiti is illegal in the city limits." Crash stood there, so still and his voice was so quiet that he could have been a hallucination.

Rion's heart kicked like crazy.

"I...um..." Rion swallowed the bubble of panic that had started to form inside her, the pocket of weakness that could ruin everything all over again. "It's just chalk."

Crash nodded and started toward her, calm and quiet, like she had woken him out of sleep to ask him whether he had any clean towels. The only difference was that his eyes were focused on her, unfeeling. Hiding something behind them that Rion couldn't decipher.

Is this how she had always looked to him? Unreadable, just out of reach?

He was so close she could touch him, then, heartbreakingly, so close she could have leaned in and kissed him. She didn't dare move an inch, afraid if she so much as turned her head to him, she'd completely break down.

The Broken Hearts Society of Suite 17C

Slowly, gently, he reached his hand out to hers, nudging open the fingers that still held the chalk so tight. He pulled it from her and raised it to the wall.

Right underneath where she had written, "I MISS YOU," he scrawled in all caps, "COME BACK."

Rion blinked, taking in the words. It took a long time for her heart to convince her voice to work. "Do you want me to?"

"If you can," Crash said, his voice so measured it was unbelievable. "But you have to be able to trust me. I know you said you love me, but for me, that means trusting me, too."

Rion pressed the heels of her hands into her eyes, begging the burning that cropped up there to subside. "It's not about you. The drug stuff, my reaction…it's not about you."

"Except it was, because I was in the middle of it." Crash sighed and pushed his hand back through his hair. "Look, Rion. I won't fucking lie. I can't make myself lie to you, no matter how much I should. I miss the hell out of you. Being with you…it was different than being with anyone else. I can't tell you to get out of my face again, because I honestly think it would fucking destroy me."

Rion whimpered. That was how she felt. Destroyed. Like she'd broken into more pieces than she could handle or keep track of.

"But I have to know we're in this together. I have to know you're not giving me the fucking side-eye every time

I'm out late or have a new tattoo or a little extra cash. I have to know that you have faith in me, to put myself—and you, for fuck's sake—first, before any stupid shit like pot."

"Crash, you know what happened to me. I can't just make that go away."

"No, you can't. And I wouldn't want you to, because it made you who you are. But you have to go back and figure out what about your stupid ex and your mom you refuse to talk to makes you unable to trust me. The guy who so obviously loves you."

"I can't." The truth hurt like hell, but doing exploratory surgery on her own heart would hurt even more. She needed someone to help her forget about mom and dad and the group home and how badly all of it had ravaged her ability to trust. Maybe Crash was right. Maybe she wasn't capable of really loving him, or anyone, anymore.

"Not even for me? You can't take a risk and say, yeah, I know shit has happened, but what the hell, maybe this time won't destroy me?" It wasn't attacking, wasn't judgmental. It was fair, and there was a clarity to the way he said it that made Rion feel just how fair it was. "Because I swear it won't, Rion. I won't. I would never."

"I don't do complicated emotions. I hate them. They make me vulnerable and weak and that makes me nervous because for so long I was all on my own. When you're on your own, you can't be weak."

The Broken Hearts Society of Suite 17C

"Well if you want to keep being fucking alone, then fine, Rion! You can keep being hard and closed off and distrusting. But as long as you are those things, I'm pretty sure alone is all you'll ever be. You can't love someone and be all those things. They just can't exist together." Crash chucked the chalk to the ground and growled.

"I do love you. And, Crash, I'm only eighteen. I have a whole lot of shit behind me and probably plenty of it ahead, too. I didn't figure out how to survive on my own for nothing."

"I know that, Rion. I do. But here's the thing. Loving somebody means you put yourself out there, you have faith in things that don't always make sense to you, and sometimes, even though it's a leap, it can expose your weakness. Really loving someone means letting yourself be vulnerable."

Crash just looked at her, then the ground, scuffing his toe on the gravel. "I told you I loved you, Rion, and I meant it. I should have said more, though."

Rion looked up. The tears had started to collect at the bottom rims of her eyes, and she knew that his sharp challenges, plus the surprise of seeing him there at all, had punched a tiny hole in the dam that had been holding back every soul-shattering feeling for so very long. It wouldn't be long until buckets of tears burst forth.

"I should have been more clear. I should have told you that you are so beautiful it makes me want to paint you a thousand different ways on a thousand different walls. I should have told you how the smell of your skin can distract me from pretty much anything. How you're the first person who I thought could really understand me in the longest fucking time, and how losing that would destroy me. I should have said that you're so easy to be around, and that that's a goddamn treasure, because that does not come along every day, or even every year, for a guy like me. I should have told you that, so many times, I would stay awake while you slept watching you breathe and trying to figure out exactly how to tell you how damn much you mean to me, to make you understand that, to me, you are the best person in the world. You are funny and smart and you have so much fucking love inside you, and sometimes you let it out, and I was so goddamn lucky to be there to catch so much of it.

"I should have told you that I never, ever, ever wanted to lose that. I should have fought for you harder, but Rion, I'm so tired. I was, and I am, and I don't want to go another day without you, but if you can't trust me, I'll have to."

At that, his voice broke, and Rion's heart broke, and she launched herself at him, folding him in her arms and feeling the sorrow and the stress and the frustration she'd caused him—*she* had contributed to this whole fucking mess—flow through him and into her where it really belonged.

And then, she cried.

Crash pulled back and studied her while she did, while

The Broken Hearts Society of Suite 17C

her chest heaved and she fought to find enough breath to say, as clearly and as surely as she should have six weeks ago, that she was sorry, and that she trusted him, and that even though she only had enough of that to give to one person in her life, she wanted it to be him.

But instead, all she managed was, "I love you. I trust you. I'm so, so sorry."

He watched her, wiping away tears and brushing the hair back from her face, like he was appraising a piece of art, trying to weigh risks and benefits and decide whether it would be worth the cost.

It didn't take him long to decide.

He wrapped an arm around her shoulders and pulled her to him, whispering "Shhhh...I'm sorry I didn't say all this sooner," and pressing kisses onto her head. With the other arm, he pulled the other piece of chalk out of her pocket, reached up and drew two hearts, interlocking, and then let it drop to the ground.

"Why two?" Rion sniffled.

"In all the other pictures I only painted one because I wasn't sure you were really in this. Now, I am."

Without another word, Crash reached down, twined his fingers with hers, and led her silently out of the alley. Rion didn't know what came next, but for the first time in a very long time, she was trusting someone else to help her figure it out.

Epilogue

Ariel

A school year practically ending in April, with only finals left in May, it just felt wrong to Arielle, who had spent her entire life on a "Passover means you still have six weeks left" schedule. Lauren, who had never tasted Manischewitz, had passed out after the third glass of wine at the Duval family Seder, and a couple hours later, Arielle had wandered from her room, bored with reading in the dark and watching Lauren sleep.

Wrinkling her nose as she bit into the first of what would be dozens of matzah peanut butter sandwiches, Arielle jumped when the garage door rattled.

Rion and Amy shouldered in through a tiny gap, like they were hiding the fact that they were sneaking back in—because, presumably, they had snuck out. They

The Broken Hearts Society of Suite 17C

clutched fast-food bags in their hands, and met Arielle with a shock on their faces that was completely comical.

"Passover food not good enough for you?" Arielle deadpanned, and Rion rolled her eyes while Amy still looked mortified.

"We were so fucking hungry, Ari. You have to give us that. Gentiles are not made for this. What the fuck do you even eat on this damn holiday, anyway?"

Arielle held up her peanut butter and matzah, and Amy frowned.

"What?" Arielle laughed. "It's not so bad. Plus, there's also ice cream."

Five minutes later, the girls sat with two half-gallons between them in a dark circle of the family room. "It's just like old times," Rion said with a mouthful of raspberry chip.

"Yeah, when we were all miserable and limping through freshman year. Look at us now, all self-assured and grown up and mature."

Something about that sentence sobered the other two girls. Amy was the first to speak again. "Is this our last Society meeting?"

"Do you want it to be?" Arielle asked. Everyone's eyes were still sad.

"I know this is a touchy topic, mostly because of our…situations," Amy said. "But did you guys get that email from the housing director today?"

"I still haven't figured out how to get my email onto this goddamn phone," Rion grumbled, but Arielle looked panicked and scrolled through her email. "Oh, shit. We have to give him our decision."

Amy cast her eyes down. "Matt and I aren't going to live together. I'm not ready, and I don't think he is either."

"Crash wants me to move in," Rion offered.

"Really?" Arielle said. "That's fast."

"I love him," Rion shrugged. "But not enough to clean his pubes off the toilet. Not yet. Maybe not ever."

Amy's gaze shot up. "So you'd think about staying in Harrison?"

Rion shrugged. "It's cheap. And if you'll swipe me for free meals in the dining hall, I don't see why not."

"I'm in too," Arielle said. "As much as I love those Alpha Chi girls, there's too much drama to live with them 24/7."

"I thought you had to live there," Amy said, relief flooding her voice.

Arielle brushed the scattered matzah crumbs from her lap for the millionth time that night. "Common sorority myths. There's actually not enough space in the house for all of us. If I sit on the board of the sorority, I have to live there, but that wouldn't happen til next year anyway."

For one cheesy moment, they all shared a smile. Then Arielle shot to her feet. "Come on."

The Broken Hearts Society of Suite 17C

"We can't abandon the ice cream!" Rion said with a full mouth. Ari swore that girl could eat three meals of ice cream a day and not gain an ounce.

"It's just for a second," Arielle said. "Stay here." She ran up the stairs and slunk into her room, deftly grabbing the pink notebook, now ragged and stuffed full of notes from every Society meeting, without waking Lauren. Then she grabbed her bag and headed to the printer. "Gather around it so the noise doesn't wake up the house." She pulled up her email and printed the Harrison Tower housing contract, then handed a pen to Rion first.

"Let's sign now. Then we'll know for sure this isn't our last meeting. As soon as we all sign, we'll schedule our first meeting for next year."

"I don't know. I was kind of worried we might decide we don't even need the Society anymore," Amy said, picking at her nails.

Arielle shrugged, making sure Amy saw her smile. "I figure we'll never be one hundred percent happy, and the world has plenty of heartbreak. There's nobody I would rather have hear all about mine than you girls."

"You know I'm just doing this to stay in touch with my mushy-gushy side, right?" Rion halfheartedly grumbled.

"Yeah, and I'm only doing it for the exposure to swear words." Amy smiled. "Don't start slacking, Ri."

"Oh, shut up. If you girls loved me and each other any more, you'd be as gay as I am." Arielle was the last to sign.

The swooping blue ink that marked their signatures felt just as much like a promise as a prayer. Their hearts had been broken and put back together again, and they'd helped each other through. Everything in life changed, and there was no such thing as a guarantee when it came to love and friendship–they'd learned that much.

Still, Arielle knew, deep down in her soul, that she wouldn't have survived this year without these two accidental, perfectly imperfect friends.

She slung her arms around their necks and grinned when they returned the hug. All three of them squeezed tight, and Arielle felt it down to her bones—their silent promise to keep holding each other up, no matter what.

The End.

Acknowledgements

First and foremost, to Jamie Grey and Trisha Leigh, the two women who nudge, push, nag, encourage and support me until the smallest of ideas I share with them turns into a real-life book – thank you, thank you, thank you. I can never say it enough, but I'll keep trying anyway.

Over-the-top, teary thanks to Valerie Cole and Julie Daly, who took on this monstrous triple-main character manuscript for second-round critique sight unseen. Your confidence and generosity are extraordinary.

Arielle Cronig (A.K.A. "Real Life Arielle,") thank you for being so very cool with the fact that I put you in not one, but two books. Hopefully my writing is like some kind of voodoo magic and you find your happily ever after just like Book Arielle did.

To my beta readers, Kayti McGee, Michelle Smith, Brett Jonas, Marlana Fireman, Taylor Mandel, Rion

Caldwell, Tara Marshall, Bethany Voyles, Tiffany Brun, and Adrianne Russell – thanks for volunteering to read this book with an enthusiastic, open heart, even though you knew it was still riddled with typos, grammar issues, and rogue yellow highlights. You are incredible.

I never thought the memory of doing copyedits would bring a smile to my face, but Shannon Ford made it happen. Thank you for taking on this behemoth of a novel and making it shiny and ready to read.

A book's beauty lies just as much in its presentation as in its words. Thank you, Cait Greer, for once again designing something completely unique and absolutely perfect for Suite 17C. You are making magic, my friend.

Thank you to David, who supports this crazy book-writing career of mine 100%, even though he probably never would have dreamed I'd ever be doing something like this. I picked a good one.

And, last but never least, thank you to my readers. Your enthusiasm and support for these stories of love lost and regained, and the friends found along the way, keeps me writing them, which brings me more joy than I could ever say.

About the Author

Raised on comic books and classic novels, LeighAnn developed an early love of science fiction and great literature. As an adult, she rediscovered her love for not only reading, but also writing the types of fiction that enchanted her as a teen. Her novels are packed full of flights of fancy, first loves, unexpected friendships, and all the other things that make self-discovery stories so fun to tell.

LeighAnn, her husband, and four children live in Columbus, Ohio. When she's not immersed in the world of fiction, you can find her with her nose buried in her Kindle, obsessing over the latest superhero movie, or using her kids as an excuse to go out for ice cream (again).

Made in the USA
Charleston, SC
21 May 2015